JUDY BLUME

Are you there, God? It's me, Margaret

Blubber

Starring Sally J. Freedman As Herself

DEAN

Are you there, God? It's me, Margaret first published in Great Britain by
Victor Gollancz Limited in 1978
Blubber first published in Great Britain by William Heinemann Limited in 1980
Starring Sally J. Freedman As Herself first published in Great Britain by
William Heinemann Limited in 1983

This edition published 1993 by Dean,
an imprint of Reed Consumer Books Limited
Michelin House, 81 Fulham Road, London SW3 6RB
and Auckland, Melbourne, Singapore and Toronto
Text copyright © 1970, 1974, 1977

ISBN 0 603 55224 2

Printed in Great Britain by The Bath Press

Contents

Are you there, God? It's me, Margaret

To My Mother

one

*Are you there, God? It's me, Margaret. We're moving today. I'm
so scared, God. I've never lived anywhere but here. Suppose I
hate my new school? Suppose everybody there hates me? Please
help me, God. Don't let New Jersey be too horrible. Thank you.*

We moved on the Tuesday before Labor Day. I knew what the
weather was like the second I got up. I knew because I caught
my mother sniffing under her arms. She always does that when
it's hot and humid, to make sure her deodorant's working. I
don't use deodorant yet. I don't think people start to smell bad
until they're at least twelve. So I've still got a few months to go.

I was really surprised when I came home from camp and
found out our New York apartment had been rented to another
family and that *we* owned a house in Farbrook, New Jersey.
First of all I never even heard of Farbrook. And second of all,
I'm not usually left out of important family decisions.

But when I groaned, 'Why New Jersey?' I was told, 'Long
Island is too social – Westchester is too expensive – and
Connecticut is too inconvenient.'

So Farbrook, New Jersey it was, where my father could
commute to his job in Manhattan, where I could go to public
school, and where my mother could have all the grass, trees and
flowers she ever wanted. Except I never knew she wanted that
stuff in the first place.

The new house is on Morningbird Lane. It isn't bad. It's part
brick, part wood. The shutters and front door are painted
black. Also, there is a very nice brass knocker. Every house on
our new street looks a lot the same. They are all seven years old.
So are the trees.

I think we left the city because of my grandmother, Sylvia
Simon. I can't figure out any other reason for the move.
Especially since my mother says Grandma is too much of an
influence on me. It's no big secret in our family that Grandma

7

sends me to summer camp in New Hampshire. And that she enjoys paying my private school tuition (which she won't be able to do any more because now I'll be going to public school). She even knits me sweaters that have labels sewn inside saying MADE EXPRESSLY FOR YOU . . . BY GRANDMA.

And she doesn't do all that because we're poor. I know for a fact that we're not. I mean, we aren't rich but we certainly have enough. Especially since I'm an only child. That cuts way down on food and clothes. I know this family that has seven kids and every time they go to the shoe store it costs a bundle. My mother and father didn't plan for me to be an only child, but that's the way it worked out, which is fine with me because this way I don't have anybody around to fight.

Anyhow, I figure this house-in-New-Jersey business is my parents' way of getting me away from Grandma. She doesn't have a car, she hates buses *and* she thinks all trains are dirty. So unless Grandma plans to walk, which is unlikely, I won't be seeing much of her. Now some kids might think, who cares about seeing a grandmother? But Sylvia Simon is a lot of fun, considering her age, which I happen to know is sixty. The only problem is she's always asking me if I have boyfriends and if they're Jewish. Now *that* is ridiculous because number one I don't have boyfriends. And number two what would I care if they're Jewish or not?

two

We hadn't been in the new house more than an hour when the doorbell rang. I answered. It was this girl in a bathing suit.

'Hi,' she said. 'I'm Nancy Wheeler. The real estate agent sent out a sheet on you. So I know you're Margaret and you're in sixth grade. So am I.'

I wondered what else she knew.

'It's plenty hot, isn't it?' Nancy asked.

'Yes,' I agreed. She was taller than me and had bouncy hair. The kind I'm hoping to grow. Her nose turned up so much I could look right into her nostrils.

Nancy leaned against the door. 'Well, you want to come over and go under the sprinklers?'

'I don't know. I'll have to ask.'

'Okay. I'll wait.'

I found my mother with her rear end sticking out of a bottom kitchen cabinet. She was arranging her pots and pans.

'Hey, Mom. There's a girl here who wants to know if I can go under her sprinklers?'

'If you want to,' my mother said.

'I need my bathing suit,' I said.

'Gads, Margaret! I don't know where a bathing suit is in this mess.'

I walked back to the front door and told Nancy, 'I can't find my bathing suit.'

'You can borrow one of mine,' she said.

'Wait a second,' I said, running back to the kitchen. 'Hey, Mom. She says I can wear one of hers. Okay?'

'Okay,' my mother mumbled from inside the cabinet. Then she backed out. She spit her hair out of her face. 'What did you say her name was?'

'Umm . . . Wheeler. Nancy Wheeler.'

'Okay. Have a good time,' my mother said.

Nancy lives six houses away, also on Morningbird Lane. Her house looks like mine but the brick is painted white and the front door and shutters are red.

'Come on in,' Nancy said.

I followed her into the foyer, then up the four stairs leading to the bedrooms. The first thing I noticed about Nancy's room was the dressing table with the heartshaped mirror over it. Also, everything was very neat.

When I was little I wanted a dressing table like that. The kind that's wrapped up in a fluffy organdie skirt. I never got one though, because my mother likes tailored things. Nancy opened her bottom dresser drawer. 'When's your birthday?' she asked.

'March,' I told her.

'Great! We'll be in the same class. There are three sixth grades and they arrange us by age. I'm April.'

'Well, I don't know what class I'm in but I know it's Room Eighteen. They sent me a lot of forms to fill out last week and that was printed on all of them.'

'I told you we'd be together. I'm in Room Eighteen too.' Nancy handed me a yellow bathing suit. 'It's clean,' she said. 'My mother always washes them after a wearing.'

'Thank you,' I said, taking the suit. 'Where should I change?'

Nancy looked around the room. 'What's wrong with here?'

'Nothing,' I said. 'I don't mind if you don't mind.'

'Why should I mind?'

'I don't know.' I worked the suit on from the bottom. I knew it was going to be too big. Nancy gave me the creeps the way she sat on her bed and watched me. I left my polo on until the last possible second. I wasn't about to let her see I wasn't growing yet. That was my business.

'Oh, you're still flat.' Nancy laughed.

'Not exactly,' I said pretending to be very cool. 'I'm small boned, is all.'

'I'm growing already,' Nancy said, sticking her chest way out. 'In a few years I'm going to look like one of those girls in *Playboy*.'

Well, I didn't think so, but I didn't say anything. My father gets *Playboy* and I've seen those girls in the middle. Nancy looked like she had a long way to go. Almost as far as me.

'Want me to do up your straps?' she asked.

'Okay.'

'I figured you'd be real grown up coming from New York. City girls are supposed to grow up a lot faster. Did you ever kiss a boy?'

10

'You mean really kiss? On the lips?' I asked.

'Yes,' Nancy said impatiently. 'Did you?'

'Not really,' I admitted.

Nancy breathed a sigh of relief. 'Neither did I.'

I was overjoyed. Before she said that I was beginning to feel like some kind of underdeveloped little kid.

'I practise a lot though,' Nancy said.

'Practise what?' I asked.

'Kissing! Isn't that what we were talking about? *Kissing!*'

'How can you practise that?' I asked.

'Watch this.' Nancy grabbed her bed pillow and embraced it. She gave it a long kiss. When she was done she threw the pillow back on the bed. 'It's important to experiment, so when the time comes you're all ready. I'm going to be a great kisser some day. Want to see something else?'

I just stood there with my mouth half open. Nancy sat down at her dressing table and opened a drawer. 'Look at this,' she said.

I looked. There were a million little bottles, jars and tubes. There were more cosmetics in that drawer than my mother had all together. I asked, 'What do you do with all that stuff?'

'It's another one of my experiments. To see how I look best. So when the time comes I'll be ready.' She opened a lipstick and painted on a bright pink mouth. 'Well, what do you think?'

'Umm . . . I don't know. It's kind of bright, isn't it?'

Nancy studied herself in the heartshaped mirror. She rubbed her lips together. 'Well, maybe you're right.' She wiped off the lipstick with a tissue. 'My mother would kill me if I came out like this anyway. I can't wait till eighth grade. That's when I'll be allowed to wear lipstick every day.'

Then she whipped out a hairbrush and started to brush her long, brown hair. She parted it in the middle and caught it at the back with a barrette. 'Do you always wear your hair like that?' she asked me.

My hand went up to the back of my neck. I felt all the bobby pins I'd used to pin my hair up so my neck wouldn't sweat. I knew it looked terrible. 'I'm letting it grow,' I said. 'It's at that in-between stage now. My mother thinks I should wear it over my ears though. My ears stick out a little.'

'I noticed,' Nancy said.

I got the feeling that Nancy noticed *everything*!

'Ready to go?' she asked.

'Sure.'

She opened a linen closet in the hall and handed me a purple towel. I followed her down the stairs and into the kitchen, where she grabbed two peaches out of the refrigerator and handed one to me. 'Want to meet my mom?' she asked.

'Okay,' I said, taking a bite of my peach.

'She's thirty-eight, but tells us she's twenty-five. Isn't that a scream!' Nancy snorted.

Mrs Wheeler was on the porch with her legs tucked under her and a book on her lap. I couldn't tell what book it was. She was suntanned and had the same nose as Nancy.

'Mom, this is Margaret Simon who just moved in down the street.'

Mrs Wheeler took off her glasses and smiled at me.

'Hello,' I said.

'Hello, Margaret. I'm very glad to meet you. You're from New York, aren't you?'

'Yes, I am.'

'East side or West?'

'We lived on West Sixty-seventh. Near Lincoln Center.'

'How nice. Does your father still work in the city?'

'Yes.'

'And what does he do?'

'He's in insurance.' I sounded like a computer.

'How nice. Please tell your mother I'm looking forward to meeting her. We've got a Morningbird Lane bowling team on Mondays and a bridge game every other Thursday afternoon and a . . .'

'Oh, I don't think my mother knows how to bowl and she wouldn't be interested in bridge. She paints most of the day,' I explained.

12

'She paints?' Mrs Wheeler asked.

'Yes.'

'How interesting. What does she paint?'

'Mostly pictures of fruits and vegetables. Sometimes flowers too.'

Mrs Wheeler laughed. 'Oh, you mean *pictures*! I thought you meant walls! Tell your mother we're making our car pools early this year. We'd be happy to help her arrange hers . . . especially Sunday school. That's always the biggest problem.'

'I don't go to Sunday school.'

'You don't?'

'No.'

'*Lucky!*' Nancy shouted.

'Nancy, *please*!' Mrs Wheeler said.

'Hey, Mom . . . Margaret came to go under the sprinkler with me, not to go through the third degree.'

'All right. If you see Evan tell him I want to talk to him.'

Nancy grabbed me by the hand and pulled me outside. 'I'm sorry my mother's so nosy.'

'I didn't mind,' I said. 'Who's Evan?'

'He's my brother. He's disgusting!'

'Disgusting how?' I asked.

'Because he's fourteen. All boys of fourteen are disgusting. They're only interested in two things – pictures of naked girls and dirty books!'

Nancy really seemed to know a lot. Since I didn't know any boys of fourteen I took her word for it.

Nancy turned on the outside faucet and adjusted it so that the water sprayed lightly from the sprinkler. 'Follow the leader!' she called, running through the water. I guessed Nancy was the leader.

She jumped through the spray. I followed. She turned cartwheels. I tried but didn't make it. She did leaps through the air. I did too. She stood straight under the spray. I did the same. That's when the water came on full blast. We both got drenched, including our hair.

'Evan, you stinker!' Nancy shrieked. 'I'm telling!' She ran off to the house and left me alone with two boys.

'Who're you?' Evan asked.

'I'm Margaret. We just moved in.'

'Oh. This is Moose,' he said, pointing to the other boy.

I nodded.

'Hey,' Moose said. 'If you just moved in, ask your father if he's interested in having me cut his lawn. Five bucks a week and I trim too. What'd you say your last name was?'

'I didn't. But it's Simon.' I couldn't help thinking about what Nancy said – that all they were interested in was dirty books and naked girls. I held my towel tight around me in case they were trying to sneak a look down my bathing suit.

'*Evan! Come in here this instant!*' Mrs Wheeler hollered from the porch.

'I'm coming . . . I'm coming,' Evan muttered.

After Evan went inside Moose said, 'Don't forget to tell your father. *Moose Freed*. I'm in the phone book.'

'I won't forget,' I promised.

Moose nibbled a piece of grass. Then the back door slammed and Nancy came out, red-eyed and sniffling.

'Hey, Nancy baby! Can't you take a joke?' Moose asked.

'Shut up, animal!' Nancy yelled. Then she turned to me. 'I'm sorry they had to act like that on your first day here. Come on, I'll walk you home.'

Nancy had my clothes wrapped up in a little bundle. She was still in her wet suit. She pointed out who lived in each house between mine and hers.

'We're going to the beach for Labor Day weekend,' she said. 'So call for me on the first day of school and we'll walk together. I'm absolutely dying to know who our teacher's going to be. Miss Phipps, who we were supposed to have, ran off with some guy to California last June. So we're getting somebody new.'

When we got to my house I told Nancy if she'd wait a minute I'd give her back her bathing suit.

'I don't need it in a hurry. Tell your mother to wash it and you can give it back next week. It's an old one.'

I was sorry she told me that. Even if I'd already guessed it. I mean, probably I wouldn't lend a stranger my best bathing suit either. But I wouldn't come right out and say it.

'Oh, listen, Margaret,' Nancy said. 'On the first day of school wear loafers, but no socks.'

'How come?'

'Otherwise you'll look like a baby.'

'Oh.'

'Besides, I want you to join my secret club and if you're wearing socks the other kids might not want you.'

'What kind of secret club?' I asked.

'I'll tell you about it when school starts.'

'Okay,' I said.

'And remember – no socks!'

'I'll remember.'

We went to a hamburger place for supper. I told my father about Moose Freed. 'Only five bucks a cutting and he trims too.'

'No, thanks,' my father said. 'I'm looking forward to cutting it myself. That's one of the reasons we moved out here. Gardening is good for the soul.' My mother beamed. They were really driving me crazy with all that good-for-the-soul business. I wondered when they became such nature lovers!

Later, when I was getting ready for bed, I walked into a closet, thinking it was the bathroom. Would I ever get used to living in this house? When I finally made it into bed and turned out the light, I saw shadows on my wall. I tried to shut my eyes and not think about them but I kept checking to see if they were still there. I couldn't fall asleep.

Are you there, God? It's me, Margaret. I'm in my new bedroom but I still have the same bed. It's so quiet here at night – nothing like the city. I see shadows on my wall and hear these funny creaking sounds. It's scary, God! Even though my father says all houses make noises and the shadows are only trees. I hope he knows what he's talking about! I met a girl today. Her name's Nancy. She expected me to be very grown up. I think she was disappointed. Don't you think it's time for me to start growing, God? If you could arrange it I'd be very glad. Thank you.

My parents don't know I actually talk to God. I mean, if I told them they'd think I was some kind of religious fanatic or something. So I keep it very private. I can talk to him without moving my lips if I have to. My mother says God is a nice idea. He belongs to everybody.

three

The next day we went to the hardware store where my father bought a deluxe power lawn mower. That evening, after our first at-home-in-New-Jersey supper (turkey sandwiches from the local delicatessen), my father went out to cut the grass with his new mower. He did fine on the front, but when he got around to the backyard he had to check to see how much grass was in the bag on the mower. It's a very simple thing to do. The man at the hardware store demonstrated just how to do it. Only you have to turn the mower off before you reach inside and my father forgot that.

I heard him yell, 'Barbara – I've had an accident!' He ran to the house. He grabbed a towel and wrapped it around his hand before I had a chance to see anything. Then he sat down on the floor and turned very pale.

'Oh, my God!' my mother said when the blood seeped through the towel. 'Did you cut it off?'

When I heard that I raced outside to look for the limb. I didn't know if they were talking about the whole hand or what,

16

but I had read about how you're supposed to save limbs if they get cut off because sometimes the doctor can sew them back on. I thought it was a good thing they had me around to think of those things. But I couldn't find a hand or any fingers and by the time I came back into the house the police were there. My mother was on the floor too, with my father's head in her lap.

I rode in the police car with them since there was no one at home to stay with me. I had a silent talk with God on the way to the hospital. I said this inside my head so no one would notice.

Are you there, God? It's me, Margaret. My father's had an awful accident. Please help him, God. He's really very kind and nice. Even though he doesn't know you the way I do, he's a good father. And he needs his hand, God. So please, please let him be all right. I'll do anything you say if you help him. Thank you, God.

It turned out that my father hadn't cut off anything, but it took eight stitches to sew up his finger. The doctor who sewed him was Dr Potter. After he was through with my father, he came out to chat. When he saw me he said, 'I have a daughter about your age.'

I love the way people always think they know somebody your age until you tell them how old you *really* are!

'I'm going on twelve,' I said.

'Gretchen is almost twelve too,' the doctor said.

Well! He was right about my age.

'She'll be in sixth grade at Delano School.'

'So will you, Margaret,' my mother reminded me. As if I needed reminding.

'I'll tell Gretchen to look for you,' Dr Potter said.

'Fine,' I told him.

As soon as we got home from the hospital my father told my mother to look up Moose Freed in the phone book and arrange for him to cut our lawn once a week.

★

On Labor Day I got up early. I wanted to fix up my desk in my room before school started. I'd bought a pile of paper, pencils, erasers, reinforcements and paper clips. I'm always real neat until about October. While I was in the middle of this project I heard a noise. It sounded like somebody knocking. I waited to see if my parents would wake up. I tiptoed to their room but the door was still closed and it was quiet so I knew they were asleep.

When I heard the knocking again I went downstairs to investigate. I wasn't scared because I knew I could always scream and my father would rescue me if it turned out to be a burglar or a kidnapper.

The knocking came from the front door. Nancy was away for the weekend so it couldn't be her. And we really didn't know anybody else.

'Who is it?' I asked, pressing my ear to the door.

'It's Grandma, Margaret. Open up.'

I unlatched the chain and both locks and flung open the door. 'Grandma! I can't believe it. You're really here!'

'Surprise!' Grandma called.

I put a finger over my lips to let her know my parents were still asleep.

Grandma was loaded down with Bloomingdale's shopping bags. But when she stepped into the house she lined them up on the floor and gave me a big hug and kiss.

'My Margaret!' she said, flashing her special smile. When she smiles like that she shows all her top teeth. They aren't her real teeth. It's what Grandma calls a bridge. She can take out a whole section of four top teeth when she wants to. She used to entertain me by doing that when I was little. Naturally I never told my parents. When she smiles without her teeth in place she looks like a witch. But with them in her mouth she's very pretty.

'Come on, Margaret. Let's get these bags into the kitchen.'

I picked up one shopping bag. 'Grandma, this is so heavy! What's in it?'

'Hotdogs, potato salad, cole slaw, corned beef, rye bread . . .'

I laughed. 'You mean it's food?'

'Of course it's food.'

'But they have food in New Jersey, Grandma.'

'Not this kind.'

'Oh yes,' I said. 'Even delicatessen.'

'No place has delicatessen like New York!'

I didn't argue about that. Grandma has certain ideas of her own.

When we got all the bags into the kitchen Grandma scrubbed her hands at the sink and put everything into the refrigerator.

When she was done I asked, 'How did you get here?'

Grandma smiled again but didn't say anything. She was measuring coffee into the pot. You can't make her talk about something until she's ready.

Finally she sat down at the kitchen table, fluffed out her hair and said, 'I came in a taxi.'

'All the way from New York?'

'No,' Grandma said. 'From the centre of Farbrook.'

'But how did you get to the centre of Farbrook?'

'On a train.'

'Oh, Grandma – you didn't!'

'Yes, I did.'

'But you always said trains are so dirty!'

'So what's a little dirt? I'm washable!'

We both laughed while Grandma changed her shoes. She brought a spare pair along with her knitting in one of the shopping bags.

'Now,' she said, 'take me on a tour of the house.'

I led her everywhere except upstairs. I pointed out closets, the downstairs bathroom, my mother's new washer and dryer, and where we sat to watch TV.

When I was finished Grandma shook her head and said, 'I just don't understand why they had to move to the country.'

'It's not really country, Grandma,' I explained. 'There aren't any cows around.'

'To me it's country!' Grandma said.

I heard the water running upstairs. 'I think they're up. Should I go see?'

'You mean should you go *tell*!'

'Well, should I?'

'Of course,' Grandma said.

I ran up the stairs and into my parents' bedroom. My father was putting on his socks. My mother was brushing her teeth in their bathroom.

'Guess who's here?' I said to my father.

He didn't say anything. He yawned.

'Well, aren't you going to guess?'

'Guess what?' he asked.

'Guess who's here in this very house at this very minute?'

'Nobody but us, I hope,' my father said.

'Wrong!' I danced around the bedroom.

'Margaret,' my father said in his disgusted-with-me voice. 'What is it you're trying to say?'

'Grandma's here!'

'That's impossible,' my father told me.

'I mean it, Daddy. She's right downstairs in the kitchen making your coffee.'

'Barbara . . .' My father went into the bathroom and turned off the water. I followed him. My mother had a mouthful of toothpaste.

'I'm not done, Herb,' she said, turning on the water again.

My father shut it off. 'Guess who's here?' he asked her.

'What do you mean who's here?' my mother said.

'Sylvia! That's who's here!' My father turned the water back on so my mother could finish brushing her teeth.

My mother turned it off and followed my father into the bedroom. I followed too. This was fun! I guess by then my mother must have swallowed her toothpaste.

'What do you mean, *Sylvia*?' my mother asked my father.

'I mean my *mother*!' my father said.

My mother laughed. 'That's impossible, Herb. How would she even get here?'

My father pointed at me. 'Ask Margaret. She seems to know everything.'

'In a taxi,' I said.

They didn't say anything.

'And a train,' I said.

Still nothing.

'It wasn't so dirty after all.'

Ten minutes later my mother and father joined Grandma in the kitchen where the table was set and the breakfast all ready. It's hard to get mad at Grandma, especially when she flashes her super smile. So my mother and father didn't say anything except what a wonderful surprise! And how clever of Grandma to take a train and a taxi to our new house when she'd never been to Farbrook before.

After breakfast I went upstairs to get dressed. Grandma came up with me to see my room.

'It's a lot bigger than my old one,' I said.

'Yes, it's bigger,' Grandma agreed. 'You could use new bedspreads and curtains. I saw some the other day – pink and red plaid. Then we could get red carpeting to match and a –' Grandma sighed. 'But I guess your mother wants to fix it up herself.'

'I guess so,' I said.

Grandma sat down on my bed. 'Margaret darling,' she said, 'I want to make sure you understand that we'll still be as close as always.'

'Of course we will,' I said.

'A few miles doesn't mean a thing,' Grandma said. 'Just because I can't drop in after school doesn't mean I won't think of you every day.'

'I know that, Grandma.'

'I tell you what – I'll call you every night at seven-thirty. How does that sound?'

'You don't have to call *every* night,' I said.

'I want to! It's my dime,' Grandma laughed. 'That way you can tell me what's going on and I'll keep you posted about New York. Okay?'

'Sure, Grandma.'

'But, Margaret . . .'

'What?'

'You answer the phone. Your mother and father might not like me calling so much. This is just between you and me. All right?'

'Sure, Grandma. I love to get phone calls.'

We spent the rest of the day sitting around in our yard. Grandma was knitting me a new sweater, my mother planted some fall flowers, and my father read a book. I sunbathed, thinking it would be nice to start school with a tan.

We ate Grandma's food for supper and every time she bit into a pickle she said, 'Mmm . . . nothing like the real thing!'

We drove her back to the Farbrook station while it was still light. Grandma has this thing about walking in New York at night. She's positive she's going to get mugged. Before she got out of the car she kissed me goodbye and told my parents, 'Now don't worry. I promise I'll only come once a month. Well . . . maybe twice. And it's not to see you, Herb. Or you either, Barbara. I've got to keep my eye on my Margaret – that's all.' Grandma winked at me.

With that she grabbed the shopping bag with her shoes and knitting and left, waving goodbye until we couldn't see her any more.

four

On Wednesday night my mother helped me wash my hair. She set it in big rollers for me. I planned to sleep like that all night but after an hour they hurt my head so I took them out. On Thursday morning I got up early but I had trouble eating. My mother said it was natural for me to feel uneasy on the first day of school. She said when she was a girl she felt the same way. My mother's always telling me about when she was a girl. It's supposed to make me feel that she understands everything.

I put on my new blue plaid cotton back-to-school dress. My mother likes me in blue. She says it brings out the colour in my eyes. I wore my brown loafers without socks. My mother thought that was dumb.

'Margaret, you have to walk three quarters of a mile.'
'So?'
'So, you know you get blisters every time you go without socks.'
'Well then, I'll just have to suffer.'
'But why suffer? Wear socks!'

Now that's my point about my mother. I mean if she understands so much about me then why couldn't she understand that I had to wear loafers without socks? I told her, 'Nancy says nobody in the sixth grade wears socks on the first day of school!'

'Margaret! I don't know what I'm going to do with you when you're a teenager if you're acting like this now!'

That's another thing. My mother's always talking about when I'm a teenager. Stand up straight, Margaret! Good posture now makes for a good figure later. Wash your face with soap, Margaret. Then you won't get pimples when you're a teenager. If you ask me, being a teenager is pretty rotten – between pimples and worrying about how you smell!

Finally my mother told me to have a good day. She kissed my cheek and gave me a pat on the back. I walked down to Nancy's house.

By the time I got to Room Eighteen of the Delano Elementary School my feet hurt so much I thought I wouldn't make it through the day. Why are mothers always right about those things? As it turned out, half the girls had on knee socks anyway.

The teacher wasn't in the room when we got there. That is, the *real* teacher. There was this girl, who I thought *was* the

23

teacher, but she turned out to be a kid in our class. She was very tall (that's why I thought she was the teacher) with eyes shaped like a cat's. You could see the outline of her bra through her blouse and you could also tell from the front that it wasn't the smallest size. She sat down alone and didn't talk to anyone. I wondered if maybe she was new too, because everybody else was busy talking and laughing about summer vacations and new hair styles and all that.

The class quieted down in a big hurry when a man walked into the room, nodded at us and wrote a name on the blackboard.

MILES J. BENEDICT JR.

When he turned away from the blackboard he cleared his throat. 'That's me,' he said, pointing to the name on the board. Then he cleared his throat two more times. 'I'm your new teacher.'

Nancy poked me in the ribs and whispered, 'Can you believe it?' The whole class was whispering and grinning.

Mr Benedict went back to the board. He wrote six phrases. Then he turned to us. He put his hands behind his back and kind of rocked back and forth on his feet. He cleared his throat so I knew he was going to say something.

'Now then . . . uh . . . you know my name. I'll tell you something about myself. Uh . . . I'm twenty-four years old. I'm uh . . . a graduate of Columbia Teachers College and uh . . . this is my first teaching position. Now that you know about me, I want to uh . . . find out about you. So, if you will copy these six phrases off the board and then complete them I'd uh . . . appreciate it. Thank you.' He coughed. I thought he was going to wind up with a very sore throat.

Mr Benedict Jr. handed out the paper himself. I read his phrases.

MY NAME IS
PLEASE CALL ME
I LIKE

24

I HATE
THIS YEAR IN SCHOOL
I THINK MALE TEACHERS ARE

I nibbled on the edge of my pencil. The first two were easy. I wrote:

My name is Margaret Ann Simon.
Please call me Margaret.

The next two were harder. I liked and hated a million things. And I didn't know what he wanted to know about. Also, he wouldn't answer any questions. He sat at his desk and watched us. He tapped his fingers and crossed his legs. Finally I wrote:

I like long hair, tuna fish, the smell of rain
and things that are pink.
I hate pimples, baked potatoes, when my
mother's mad and religious holidays.
This year in school I want to have fun.
And also learn enough to go to
seventh grade.
I think male teachers are . . .

That was the worst! How was I supposed to know? Every teacher is different. But I couldn't think of a way to fit that in. So I wrote:

I think male teachers are the opposite of
female teachers.

There! That ought to do it. It was a stupid answer but I thought it was also a pretty stupid question.

At two-thirty Nancy slipped me a note. It said: *Secret club meets today after school my house — no socks!*

★

I went home to change before going to Nancy's. My mother was waiting for me. 'Let's have a snack and you can tell me all about your first day of school,' she said.

'I can't,' I told her. 'No time now. I've got to go to Nancy's house. I'm joining her secret club.'

'Oh, that's nice,' my mother said. 'Just tell me about your teacher. What's she like?'

'It's a *he*,' I said. 'His name is Mr Benedict and this is his first job.'

'Oh gads! A first-year teacher. What could be worse?'

'He's not bad,' I told my mother. 'I thought he was very nice.'

'We'll see how much you learn,' my mother said.

I changed into shorts and a polo and walked to Nancy's.

five

The others were already there. Janie Loomis, Gretchen Potter and Nancy. That was it. We sat around on the porch and Nancy brought us Cokes and cookies. When Gretchen helped herself to six Oreos at once Nancy asked her how much weight she'd gained over the summer. Gretchen put back four cookies and said, 'Not much.'

'Did you see Laura Danker come in this morning?' Janie asked.

'Which one is she?' I said.

They all giggled. Nancy spoke to me as if she were my mother. 'Margaret dear – you can't possibly miss Laura Danker. The big blonde with the big *you know whats*!'

'Oh, I noticed her right off,' I said. 'She's very pretty.'

'Pretty!' Nancy snorted. 'You be smart and stay away from her. She's got a bad reputation.'

'What do you mean?' I asked.

26

'My brother says she goes behind the A&P with him and Moose.'

'And,' Janie added, 'she's been wearing a bra since fourth grade and I'll bet she gets her period.'

'Did you get it yet, Margaret?' Nancy asked.

'Get what?'

'Your period,' Nancy said, like I should have known.

'Oh – no, not yet. Did you?'

Nancy swallowed some soda and shook her head. 'None of us has yet.'

I was glad to hear that. I mean, suppose they all got it already and I was the only one who didn't. I'd feel awful.

Gretchen smacked her lips, brushed the cookie crumbs off her lap and said, 'Let's get down to business.'

'Agreed,' Nancy said. 'First of all we need a good club name this year. Everybody think up a name for our club.'

It got quiet. Everybody thought. I didn't really think but I pretended to. I didn't even know anything about the club so how could I pick out a name?

Gretchen suggested the SGCT which meant the Sixth Grade Cu-Tees. Janie said that sounded really dumb. So Gretchen told Janie if she was so smart why didn't she suggest a name. Janie suggested the MJB Girls which meant the Miles J. Benedict Girls. Nancy told Janie she'd forgotten the Jr. on the end of his name. Janie got mad and excused herself to go to the bathroom.

'As long as we're on the subject,' Nancy said, 'what do you think of Miles J.?'

'I think he's cute!' Gretchen giggled.

'He is – but he's too skinny,' Nancy said.

Then I finally thought of something to say. 'I wonder if he's married!'

Janie joined us again. 'My guess is no. He doesn't look married.'

'Anyhow, did you see the way he looked at Laura?' Nancy asked.

'No! Did he?' Gretchen opened her eyes wide.

'Naturally! Men can't help looking at her,' Nancy said.

'But do you think she looks that way on purpose?' I asked.

The others laughed and Nancy said, 'Oh, Margaret!' Nancy had a great way of making me feel like a dope.

Then we talked about Mr Benedict's questions and Gretchen told us that she wrote male teachers are very strict – because if Mr Benedict thought we were afraid of him he'd bend over backwards to be really easy going and nice. I thought that was pretty clever and wished I had written it myself.

'Well, the whole idea of those questions is just to find out if we're normal,' Janie said.

I hadn't thought about that. Now it was too late. 'How can he tell if we're normal?' I asked.

'That's easy,' Nancy said. 'From the way you answered. Like if you said, I hate my mother, my father and my brother you might be weird. Get it?'

I got it.

Nancy snapped her fingers. 'I have the perfect name for our club,' she said.

'What is it?' Gretchen asked.

'Tell us,' Janie said.

'We'll be the Four PTS's.'

'What's it stand for?' Janie asked.

Nancy tossed her hair around and smiled. 'The Pre-Teen Sensations!'

'Hey, that's good,' Gretchen said.

'I love it,' Janie squealed.

We had a secret vote to pass the club name and naturally it passed. Then Nancy decided we should all have secret sensational names such as Alexandra, Veronica, Kimberly and Mavis. Nancy got to be Alexandra. I was Mavis.

Nancy reminded us that nobody in school was to know anything about our secret club and that at secret meetings such as this we were to use our secret names. We all had to solemnly swear. Then we all had to think up a rule.

28

Nancy's rule was, we all had to wear bras. I felt my cheeks turn red. I wondered if the others wore them already. I didn't think Janie did because she looked down at the floor after Nancy said it.

Gretchen's rule was, the first one to get her period had to tell the others all about it. Especially how it feels. Janie's rule was, we all had to keep a Boy Book, which was a notebook with a list of boys' names in order of how we liked them. Each week we had to change our lists and pass the Boy Books around.

Finally Nancy asked me what my rule was. I couldn't think of one to equal the others so I said, 'We meet on a certain day each week.'

'Naturally!' Nancy said. 'But *what* day?'

'Well, I don't know,' I told her.

'Okay, let's think up a good day,' Gretchen said. 'Tuesday and Thursday are out. I have to go to Hebrew school.'

'Oh, Gretchen!' Janie said. 'You and that Hebrew school business. Can't you get out of it?'

'I'd love to,' Gretchen explained. 'But I've got to go one more year and then I'm through.'

'What about you, Margaret? Do you go?' Janie asked me.

'You mean to Hebrew school?'

'Yes.'

'No, I don't go,' I said.

'Margaret doesn't even go to Sunday school. Isn't that right?' Nancy asked.

'Yes,' I answered.

'How'd you arrange that?' Gretchen asked.

'I'm not any religion,' I said.

'You're not!' Gretchen's mouth fell open.

'What are your parents?' Janie asked.

'Nothing,' I said.

'How positively neat!' Gretchen said.

Then they all just looked at me and nobody said anything and I felt pretty silly. So I tried to explain. 'See uh . . . my father was Jewish and uh . . . my mother was Christian and . . .'

Nancy's face lit up. 'Go on,' she said.

This was the first time they were interested in anything I had to say. 'Well, my mother's parents, who live in Ohio, told her they didn't want a Jewish son-in-law. If she wanted to ruin her life that was her business. But they would never accept my father for her husband.'

'No kidding!' Gretchen said. 'How about your father's family?'

'Well, my grandmother wasn't happy about getting a Christian daughter-in-law, but she at least accepted the situation.'

'So what happened?' Janie asked.

'They eloped.'

'How romantic!' Nancy sighed.

'So that's why they're not anything.'

'I don't blame them,' Gretchen said. 'I wouldn't be either.'

'But if you aren't any religion, how are you going to know if you should join the Y or the Jewish Community Center?' Janie asked.

'I don't know,' I said. 'I never thought about it. Maybe we won't join either one.'

'But *everybody* belongs to one or the other,' Nancy said.

'Well, I guess that will be up to my parents,' I said, ready to change the subject. I never meant to tell them my story in the first place. 'So uh . . . what day should we meet?'

Nancy announced that Friday was no good for a meeting day because she had piano lessons. Janie said she had ballet on Wednesday so I said that only left Mondays and we agreed that Monday would be our meeting day. Next week we had to bring our Boy Books and get checked to make sure we were all wearing bras.

When the meeting was over Nancy raised her arms high above her head. She closed her eyes and whispered, 'Here's to the Four PTS's. Hurray!'

'Long live the PTS's,' we chanted.

★

All through supper I thought about how I was going to tell my mother I wanted to wear a bra. I wondered why she hadn't ever asked me if I wanted one, since she knew so much about being a girl.

When she came in to kiss me goodnight I said it. 'I want to wear a bra.' Just like that – no beating around the bush.

My mother turned the bedroom light back on. 'Margaret . . . how come?'

'I just do is all.' I hid under the covers so she couldn't see my face.

My mother took a deep breath. 'Well, if you really want to we'll have to go shopping on Saturday. Okay?'

'Okay.' I smiled. My mother wasn't bad.

She turned out the light and closed my door halfway. Was I glad that was over!

Are you there, God? It's me, Margaret. I just told my mother I want a bra. Please help me grow, God. You know where. I want to be like everyone else. You know, God, my new friends all belong to the Y or the Jewish Community Center. Which way am I supposed to go? I don't know what you want me to do about that.

six

The next day after school Mr Benedict called me up to his desk. 'Margaret,' he said. 'I'd like to discuss your getting-to-know-you paper. For instance, why do you hate religious holidays?'

Was I sorry I wrote that! How positively stupid of me. If it was true that he was trying to find out if we were normal, I guess he thought I wasn't.

I half laughed. 'Oh, I just wrote that,' I said. 'I really don't hate them at all.'

'You must have had a reason. You can tell me. It's confidential.'

I raised my right eyebrow at Mr Benedict. I can do that really good. Raise one without the other. I do it whenever I can't think of anything to say. People notice it right away. Some people actually ask me how I do it. They forget what we were talking about and concentrate on my right eyebrow. I don't know exactly how I do it. What I do is think about it and the eyebrow goes up. I can't do it with my left. Only my right.

Mr Benedict noticed. But he didn't ask me anything about how I do it. He just said, 'I'm sure you have a perfectly good reason for hating religious holidays.'

I knew he was waiting for me to say something. He wasn't going to just forget about it. So I decided to get it over with in a hurry. 'None of those holidays are special to me. I don't belong to any religion,' I said.

Mr Benedict seemed pleased. Like he had uncovered some deep, dark mystery. 'I see. And your parents?'

'They aren't any religion. I'm supposed to choose my own when I grow up. If I want to, that is.'

Mr Benedict folded his hands and looked at me for a while. Then he said, 'Okay, Margaret. You can go now.'

I hoped he decided I was normal, after all. I lived in New York for eleven and a half years and I don't think anybody ever asked me about my religion. I never even thought about it. Now, all of a sudden, it was the big thing in my life.

That night when Grandma called she told me she'd gotten a subscription to Lincoln Center for the two of us. We'd meet one Saturday a month, have lunch and then go to a concert. Grandma really is clever. She knew my parents would never say no to one Saturday a month at Lincoln Center. That was culture. And they thought culture was very important. And now Grandma and I would have a chance to spend some time alone. But I was glad that Lincoln Center didn't start right away because I didn't want anything to interfere with Bra Day.

First thing on Saturday morning Moose Freed arrived to cut

our lawn. My father sulked behind a sports magazine. His finger was a lot better but it was still bandaged.

I sat around outside while Moose cut the grass. I liked the way he sang as he worked. I also liked his teeth. I saw them when he smiled at me. They were very clean and white and one in the front was a little crooked. I pretended to be really busy reading a book but the truth is – I was watching Moose. If he looked toward me I put my nose back in the book in a hurry. Moose would be number one in my Boy Book if only I was brave enough, but what would Nancy think? She hated him.

After lunch my mother told my father we were going shopping. We still had our same car but my mother thought we needed two now, because there weren't any buses in Farbrook and taxis were so expensive. My father said he'd see, but I knew we'd be getting another one soon. My mother can talk my father into anything.

My mother drove to a shopping centre where there was a Lord & Taylor. I had on my blue plaid dress and my loafers without socks and three Band Aids on my blisters.

First we went to the ladies' lingerie department where my mother told the saleslady we wanted to see a bra for me. The saleslady took one look and told my mother we'd be better off in the teen department where they had bras in very small sizes. My mother thanked the lady and I almost died! We went down on the escalator and headed for the teen shop. They had a whole display of underwear there. Bras and panties and slips to match. All I ever wore was white underpants and regular undershirts. Sometimes a slip if I was going to a party. My mother went to the counter and told the saleslady we were interested in a bra. I stood back and pretended not to know a thing. I even bent down to scratch a new mosquito bite.

'Come here, dear,' the saleslady called.

I hate people who call you dear. I walked over to the counter and raised my right eyebrow at her.

She reached over the top of the counter and said, 'Let's measure you, dear.' She put the tape measure all the way

around me and smiled at my mother. 'Twenty-eight,' she said.
I felt like giving her a pinch.

Then she took out a bunch of bras and put them on the
counter in front of us. My mother felt them all.

'Now, dear – I suggest the Gro-Bra. It grows *with* you.
You're not quite ready for a double A. Suppose you try them on
and see which is most comfortable.' She led us to a dressing
room with a pink door that locked. My mother sat in the
dressing room on a chair. I took off my dress. I wasn't wearing
anything underneath but pants. I picked up the first bra and
stuck my arms into the straps. I couldn't fasten it in back. My
mother had to help me. She adjusted the straps and felt the
front of me. 'How does it feel?' she asked.

'I don't know,' I said.

'Is it too tight?'

'No.'

'Too loose?'

'No.'

'Do you like it?'

'I guess . . .'

'Try on this one.'

She got me out of the first bra and into the next one. I
wondered how I'd ever learn to do it by myself. Maybe my
mother would have to dress me every day.

The next bra was softer than the first. My mother explained
it was made of Dacron. I liked the way it felt. My mother
nodded. The third one was fancy. It was lace and it made me
itch. My mother said it was impractical.

The saleslady knocked on the door as I was getting back into
my dress. 'How did we do? Did we find something?'

My mother told her *we* did. 'We'll take three of these,' she
said, holding up the soft bra.

When we got back to the counter who should be there but
Janie Loomis and her mother.

'Oh, hi, Margaret,' she said. 'I'm getting some winter
pyjamas.' Her cheeks were bright red and I saw the selection of

bras on the counter in front of her.

'Me too,' I said. 'I'm getting some flannel pyjamas for winter.'

'Well, see you Monday,' Janie said.

'Right – Monday.' I was plenty glad that my mother was down at the other end of the counter paying for my bras.

seven

When I got home I carried my package straight to my room. I took off my dress and put on the bra. I fastened it first around my waist, then wiggled it up to where it belonged. I threw my shoulders back and stood sideways. I didn't look any different. I took out a pair of socks and stuffed one sock into each side of the bra, to see if it really grew with me. It was too tight that way, but I liked the way it looked. Like Laura Danker. I took the socks out and put them away.

My father congratulated me at dinner. 'Well, you're really growing up, Margaret. No more little girl.'

'Oh, Daddy!' was all I could think of to say.

On Monday I studied the boys in my class. I had to have some names for my Boy Book before three o'clock. I picked Philip Leroy because he was the best-looking one. Also Jay Hassler because he had nice brown eyes and clean fingernails. I decided to leave it at that and explain I didn't know anybody else.

Right before the bell rang Mr Benedict told us that he was going to ask us each to do a year-long individual project.

Everybody groaned.

Mr Benedict held up his hands. 'Now it's not as bad as it sounds, class. For one thing, it's personal – between each of you and me. I'm not going to ask what your topic is. I expect you to choose it yourself and work it up in your own way. The only thing I insist on is that it be something . . . uh . . . meaningful.'

More groans.

Mr Benedict looked crushed. 'I had hoped you would find this interesting.'

Poor Mr Benedict. He was really disappointed. The way he talked to us I got the feeling we made him nervous. Nobody seemed scared of him at all and you should always be a little scared of your teacher. Sometimes he just sat at his desk and looked out at us like he couldn't believe we were really there. Of course Nancy pointed out that he *never ever* called on Laura Danker. I hadn't noticed.

As we were getting in line to go home he reminded us that on Thursday we'd have a test on the first two chapters in our social studies book. He asked us to please be prepared. Most teachers never say please.

After school we went straight to Nancy's. Before we started our official meeting we talked about Mr Benedict and his project. We all agreed it was crazy and none of us could think of a single idea.

Then Nancy called the roll. 'Veronica?'

'I'm here,' Gretchen said.

'Kimberly?'

'I'm here,' Janie said.

'Mavis?'

'I'm here,' I said.

'And so am I . . . Alexandra.' Nancy closed the roll book. 'Well, let's get to it. We all feel each other's backs to make sure we're wearing our bras.'

We all were.

'What size did you get, Janie?' Gretchen asked.

'I got a Gro-Bra,' Janie said.

'Me too,' I said.

'Me too!' Gretchen laughed.

'Not me,' Nancy said, proudly. 'Mine's thirty-two double A.'

We were all impressed.

'If you ever want to get out of those baby bras you have to exercise,' she told us.

'What kind of exercise?' Gretchen asked.

'Like this,' Nancy said. She made fists, bent her arms at the elbow and moved them back and forth, sticking her chest way out. She said, 'I must – I must – I must increase my bust.' She said it over and over. We copied her movements and chanted with her. 'We must – we must – we must increase our bust!'

'Good,' Nancy told us. 'Do it thirty-five times a day and I promise you'll see the results.'

'Now, for our Boy Books,' Gretchen said. 'Is everybody ready?'

We put our Boy Books on the floor and Nancy picked them up, one at a time. She read each one and passed it around for the rest of us to see. Janie's was first. She had seven names listed. Number one was Philip Leroy. Gretchen had four names. Number one was Philip Leroy. Nancy listed eighteen boys. I didn't even know eighteen boys! And number one was Philip Leroy. When Nancy got to my Boy Book she choked on an ice cube from her glass of Coke. When she stopped choking she read, 'Number one – Philip Leroy.' Everybody giggled. 'Number two – Jay Hassler. How come you picked him?'

I was getting mad. I mean, she didn't ask the others why they liked this one or that one, so why should I have to tell? I raised my eyebrow at Nancy, then looked away. She got the message.

When we were through, Nancy opened her bedroom door. There were Evan and Moose, eavesdropping. They followed us down the stairs and outside. When Nancy said, 'Get lost, we're busy,' Evan and Moose burst out laughing.

They shouted, 'We must – we must – we must increase our bust!' Then they fell on the grass and rolled over and over laughing so hard I hoped they would both wet their pants.

On Wednesday, during an arithmetic review, I heard a bird go *peep*. Lots of other kids heard it too and so did Mr Benedict. I know because he looked up. I went back to my problems but pretty soon I heard it again. *Peep.*

After the second *peep*, Mr Benedict walked to the window and opened it wide. He stuck his head way out looking all round. While he was doing that three more *peeps* came from the room. Mr Benedict walked to his deck and stood with his hands behind his back. *Peep.* I looked at Nancy. I was sure it came from her. But she didn't look at me or say anything. Mr Benedict sat down and tapped his fingers on the top of his desk. Pretty soon our room sounded like a pet store full of birds. Every second there was another *peep*. It was hard not to giggle. When Nancy kicked me under the table I knew it was my turn. I looked down and erased my answer to a problem. While I was blowing the eraser dust away I said it – *peep*. By the time Mr Benedict looked my way another *peep* came from across the room. I think it was Philip Leroy. We kept waiting for Mr Benedict to say something, but he didn't.

When we came in the next morning our desks had been rearranged. Instead of four tables our desks formed one big U shape across the room. There were name cards taped on to each desk. On one side I was next to Freddy Barnett, who I didn't like at all. I knew for a fact that he was a troublemaker because I saw him stand behind Jay Hassler on the first day of school and just as Jay was about to sit down, Freddy Barnett pulled his chair away. Jay wound up on the floor. I hate kids who do that! I'd have to be very careful not to fall into the trap of the Lobster. That's what we call him because on the first day of school he was sunburned bright red.

But on the other side of me things were even worse. I was next to Laura Danker! I was afraid to even look her way. Nancy warned me that reputations were catching. Well, I didn't have to worry because Laura didn't look my way either. She looked straight ahead. Naturally, the Four PTS's were all separated. But Nancy (that lucky!) got to sit next to Philip Leroy!

There wasn't any more *peeping*. Mr Benedict reminded us of our social studies test the next day. That afternoon we had gym. The boys got to play baseball with Mr Benedict. The girls

38

were left with the gym teacher, Miss Abbott, who told us to line up in order of size. I was third from the front end. Janie was first. Laura Danker was last. Gretchen and Nancy were in the middle. After we lined up Miss Abbott talked about posture and how important it is to stand up straight. 'No matter how tall you are you must never slouch, because height is such a blessing.' With that Miss Abbott stood up and took some deep breaths. She must have been at least six feet tall. Janie and I looked at each other and giggled. We were not blessed.

Then Miss Abbott told us since we were in sixth grade and very grown up, there were certain subjects we would cover during the school year. 'Certain very private subjects just for girls.' That was all she said but I got the idea. Why do they wait until sixth grade when you already know everything!

That night I really worked hard. I read the first two chapters in my social studies book four times. Then I sat on my bedroom floor and did my exercise. 'I must – I must – I must increase my bust!' I did it thirty-five times and climbed into bed.

Are you there, God? It's me, Margaret. I just did an exercise to help me grow. Have you thought about it, God? About my growing, I mean. I've got a bra now. It would be nice if I had something to put in it. Of course, if you don't think I'm ready I'll understand. I'm having a test in school tomorrow. Please let me get a good grade on it, God. I want you to be proud of me. Thank you.

The next morning Mr Benedict passed out the test paper himself. The questions were already on the board. He said to begin as soon as we got our paper. Freddy the Lobster poked me and whispered, 'No name.'

'What do you mean, no name?' I whispered back.

Freddy whispered, 'Nobody signs his name. Benedict won't know whose paper is whose. Get it?'

I got it all right but I didn't like it. Especially since I'd read the chapters four times. But if nobody was going to put a name on the test paper, I wasn't going to either. I felt cheated because Mr Benedict would never know how hard I'd studied.

I answered all the questions in fifteen minutes. Mr Benedict asked Janie to collect the papers for him. I couldn't imagine what he would do to us when he found out nobody had put a name on the test. I figured he'd be plenty mad but you can't do much to a whole class except keep them after school. We couldn't all be expelled, could we?

eight

On Friday morning when we walked into our room, there was a test paper on everyone's desk. Every paper was marked and had the proper name on it. I got a ninety-eight. I felt great. Freddy Barnett didn't feel great at all. He got a fifty-three! Mr Benedict didn't say anything about our names not being on the test papers. He just stood there and smiled. 'Good morning, class,' he said without clearing his throat. I think he knew he'd won the battle.

Later that day Mr Benedict reminded us of our individual projects again. He told us not to wait until the last minute and think we could whip something up then. He said by the end of next week we should all know our topic and start in on our notes.

I thought a lot about it, but I didn't know anything meaningful that I was willing to share with Mr Benedict. I mean, I couldn't very well come up with a year-long study about bras and what goes in them. Or about my feelings towards Moose. Or about God. Or could I? I mean, not about God exactly – I could never tell Mr Benedict that – but maybe about religion. If I could figure out which religion to be I'd know if I wanted to join the Y or the Jewish Community

Center. That was meaningful, wasn't it? I'd have to think about it.

Are you there, God? It's me, Margaret. What would you think of me doing a project on religion? You wouldn't mind, would you, God? I'd tell you all about it. And I won't make any decisions without asking you first. I think it's time for me to decide what to be. I can't go on being nothing forever, can I?

The following Saturday morning my mother drove me to the highway to get the New York bus. It was my first time going alone and my mother was nervous.

'Listen, Margaret – don't sit next to any men. Either sit alone or pick out a nice lady. And try to sit up front. If the bus isn't air-conditioned open your window. And when you get there ask a *lady* to show you the way downstairs. Grandma will meet you at the information desk.'

'I know, I know.' We'd been over it three dozen times but when the bus came my mother got out of the car and shouted to the bus driver.

'This little girl is travelling alone. Please keep an eye on her. It's her first trip.'

'Don't worry, lady,' the bus driver told my mother. Then my mother waved to me. I made a face at her and looked the other way.

I found Grandma right where she was supposed to be. She gave me a big kiss. Grandma smelled delicious. She was wearing a green suit and had on lots of green eyeshadow to match. Her hair was silver blonde. Grandma's hair colour changes about once a month.

When we were out of the bus terminal Grandma said, 'You look beautiful, Margaret. I love your hair.'

Grandma always has something nice to say to me. And my hair did look better. I read that if you brush it good it can grow up to an inch a month.

We went to lunch at a restaurant near Lincoln Center.

During my chocolate parfait I whispered, 'I'm wearing a bra. Can you tell?'

'Of course I can tell,' Grandma said.

'You can?' I was really surprised. I stopped eating. 'Well, how do you think it makes me look?'

'Much older,' Grandma said, between sips of her coffee. I didn't know whether to believe her or not so I believed her.

Then we went to the concert. I didn't fidget like when I was a little kid. I sat very still and paid attention to the music. During intermission Grandma and I walked around outside. I love that fountain in the middle of Lincoln Center. I love it more than the concerts themselves. And I love to watch the people walk by. Once I saw a model having her picture taken by the fountain. It was freezing cold and she was wearing a summer dress. That's when I decided not to be a model. Even if I did get beautiful some day.

In the cab, on the way back to the bus terminal, I thought about Grandma being Jewish. She was the perfect person to help me start my project. So I asked her, 'Can I go to temple with you sometime?'

Grandma absolutely stared at me. I never knew anyone could open her eyes so wide.

'What are you saying? Are you saying you want to be Jewish?' She held her breath.

'No. I'm saying I'd like to go to temple and see what it's all about.'

'My Margaret!' Grandma threw her arms around me. I think the cab driver thought we were crazy. 'I knew you were a Jewish girl at heart! I always knew it!' Grandma took out a lace hanky and dabbed her eyes.

'I'm not, Grandma,' I insisted. 'You know I'm not anything.'

'You can say it, but I'll never believe it. Never!' She blew her nose. When she finished blowing she said, 'I know what it is. You've made a lot of Jewish friends in Farbrook. Am I right?'

'No, Grandma. My friends have nothing to do with this.'

'Then what? I don't understand.'

42

'I just want to see what it's all about. So can I?' I certainly was not going to tell Grandma about Mr Benedict.

Grandma sat back in her seat and beamed at me. 'I'm thrilled! I'm going right home to call the rabbi. You'll come with me on Rosh Hashanah.' Then she stopped smiling and asked. 'Does your mother know?'

I shook my head.

'Your father?'

I shook it again.

Grandma slapped her hand against her forehead. 'Be sure to tell them it's not my idea! Would I be in trouble!'

'Don't worry, Grandma.'

'That's ridiculous!' my mother said when I told her. 'You know how Daddy and I feel about religion.'

'You said I could choose when I grow up!'

'But you're not ready to choose yet, Margaret!'

'I just want to try it out,' I argued. 'I'm going to try church too, so don't get hysterical!'

'I am *not* hysterical! I just think it's foolish for a girl of your age to bother herself with religion.'

'Can I go?' I asked.

'I'm not going to stop you,' my mother said.

'Fine. Then I'll go.'

On Rosh Hashanah morning, while I was still in bed, I said.

Are you there, God? It's me, Margaret. I'm going to temple today – with Grandma. It's a holiday. I guess you know that. Well, my father thinks it's a mistake and my mother thinks the whole idea is crazy, but I'm going anyway. I'm sure this will help me decide what to be. I've never been inside a temple or a church. I'll look for you, God.

nine

I had a new suit and a small velvet hat. My mother said
everyone wears new clothes for the Jewish holidays. It was hot
for October and my father said he remembered it was always
hot on the Jewish holidays when he was a kid. I had to wear
white gloves. They made my hands sweat. By the time I got to
New York the gloves were pretty dirty so I took them off and
stuffed them into my pocketbook. Grandma met me at our
usual spot in the bus terminal and took me in a taxi to her
temple.

We got there at ten-thirty. Grandma had to show a card to an
usher and then he led us to our seats which were in the fifth row
in the middle. Grandma whispered to the people sitting near
her that I was her granddaughter Margaret. The people looked
at me and smiled. I smiled back. I was glad when the rabbi
stepped out on the stage and held up his hands. While this was
going on soft organ music played. I thought it sounded
beautiful. The rabbi was dressed in a long black robe. He
looked like a priest except he didn't have on the backwards
collar that priests wear. Also, he had a little hat on his head that
Grandma called a yarmulke.

The rabbi welcomed us and then started a lot of things I
didn't understand. We had to stand up and sit down a lot and
sometimes we all read together in English from a prayer book. I
didn't understand too much of what I was reading. Other times
the choir sang and the organ played. That was definitely the
best part. Some of the service was in Hebrew and I was
surprised to see that Grandma could recite along with the rabbi.

I looked around a lot, to see what was going on. But since I
was in the fifth row there wasn't much for me to see, except for
four rows in front of me. I knew it wouldn't be polite to actually
turn my head and look behind me. There were two big silver
bowls filled with white flowers up on the stage. They were very
pretty.

At eleven-thirty the rabbi made a speech. A sermon, Grandma called it. At first I tried very hard to understand what he was talking about. But after a while I gave up and started counting different coloured hats. I counted eight brown, six black, three red, a yellow and a leopard before the rabbi finished. Then we all stood up again and everyone sang a song in Hebrew that I didn't know. And that was it! I expected something else. I don't know what exactly. A feeling, maybe. But I suppose you have to go more than once to know what it's all about.

As we filed out of the aisles Grandma pulled me to one side, away from the crowd. 'How would you like to meet the rabbi, Margaret?'

'I don't know,' I said. I really wanted to get outside.

'Well, you're going to!' Grandma smiled at me. 'I've told him all about you.'

We stood in line waiting to shake hands with the rabbi. After a long time it was our turn. I was face to face with Rabbi Kellerman. He was kind of young and looked a little like Miles J. Benedict Jr. He wasn't skinny though.

Grandma whispered to me, 'Shake hands, Margaret.'

I held out my hand.

'This is my granddaughter, Rabbi. The one I told you about . . . Margaret Simon.'

The rabbi shook my hand. 'Yes, of course. Margaret! Good Yom Tov.'

'Yes,' I said.

The rabbi laughed. 'It means Happy New Year. That's what we're celebrating today.'

'Oh,' I said. 'Well, Happy New Year to you, Rabbi.'

'Did you enjoy our service?' he asked.

'Oh, yes,' I said. 'I just loved it.'

'Good – good.' He pumped my hand up and down some more. 'Come back any time. Get to know us, Margaret. Get to know us and God.'

★

I had to go through the third degree when I got home.

'Well,' my mother said. 'How was it?'

'Okay, I guess.'

'Did you like it?' she asked.

'It was interesting,' I said.

'Did you learn anything?' my father wanted to know.

'Well,' I said. 'In the first five rows there were eight brown hats and six black ones.'

My father laughed. 'When I was a kid I used to count feathers on hats.' Then we laughed together.

Are you there, God? It's me, Margaret. I'm really on my way now. By the end of the school year I'll know all there is to know about religion. And before I start junior high I'll know which one I am. Then I'll be able to join the Y or the Center like everybody else.

ten

Three things happened the first week in November. Laura Danker wore a sweater to school for the first time. Mr Benedict's eyes almost popped out of his head. Actually, I didn't notice Mr Benedict's eyes, but Nancy told me. Freddy the Lobster noticed too. He asked me, 'How come you don't look like that in a sweater, Margaret?' Then he laughed hard and slapped his leg. Very funny, I thought. I wore sweaters every day since I had so many of them. All *made expressly* for me by Grandma. Even if I stuffed my bra with socks I still wouldn't look like Laura Danker. I wondered if it was true that she went behind the A&P with Evan and Moose. Why would she do a stupid thing like that?

What reminded me of Moose was that he cut our grass and cleaned up our leaves and said he'd be back in the spring. So unless I bumped into him at Nancy's house I wouldn't see him all winter. Not that he even knew I existed – I'd had to hide from him ever since that *We must – we must* incident. But I watched him secretly from my bedroom window.

The second thing that happened was that I went to church with Janie Loomis. Janie and I had gotten pretty friendly. We were especially friendly in gym because Ruth, the girl who was second in line, was absent a lot. So Janie and I got to talk and once I came right out and asked her if she went to church.

'When I have to,' she said.

So I asked her if I could go with her some time just to see what it was like and she said, 'Sure, how about Sunday?'

So I went. The funniest thing was it was just like temple. Except it was all in English. But we read from a prayer book that didn't make sense and the minister gave a sermon I couldn't follow and I counted eight black hats, four red ones, six blue and two fur. At the end of the service everyone sang a hymn. Then we stood in line to shake hands with the minister. By then I was a pro at it.

Janie introduced me. 'This is my friend Margaret Simon. She's no religion.'

I almost fainted. What did Janie have to go and say that for? The minister looked at me like I was a freak. Then he smiled with an Aha – maybe-I'll-win-her look.

'Welcome to the First Presbyterian Church, Margaret. I hope you'll come back again.'

'Thank you,' I said.

Are you there, God? It's me, Margaret. I've been to church. I didn't feel anything special in there, God. Even though I wanted to. I'm sure it has nothing to do with you. Next time I'll try harder.

During this time I talked to Nancy every night. My father wanted to know why we had to phone each other so often when we were together in school all day. 'What can you possibly discuss after only three hours?' he asked. I didn't even try to explain. Lots of times we did our maths homework over the phone. When we were done Nancy called Gretchen to check answers and I called Janie.

The third thing that happened that week was the principal of our school announced over the loudspeaker that the PTA was giving a Thanksgiving square dance for the three sixth-grade classes. Mr Benedict asked us if we knew how to square dance. Most of us didn't.

Nancy told the Four PTS's the square dance was going to be really super. And she knew all about it because her mother was on the committee. She said we should all write down who we wanted to dance with and she'd see what she could do about it. It turned out that we all wanted Philip Leroy, so Nancy said, 'Forget it – I'm no magician.'

For the next two weeks our gym period was devoted to square-dancing lessons. Mr Benedict said if we were being given this party the least we could do to show our appeciation was to learn to do the basic steps. We practised with records and Mr Benedict jumped around a lot, clapping his hands. When he had to demonstrate a step he used Laura Danker as his partner. He said it was because she was tall enough to reach his shoulder properly, but Nancy gave me a knowing look. Anyway, none of the boys in our class wanted to be Laura's partner because they were all a lot smaller than her. Even Philip Leroy only came up to her chin, and he was the tallest.

The problem with square-dance lessons was that most of the boys were a lot more interested in stepping on our feet than they were in learning how to dance. And a few of them were so good at it they could step on us in time to the music. Mostly, I concentrated on not getting my feet squashed.

On the morning of the square dance I dressed in my new skirt and blouse.

Are you there, God? It's me, Margaret. I can't wait until two o'clock, God. That's when our dance starts. Do you think I'll get

Philip Leroy for a partner? It's not so much that I like him as a person, God, but as a boy he's very handsome. And I'd love to dance with him . . . just once or twice. Thank you, God.

The PTA decorated the gym. It was supposed to look like a barn, I think. There were two piles of hay and three scarecrows. And a big sign on the wall in yellow letters saying WELCOME TO THE SIXTH GRADE SQUARE DANCE . . . as if we didn't know.

I was glad my mother wasn't a chaperone. It's bad enough trying to act natural at a dance, but when your mother's there it's impossible. I know because Mrs Wheeler was a chaperone and Nancy was a wreck. The chaperones were dressed funny, like farmers or something. I mean, Nancy's mother wore dungarees, a plaid shirt and a big straw hat. I didn't blame Nancy for pretending not to know her.

We had a genuine square-dance caller. He was dressed up a lot like Mrs Wheeler. He stood on the stage and told us what steps to do. He also worked the record player. He stamped his feet and jumped around and now and then I saw him mop his face off with a red handkerchief. Mr Benedict kept telling us to get into the spirit of the party. 'Relax and enjoy yourselves,' he said.

The three sixth grades were supposed to mingle but the Four PTS's stuck together. We had to line up every time there was a new dance. The girls lined up on one side and the boys on the other. That's how you got a partner. The only trouble was there were four more girls than boys, so whoever wound up last on line had to dance with another leftover girl. That only happened to me and Janie once, thank goodness!

What we did was try to figure out who our partner was going to be in advance. Like, I knew when I was fourth in line that Norman Fishbein was going to be my partner because he was fourth in line on the boys' side. So I switched around fast because Norman Fishbein is the biggest drip in my class. Well, at least one of the biggest drips. Also, Freddy Barnett was to be avoided because all he would do was tease me about how come I didn't look like Laura Danker in a sweater. But I noticed that once when he danced with her his face was so red he looked more like a lobster than he did when he was all sunburned.

The girls shuffled around more than the boys because most of us wanted to get Philip Leroy for a partner. And finally I got him. This is how it happened. After everyone had a partner we had to make a square. My partner was Jay Hassler who was very polite and didn't try to step on my foot once. Then the caller told us to switch partners with whoever was on our right side. Well, Philip Leroy was with Nancy on my right side, and Nancy was so mad she almost cried right in front of everyone. Even though I was thrilled to have Philip Leroy all to myself for a whole record, he *was* one of the foot steppers! And dancing with him made my hands sweat so bad I had to wipe them off on my new skirt.

At four o'clock the chaperones served us punch and cookies and at quarter to five the dance was over and my mother picked me up in our new car. (My father gave in around Hallowe'en when my mother explained that she couldn't even get a quart of milk because she had no car. And that *Margaret* couldn't possibly walk to and from school in bad weather and that bad weather would be coming very soon. My mother didn't like my father's suggestion that if she got up early and drove him to the station she could use his car all day long.) Our new car is a Chevy. It's green.

My mother was in a hurry to drive home from the square dance because she was in the middle of a new painting. It was a picture of a lot of different fruits in honour of Thanksgiving. My mother gives away a whole bunch of pictures every Christmas. My father thinks they wind up in other people's attics.

eleven

By the first week in December we no longer used our secret names at PTS meetings. It was too confusing, Nancy said. Also, we just about gave up on our Boy Books. For one thing the names never changed. Nancy managed to shift hers around. It was easy for her – with eighteen boys. But Janie and Gretchen and I always listed Philip Leroy number one. There was no suspense about the whole thing. I wondered, did they list Philip Leroy because they really liked him or were they doing what I did – making him number one because he was so good-looking. Maybe they were ashamed to write who they really liked too.

The day that Gretchen finally got up the guts to sneak out her father's anatomy book we met at my house, in my bedroom, with the door closed and a chair shoved in front of it. We sat on the floor in a circle with the book opened to the male body.

'Do you suppose that's what Philip Leroy looks like without his clothes on?' Janie asked.

'Naturally, dope!' Nancy said. 'He's male, isn't he?'

'Look at all those veins and stuff,' Janie said.

'Well, we *all* have them,' Gretchen said.

'I think they're ugly,' Janie said.

'You better never be a doctor or a nurse,' Gretchen told her. 'They have to look at this stuff all the time.'

'Turn the page, Gretchen,' Nancy said.

The next page was the male reproductive system.

None of us said anything. We just looked until Nancy told us, 'My brother looks like that.'

'How do you know?' I asked.

'He walks around naked,' Nancy said.

'My father used to walk around naked,' Gretchen said. 'But lately he's stopped doing it.'

'My aunt went to a nudist colony last summer,' Janie said.

'No kidding!' Nancy looked up.

'She stayed a month,' Janie told us. 'My mother didn't talk to her for three weeks after that. She thought it was a disgrace. My aunt's divorced.'

'Because of the nudist colony?' I asked.

'No,' Janie said. 'She was divorced before she went.'

'What do you suppose they do there?' Gretchen asked.

'Just walk around naked is all. My aunt says it's very peaceful. But I'll never walk around naked in front of anybody!'

'What about when you get married?' Gretchen asked.

'Even then,' Janie insisted.

'You're a prude!' Nancy said.

'I am not! It has nothing to do with being a prude!'

'When you grow you'll change your mind,' Nancy told her. 'You'll want everybody to see you. Like those girls in *Playboy*.'

'What girls in *Playboy*?' Janie asked.

'Didn't you *ever* see a copy of *Playboy*?'

'Where would I see it?' Janie asked.

'My father gets it,' I said.

'Do you have it around?' Nancy asked.

'Sure.'

'Well, get it!' Nancy told me.

'Now?' I asked.

'Of course.'

'Well, I don't know,' I said.

'Listen, Margaret – Gretchen went to all the trouble of sneaking out her father's medical book. The least you could do is show us *Playboy*.'

So I opened my bedroom door and went downstairs, trying to remember where I had seen the latest issue. I didn't want to ask my mother. Not that it was so wrong to show it to my friends. I mean, if it was so wrong my father shouldn't get it at all, right? Although lately I think he's been hiding it because it's never in the magazine rack where it used to be. Finally, I found it in his night table drawer and I thought if my mother caught me and asked me what I was doing I'd say we were making booklets and I needed some old magazines to cut up. But she didn't catch me.

Nancy opened it right up to the naked girl in the middle. On the page before there was a story about her. It said 'Hillary Brite is eighteen years old'.

'Eighteen! That's only six more years,' Nancy squealed.

'But look at the size of her. They're huge!' Janie said.

'Do you suppose we'll look like that at eighteen?' Gretchen asked.

'If you ask me, I think there's something wrong with her,' I said. 'She looks out of proportion!'

'Do you suppose that's what Laura Danker looks like?' Janie asked.

'No. Not yet,' Nancy said. 'But she might at eighteen!'

Our meeting ended with fifty rounds of '*We must – we must – we must increase our bust!*'

twelve

On December eleventh Grandma sailed on a three-week cruise to the Caribbean. She went every year. She had a bon voyage party in her room on the ship. This year I was allowed to go. My mother gave Grandma a green silk box to keep her jewellery safe. It was very nice – all lined in white velvet. Grandma said thank you and that all her jewellery was for 'her Margaret' anyway so she had to take good care of it. Grandma's always reminding me of how nobody lives forever and everything she has is for me and I hate it when she talks like that. She once told me she had her lawyer prepare her funeral instructions so things would go the way she planned. Such as, the kind of box she wants to be buried in and that she doesn't want any speeches at all and that I should only come once or twice a year to see that her grave is looking nice and neat.

We stayed on the ship half an hour and then Grandma kissed me goodbye and promised to take me along with her one of these days.

The next week my mother started to address her Christmas cards and for days at a time she was frantically busy with them. She doesn't call them Christmas cards. Holiday greetings, she says. We don't celebrate Christmas exactly. We give presents but my parents say that's a traditional American custom. My father says my mother and her greeting cards have to do with her childhood. She sends them to people she grew up with and they send cards back to her. So once a year she finds out who married whom and who had what kids and stuff like that. Also, she sends one to her brother, whom I've never met. He lives in California.

This year I discovered something really strange. I discovered that my mother was sending a Christmas card to her parents in Ohio. I found out because I was looking through the pile of cards one day when I had a cold and stayed at home from school. There it was – just like that. The envelope said Mr and Mrs Paul Hutchins, and that's them. My grandparents! I didn't mention anything about it to my mother. I had the feeling I wasn't supposed to know.

In school, Mr Benedict was running around trying to find out what happened to the new choir robes. The whole school was putting on a Christmas – Hanukkah pageant for the parents and our sixth-grade class was the choir. We didn't even have to try out. 'Mr Benedict's class will be the choir,' the principal announced. We practised singing every day with the music teacher. I thought by the time Christmas finally rolled around I wouldn't have any voice left. We learned five Christmas carols and three Hanukkah songs – alto and soprano parts. Mostly the boys sang alto and the girls sang soprano. We'd been measured for our new choir robes right after Thanksgiving. The PTA decided the old ones were really worn out. Our new ones would be green instead of black. We all had to carry pencil-sized flashlights instead of candles.

We practiced marching down the halls and into the auditorium singing '*Adeste Fidelis*' in English and Latin. We marched in two lines, boys and girls. And naturally in size places. I walked right behind Janie because Ruth had moved away. My partner turned out to be Norman Fishbein. I never looked at him. I just marched looking straight ahead singing very loud.

A week before the pageant Alan Gordon told Mr Benedict that he wasn't going to sing the Christmas songs because it was against his religion. Then Lisa Murphy raised her hand and said that she wasn't going to sing the Hanukkah songs because it was against *her* religion.

Mr Benedict explained that songs were for everyone and had nothing at all to do with religion, but the next day Alan brought in a note from home and from then on he marched but he didn't sing. Lisa sang when we marched but she didn't even move her lips during the Hanukkah songs.

Are you there, God? It's me, Margaret. I want you to know I'm giving a lot of thought to Christmas and Hanukkah this year. I'm trying to decide if one might be special for me. I'm really thinking hard, God. But so far I haven't come up with any answers.

Our new green choir robes were delivered to school the day of the pageant and were sent home with us to be pressed. The best thing about the pageant, besides wearing the robe and carrying the flashlight, was that I got to sit in the first row of choir seats, facing the audience, which meant that the kindergarten kids were right in front of me. Some of them tried to touch our feet with their feet. One little kid wet his pants during the scene where Mary and Joseph come to the inn. He made a puddle on the floor right in front of Janie. Janie had to keep on singing and pretend she didn't know. It was pretty hard not to laugh.

School closed for vacation right after the pageant. When I got home my mother told me I had a letter.

thirteen

'Margaret – you've got a letter,' my mother called from the studio. 'It's on the front table.'

I just about never get any letters. Probably because I never write anybody back. So I dashed over to the front table and picked it up. *Miss Margaret Simon*, it said. I turned the envelope around but there was no return address. I wondered who sent it. Wondering made it much more fun than ripping it open and knowing right away. It was probably just an advertisement anyway. Finally, when I couldn't stand it any more I opened it – very slowly and *very* carefully so I wouldn't rip up the envelope. It was an invitation! I knew right away because of the picture – a bunch of kids dancing around a record. Also, it said, HAVING A PARTY.

Who's having a party, I thought. Who's having a party and invited me? Naturally I could have found out right away. I could have looked inside. But this was better. I considered the possibilities. It couldn't be a PTS because I would have known. It could be somebody I knew from New York or camp, except I hadn't written to any old friends to tell them my new address. Anyway, the envelope was postmarked New Jersey. Let's see, I thought. Who could it be? Who? Finally, I opened it.

> *Come on over on Saturday, Dec. 20*
> *from 5 PM to 9 PM (supper)*
> *1334 Whittingham Terrace*
> *Norman Fishbein*

'Norman Fishbein!' I yelled. That drip! I never even talked to him. Why would he invite me to his party? Still, a party is a

56

party. And for supper too!

'Hey, Mom!' I yelled, running into the studio. My mother was standing away from her canvas, studying her work. Her paint brush was in her mouth, between her teeth. 'Guess what, Mom?'

'What?' she said, not taking the paint brush away.

'I'm invited to a supper party. Here – look –' I showed her my invitation.

She read it. 'Who's Norman Fishbein?' She took the paint brush out of her mouth.

'A kid in my class.'

'Do you like him?'

'He's okay. Can I go?'

'Well . . . I suppose so.' My mother dabbed some red paint on her canvas. Then the phone rang.

'I'll get it.' I ran into the kitchen and said a breathless hello.

'It's Nancy. Did you get invited?'

'Yes,' I said. 'Did you?'

'Mmm. We all did. Janie and Gretchen too.'

'Can you go?'

'Sure.'

'Me too.'

'I've never been to a supper party,' Nancy said.

'Me either. Should we dress up?' I asked.

'My mother's going to call Mrs Fishbein. I'll let you know.' She hung up.

Ten minutes later the phone rang again. I answered.

'Margaret. It's me again.'

'I know.'

'You'll never believe this!' Nancy said.

'What? What won't I believe?'

'We're all invited.'

'What do you mean *all*?'

'Our whole class.'

'All twenty-eight of us?'

'That's what Mrs Fishbein told my mother.'

'Even Laura?'

'I guess so.'

'Do you think she'll come?' I asked, trying to picture Laura at a party.

'Well, her mother and Mrs Fishbein work on a lot of committees together. So maybe her mother will make her.'

'How about Philip Leroy?'

'He's invited. That's all I know. And Mrs Fishbein said definitely party clothes.'

When I hung up I raced back to the studio. 'Mom – our whole class is invited!'

'Your *whole* class?' My mother put her paint brush down and looked at me.

'Yes. All twenty-eight of us.'

'Mrs Fishbein must be crazy!' my mother said.

'Should I wear my velvet, do you think?'

'It's your best. You might as well.'

On the day of the party I talked to Nancy six times, to Janie three times and to Gretchen twice. Nancy called me back every time she changed her mind about what to wear. And each time she asked me if I was still wearing my velvet. I told her I was. The rest of the time we made our arrangements. We decided that Nancy would sleep over at my house and that Gretchen would sleep over at Janie's. Mr Wheeler would drive us all to the party and Mr Loomis would drive us home.

My mother washed my hair at two o'clock. She gave me a cream rinse too, so I wouldn't get tangles. She set it in big rollers all over my head. I sat under her hair dryer. Then she *filed* my nails with an emery board instead of just cutting them like usual. My velvet dress was already laid out on my bed along with my new underwear, party shoes and tights. My new underwear was not the ordinary cotton kind. It was nylon, trimmed with lace around the edges. It was supposed to be one of my December tradition gifts. All afternoon I kept thinking that maybe Norman Fishbein wasn't such a drip.

58

After my bath I was supposed to go to my room and rest so I'd be in good shape for the party. I went to my room and closed the door – only I didn't feel like resting. What I did was move my desk chair in front of my dresser mirror. Then I stood on the chair and took off my robe. I stood naked in front of the mirror. I was starting to get some hairs. I turned around and studied myself sideways. Then I got off the chair and moved it closer to the mirror. I stood back up on it and looked again. My head looked funny with all those rollers. The rest of me looked the same.

Are you there, God? It's me, Margaret. I hate to remind you, God . . . I mean, I know you're busy. But it's already December and I'm not growing. At least I don't see any real difference. Isn't it time, God? Don't you think I've waited patiently? Please help me.

I hopped off the chair and sat down on the edge of my bed, putting on my clean underwear and tights. Then I stood in front of the mirror again. I didn't look at myself for very long this time.

· I went into the bathroom and opened the bottom cabinet. There was a whole box of cotton balls. *Sterile until opened*, the package said. I reached in and grabbed a few. My heart was pounding, which seemed stupid because what was I so afraid of anyway? I mean, if my mother saw me grab some cotton balls she wouldn't say anything. I use them all the time – to put calamine on my summer mosquito bites – to clean off cuts and bruises – to put on my face lotion at night. But my heart kept pounding anyway, because I knew what I was going to do with the cotton balls.

I tiptoed back to my room and closed the door. I stepped into my closet and stood in one corner. I shoved three cotton balls into each side of my bra. Well, so what if it was cheating! Probably other girls did it too. I'd look a lot better, wouldn't I? So why not!

I came out of the closet and got back up on my chair. This time when I turned sideways I looked like I'd grown. I liked it!

Are you still there, God? See how nice my bra looks now! That's all I need – just a little help. I'll really be good around the house, God. I'll clear the table every night for a month at least! Please, God . . .

fourteen

Later, my mother brushed my hair. It came out just right, except for one piece on the left that turned the wrong way. My mother said that piece made it look very natural.

My mother and father smiled at me a lot while I was waiting for Nancy's father to pick me up. I smiled back. It was like we all knew some special secret. Only I knew they didn't know *my* special secret! At least they didn't say anything dumb like doesn't she look sweet – going to her first supper party! I'd have died!

Mr Wheeler tooted his horn at quarter to five. My mother kissed me goodbye and my father waved from his chair. 'Have fun,' he called.

The Four PTS's squeezed into the back seat of the Wheeler car (not the station wagon). Nancy's father told us it was silly to sit like that and besides it made him feel like a hired chauffeur. But all we did was giggle. Janie got her hair cut without telling us she was going to. She said she didn't know it herself until that afternoon when her mother took her to the beauty parlour and had a private talk with Mr Anthony. Then Mr Anthony started clipping away and next thing she knew – she had this new haircut. She looked like an elf. It did a lot for her. And for a minute I thought about how I would look with the same haircut. But then I remembered how long I'd been suffering to let my hair grow. I decided it would be stupid to cut it all off.

When we got to the party Norman's mother opened the door for us. She was very tall and thin with a face like Norman's. I remembered her from the PTA square dance. Tonight she wasn't dressed like a farmer. She had on black velvet pants and some kind of top that looked like it had diamonds and rubies all over it.

'Good evening, Mrs Fishbein,' Nancy said, in a voice I'd never heard. 'Please meet my friend Margaret Simon.'

Mrs Fishbein smiled at me and said, 'Glad to meet you, Margaret.' Then she took our coats away and handed them to a maid who carried them up the stairs.

'My, you all look so pretty!' Mrs Fishbein said. 'Everyone is downstairs. Nancy, you know the way.'

I followed Nancy past the living room. The furniture was all very modern. The chairs looked like carved-out boxes and the tables were all glass. Everything was beige. At Nancy's house the furniture all has lion's paws for feet and there are a million colours. At my house the living room is carpeted but empty. My mother is trying to decide what kind of stuff she wants.

Norman's house was pretty big, because I had to follow Nancy through at least four more rooms before we got to a door leading downstairs.

It looked like most of my class was already there. Including Laura Danker, who I thought looked gorgeous in a soft pink dress with her hair all loose, kind of hanging in her face.

The boys had on sports jackets and some wore ties. Philip Leroy had on a tie the first time I saw him but a few minutes later the tie was gone and his shirt was unbuttoned around the neck. Soon after that, not one boy had his jacket on. They were all in a big heap in the corner.

Mostly, the girls stayed on one side of the room, and the boys on the other. As soon as everyone was there Mrs Fishbein brought out the food. All kinds of sandwiches and a big dish of cut-up hotdogs in beans. I took some of that and some potato salad and sat down at a table with Janie, Nancy and Gretchen.

There were six little tables so practically everyone had a place to sit. As soon as we were all served Mrs Fishbein and the maid went back upstairs.

I'm not sure who started blowing the mustard through a straw up at the ceiling. I only know that I saw Philip Leroy yell, 'Watch this, Freddy!' as he aimed his straw. I saw the mustard fly up and make a yellow splotch on the white ceiling.

Mrs Fishbein didn't come downstairs again until dessert time. At first she didn't see the ceiling. But she did see the mess on the buffet table. When she looked up she sucked in her breath and the room got very quiet. 'What is that on my ceiling?' she asked Norman.

'Mustard,' Norman answered.

'I see,' Mrs Fishbein replied.

That was all she said but she looked at every one of us with an I-don't-know-why-your-parents-never-taught-you-any-manners look. Then Mrs Fishbein stood close to our table and said, 'I'm sure these girls aren't responsible for this mess.' We smiled at her, but I saw Philip Leroy stick out his tongue at us.

'Now I'm going upstairs to get your dessert,' Mrs Fishbein said, 'and I expect you to behave like ladies and gentlemen.'

Dessert was tiny cupcakes in all different colours. I ate two chocolate ones before Freddy Barnett came over to our table. 'I'm sure these girls didn't do anything naughty!' he mimicked. 'These girls are so sweet and good.'

'Oh shut up!' Nancy told him, standing up. She was as tall as he was.

'Why don't you shut up, *know it all*!'

'Cut it out, Lobster!' Nancy hollered.

'Who's a lobster?'

'You are!' Nancy gritted her teeth.

Freddy grabbed hold of Nancy and for a minute I thought he was going to hit her.

'Take your lobster claws off me!' Nancy yelled.

'Make me,' Freddy told her.

Nancy whirled around but Freddy had hold of her dress by

62

the pocket and next thing we knew Freddy still had the pocket but Nancy was across the room.

'Oh! He ripped off my pocket!' Nancy screamed.

Freddy looked like he couldn't believe it himself. But there he was, holding Nancy's pocket. There wasn't any hole in Nancy's dress – just some loose threads where her pocket used to be. Nancy ran up the stairs and returned a few minutes later with Mrs Fishbein.

'He tore off my pocket,' Nancy said, pointing to Freddy Barnett.

'I didn't mean to,' Freddy explained. 'It just came off.'

'I am shocked at your behaviour. *Simply shocked!*' Mrs Fishbein said. 'I don't know what kind of children you are. I'm not going to send you home because your parents expect you to be here until nine and it's only seven now. But I'm telling you this – any more hanky-panky and I'll call each and every one of your mothers and fathers and report this *abominable* behavior to them!'

Mrs Fishbein marched back up the stairs. We couldn't hold back our giggles. It was all so funny. *Hanky-panky* and *abominable*!

Even Nancy and Freddy had to laugh. Then Norman suggested that we play games to keep out of trouble. 'The first game is Guess Who,' Norman said.

'Guess Who?' Janie asked. 'How do you play that?'

Norman explained. 'See, I turn off the lights and the boys line up on one side and the girls on the other and then when I yell *Go* the boys run to the girls' side and try to guess who's who by the way they feel.'

'No, thank you,' Gretchen said. 'That's disgusting!'

'Above the neck, Gretchen,' Norman said. 'Only above the neck.'

'Forget it,' Gretchen said and we all agreed. Especially me – I kept thinking of those six cotton balls. They weren't so far below my neck.

'Okay,' Norman said. 'We'll start with Spin the Bottle.'

'That's corny!' Philip Leroy shouted.

'Yeah,' the other boys agreed.

'We have to start with something,' Norman said. He put a green bottle on the floor.

We sat in a big circle, around the green bottle. Norman told us his rules. 'You got to kiss whoever's nearest to where the bottle points. No fair boy kissing boy or girl kissing girl.'

Norman spun first. He got Janie. He bent down and gave her a kiss on the cheek, near her ear but up higher. He ran back to his place in the circle. Everybody laughed. Then Janie had to spin. She got Jay. She put her face next to his but she kissed the air instead of him.

'Not fair!' Norman called out. 'You've got to *really* kiss him.'

'Okay, okay,' Janie said. She tried again. She made it this time, but far away from his mouth.

I felt a lot safer knowing it would all be cheek kissing. I held my breath every time somebody turned the bottle, waiting to see who would get me and wondering who I would get. When Gretchen got Philip Leroy she could hardly stand up. She kept biting her lip and finally she went over to him and gave him the quickest kiss you ever saw. Then I really couldn't breathe because I thought, if he gets me I'll faint. I closed my eyes. When I opened them I saw the bottle pointing straight at Laura Danker. She looked down and when Philip bent to kiss her I think all he got was her forehead and some loose hair.

That's when Jay said, 'This is *really* stupid. Let's play Two Minutes in the Closet.'

'What's that?' Norman asked.

Jay explained. 'We all get a number and then somebody starts by calling like – number six – and those two go in the closet for two minutes and uh . . . well, you know.'

'We don't have a closet down here,' Norman said. 'But we do have a bathroom.'

Norman didn't waste any time getting some paper and pencils. He scribbled the numbers on a big sheet of paper – odd ones for the boys, evens for the girls. Then he tore each number off and put first the evens, then the odds in his father's hat. We all picked. I got number twelve.

I was half scared and half excited and I wished I had been experimenting like Nancy. Nancy would know what to do with a boy in the dark, but what did I know? Nothing!

Norman said he'd go first because it was his party. Nobody argued. He stood up and cleared his throat. 'Number uh . . . number sixteen,' he said.

Gretchen squealed and jumped up.

'Bye bye, you two,' Nancy said. 'Don't be long!'

Long! They were back in three seconds.

'Hey! I thought you said two minutes,' Philip Leroy called.

'Two minutes is as long as you can stay,' Norman said. 'But you don't have to stay that long if you don't want to.'

Gretchen called number three which was Freddy Barnett and I hoped I'd remember to never call number three.

Then Freddy called number fourteen and got Laura Danker. We all giggled. I wondered how he would kiss her because I didn't think he could reach her face unless he stood on something. Maybe he'll stand on the toilet seat, I thought. And then I couldn't stop laughing at all.

When they came out of the bathroom Laura's face was as red as Freddy's and I thought that was pretty funny for a girl who goes behind the A&P with boys,

Laura called her number very softly. 'Seven,' she said.

Philip Leroy stood up and smiled at the boys. He pushed his hair off his face and walked to the bathroom with his hands stuffed in his pockets. I kept thinking that if he really liked her he'd call her number back and the two of them would be in the bathroom together for the rest of the party.

When they came out Philip was still smiling but Laura wasn't. Nancy poked me and gave me her knowing look. I was so busy watching Laura that I didn't hear Philip call number twelve.

'Who's twelve?' Philip asked. 'Somebody must be twelve.'

'Did you say twelve?' I asked. 'That's me.'

'Well, come on, Margaret.'

I stood up knowing I'd never be able to make it across the recreation room to the bathroom, where Philip Leroy was waiting to kiss me. I saw Janie, Gretchen and Nancy smiling at me. But I couldn't smile back. I don't know how I got to the bathroom. All I know is I stepped in and Philip shut the door. It was hard to see anything.

'Hi, Margaret,' he said.

'Hi, Philip,' I whispered. Then I started to giggle.

'I can't kiss you if you don't stop laughing,' he said.

'Why not?'

'Because your mouth is open when you laugh.'

'You're going to kiss me on the mouth?'

'You know a better place?'

I stopped laughing. I wished I could remember what Nancy said that day she showed me how to kiss her pillow.

'Stand still, Margaret,' Philip told me.

I stood still.

He put his hands on my shoulders and leaned close. Then he kissed me. A really fast kiss! Not the kind you see in the movies where the boy and girl cling together for a long time. While I was thinking about it, Philip kissed me again. Then he opened the bathroom door and walked back to his place.

'Call a number, Margaret,' Norman said. 'Hurry up.'

I couldn't even think of a number. I wanted to call Philip Leroy's number. But I couldn't remember it. So I called number nine and got Norman Fishbein!

He was really proud. Like I'd picked him on purpose. Ha! He practically ran to the bathroom.

After he closed the door he said, 'I really like you, Margaret. How do you want me to kiss you?'

'On the cheek and fast,' I said.

He did it just that way and I quickly opened the door and walked away from the bathroom. And that was it!

Later, at my house, Nancy told me she thought I was the luckiest girl in the world and maybe it was fate that brought me and Philip Leroy together.

'Did he kiss good?' she asked.

'Pretty good,' I said.

'How many times?' she asked.

'About five. I lost count,' I told her.

'Did he *say* anything?'

'Nothing much.'

'Do you still like him?'

'Of course!'

'Me too.'

'Good night, Nancy.'

'Good night, Margaret.'

fifteen

I went to Christmas Eve services with the Wheelers, at the United Methodist Church of Farbrook. I asked Nancy if I had to meet the minister.

'Are you kidding!' she said. 'The place will be mobbed. He doesn't even know *my* name.'

I relaxed after that and enjoyed most of the service, especially since there wasn't any sermon. The choir sang for forty-five minutes instead.

I got home close to midnight. I was so tired my parents didn't question me. I fell into bed without brushing my teeth.

Are you there, God? It's me, Margaret. I just came home from church. I loved the choir – the songs were so beautiful. Still, I didn't really feel you, God. I'm more confused than ever. I'm trying hard to understand but I wish you'd help me a little. If only you could give me a hint, God. Which religion should I be? Sometimes I wish I'd been born one way or the other.

★

Grandma came back from her cruise in time to pack up and head for Florida. She said New York had nothing to offer since I was gone. She sent me two postcards a week, called every Friday night and promised to be home before Easter.

Our phone conversations were always the same. I talked first: 'Hello, Grandma . . . Yes, I'm fine . . . They're fine . . . School's fine . . . I miss you too.'

Then my father talked: 'Hello, Mother . . . Yes, we're fine . . . How's the weather down there? . . . Well, it's bound to come out sooner or later. That's why they call it the Sunshine State.'

Then my mother talked: 'Hello, Sylvia . . . Yes, Margaret's really fine . . . Of course I'm sure . . . Okay – and you take care too.'

Then I talked a second time: 'Bye, Grandma. See you soon.'

During the second week in January Mr Benedict announced that the sixth-grade girls were going to see a movie on Friday afternoon. The sixth-grade boys were not going to see the movie. At that time they would have a discussion with the boy's gym teacher from the junior high.

Nancy passed me a note. It said, *Here we go – the big deal sex movie.*

When I asked her about it she told me the PTA sponsors it and it's called *What Every Girl Should Know.*

When I went home I told my mother. 'We're going to see a movie in school on Friday.'

'I know,' my mother said. 'I got a letter in the mail. It's about menstruation.'

'I already know all about that.'

'I know you know,' my mother said. 'But it's important for *all* girls to see it in case their mothers haven't told them the facts.'

'Oh.'

On Friday morning there was a lot of giggling. Finally, at two o'clock, the girls lined up and went to the auditorium. We took up the first three rows of seats. There was a lady on the stage, dressed in a grey suit. She had a big behind. Also, she wore a hat.

'Hello, girls,' she said. She clutched a hanky which she waved at us sometimes. 'I'm here today to tell you about *What Every Girl Should Know*, brought to you as a courtesy of the Private Lady Company. We'll talk some more after the film.' Her voice was smooth, like a radio announcer's.

Then the lights went out and we saw the movie. The narrator of the film pronounced it menstroo-ation. 'Remember,' the voice said, 'it's menstroo-ation.' Gretchen, who was next to me, gave me a kick and I kicked Nancy on the other side. We held our hands over our mouths so we wouldn't laugh.

The film told us about the ovaries and explained why girls menstroo-ate. But it didn't tell us how it feels, except to say that it is not painful, which we knew anyway. Also, it didn't really show a girl getting it. It just said how wonderful nature was and how we would soon become women and all that. After the film the lady in the grey suit asked if there were any questions.

Nancy raised her hand and when Grey Suit called on her Nancy said, 'How about Tampax?'

Grey Suit coughed into her hanky and said, 'We don't advise *internal protection* until you are considerably older.'

Then Grey Suit came down from the stage and passed out booklets called *What Every Girl Should Know*. The booklet recommended that we use Private Lady sanitary supplies. It was like one big commercial. I made a mental note never to buy Private Lady things *when* and *if* I ever needed them.

For days after that whenever I looked at Gretchen, Janie or Nancy we'd pretend to be saying menstroo-ation. We laughed a lot. Mr Benedict told us we'd have to settle down since we had a lot to learn before we'd be ready for seventh grade.

One week later Gretchen got it. We had a special PTS meeting that afternoon.

'I got it last night. Can you tell?' she asked us.

'Oh, Gretchen! You lucky!' Nancy shrieked. 'I was sure I'd be first. I've got more than you!'

'Well, that doesn't mean much,' Gretchen said, knowingly.

'How did it happen?' I asked.

'Well, I was sitting there eating my supper when I felt like something was dripping from me.'

'Go on – go on,' Nancy said.

'Well, I ran to the bathroom, and when I saw what it was I called my mother.'

'And?' I asked.

'She yelled that she was eating.'

'And?' Janie said.

'Well, I yelled back that it was important.'

'So – so –' Nancy prompted.

'So . . . uh . . . she came and I showed her,' Gretchen said.

'Then what?' Janie asked.

'Well, she didn't have any stuff in the house. She uses Tampax herself – so she had to call the drugstore and order some pads.'

'What'd you do in the meantime?' Janie asked.

'Kept a wash cloth in my pants,' Gretchen said.

'Oh – you didn't!' Nancy said, laughing.

'Well, I had to,' Gretchen said.

'Okay – so then what?' I asked.

'Well . . . in about an hour the stuff came from the drugstore.'

'Then what?' Nancy asked.

'My mother showed me how to attach the pad to the belt. Oh . . . you know . . .'

Nancy was mad. 'Look Gretchen, did we or did we not make a deal to tell each other absolutely everything about getting it?'

'I'm telling you, aren't I?' Gretchen asked.

'Not enough,' Nancy said. 'What's it *feel* like?'

'Mostly I don't feel anything. Sometimes it feels like it's dripping. It doesn't hurt coming out – but I had some cramps last night.'

70

'Bad ones?' Janie asked.

'Not bad. Just different,' Gretchen said. 'Lower down, and across my back.'

'Does it make you feel older?' I asked.

'Naturally,' Gretchen answered. 'My mother said now I'll really have to watch what I eat because I've gained too much weight this year. And she said to wash my face well from now on – with soap.'

'And that's it?' Nancy said. 'The whole story?'

'I'm sorry if I've disappointed you, Nancy. But really, that's all there is to tell. Oh, one thing I forgot. My mother said I may not get it every month yet. Sometimes it takes a while to get regular.'

'Are you using that Private Lady stuff?' I asked.

'No, the drugstore sent Teenage Softies.'

'Well, I guess I'll be next,' Nancy said.

Janie and I looked at each other. We guessed so too.

When I went home I told my mother. 'Gretchen Potter got her period.'

'Did she really?' my mother asked.

'Yes,' I said.

'I guess you'll begin soon too.'

'How old were you, Mom – when you got it?'

'Uh . . . I think I was fourteen.'

'*Fourteen!* That's crazy. I'm not waiting until I'm fourteen.'

'I'm afraid there's not much you can do about it, Margaret. Some girls menstruate earlier than others. I had a cousin who was sixteen before she started.'

'Do you suppose that could happen to me? I'll die if it does!'

'If you don't start by the time you're fourteen I'll take you to the doctor. Now stop worrying!'

'How can I stop worrying when I don't know if I'm going to turn out normal?'

'I promise, you'll turn out normal.'

★

*Are you there, God? It's me, Margaret. Gretchen, my friend, got
her period. I'm so jealous, God. I hate myself for being so
jealous, but I am. I wish you'd help me just a little. Nancy's sure
she's going to get it soon, too. And if I'm last I don't know what
I'll do. Oh please, God. I just want to be normal.*

Nancy and her family went to Washington over Lincoln's
birthday weekend. I got a postcard from her before she got
back which means she must have mailed it the second she got
there. It only had three words on it.

I GOT IT!!

I ripped the card into tiny shreds and ran to my room. There
was something wrong with me. I just knew it. And there wasn't
a thing I could do about it. I flopped on to my bed and cried.
Next week Nancy would want to tell me about her period and
about how grown up she was. Well, I didn't want to hear her
good news!

*Are you there, God? It's me, Margaret. Life is getting worse
every day. I'm going to be the only one who doesn't get it. I know
it, God. Just like I'm the only one without a religion. Why can't
you help me? Haven't I always done what you wanted?
Please . . . let me be like everybody else.*

sixteen

My mother took me to Lincoln Center twice. We used
Grandma's subscription tickets. It wasn't as much fun as with
Grandma, because number one, I didn't get to ride the bus
alone, and number two, my mother thought the concert itself
was more important than looking at the people. I wrote
Grandma a letter.

Dear Grandma,

I miss you. Florida sure sounds like fun. School is fine. So are Mom and Dad. I am fine too. I've only had one cold so far and two viruses. One was the throwing up kind. I forgot to tell you this over the phone, but when we went to Lincoln Center there was slush all over the place so I couldn't sit by the fountain. I had to wear boots too, and my feet sweated during the concert. Mom wouldn't let me take them off, the way you do. It snowed again yesterday. I'll bet you don't miss that, do you! But snow is more fun in New Jersey than in New York. For one thing, it's cleaner.
    Love,
    Margaret

Grandma wrote back:

Dear Margaret,

I miss you too. Thank you for your nice letter. I hope when you were sick your mother took you to a good doctor. If I had been home I would have asked Dr Cohen who he recommends in New Jersey. There must be one or two good doctors there. You probably caught cold because you kept your boots on at Lincoln Center. Your mother should know better! From now on, take off your boots the way we always do – no matter what your mother says! Only don't tell her I said so. I met a very nice man at my hotel. His name is Mr Binamin. He comes from New York too. We have dinner together and sometimes see a show. He is a widower with three children (all married). They think he should get married again. He thinks he should get married again. But I'm not saying anything! I hope your mother and father will let you come stay with me during spring vacation. Would you like that? I'm writing a letter to ask their permission.
Be careful and dress warmly! Write to me again.
    All my love,
    Grandma

Dear Grandma,

Mom and Dad say I can probably visit you during spring vacation, but that it's too soon to make definite plans. I'm so excited I could die! I'm counting the days already. I've never been on a plane, as you know. And Florida sounds like so much fun! Also, I want to see what's going on with you and that Mr Binamin. You never tell us a thing when you call!
I am fine. The snow melted. Mom is painting a new picture. This one is of apricots, grapes and ivy leaves. Did I tell you my friends Nancy and Gretchen got their periods?
See you soon, I hope.

Love and kisses,
Margaret

seventeen

On the first Sunday in March Nancy invited me to spend the day in New York with her family. Evan brought Moose. It was pretty exciting riding all the way to the city with Moose Freed in the same car, except the Wheelers used their station wagon. The boys sat in the back and Nancy and I were in the middle, so if I wanted to see Moose I had to turn around and if I ride looking backwards like that I get car sick.

We went to Radio City Music Hall. Grandma used to take me there when I was little. My parents always say it's strictly for the tourists. I wanted to sit next to Moose but he and Evan found two seats off by themselves.

After the show the Wheelers took us to the Steak Place for dinner. Nancy and I ordered, then excused ourselves to go to the Ladies' Room. We were the only two in there, which was lucky for us because there were only two toilets and we both had to go pretty bad. Just as I was finishing up I heard Nancy moan.

'Oh no – oh no –'

'What is it, Nancy?' I asked.

'Oh please – oh no –'

'Are you okay?' I banged on the wall separating us.

'Get my mother – quick!' she whispered.

I stood in front of her booth then. 'What's wrong?' I tried the door but it was locked. 'Let me in.'

Nancy started to cry. 'Please get my mother.'

'Okay. I'm going. I'll be right back.'

I raced to our table in the dining room, hoping Nancy wouldn't faint or anything like that before I got back with her mother.

I whispered to Mrs Wheeler, 'Nancy's sick. She's in the bathroom crying and she wants you.'

Mrs Wheeler jumped up and followed me back to the Ladies' Room. I could hear Nancy sobbing.

'Nancy?' Mrs Wheeler called, trying the door.

'Oh, Mom – I'm so scared! Help me – please.'

'The door's locked, Nancy. I can't get in,' Mrs Wheeler said. 'You've got to unlock it.'

'I can't – I can't – ' Nancy cried.

'I could crawl under and open it from the other side,' I suggested. 'Should I?' I asked Mrs Wheeler.

She nodded.

I gathered my skirt around my legs so it wouldn't drag on the floor and crawled under the door. Nancy's face was buried in her hands. I unlocked the door for Mrs Wheeler, then waited outside by the sinks. I wondered if Nancy would have to go to the hospital or what. I hoped she didn't have anything catching.

In a few minutes Mrs Wheeler opened the door a crack and handed me some change. 'Margaret,' she said, 'would you get us a sanitary napkin please?' I must have given her a strange look because she said, 'From the dispenser on the wall, dear. Nancy's menstruating.'

'Does she always act like that?'

'It's her first time,' Mrs Wheeler explained. 'She's frightened.' Nancy was still crying and there was a lot of whispering going on.

I couldn't believe it! Nancy, who knew everything! She'd lied to me about her period. She'd never had it before!

I put the change into the machine and pulled the lever. The sanitary napkin popped out in a cardboard box. I handed it to Mrs Wheeler.

'Nancy, calm down,' I heard her mother say. 'I can't help you if you don't stop crying.'

Suppose I hadn't been along that day? I'd never have found out about Nancy. I almost wished I hadn't.

Finally Nancy and her mother came out of the booth and Mrs Wheeler suggested that Nancy wash up before coming back to the table. 'I'm going to tell the others not to worry,' she said. 'Don't be too long, girls.'

I didn't know what to say. I mean, what can you say when you've just found out your friend's a liar!

Nancy washed her hands and face. I handed her two paper towels to dry herself. 'Are you okay?' I asked. I felt kind of sorry for Nancy then. I want my period too, but not enough to lie about it.

Nancy faced me. 'Margaret, please don't tell.'

'Oh, Nancy . . .'

'I mean it. I'd die if the others knew. Promise you won't tell about me,' she begged.

'I won't.'

'I thought I had it that time. You know . . . I didn't just make it all up. It was a mistake.'

'Okay,' I said.

'You won't tell?'

'I said I wouldn't.'

We walked back to the table and joined the others for dinner. Our steaks were just being served. I sat next to Moose. He smelled very nice. I wondered if he shaved because the nice smell reminded me of my father's after-shave lotion. I got to touch his hand a couple of times because he was a lefty and I'm a righty so now and then we'd bump. He said he always has that trouble at round tables. He was definitely number one in my Boy Book, even if nobody knew it but me.

I could only finish half my steak. The Wheelers took the other half home in a doggie bag. I knew they didn't have a dog but naturally I didn't tell the waitress.

Are you there, God? It's me, Margaret. Nancy Wheeler is a big fake. She makes up stories! I'll never be able to trust her again. I will wait to find out from you if I am normal or not. If you would like to give me a sign, fine. If not, I'll try to be patient. All I ask is that I don't get it in school because if I had to tell Mr Benedict I know I would die. Thank you, God.

eighteen

On March eighth I was twelve years old. The first thing I did was sniff under my arms, the way my mother does. Nothing! I didn't smell a thing. Still, now that I was twelve, I decided I'd better use deodorant, just in case. I went into my parents' bathroom and reached for my mother's roll-on. When I got dressed I went down to the kitchen for breakfast.

'Happy Birthday, Margaret!' my mother sang, bending over to kiss me while I was drinking my orange juice.

'Thank you, Mom,' I said. 'I used your deodorant.'

My mother laughed. 'You don't have to use mine. I'll get you your own.'

'You will?' I asked.

'Sure, if you want to use it regularly.'

'Well, I think I'd better. I'm twelve now, you know.'

'I know – I know.' My mother smiled at me while she cut some banana on to my cereal.

Grandma sent me a hundred-dollar savings bond as she does every year – plus three new sweaters with MADE EXPRESSLY FOR YOU . . . BY GRANDMA labels in them, a new bathing suit and an airline ticket to Florida! Round trip, leaving from Newark Airport at noon on April fourth. Was I excited!

In school Mr Benedict shook my hand and wished me a lot of good luck in the coming year. He led the class in singing 'Happy Birthday' to me. Nancy, Janie and Gretchen chipped in and bought me the new Mice Men record album. They gave it to me at lunch. Nancy mailed me a separate birthday card signed, *A million thanks to the best friend a girl could ever have*. I guess she was still scared I'd give away her secret.

That afternoon Mr Benedict announced that for the next three weeks a part of each school day would be devoted to committee work. We were going to do projects on different countries. Janie, Nancy, Gretchen and I gave each other looks saying we'd work together, of course.

But that sneaky Miles J. Benedict! He said that since he wanted us to work with people we hadn't worked with before he had made up the committees already. Well, that's a first-year teacher for you! Didn't he know that was a bad idea? Didn't he know he was supposed to let us form our own committees? Teachers never come right out and say they've picked who you should work with. It's bad enough that they fool you a lot by pretending to let you choose a subject when they know all along what you're going to do. But this was ridiculous!

I guess Mr Benedict didn't think it was ridiculous because he was already reading out names of committees. Each group had four kids in it. Two boys and two girls, with one group left over that had three girls. I really couldn't believe it when he read my group. Norman Fishbein, Philip Leroy, Laura Danker and me! I glanced sideways at Janie. She rolled her eyes at me. I raised my eyebrow back at her.

Mr Benedict asked us to rearrange our desks into our groups. I was going to have to talk to Laura Danker! There would be no way of getting out of it. I was also going to be spending a lot of time with Philip Leroy, which was pretty exciting to think about.

The first thing Philip did after we moved our desks together was to sing to me.

'Happy Birthday to you,
You live in a zoo,
You look like a monkey,
And you smell like one too!'

Then he pinched me on the arm – really hard! Enough to make tears come to my eyes. He said, 'That's a pinch to grow an inch. And you know where you need that inch!'

I knew it was just a joke. I knew I shouldn't take it seriously. For one thing, I did not smell like a monkey. I was wearing deodorant! And for another thing, it was none of Philip Leroy's business whether or not I needed to grow an inch *anywhere*! As far as I was concerned, Nancy could have him. They deserved each other.

To make matters worse I had to sit facing Laura Danker. I hated her. I hated her for being so big and beautiful and having all the boys stare at her, including Mr Benedict. Also, I hated her because she knew she was normal and I didn't know a thing about me! I hated Mr Benedict too – for sticking me with Norman Fishbein. Norman was such a drip!

So all in all my birthday, which started out to be the most perfect day of my life, ended up being pretty rotten. I couldn't wait for spring vacation to come. The only good thing I had to look forward to was my trip to Florida. I was sick of school.

nineteen

At home my mother said she'd never seen me in such a bad mood. The mood lasted the whole three weeks of that dumb committee project. To top off everything else our group voted three to one to report on Belgium. I wanted a more exciting country, like France or Spain. But I lost.

So I ate, breathed and slept Belgium for three weeks. Philip Leroy was a lousy worker. I found that out right away. All he did was fool around. During project time, while Laura, Norman and I were busy looking things up in reference books, Philip was busy drawing funny faces in his notebook. On two days he snuck comic books inside his notebook and read them instead. Norman Fishbein tried hard but he was so slow! And I couldn't stand the way he read with his lips moving. Laura was a good worker. But of course, I never told her that I thought so.

During the third week of Project Belgium Laura and I got permission to stay after school and work in the library. We needed more time with the encyclopedias. My mother was going to pick me up in front of school at four-thirty. Laura was going to walk from school to church because she had to go to Confession.

Now that really started me thinking. For one thing, I never knew she was Catholic. For another, I wondered what she said in Confession. I mean, did she talk about what she did with boys? And if she did, what did the priest say to her? Did she go to Confession every time she did something bad? Or did she save it all up and go once a month?

I was so busy thinking about Laura and the Confessional that I nearly forgot about Belgium. And probably I never would have said anything at all if it hadn't been for Laura. She picked on me first. So she was really to blame for the whole thing.

'You're copying that straight out of the *World Book* word for word,' she whispered to me.

'So?'

'Well, you can't do that,' she explained. 'You're supposed to read it and then write about it in your own words. Mr Benedict will *know* if you've copied.'

Normally I don't copy word for word. I know the rules as well as Laura. But I was busy thinking about other things and anyway, who did Laura think she was giving orders like that? Big shot!

So I said: 'Oh, you think you're so great, don't you!'

And she said: 'This has nothing to do with being great.'

And I said: 'I know all about you anyway!'

And she said: 'What's *that* supposed to mean?'

And the librarian said: 'Girls – let's be more quiet.'

And then Laura went back to work. But I didn't.

'I heard all about you and Moose Freed,' I whispered.

Laura put down her pencil and looked at me. 'You heard *what* about me and Moose Freed?'

'Oh – about how you and Evan and Moose go behind the A&P,' I said.

'What would I do *that* for?' Laura asked.

She was really thick! 'I don't know what *you* do it for. But I know why *they* do it . . . they do it so they can *feel* you or something and *you* let them!'

She shut the encyclopedia hard and stood up. Her face was burning red and I saw a blue vein stick out in her neck. 'You filthy liar! You *little pig*!' Nobody ever called me such names in my whole life.

Laura scooped up her books and her coat and ran out of the library. I grabbed my things and followed her.

I was really being awful. And I hadn't even planned it. I sounded like Nancy. That's when it hit me that for all I knew Nancy made up that story about Laura. Or maybe Moose and Evan made it up just to brag. Yes, I bet they did! Moose was a big liar too!

'Hey, Laura! Wait up,' I called.

She walked fast – probably because her legs were so long. I chased her. When I finally caught up to her I could hardly breathe. Laura kept walking and wouldn't look at me. I didn't blame her. I walked alongside her. I took four steps to every two of hers.

'Look,' I told her. 'I'm not saying it's wrong to do those things.'

'I think it's disgusting that you all pick on me because I'm big!' Laura said, sniffing.

I wanted to tell her to blow her nose. 'I didn't mean to insult you,' I said. 'You're the one who started it.'

'Me? That's a good one! You think it's such a great game to make fun of me, don't you?'

'No,' I said.

'Don't you think I know all about *you* and your friends? Do you think it's any fun to be the biggest kid in the class?'

'I don't know,' I said. 'I never thought about it.'

'Well, try thinking about it. Think about how you'd feel if you had to wear a bra in fourth grade and how everybody laughed and how you always had to cross your arms in front of you. And about how the boys called you dirty names just because of how you looked.'

I thought about it. 'I'm sorry, Laura,' I said.

'I'll bet!'

'I really am. If you want to know the truth . . . well, I wish I looked more like you than like me.'

'I'd gladly trade places with you. Now, I'm going to Confession.' She walked on mumbling something about how the wrong ones always confessed.

And I thought, maybe she's right. Maybe I was the one who should confess. I followed Laura to her church. It was only two blocks from school. I still had half an hour before my mother was due. I crossed the street and hid behind a bush watching Laura climb the steps and disappear into the church.

Then I crossed back to the other side of the street and ran up the brick steps. I held open the front door and looked inside. I didn't see Laura. I stepped into the church and tiptoed up the aisle.

It was so quiet. I wondered what would happen if I decided to scream; of course I knew I wouldn't, but I couldn't help wondering about how a scream would sound in there.

I was really hot in my heavy coat, but I didn't take it off. After a while I saw Laura come out of a door and I crouched down behind a row of seats so she wouldn't see me. She never even glanced my way. I thought it didn't take her very long to confess.

I felt weird. My legs were getting weak. As soon as Laura left the church I stood up. I meant to leave too. I had to meet my mother back at school. But instead of walking to the front of the church and outside, I headed the other way.

I stood in front of the door that Laura came from. What was inside? I opened it a little. There was nobody there. It looked like a wooden phone booth. I stepped in and closed the door behind me. I waited for something to happen. I didn't know what I was supposed to do, so I just sat there.

Finally I heard a voice. 'Yes, my child.'

At first I thought it was God. I really and truly thought it was, and my heart started to pound like crazy and I was all sweaty inside my coat and sort of dizzy too. But then I realized it was only the priest in the booth next to mine. He couldn't see me and I couldn't see him but we could hear each other. Still, I didn't say anything.

'Yes, my child,' he said again.

'I . . . I . . . uh . . . uh . . .' I began.

'Yes?' the priest asked me.

'I'm sorry,' I whispered.

I flung open the door and ran down the aisle and out of the church. I made my way back to school, crying, feeling horribly sick and scared stiff I would throw up. Then I saw my mother waiting in the car and I got in the back and explained I was feeling terrible. I stretched out on the seat. My mother drove home and I didn't have to tell her any of the awful things I'd done because she thought I was sick for real.

Later that night she brought a bowl of soup to my room and she sat on the edge of my bed while I ate it. She said I must have had a virus or something and she was glad I was feeling better but I didn't have to go to school tomorrow if I didn't feel like it. Then she turned out the light and kissed me goodnight.

★

*Are you there, God? It's me, Margaret. I did an awful thing
today. Just awful! I'm definitely the most horrible person who
ever lived and I really don't deserve anything good to happen to
me. I picked on Laura Danker. Just because I felt mean I took it
all out on her. I really hurt Laura's feelings. Why did you let me
do that? I've been looking for you, God. I looked in temple. I
looked in church. And today, I looked for you when I wanted to
confess. But you weren't there. I didn't feel you at all. Not the
way I do when I talk to you at night. Why, God? Why do I only
feel you when I'm alone?*

twenty

A week before spring vacation the letter came. Only it wasn't
from Grandma and it wasn't about my trip to Florida. It was
from Mary and Paul Hutchins, my other grandparents. Now
that was really strange because since they disowned my mother
when she got married naturally they never wrote to her. My
father, having no kind thoughts about them, really hit the roof.

'How did they get our address? Answer that one simple
question please! Just how did they get our address?'

My mother practically whispered her answer. 'I sent them a
Christmas card. That's how.'

My father hollered, 'I can't believe you, Barbara! After
fourteen years you sent *them* a Christmas card?'

'I was feeling sentimental. So I sent a card. I didn't write
anything on it. Just our names.'

My father shook the letter at my mother. 'So now after fourteen
years – *fourteen years*, Barbara! Now they change their minds?'

'They want to see us. That's all.'

'They want to see *you*, not me! They want to see Margaret!
To make sure she doesn't have horns!'

'Herb! Stop it! You're being ridiculous –'

'*I'm being ridiculous!* That's funny, Barbara. That's very funny.'

'You know what I think?' I asked them. 'I think you're both being ridiculous!' I ran out of the kitchen and stormed up the stairs to my room. I slammed the door. I hated it when they had a fight in front of me. Why didn't they know how much I hated it! Didn't they know how awful they sounded? I could still hear them, shouting and carrying on. I put my hands over my ears while I crossed the room to my record player. Then I took one hand off one ear and turned on my Mice Men record as loud as it would go. There – that was much better.

A few minutes later my bedroom door opened. My father walked straight to my record player and snapped it off. My mother held the letter in her hand. Her eyes were red. I didn't say anything.

My father paced up and down. 'Margaret,' he finally said. 'This concerns you. I think before we do or say anything else you ought to read the letter from your grandparents. Barbara . . .' He held out his hand.

My mother handed the letter to my father and he handed it to me. The handwriting was slanty and perfect, the way it is in third grade when you're learning script. I sat down on my bed.

Dear Barbara,

Your father and I have been thinking about you a lot. We are growing old. I guess you find that hard to believe, but we are. Suddenly, more than anything else we want to see our only daughter. We wonder if it is possible that we made a mistake fourteen years ago. We have discussed this situation with our minister and dear friend, Reverend Baylor. You remember him, dear, don't you? My goodness, he christened you when you were a tiny baby. He says it's never too late to try again. So your father and I are flying East for a week and hope that you will let us visit you and get to know our granddaughter, Margaret Ann. Flight details are enclosed.

Your mother,
Mary Hutchins

What a sickening letter! No wonder my father was mad. It didn't even mention him.

I handed the letter back to my father, but I didn't say anything because I didn't know what I was supposed to say.

'They're coming on April fifth,' my father said.

'Oh, then I won't see them after all,' I said, brightening. 'I leave for Florida on the fourth.'

My mother looked at my father.

'Well,' I said. 'Isn't that right? I leave for Florida on the fourth!'

They still didn't say anything and after a minute I knew – I knew I wasn't going to Florida! And then I had plenty to say. Plenty!

'I don't want to see them,' I shouted 'It isn't fair! I want to go to Florida and stay with Grandma. Daddy – *please!*'

'Don't look at me,' my father said quietly. 'It's not my fault. I didn't send them a Christmas card.'

'Mom!' I cried. 'You can't do this to me. You can't! It's not fair – it's not!' I hated my mother. I really did. She was so stupid. What did she have to go and send them a dumb old card for!

'Come on, Margaret. It's not the end of the world,' my mother said, putting her arm around me. 'You'll go to Florida another time.'

I wriggled away from her as my father said, 'Somebody better call Sylvia and tell her the change in plans.'

'I'll put the call through and Margaret can tell her now,' my mother said.

'Oh no!' I shouted. '*You* tell her. It's not my idea!'

'All right,' my mother said quietly. 'All right, I will.'

I followed my parents into their bedroom. My mother picked up the phone and placed a person-to-person call to Grandma at her hotel. After a few minutes she said, 'Hello, Sylvia . . . It's Barbara . . . Nothing's wrong . . . Everything's fine . . . Yes, really . . . Of course I'm sure . . . It's just that Margaret won't be able to visit you after all . . . Of course she's here . . . she's standing right next to me . . . Yes, you can talk to her . . .'

My mother held the phone out toward me. But I shook my head and refused to take it. So she covered the mouthpiece and whispered, 'Grandma thinks you're sick. You've got to tell her you're all right.'

I took the phone. 'Grandma,' I said, 'it's Margaret.'

I heard Grandma catch her breath.

'Nothing's wrong, Grandma . . . No, I'm not sick . . . Nobody's sick . . . Of course I'm sure . . . But I do want to come, Grandma. I just can't.' I felt the tears in my eyes. My throat hurt when I swallowed. My mother motioned for me to tell Grandma the rest of the story. 'I can't come to Florida because we're having company that week.' Now my voice sounded very high and squeaky.

Grandma asked me, what company?

'My other grandparents,' I said. 'You know, Mom's mother and father . . . Nobody invited them exactly . . . but Mom sent them a Christmas card with our new address and now we got a letter saying they're coming and they want to see me . . . Well, I know you want to see me too. And I want to see you but Mom won't let me . . .'

Then I started to cry for real and my mother took the phone.

'We're all sorry, Sylvia. It's just one of those things. Margaret understands. I hope you do too. Thank you, Sylvia. I knew you would . . . Yes, Herb's fine. I'll put him on. Just a minute.' I ran upstairs while my father said, 'Hello, Mother.'

Are you there, God? It's me, Margaret. I'm so miserable! Everything is wrong. Absolutely everything! I guess this is my punishment for being a horrible person. I guess you think it's only fair for me to suffer after what I did to Laura. Isn't that right, God? But I've always tried to do what you wanted. Really, I have. Please don't let them come, God. Make something happen so I can go to Florida anyway. Please . . .

twenty-one

That week my mother went crazy cleaning the house, while I waited for something to happen. I thought it would be a telegram saying they weren't able to come after all. I was sure God only wanted to punish me for a little while. Not for the whole spring vacation.

'Cheer up, Margaret,' my mother said over dinner. 'Things are never as bad as they seem.'

'How can you be glad they're coming?' I asked. 'After all those stories you've told me about them – how?'

'I want to show them how well I've managed for fourteen years without their help. And I want them to see my wonderful family.'

My father said, 'You can't expect Margaret to be overjoyed when her plans have been changed at the last minute.'

'Look, Herb,' my mother said. 'I haven't forgiven my parents. You know that. I never will. But they're coming. I can't say no. Try to understand . . . both of you . . . please.'

My mother hadn't ever asked me to do that before. Usually it was me asking her to try to understand.

My father kissed her on the cheek as she cleared away the dishes. He promised to make the best of it. I promised too. My mother kissed us both and said she had the best family in the world.

On April fifth my mother and I drove to Newark Airport to meet them. My father didn't come. He thought it would be better if he stayed at home and greeted them there.

All the way to the airport my mother briefed me. 'Margaret, I'm not trying to make excuses for my mother and father. But I want you to know that your grandparents have their beliefs too. And fourteen years ago . . . well . . . they did what they thought was right. Even though we know it was cruel. Their beliefs were that important to them. Am I making any sense to you?'

88

'Some,' I said.

When they announced the arrival of flight #894 from Toledo I followed my mother to the gate. I knew it was them right away. I knew it by the way they walked down the airplane stairs, clutching each other. And when they got closer I knew it by my grandmother's shoes – black with laces and fat heels – old lady shoes. My grandfather had white hair around the edges and none on top. He was shorter and fatter than my grandmother.

They looked around a bit before my mother called out, 'Here we are – over here.'

They walked towards us, growing more excited as they recognized my mother. She gave each of them a short hug. I just stood there feeling dumb until my grandmother said, 'And this must be Margaret Ann.' When she said it I noticed the cross around her neck. It was the biggest one I ever saw. And it sparkled!

I didn't want them to touch me. And maybe they could tell, because when my grandmother bent over, as if to kiss me, I stiffened. I didn't mean to. It just happened.

I think my mother knew how I felt because she told them we'd better see about the luggage.

When we got home my father met us at our front door and carried in their suitcases. They had two of them. Both brown and both new.

'Hello, Herb,' my grandmother said.

'Hello, Mrs Hutchins,' my father answered.

I thought how funny it was for my father to call her 'Mrs'.

My grandfather shook hands with my father. 'You're looking well, Herb,' he said.

My father pressed his lips together but finally managed to say, 'Thank you.'

I thought, this is harder on my father than it is on me!

My mother and I showed my grandparents to their room. Then my mother went down to see about dinner. I said, 'If there's anything you need, just ask me.'

'Thank you, Margaret Ann,' my grandmother said. She had a funny way of scrunching up her mouth.

'You don't have to call me Margaret Ann,' I said. 'Nobody does. Just Margaret is fine.'

My mother really made a fancy dinner. The kind she has when she's entertaining friends and I'm sent to bed early. We had flowers on the table and a hired lady to wash the dishes.

My mother changed into a new dress and her hair looked nice too. She didn't look like her parents at all. My grandmother changed her dress too, but she still had the cross around her neck.

At dinner we all tried hard to have a conversation. My mother and my grandmother talked about old friends from Ohio and who was doing what these days. My grandfather said mostly, 'Please pass the butter . . . please pass the salt.'

Naturally I used my best possible manners. In the middle of the roast beef course my grandfather knocked over his water glass and my grandmother gave him a sharp look, but my mother said water couldn't possibly hurt anything. The lady from the kitchen wiped it up.

During dessert my mother explained to my grandparents that she had just ordered all new living-room furniture and she was sorry they wouldn't be able to see it. I knew she hadn't ordered anything yet, but I didn't tell.

After dinner we sat around in the den and my grandfather asked my father such questions as:

GRANDFATHER: 'Are you still in the insurance business?'
FATHER: 'Yes.'
GRANDFATHER: 'Do you invest in the stock market?'
FATHER: 'Occasionally.'
GRANDFATHER: 'This is a pretty nice house.'
FATHER: 'Thank you. We think so too.'

While my grandmother talked to my mother about:

GRANDMOTHER: 'We were in California over Thanksgiving.'
MOTHER: 'Oh?'
GRANDMOTHER: 'Yes, your brother has a wonderful wife.'
MOTHER: 'I'm glad.'
GRANDMOTHER: 'If only they were blessed with a child. You know, they're thinking of adopting.'
MOTHER: 'I hope they do. Everyone should have a child to love.'
GRANDMOTHER: 'Yes, I know . . . I've always wanted dozens of grandchildren, but Margaret's all I've got.'

Then my mother excused herself to pay the lady in the kitchen, who signalled that her taxi was waiting out front. So my grandmother turned to me.

'Do you like school?' she asked.

'Most of the time,' I said.

'Do you get good marks?'

'Pretty good,' I said.

'How do you do in Sunday school?'

My mother came back into the den then and sat down next to me.

'I don't go to Sunday school,' I said.

'You don't?'

'No.'

'Father . . .' (That's what Grandmother called Grandfather. He called her 'Mother'.)

'What is it, Mother?' Grandfather said.

'Margaret doesn't go to Sunday school.' Grandmother shook her head and played with her cross.

'Look,' my mother said, trying a smile. 'You know we don't practise any religion.'

Here it comes, I thought. I wanted to leave the room then but I felt like I was glued to my seat.

'We hoped by now you'd changed your minds about religion,' Grandfather said.

'Especially for Margaret's sake,' Grandmother added. 'A

person's got to have religion.'

'Let's not get into a philosophical discussion,' my father said, annoyed. He sent my mother a warning look across the room.

Grandfather laughed. 'I'm not being a philosopher, Herb.'

'Look,' my mother explained, 'we're letting Margaret choose her own religion when she's grown.'

'If she wants to!' my father said, defiantly.

'Nonsense!' Grandmother said. 'A person doesn't choose religion.'

'A person's born to it!' Grandfather boomed.

Grandmother smiled at last and gave a small laugh. 'So Margaret is Christian!' she announced, like we all should have known.

'Please . . .' my mother said. 'Margaret could just as easily be Jewish. Don't you see – if you keep this up you're going to spoil everything.'

'I don't mean to upset you, dear,' Grandmother told my mother. 'But a child is always the religion of the mother. And you, Barbara, were born Christian. You were baptized. It's that simple.'

'Margaret is nothing!' my father stormed. 'And I'll thank you for ending this discussion right now.'

I didn't want to listen any more. How could they talk that way in front of me! Didn't they know I was a real person – with feelings of my own!

'Margaret,' Grandmother said, touching my sleeve. 'It's not too late for you, dear. You're still God's child. Maybe while I'm visiting I could take you to church and talk to the minister. He might be able to straighten things out.'

'Stop it!' I hollered, jumping up. 'All of you! Just stop it! I can't stand another minute of listening to you. Who needs religion? Who! Not me . . . I don't need it. I don't even need God!' I ran out of the den and up to my room.

I heard my mother say, 'Why did you have to start? Now you've ruined everything!'

I was never going to talk to God again. What did he want

from me anyway? I was through with him and his religions!
And I was never going to set foot in the Y or the Jewish
Community Center – *never*.

twenty-two

The next morning I stayed in my room. I wouldn't even go
down for breakfast. I caught myself starting to say, *Are you
there, God*, but then I remembered that I wasn't talking to him
any more. I wondered if he would strike me down. Well, if he
wanted to, that was his business.

By afternoon I couldn't stand being in the house, so I asked
my mother to drive me downtown to meet Janie for a movie.
My mother agreed that I needed to get away for a few hours.
Janie and I met at the drugstore on the corner, across the street
from the movie theatre. We were twenty minutes early so we
went into the drugstore to look around. Mostly we liked to
inspect the sanitary napkin display.

After a few minutes of looking, I whispered to Janie, 'Let's
buy a box.' It was something I'd thought about for a while, but
wasn't ever brave enough to do. Today I was feeling brave. I
thought, so what if God's mad at me. Who cares? I even tested
him by crossing the street in the middle *and* against the light.
Nothing happened.

'Buy it for what?' Janie asked.

'Just in case,' I told her.

'You mean to keep at home?'

'Sure. Why not?'

'I don't know. My mother might not like it,' Janie said.

'So don't tell her.'

'But what if she sees it?'

'It'll be in a bag. You can say it's school supplies,' I said. 'Do
you have enough money?'

'Yes.'

'Okay. Now, what kind should we buy?' I asked.

'How about Teenage Softies?' Janie said. 'That's the kind Gretchen uses.'

'Okay.' I took a box of Teenage Softies off the shelf. 'Well, go ahead,' I said to Janie. 'Take yours.'

'Okay, okay.' Janie took a box too.

'We need a belt to go with it,' I said, getting braver by the minute.

'You're right. Which kind?' Janie asked.

'I like that one. It's pink,' I told her, pointing to a small box with a pretty girl's picture on it.

'Okay, I'll take that one too,' Janie said, reaching.

We walked to the check-out counter with our stuff and walked away just as fast when we saw that there was a boy behind the cash register.

'I can't go through with it,' Janie whispered. She put her boxes back on the shelf. 'I'm scared.'

'Don't be a dope. What's to be . . .' I was interrupted by a saleslady in a blue doctor's coat.

'Can I help you, girls?' she asked.

Janie shook her head but I said, 'We'd like these, please.' I took Janie's boxes back off the shelf and showed the saleslady what we'd selected.

'Fine, girls. Take them to the cash register and Max will wrap them for you.'

Janie didn't move, She looked like she was cemented to the floor. She had this dumb expression on her face – between crying and smiling. So I grabbed her boxes and headed for Max and the cash register. I plopped everything down in front of him and just stood there not looking at his face and not saying anything either. He added it all up and I motioned to Janie to give me her money. Then I said, 'Two bags, please.' Max took my money, gave me some change, which I didn't bother to count, and presented me with two brown bags. That was all there was to it! You'd think he sold that kind of stuff every day of the week.

When I got home from the movies my mother asked, 'What's that package?'

I said, 'School supplies.'

I went to my room with my purchases. I sat down on my bed staring at the box of Teenage Softies. I hoped God was watching. Let him see I could get along fine without him! I opened the box and took out one pad. I held it for a long time.

Then I took the pink belt out of its box and held that too. Finally I got up and went to my closet. It was dark in there. Especially with the door closed. I wished I had a huge walk-in closet with a light and a lock. But I managed anyway. I got the pink belt around me and attached the pad to it. I wanted to find out how it would feel. Now I knew. I like it. I thought about sleeping in my belt and pad that night, but decided against it. If there was a fire my secret might be discovered. So I took off the belt and pad, put them back in their boxes and hid them in my bottom desk drawer. My mother never checks there because the mess makes her positively sick!

The next morning my grandparents announced they were moving to New York.

'You told me a week!' my mother said. 'You said you were coming for a week!'

'We did say that,' my grandfather told her. 'But we've decided to spend the rest of the week in New York, at a hotel.'

'I see,' my mother said.

My father hid behind his newspaper but I saw the big smile. All I could think of was that they ruined my trip to Florida and now they weren't even staying. It wasn't fair! It was really a cheat!

When my mother got back from driving them to the bus my father said, 'How much do you want to bet it was a trip to New York all the time. They just stopped in to see you because it was convenient.'

'I don't believe that!' my mother said.

'Well, I believe it,' my father said.

'They ruined my vacation,' I said.

Nobody answered me.

twenty-three

That night the doorbell rang at eight. We were in the den. I said I'd see who was there. I opened the front door.

'Grandma!' I screamed. I threw my arms around her. 'What are you doing home?'

'If Mohammed doesn't come to the mountain – the mountain comes to Mohammed.'

I laughed, knowing that I was Mohammed and that Grandma was the mountain. There was a man standing next to Grandma. Grandma turned to him. 'Morris,' she said. 'This is my Margaret.'

Then Grandma closed the front door and told me, 'Margaret darling, this is Mr Morris Binamin.'

'Rhymes with cinnamon,' he said to me.

I smiled.

Grandma looked marvellous – very tan and pale blonde. Mr Binamin had a lot of silver hair, a moustache to match, and black-rimmed eyeglasses. He was tan too. He held Grandma's arm.

'Where are they?' Grandma asked.

'Mom and Dad are in the den,' I said.

'With your other grandparents?'

'No . . . they're gone.'

'Gone!' Grandma cried. 'But I thought they were staying all week.'

'We thought so too,' I said.

'But Morris and I came especially to see them.'

'You did!' I said. 'How come?'

Grandma and Mr Binamin gave each other a secret look. 'Well . . . we thought you might need our support.'

'Oh, Grandma! I can manage just fine by myself.'

'I know you can. You're my Margaret, aren't you? Tell me – did they try anything?'

'Like what?' I asked.

'You know,' Grandma said. 'Church business.'

'Well . . . kind of,' I admitted.

'I knew it!' Grandma cried. 'Didn't I tell you?' she asked Mr Binamin.

Mr Binamin shook his head. 'You had them pegged right all the time, Sylvia,' he said.

'Just remember, Margaret . . . no matter what they said . . . you're a Jewish girl.'

'No I'm not!' I argued. 'I'm nothing, and you know it! I don't even believe in God!'

'Margaret!' Grandma said. 'Don't ever talk like that about God.'

'Why not?' I asked. 'It's true!' I wanted to ask God did he hear that! But I wasn't speaking to him and I guess he knew it!

By that time my mother and father were in the living room and Grandma was making the introductions. My parents gave Mr Binamin the once-over and he was pretty busy sizing them up too.

Then my mother made coffee and served warm Danish. She offered me some milk and ginger snaps but I wasn't hungry. I wanted to get out of there so I yawned very loud without covering my mouth.

'Margaret dear, if you're so tired, why don't you go up to bed,' Grandma said.

'I think I will. Goodnight, everybody.'

Sometimes Grandma is almost as bad as everybody else. As long as she loves me and I love her, what difference does religion make?

twenty-four

Mr Benedict announced that our individual reports on our year-long project would be due next Friday. They wouldn't be graded so we were to be completely honest and not worry about pleasing him. He hoped we had each learned something of value. On Thursday night I wrote a letter.

May 25

Dear Mr Benedict,

I have conducted a year-long experiment in religion. I have not come to any conclusions about what religion I want to be when I grow up – if I want to be any special religion at all.
I have read three books on this subject. They are: Modern Judaism, A History of Christianity, *and* Catholicism – Past and Present. *I went to church services at the First Presbyterian Church of Farbrook. I went to the United Methodist Church of Farbrook on Christmas Eve. I attended Temple Israel of New York City on Rosh Hashanah, which is a Jewish holiday. I went to Confession at Saint Bartholomew Church, but I had to leave the Confessional because I didn't know what to say. I have not tried being a Buddhist or a Moslem because I don't know any people of these religions.*

I have not really enjoyed my religious experiments very much and I don't think I'll make up my mind one way or the other for a long time. I don't think a person can decide to be a certain religion just like that. It's like having to choose your own name. You think about it a long time and then you keep changing your mind. If I should ever have children I will tell them what religion they are so they can start learning about it at an early age. Twelve is very late to learn.
Sincerely,
Margaret Ann Simon

On Friday everybody handed in a thick booklet with a decorated cover. All I had was the letter. I couldn't put that in with the pile of booklets. I was too embarrassed. It looked like I hadn't done any work at all.

When the bell rang I sat at my desk while everyone else filed out of the room.

98

When Mr Benedict looked up he said, 'Yes, Margaret?'

I walked to his desk with my letter.

'I didn't hand in a booklet,' I said.

'Oh?'

'I, uh . . . I wrote you a letter instead.' I handed it to him, then stood there while he read it.

'I really tried, Mr Benedict. I'm – I'm sorry. I wanted to do better.' I knew I was going to cry. I couldn't say anything else. So I ran out of the classroom.

I got to the Girls' Room before the tears came. I could still hear Mr Benedict calling, 'Margaret – Margaret –' I didn't pay any attention. I splashed cold water on my face. Then I walked home slowly by myself.

What was wrong with me anyway? When I was eleven I hardly ever cried. Now anything and everything could start me bawling. I wanted to talk it over with God. But I wasn't about to let him know that, even though I missed him.

twenty-five

On June seventeenth the PTA gave us a farewell party in the gym and none of the sixth-grade girls wore socks. I wore my first pair of sheer stockings and got my first run in them one hour later. All I could think of was I'd be in seventh grade in September and I was growing up. My mind knew it – even if my body didn't.

The party in the gym was a lot like the Thanksgiving square dance. Mrs Wheeler and Mrs Fishbein were chaperones but this time they were dressed in regular clothes.

Our class presented Mr Benedict with a pair of silver cufflinks that Gretchen's mother had gotten wholesale. He seemed very pleased, because he cleared his throat a lot and sounded like he didn't know what to say except thank you – and that although we hadn't started out to be the greatest sixth grade in the world, we'd come a long way. And thanks to us, next year, he'd be an experienced teacher – *very experienced!* Then we all laughed and some of the girls cried but I didn't.

Nancy, Gretchen, Janie and I had lunch downtown by ourselves and talked about how it would feel to go to junior high. Janie was afraid she wouldn't be able to find her way around and she'd get lost. Gretchen said probably the teachers would all be mean and Nancy said suppose we weren't in any classes together and then we all went home and cried.

Later that day my mother started packing my camp trunk. I watched her put the stacks of shorts and polos into it. Then I heard the lawn mower. Moose was back. First I got excited about seeing him and then I got mad, thinking about Laura and those stories he helped spread around.

I ran downstairs and outside and yelled, 'Hey, Moose!' He didn't hear me because the mower made too much noise. So I ran over to where he was cutting and I stood right in his way so he'd have to notice me and I shouted again. 'Hey, Moose!'

He shut off the mower. 'You're in my way,' he said.

'I want to tell you something,' I said.

'Go ahead.'

I put my hands on my hips. 'You know what, Moose! You're a liar! I don't believe you ever took Laura Danker behind the A&P.'

'Who said I did?'

'What do you mean who said it!'

'Well, who?'

'Nancy told me that Evan told her that you and Evan – ' I stopped. I sounded like an idiot.

Moose shook his head at me. 'You always believe everything you hear about other people?' he asked.

I didn't know what to say.

Moose kept talking. 'Well, next time, don't believe it unless you see it! Now if you'll move out of my way, I've got things to do!'

I didn't move. 'You know what, Moose?' I asked.

'What now?'

'I'm sorry I thought you were a liar.'

'You know what, Margaret?' Moose asked me.

'No, what?'

'You're still in my way!'

I jumped away and Moose turned the mower on again. I heard him singing his favourite song – about the Erie Canal.

I went back into the house. I had to go to the bathroom. I was thinking about Moose and about how I liked to stand close to him. I was thinking that I was glad he wasn't a liar and I was happy that he cut our grass. Then I looked down at my underpants and I couldn't believe it. There was blood on them. Not a lot – but enough. I really hollered, *'Mom – hey, Mom – come quick!'*

When my mother got to the bathroom she said, 'What is it? What's the matter?'

'I got it,' I told her.

'Got what?'

I started to laugh and cry at the same time. 'My period. I've got my period!' My nose started running and I reached for a tissue.

'Are you sure, Margaret?' my mother asked.

'Look – look at this,' I said, showing her my underpants.

'My God! You've really got it. My little girl!' Then her eyes filled up and she started sniffling too. 'Wait a minute – I've got equipment in the other room. I was going to put it in your camp trunk, just in case.'

'You were?'

'Yes. Just in case.' She left the bathroom.

When she came back I asked her, 'Is it that Private Lady stuff?'

'No, I got you Teenage Softies.'

'Good,' I said.

'Now look, Margaret – here's how you do it. The belt goes around your waist and the pad – '

'Mom,' I said. 'I've been practising in my room for two months!'

Then my mother and I laughed together and she said, 'In that case, I guess I'll wait in the other room.'

I locked the bathroom door and attached a Teenage Softie to the little hooks on my pink belt. Then I got dressed and looked at myself in the mirror. Would anyone know my secret? Would it show? Would Moose, for instance, know if I went back outside to talk to him? Would my father know it right away when he came home for dinner? I had to call Nancy and Gretchen and Janie right away. Poor Janie! She'd be the last of the PTS's to get it. And I'd been so sure it would be me! How about that! Now I am growing for sure. Now I am almost a woman!

Are you still there, God? It's me, Margaret. I know you're there, God. I know you wouldn't have missed this for anything! Thank you, God. Thanks an awful lot . . .

Blubber

for Randy and Larry
my experts on fifth grade, loose teeth, the *Book of World Records*, stamp collecting and school bus action

one

'It's very foolish to laugh if you don't know what's funny in the first place.'

My best friend, Tracy Wu, says I'm really tough on people. She says she wonders sometimes how I can like her. But we both know that's a big joke. Tracy's the best friend I'll ever have. I just wish we were in the same fifth-grade class.

My teacher is Mrs Minish. I'm not crazy about her. She hardly ever opens the windows in our room because she's afraid of getting a stiff neck. I never heard anything so dumb. Some days our room gets hot and stuffy and it smells – like this afternoon. We'd been listening to individual reports on The Mammal for almost an hour. Donna Davidson was standing at the front of the room reading hers. It was on the horse. Donna has this *thing* about horses.

I tried hard not to fall asleep but it wasn't easy. For a while I watched Michael and Irwin as they passed a *National Geographic* back and forth. It was open to a page full of naked people. Wendy and Caroline played Tic-Tac-Toe behind Wendy's notebook. Wendy won three games in a row. I wasn't surprised. Wendy is a very clever person. Besides being class president, she is also group science leader, recess captain and head of the goldfish committee.

Did Mrs Minish notice anything that was going on or was she just concentrating on Donna's boring report? I couldn't tell from looking at her. She had a kind of half-smile on her face and sometimes she kept her eyes closed for longer than a blink.

To make the time go faster I thought about Hallowe'en. It's just two days away. I love to dress up and go Trick-or-Treating, but I'm definitely not going to be a dumb old witch again this year. Donna will probably be a horse. She dresses up like one every Hallowe'en. Last year she said when she grows up she is going to marry a horse. She has him all picked out and everything. His name is San Salvador. Most of the time Donna smells like a horse but I wouldn't tell her that because she might think it's a compliment.

I yawned and wiggled around in my chair.

'In closing,' Donna said, 'I would like you to remember that even though some people say horses are stupid that is a big lie! I personally happen to know some very smart horses. And that's the end of my report.'

The whole class clapped, not because Donna's report was great, but because it was finally over. Mrs Minish opened her eyes and said, 'Very nice, Donna.'

Earlier, when I had finished my report on the lion, Mrs Minish said the same thing to me. *Very nice, Jill.* Just like that. Now I couldn't be sure if she really meant it. My report wasn't as dull as Donna's but it wasn't as long either. Maybe the longer you talk the better grade you get. That wouldn't be fair though. Either way, I'm glad Mrs Minish calls on us alphabetically and that my last name is Brenner. I come right after Bruce Bonaventura.

Mrs Minish cleared her throat. 'Linda Fischer will give the last report for today,' she said. 'We'll hear five more tomorrow and by the middle of next week everyone will have had a turn.'

I didn't think I'd be able to live through another report.

'Are you ready, Linda?' Mrs Minish asked.

'Yes,' Linda said, as she walked to the front of the room. 'My report is uh . . . on the whale.'

Caroline and Wendy started another game of Tic-Tac-Toe while Bruce went to work on his nose. He has a very interesting way of picking it. First he works one nostril and then the other and whatever he gets out he sticks on a piece of yellow paper inside his desk.

The hand on the wall clock jumped. Only ten minutes till the bell. I took a piece of paper out of my desk to keep a record of how many times Linda said *And uh* . . . while she gave her report. So far I'd counted seven. Linda's head is shaped like a potato and sits right on her shoulders as if she hasn't got any neck. She's also the pudgiest girl in our class, but not in our grade. Ruthellen Stark and Elizabeth Ryan are about ten times fatter than Linda, but even they can't compare to Bruce. If we had a school fat contest he would definitely win. He's a regular butterball.

'Blubber is a thick layer of fat that lies under the skin and over the muscles of whales,' Linda said. 'And uh . . . it protects them and keeps them warm even in cold water. Blubber is very important. Removing the blubber from a whale is a job done by men called flensers. They peel off the blubber with long knives and uh . . . cut it into strips.' Linda held up a picture. 'This is what blubber looks like,' she said.

Wendy passed a note to Caroline. Caroline read it, then turned around in her seat and passed it to me. I unfolded it. It said: *Blubber is a good name for her!* I smiled, not because I thought the note was funny, but because Wendy was watching me. When she turned away I crumpled it up and left it in the corner of my desk. The next thing I knew, Robby Winters, who sits next to me, reached out and grabbed it.

Linda kept talking. 'And uh . . . whale oil is obtained by heating the blubber of the whale. European margarine companies are the chief users of whale oil and uh . . . it also goes into glycerine and some laundry soaps and has other minor uses. Sometimes Eskimos and Japanese eat blubber . . .'

When Linda said that Wendy laughed out loud and once she started she couldn't stop. Probably the reason she got the hiccups was she laughed too hard. They were very loud hiccups. The kind you can't do anything about.

Pretty soon Robby Winters was laughing too. He doesn't laugh like an ordinary person – that is, no noises come out. But his whole body shakes and tears run out of his eyes and just watching him is enough to make anybody start in, so the next minute we were all roaring – all except Linda and Mrs Minish. She clapped her hands and said, 'Exactly what is going on here?'

Wendy let out a loud hiccup.

Mrs Minish said, 'Wendy, you are excused. Go and get a drink of water.'

Wendy stood up and ran out of the room.

By then Wendy's note about Blubber had travelled halfway around the class and I couldn't stop laughing, even when Mrs Minish looked right at me and said, 'Jill Brenner, will you please explain the joke.'

I didn't say anything.

'Well, Jill . . . I'm waiting . . .'

'I don't know the joke,' I finally said, finding it hard to talk at all.

'You don't know why you're laughing?' Mrs Minish asked.

I shook my head.

'It's very foolish to laugh if you don't know what's funny in the first place.'

I nodded.

'If you can't control yourself you can march straight to Mr Nichols' office and explain the situation to him.'

I nodded again.

'I'm waiting for your answer, Jill.'

'I forgot the question, Mrs Minish.'

'The question is, can you control yourself?'

'Oh . . . yes, Mrs Minish . . . I can.'

'I hope so. Linda, you may continue,' Mrs Minish said.

'I'm done,' Linda told her.

'Well . . . that was a very nice report.'

The bell rang then. We pushed back our chairs and ran for the row of lockers behind our desks. Mrs Minish has to dismiss us at exactly two thirty-five. Otherwise we'd miss our buses.

It's very important to get on the right one. On the first day of school my brother, Kenny, got on the wrong bus and wound up all the way across town. Since my mother and father were both at work the principal of Longmeadow School had to drive Kenny home. I would never make such a mistake. My bus is H-4. That means Hillside School, route number four. I'm glad Kenny doesn't go to my school. Next year he will, but right now he is just in fourth grade and only fifth and sixth graders go to Hillside.

When I got on the bus Tracy was saving me a seat. Caroline and Wendy found two seats across from us. Before this year I'd never been in either one of their classes but this is my second time with Linda Fischer and I've been with Donna, Bruce and Robby since kindergarten.

'We had the best afternoon,' Tracy said. 'Mr Vandenburg invented this game to help us get our multiplication facts straight and I was *forty-eight* and every time he called out *six times eight* or *four times twelve* I had to jump up and yell *Here!* It was so much fun.'

'You're lucky to be in his class,' I said. 'I wish he'd give Mrs Minish some ideas.'

'She's the wrong type.'

'You're telling me!'

As Linda climbed on to the bus Wendy shouted, 'Here comes Blubber!' And a bunch of kids called out, 'Hi, Blubber.'

Our bus pulled out of the driveway and as soon as we turned the corner and got going Robby Winters sailed a paper airplane down the aisle. It landed on my head.

'Pass it here, Jill,' Wendy called. When I did, she whipped out a magic marker and wrote *I'm Blubber – Fly Me* on the wing. Then she stood up and aimed the plane at Linda.

The group of girls who always sit in the last row of seats started singing to the tune of 'Beautiful Dreamer', *Blubbery blubber . . . blub, blub, blub, blub . . .*

At the same time, the airplane landed on two sixth-grade boys who ripped it up to make spit balls. They shot them at Linda. Then Irwin grabbed her jacket off her lap. 'She won't need a coat this winter,' he said. 'She's got her blubber to keep her warm.' He tossed the jacket up front and we played Keep-Away with it.

'Some people even eat blubber!' Caroline shrieked, catching Linda's jacket. 'She said so herself.'

'Ohhh . . . disgusting!' Ruthellen Stark moaned, clutching her stomach.

'Sick!'

The girls in the back started their song again. *Blubbery blubber . . . blub, blub, blub, blub . . .*

The bus driver yelled, 'Shut up or I'll put you all off!'

Nobody paid any attention.

Linda picked the spit balls out of her hair but she still didn't say anything. She just sat there, looking out the window.

When we reached the first stop Wendy threw Linda's jacket to me. She and Caroline ran down the aisle and as Linda stood up, Wendy called back, ''Bye, Blubber!'

Linda stopped at my row. I could tell she was close to crying because last year, when Robby stepped on her finger by mistake, she got the same look on her face, right before the tears started rolling.

'Oh, here,' I said and I tossed her the jacket. She got off and I saw her race down the street away from Wendy and Caroline. They were still laughing.

two

'That's what you're going to be for Hallowe'en?'

Linda lives in Hidden Valley. So do Wendy, Caroline, Robby and a bunch of other kids. It's a big group of houses with a low brick wall around it and a sign that says WELCOME TO HIDDEN VALLEY – SPEED LIMIT 25 MILES PER HOUR. Across the street there is another sign saying WATCH OUR CHILDREN. It's called Hidden Valley because there are a million trees and in the summer you can't see any of the houses. Nobody told me this. It's something I figured out by myself.

My stop is next. Me and Tracy are the only ones who get off there. The Wu family lives across the road from us. They have

110

a lot of animals. All of this doesn't mean we live in the country. It's kind of pretend country. That is it looks like country because of all the woods but just about everyone who lives here works in the city, like my mother and father. I don't know one single farmer unless you count the woman who sells us vegetables in the summer.

'Can you come over?' Tracy asked, as we collected the mail from our mailboxes.

'As soon as I change,' I told her.

'Bring your stamps,' Tracy said.

'I will.' Me and Tracy are practically professional stamp collectors. We both have the *Master Global Album*. And I have this deal going with my father – if I let my nails grow between now and Christmas he will give me twenty-five dollars to spend in Gimbels, which has the best stamp department in the whole world. So even though it is just about killing me, I'm not going to bite my nails. Sometimes I have to sit on my fingers to keep from doing it.

When I got home Kenny was waiting at the front door. He was holding his *Guinness Book of World Records* in one hand and with the other was shoving a cupcake into his mouth. 'Did you know the oldest woman to ever give birth to a baby was fifty-seven years old?' As he talked he blew crumbs out of his mouth.

'So?' I said, to show I wasn't interested, because if Kenny gets the idea I'm interested he will tell me facts from his *Book of World Records* all day.

'So . . . that means Grandma is too old to have a baby.'

'Well, of course she is! She's past sixty.'

'And Mrs Sandmeier's too old, too.'

Mrs Sandmeier is our housekeeper. She takes care of me and Kenny after school.

'Too old for what?' she asked, as we walked into the kitchen.

'Too old to have a baby,' Kenny said.

Mrs Sandmeier laughed. 'Who says so?'

'My *Book of World Records*,' Kenny told her. 'The oldest

woman to give birth was fifty-seven and you're fifty-eight.'

'Don't remind me!' Mrs Sandmeier said.

Mrs Sandmeier is always telling us she's getting old but she can still take on Kenny and his friends at basketball and beat them single-handed.

'How was your day, Jill?' Mrs Sandmeier asked me in French, as she poured a glass of milk.

I answered in English. 'Pretty good.'

Mrs Sandmeier made a face. Part of her job is to teach me and Kenny to speak French. She's from Switzerland and can speak three languages. I understand what she says when she speaks French but I always answer in English because most of the time I'm too busy to think of the right words in French.

After my snack, I changed into my favourite jeans, collected my stamp equipment, and headed for Tracy's. Kenny and Mrs Sandmeier were already outside, practising lay-ups.

'Be back at five-thirty,' Mrs Sandmeier called, as I walked up the driveway.

'I will.'

Our street isn't big enough to have a name. There's just a sign saying PRIVATE ROAD, and our house and Tracy's. Dr Wu was outside planting tulip bulbs. Tuesday is his day off.

'Hi, Dr Wu,' I said. He is our family doctor and makes house calls only to us. I like him a lot. He's always smiling. Also, he doesn't gag me with a stick when he looks down my throat.

'Hi, yourself,' he called to me.

Tracy was in the backyard, feeding her chickens. She has ten of them and a beautiful white rooster called Friendly, whom I love. Sometimes Tracy lets me hold him. His crown is red and it feels like a cat's tongue. I know this because last year one of Tracy's cats licked me. She has seven cats but they don't live in the house. They come into the garage to get food and water and the rest of the time they stay outside. Tracy also has two dogs. They live in the house.

When the chickens were fed we went inside to Tracy's room to look over our latest approvals from the Winthrop Stamp

112

Company. We decided we'd each buy two stamps.

Tracy showed me the Hallowe'en costume her mother is making for her – Big Bird from Sesame Street. It has yellow feathers and everything.

'It's beautiful!' I said. I still didn't have an idea for my costume.

We went to work on our albums, trading doubles and fastening loose stamps to the page. And then, right in the middle of licking a stamp hinge, I thought up a costume so clever I didn't even tell Tracy. I decided it would be a surprise.

That night, when my mother and father got home, they brought two big pumpkins with them.

I waited until we were halfway through with dinner before I brought up the subject of my Hallowe'en costume. 'I don't think I want to be a witch this year,' I said. I hoped I wouldn't hurt Mom's feelings because the witch's costume was hers when she was a kid. It has funny, pointy-toed shoes with silver buckles, a high black silk hat and a long black robe with a bow at the neck. The whole thing smells like mothballs. Besides, the shoes hurt my feet.

'You can be whatever you want,' my mother said and she didn't sound insulted.

'If she doesn't want to wear the witch's suit, can I?' Kenny asked.

'A boy witch?' I said.

'Sure. What's wrong with that?'

'Nothing,' Mom told him. 'I'd love to have you wear my costume.'

'And I'm going to carry a broom,' Kenny said. 'And remember that fake cigar from my last year's disguise . . . I'm going to use that too. I'll bet there aren't many witches around who smoke cigars.'

'Smoking is dangerous to your health!' I said.

'My cigar's fake, stupid!'

I gave him a kick under the table and was pleased to see that

113

Mom ground out the cigarette she'd been smoking.

'What about you, Jill?' my father asked. 'What do you want to be?'

'Oh . . . I've been thinking I might like to be a flenser.'

'What's that?' Kenny asked.

'You mean you don't know?' I said.

'Never heard of it.'

'With all your facts in the *Book of World Records* you never learned about the oldest flenser and the youngest flenser and the flenser who did the best job and all that?'

'Dad . . .' Kenny said. 'She's starting in again.'

I absolutely love to tease Kenny.

'Jill, that's enough,' my father said. 'Tell Kenny what a flenser is.'

'Yes,' Mom said. 'I can hardly wait to hear myself.'

'You mean you don't know either?' I asked my mother.

'Never heard the word. Did you, Gordon?'

'Nope,' Dad said.

Kenny jumped up. 'I'll be right back,' he told us, as he ran out of the room.

I knew where he was going – to look up 'flenser' in his dictionary.

In a few minutes he was back, carrying it. 'A flenser strips the blubber off whales,' he read, looking at me. 'That's what you're going to be for Hallowe'en?' he asked, like he couldn't believe it.

I smiled.

'Where did you get that idea, Jill?' Mom asked.

'From this girl in my class. She gave a report on whales.'

'Well . . . that's certainly original,' Dad said.

'What kind of costume does a flenser wear?' Kenny asked.

'A flenser suit,' I told him.

'Yeah . . . but what's it made of?'

'Oh . . . jeans and shirt and a special kind of hat and a long knife.'

'No knife,' my father said. 'That's too dangerous.'

114

'Not a *real* knife,' I said. 'One made out of cardboard.'

'What kind of hat?' Kenny asked.

'A flenser hat, naturally,' I told him.

'Yeah . . . but what's it look like?'

'I can't begin to describe it. You'll just have to wait and see.'

'I'd wear boots if I was a flenser,' Kenny said.

'What for?' I asked him.

'Because of walking around in all that yucky blubber stuff.'

Kenny was right. I'd have to wear boots too.

After dinner we went into the living room for our family poker game. I handed out the Monopoly money. We each get one hundred and fifty dollars from the bank. My father shuffled the cards, Mom cut them and Kenny dealt.

I got a pair of kings and three junk cards. I'm careful not to give my hand away by the expression on my face. You can always tell what Kenny is holding. If it's something good he makes all kinds of noises and he laughs a lot. Even if he doesn't have anything good he stays in and takes three new cards. He never drops out when he should because he can't stand not betting against the rest of us.

When it comes to bluffing my father is the best. Every time he stays in and starts raising I think he has three aces and unless I have something really great I drop out. Then I'll find out Dad didn't even have a pair. My mother is not an experienced poker player. She can never remember which is higher – a flush or a straight. Sometimes I have to help her out.

Later, when me and Kenny were in our pyjamas and ready for bed, my father said we could carve our pumpkins. Mom had to go to her room because the smell of pumpkin guts makes her sick to her stomach.

Last year, when I cut out my pumpkin's face, it was all lopsided, but this time I got both eyes even and the nose in between. Dad made the teeth for me. Kenny wouldn't let anyone touch his pumpkin, which is why it turned out looking like it had three eyes and no teeth.

three

'And now . . . for the most original costume of the day . . .'

The next night I turned my mother's old beach hat into part of my flenser suit. Mom didn't mind because she'd worn the hat for four years and was getting tired of it. My mother never sets foot on the beach without wearing a floppy hat. She thinks it's very bad to get sun on her face. She's always saying that sun makes wrinkles and wrinkles make people look older and that someday I will know what she means. My father doesn't worry about wrinkles so he never has to wear anything on his head. I'll be like him when I grow up. How can you dive under the waves with a floppy hat on your head?

I look much older in the beach hat. I could pass for twelve, I think, maybe even thirteen with sun glasses. The beach hat is so big it covers most of my face. It used to be lots of different colours but now it's faded into a kind of bluish-grey.

I tried to find pictures of whales to decorate the hat but I couldn't so I settled for some of dolphins instead. I cut them out and stampled them all over the brim. Then I cut a piece of black construction paper into thin strips and attached them too. They hung down the sides, kind of like hair.

I shaped my flenser knife like a sword, but with a big curl at one end. I covered it with gold sparkle and painted my boots to match. Then I tried on my whole costume.

I went to my mother's room to have a look in her long mirror but Kenny was already there, admiring himself in the witch's suit. He had on his yellow goggles and the fake cigar dangled out of the corner of his mouth. He was doing some strange dance but as soon as he saw me he stopped.

'I just wanted to see if it fits okay,' he said. He walked away from the mirror, tripping over the pointy witch's shoes. 'It's hard to walk in these things,' he told me, kicking them off.

'Can I ask you a very simple question?' I said.

116

'Go ahead . . .'

'Why are you wearing your goggles?'

'If you have to ask, you wouldn't understand,' Kenny told me. 'But speaking of goggles . . . did you know that the first motorcycle race was in France, in 1897?'

'No, I didn't. But thanks for telling me.'

Kenny looked me up and down. 'Is that what you're wearing tomorrow?'

'Yes, it's my flenser suit.' I stood in front of the mirror and held the sword out.

'What'd you do to your boots?'

'Painted them.'

'Gold?'

'Why not . . .'

'Does Mom know?'

'They're *my* boots, Kenny. Why should Mom care if I had to paint them to match my sword?'

'Speaking of swords . . .' Kenny began.

'We were *not* speaking of swords,' I told him. 'We were speaking about my flenser suit!'

'Yeah . . . well, if I were you I'd wear a sign telling people what you are . . . because I don't think anybody's going to know otherwise.'

'Oh, Kenny . . . you are *so* dumb! Of course they'll know. Just look at my hat . . . can't you see all the picture of whales up there?'

'They're dolphins,' Kenny said.

'Only *you* would know that!'

'And speaking of dolphins,' Kenny said.

'Never mind . . . never mind! I don't want to hear it.'

Later, I made a sign saying *FLENSER*, just in case Kenny was right. I punched two holes through it, ran a string across and hung it around my neck.

The next morning my mother was surprised when she saw my boots. 'They're gold!' Mom said in a very loud voice. She puffed hard on her cigarette.

'Smoking causes cancer and heart disease,' I told her, ignoring my boots.

Mom mashed her cigarette out and reached for her coffee. 'What did you do to your new boots, Jill?'

'I painted them.'

'Jill . . . they have to last you all winter. You haven't even worn them yet.'

'I know it, Mother!'

'Well . . . how could you do such a thing?'

'A flenser wouldn't wear plain brown boots.'

'I just hope you used washable paint.'

'I think I did.'

'You checked first, didn't you?'

'I'm almost sure it's washable.'

'You didn't check before you used it?'

'Not exactly.'

Mom lit another cigarette.

I called for Tracy. She was in her Big Bird costume and her mother was adjusting a crown of feathers on her head. 'How do you like it?' she asked, twirling around.

'Oh, Tracy . . . you look fantastic!' Next to her I felt very plain.

Tracy looked me over. 'What's a flenser?' she asked, reading my sign.

'That's what I'm supposed to be,' I told her.

'I know . . . but what is one?'

'Oh . . . a flenser's a guy who strips the blubber off whales.'

'Where'd you get such a weird idea?' Tracy asked.

'From Linda Fischer . . . you know . . . the one Wendy calls Blubber. She gave a report on whales.'

'Well,' Tracy said, 'at least you don't have to worry that everyone will be dressed like you.' She went to the mirror and combed her hair. She has the nicest hair I've ever seen. It hangs straight down her back. She can even sit on it. And it never

118

looks dirty or has tangles. I'm growing mine but no matter how long it gets it will never look like Tracy's.

Mrs Wu drove us to school so Tracy wouldn't mess up her costume. When I got to my class Wendy was already there. She was dressed like a queen. She wore a very high crown with lots of fake emeralds and rubies pasted to it. She also wore her mother's long bathrobe and had this crazy-looking fur thing wrapped around her neck. It had eyes, paws, a tail and everything.

'Animals are for loving, not wearing,' I told her.

'I know it,' Wendy said, 'but this thing is very old. It belonged to my grandmother. And in those days they didn't know about ecology.'

'Oh . . .' I said. 'Then I guess it's all right.'

Donna Davidson really fooled me. Instead of dressing up like a horse, this year she was a jockey. 'My things are all *genuine*,' she bragged. 'My father knows this jockey who's very famous and he's just my size and these are his *real life* jockey clothes.'

Donna looked pretty good, but I didn't tell her I thought so. And I wasn't worried about winning the prize for most original costume because a flenser is a lot more clever than a jockey or a queen with a tall crown. Practically everyone else in our class was dressed like a bum, with old baggy pants and shirts hanging out and charcoal smudges on their faces. Caroline even carried a stick with a pouch tied on one end. There is nothing very original about dressing up like that.

Right after Mrs Minish took the attendance she told us to line up for the Hallowe'en assembly. 'Remember, no talking in the halls or the auditorium.'

I stood on line between Wendy and Linda, who was wearing a long, red cape. As we walked down the hall Linda tapped me and said, 'What are you supposed to be?'

'Can't you read?' I asked, holding up my sign.

'Oh . . . a flenser. I'll bet you got that idea from my report.'

'What makes you think so?'

'Jill Brenner!' Mrs Minish snapped. 'I said *no* talking!'

In the auditorium our class sat in the third and fourth rows. I whispered to Linda, 'What are *you* supposed to be?'

'Never mind.'

'Don't you know?'

'I know.'

'Then tell me.'

'No . . . it's my own business.'

'I'll bet you're supposed to be Little Red Riding Hood.'

'I am not.'

I turned to Wendy. 'Get a load of Little Red Riding Hood,' I said.

Wendy leaned across me and told Linda. 'You better watch out for the Big Bad Wolf!'

'Yeah . . .' I said, 'you better . . .' I felt a hand on my head. I turned around in my seat. It was Mrs Minish.

'If I have to speak to you again you'll go back to the classroom.'

I didn't say a word during the Pledge of Allegiance or 'The Star-Spangled Banner'. Linda sang in a very loud voice and when I looked at her I could see her grey tooth. Wendy says if she isn't more careful about the way she brushes all her teeth will turn grey and rotten and fall out.

The Hallowe'en Parade was next. Every class had a turn to march across the stage. The costume judges all sat in the first row. They were mothers from the PTA. It's against the rules for them to vote for their own kids.

I watched carefully as the other classes had their turns. I pretended to be a judge. Only two sixth graders were dressed as anything besides bums. Jerry Pochuk was a doctor and Fred Yarmouth was something I couldn't figure out. I certainly didn't see any costumes as original as mine or any that were prettier than Tracy's.

After the parade Mrs Runyon, the librarian, stood on the stage and said, 'I'm happy to be here today to present the prizes for the most beautiful and the most original costumes.'

I sat on my hands to keep from chewing my nails.

'But before I do, I want to share with you the fine prizes the PTA has selected and donated.' Mrs Runyon held up two paperback books. They both had medals printed on the covers. I read them last year. One wasn't too bad but the other was so boring I never got past the first chapter. Still, it wasn't the prize that mattered. It was the idea of winning.

'And now . . . for our winner . . .' Mrs Runyon said. 'For the most beautiful costume . . . Tracy Wu, the Big Bird!'

Everyone clapped as Tracy ran to the stage, dripping yellow feathers all over the aisle. She got the boring book.

'And now . . . for the most original costume of the day . . .'

I sat up in my seat.

'To Fred Yarmouth, the fried egg,' Mrs Runyon called.

I couldn't believe it! I was so sure the prize would be mine. And how did the judges know Fred was supposed to be a fried egg when I had no idea what he was?

Fred ran to the stage. Mrs Runyon said, 'Tell us, Fred, how did you decide to be a fried egg?'

'Oh, I don't know,' Fred said. 'I had this white sheet and some yellow felt and when I put it all together that's what it looked like to me.'

He hadn't even planned to be an egg. That made everything worse. Now I'd be stuck wearing gold boots for the rest of the year – and all for nothing.

four

'What's the magic word?'

We were back in our classroom at ten-thirty and Mrs Minish said we'd work on maths and science until the lunchtime. I tried to concentrate on my maths but when Mrs Minish asked to see my paper she drew red lines across every problem.

'They're all wrong?' I asked.

'Not the answers,' Mrs Minish said.

'Then what?'

'You didn't set up the problems properly.'

'But if I got the right answers what's the difference?'

'Your equations are backwards. You'll have to do the paper over.'

'I don't see why,' I told her.

'Because you're supposed to be learning how to think the problems through and you aren't thinking the right way.'

'Isn't there more than one way to think?'

'Really, Jill . . . I don't care for this talking back!'

'But, Mrs Minish . . .'

'No buts,' Mrs Minish said. 'Take it home and do it over.'

Before lunch Mrs Minish excused us to go to the Girls' and Boys' Rooms. I took my sword with me. I was afraid if I left it at my desk Robby Winters might get his hands on it and ruin it. And I needed it for later, to go Trick-or-Treating for UNICEF.

'Mrs Minish is such a bitch!' I said to Wendy and Caroline, as we stood by the sinks in the Girls' Room. 'She marked all my maths problems wrong.'

'I got a hundred,' Caroline said.

'That's because I let you copy off me,' Wendy told her.

'Not that my morning wasn't already ruined,' I said. 'I still can't believe they gave that smelly fried-egg costume the prize.'

'Yeah,' Wendy said. 'My costume was much more original than that.'

Caroline said, 'Personally, I thought Donna Davidson would win. Her things were all genuine.'

'There's nothing original about being a jockey,' I said. 'Being a flenser is original but those judges were too dumb to know it.'

'One of them was my aunt,' Caroline said.

'Oh . . . I didn't mean to insult her.'

'That's all right. She is dumb. My mother's always saying so.'

'Oh.'

122

The other girls finished and went back to the classroom while me, Caroline and Wendy stood around talking.

I heard a toilet flush, then Linda Fischer came out of a booth, pulling her red cape around her.

'Look who's here,' Wendy said. 'It's Blubber!'

'In the flesh,' Caroline added.

'I wonder what's under her cape?' Wendy asked.

'Probably nothing,' Caroline said.

'Oh, there's got to be something,' Wendy said. 'There's got to be her blubber . . . at least.'

'Yeah . . . her blubber's under her cape!' Caroline said and she and Wendy started laughing. I giggled a little too.

Wendy moved closer to Linda, humming 'Beautiful Dreamer'.

'Stay away from me!' Linda told her, walking backwards.

'I'm not going to hurt you, stupid,' Wendy said. 'I just want to see what's under your cape.'

'Don't touch me.'

'Oh, don't worry . . . that's not my job . . . Jill's the flenser.'

'That's true,' I said. 'I am.'

'And the flenser's the one who strips the blubber,' Wendy said.

I wasn't sure exactly what Wendy had in mind.

Linda tried to run but Caroline and Wendy blocked her way.

'Strip her, flenser!' Wendy called. 'Now! Then we'll throw her cape out the window and she'll have to walk down the hall in her blubbery birthday suit.'

'No!' Linda said. 'Don't you dare strip me!'

Caroline and Wendy grabbed hold of Linda's arms and held her still.

'Do your job,' Wendy said. 'Prove what a good flenser you are.'

'Okay,' I said, pulling off Linda's cape. She had on a regular skirt and shirt under it.

'Strip her some more!' Wendy said, yanking up Linda's

123

skirt. 'Hey . . . Blubber wears flowered underpants.'

'Let go of me!' Linda squirmed and tried to kick but Caroline grabbed her shirt and tugged until two buttons popped off.

'She wears an undershirt!' Caroline said.

Linda started to cry.

'Oh my . . . Blubber's blubbering,' Wendy said.

'Stop it . . . stop it!' Linda cried.

'What's the magic word?' I asked.

'*Please!*' Linda's nose was running.

'Blubber knows the magic word,' I said, 'so the flenser won't strip her today.'

'But she still has to obey the queen,' Wendy said. 'I am Her Majesty, Queen Wendy. Get it, Blubber?'

Linda nodded and tried to catch her breath. She had red splotches all over her face.

'Curtsy to the queen,' Wendy said.

Linda tried to tuck her shirt back into her skirt.

'Didn't you hear me, Blubber? I said, curtsy to the queen.'

Linda curtsied to Wendy.

'That's better,' Wendy said. 'Now kiss my foot.'

'I don't want to.' Linda started sniffling.

I raised my sword. 'Do whatever Queen Wendy says, Blubber.'

Linda bent down and kissed Wendy's sneaker.

'Now, cut out that stupid crying,' Wendy told her, as she threw Linda her cape. 'Here . . . put this on . . . and remember . . . one word to anyone about this and we'll *really* get you next time.' Wendy looked at me and smiled.

I wasn't worried about Linda telling on us. Besides, everybody knows you don't cross Wendy.

five

'A person gets what she deserves.'

'I won the prize for the most original costume in my school,' Kenny said. He was still in his witch's suit, standing at the front door, when I got home.

'I don't believe you.'

Kenny held up an envelope. 'See for yourself.' He handed it to me.

I opened the envelope and pulled out a piece of stiff red paper. It said, *One Free Meal at Opie's/Awarded by the PTA of Longmeadow School for the most Original Hallowe'en Costume.* Under that, *Kenny Brenner* was printed in blue ink.

'You see?' Kenny said. 'I told you I won.'

'Opie's has rat tails in their food.'

'Just in the chicken,' Kenny said. 'The hamburgers are okay.'

'I wouldn't eat there if it was the last place on earth!'

'You don't have to,' Kenny said.

'At my school they at least gave away paperback books.'

'Did you get one?'

'I already read them both,' I told him.

'But did you get one?'

'They gave it to Fred Yarmouth, just because he's in sixth grade.'

Kenny smiled and went tripping down the hall to his room.

I kicked the front door shut and went to the kitchen. 'I don't understand it,' I told Mrs Sandmeier. 'I wore that witch's suit three years in a row and I never won anything.'

Mrs Sandmeier offered me a plate of gingersnaps. 'It was the cigar that did it,' she said. 'That and the yellow goggles. He was an unusual witch.'

'Next year he'll probably be an unusual flenser and win again.'

'Probably,' Mrs Sandmeier said.

'Hmph!' I took three gingersnaps and went to my room. I opened my closet and took out my special suitcase. I keep my stamp collection in it. Grandma gave me the suitcase last year, before she moved to her apartment. She kept it in her basement for fifteen years, ever since Grandpa died. All that time she was just waiting to find someone who would really appreciate it. She chose me because she knew I would take good care of it, and I do. I polish it with a special leather cream once a week.

I turned the pages of my *Master Global Album*, admiring all my stamps. The ones from Nagaland are my favourites.

Tracy called at five. 'What time will you be ready to go Trick-or-Treating?'

I swallowed the meatball I'd been chewing and said, 'As soon as my parents get home. I'm eating now.'

'Don't forget your pillowcase.'

'I won't. I cut out eyes and everything.'

'Good . . . because if Mr Machinist takes pictures this year I don't want him getting me.'

'Me neither.'

'I'll meet you outside at six-thirty.'

'Okay . . .'

'And bring a flashlight.'

'Right.'

''Bye . . .'

Mr Machinist lives in Hidden Valley and every Hallowe'en he hides in his bushes, snapping pictures of kids on his property. Last year he caught some boy soaping up his car windows and besides taking his picture, which he sent to the police, he also turned the hose on him. Mr Machinist has no sense of humour.

After supper I packed a shopping bag with a flashlight, a can of pink Silly String, a roll of toilet paper and my UNICEF collection box. In my free hand I carried my flenser sword.

When my parents got home my mother said, 'It's freezing out. You can't go like that.'

'But if I wear a jacket no one will be able to see my flenser suit.'

'Not only do you have to wear a jacket,' Mom said, 'but it has to be a heavy one . . . zipped up!'

'Oh, Mom! You do this to me every Hallowe'en.'

'I'm sorry, Jill. It's the weather, not me. Hallowe'en should be in August. Then you wouldn't have to wear anything.'

'Ha ha,' I said, pulling the pillowcase over my head. I put my flenser hat on top of that.

'Are you sure you can see?' Dad asked me.

'Hold up your fingers and I'll tell you how many,' I said.

My father held up two. I said, 'Um . . . six . . . right?' Then I laughed. So did Dad.

'Gordon . . . I'm afraid she's going to suffocate in that get-up,' my mother said.

'Can you breathe?' Dad asked.

'Yes . . . I can see and I can breathe and Tracy's waiting for me so can I please go now?'

'Have fun,' my mother said. 'But remember, if you're not home by eight-thirty, I'm sending your father to find you.'

'I'll be home . . . I promise.' I walked to the front hall and grabbed my heavy jacket from the closet. Kenny was standing at the door, waiting for Trick-or-Treaters. He never goes out on Hallowe'en night. He says it's because he likes to answer the doorbell, handing out the candy and UNICEF money, but I know the truth. Kenny is chicken. He's scared of the dark. He really believes in witches and goblins and monsters. That's why he sleeps with his closet light on every night.

I took three nickels from the bowl on the hall table.

'Hey . . .' Kenny said. 'That's UNICEF money.'

'I know it!' I dropped the nickels into my collection box. ''Bye, chicken . . . watch out for the wolf-man . . . he just loves Hallowe'en!' I snorted and jumped away as Kenny tried to slug me.

It was a very dark night. There was no moon and there aren't any street lights in our neighbourhood.

'I think we should head straight for Hidden Valley,' Tracy said. 'There aren't enough houses to bother with around here.'

'Agreed.'

We took turns holding the flashlight. Mrs Wu had made Tracy wear a heavy jacket too. All you could see of her Big Bird suit was a bunch of yellow feathers hanging out. She had her pillowcase over her head, same as me, but she had taped a few feathers to the top, sort of like an Indian headdress.

When we got to Hidden Valley it was easier to see because most families there have lamp posts down by the road. 'You brought the eggs, didn't you?' I asked Tracy.

'Yes . . . six of them.'

'Do they smell bad?'

'I don't know. When we crack them we'll find out. They should be rotten by now. I've had them in my dresser drawer for a month.'

'Good.'

There are some things I would never do on Hallowe'en. I would never smash a carved pumpkin. I know how that feels because last year somebody swiped both pumpkins off our front porch and smashed them all over the road. This year me and Kenny got smart. We put our pumpkins in the window, where they'll be safe. Also, I would never mess around with little kids, trying to steal their loot. That's mean.

But nothing is too mean for Mr Machinist, which is why me and Tracy planned to crack eggs in his mailbox. He deserves it. He won't give to UNICEF and if ever there was a person who'd put razor blades in apples, it's him.

I'm not allowed to eat much of anything I collect Trick-or-Treating, especially apples. Mrs Sandmeier makes them all into apple sauce. So far she's never found a razor blade but my mother says there are crazy people all over and she isn't taking any chances.

Mr Machinist's mailbox is next to his driveway, by the side of the street. It says MACHINIST in small stencilled letters.

128

Tracy took out an egg and handed it to me. 'Ready for action?'

I looked around, sure that Mr Machinist was lurking behind a tree, just waiting to jump out and snap my picture. But I didn't see anything so I said, 'I guess so . . .'

Tracy took another egg out of her bag and held it herself. 'You go first,' she told me.

I put my shopping bag and sword on the ground. Then I opened Mr Machinist's mailbox. It squeaked.

'Go ahead,' Tracy whispered. 'Do it.'

I expected a flashbulb to pop in my face as I cracked the egg and dumped it inside. The yolk broke and dripped all over. 'Now you go,' I told Tracy.

Tracy cracked her egg and threw it inside the box too. We looked at each other, then reached for two more eggs and did the same thing again. When we came to the last eggs we didn't bother cracking them first. We just tossed them into the mailbox, shell and all. After that we picked up our things and ran as fast as we could.

When we were far enough away we started to laugh. 'We did it!' I said. 'We really did it.'

'And they were rotten,' Tracy said. 'Did you get a whiff?'

'Yeah . . . they were just great!'

'Won't he be surprised tomorrow when he reaches in for his mail . . .'

'And comes out with a handful of raw, rotten eggs!'

'Oh, Mr Machinist . . .' Tracy sang, 'you deserve it!'

After that we went Trick-or-Treating. We stopped at every house in Hidden Valley. At Wendy's we got two miniature Hershey bars and a handful of UNICEF pennies. At Caroline's we each got a quarter for UNICEF and a napkin full of chicken corn. At Robby Winters' his mother invited us inside while she wrote a one-dollar cheque for each of us to give to UNICEF.

'I never got a cheque before,' Tracy said, when we were outside again.

'Me neither, but I think it's neat.'

'So do I.'

When we got to Linda Fischer's house, Tracy asked, 'Do you want to ring her bell?'

'No . . . Let's do her trees instead.'

'Good idea,' Tracy said.

I whipped out the roll of toilet paper and me and Tracy wound it all around the Fischers' trees. Then we ran up and down the front walk squirting pink Silly String on all bushes. I was having the best time. I wished Hallowe'en came more than once a year. I shook the can and aimed it at the hedge right next to the house. 'A person gets what she deserves,' I sang. But when I pushed the button nothing came out of the can. 'It's empty,' I told Tracy.

'So's mine,' she said.

We raced down the driveway. Tracy had a piece of blue chalk with her and she snapped it in half and both of us laughed like crazy as we wrote *Blubber lives here* all over the street.

Wendy and Caroline came along then, shining their flashlights in our faces. 'Hey,' I said, 'turn those things off.'

'Who are you?' Wendy asked.

'Who do you think? It's me, Jill.'

'Prove it,' Wendy said.

I took off my hat and pillowcase.

'Oh, it really is you,' Wendy said. 'Is that Tracy?'

'Naturally.'

'We smashed six pumpkins,' Caroline said.

'I don't think it's fair to smash pumpkins,' I said.

'Fair or not fair, it was great fun,' Wendy told me.

'Yeah . . .' Caroline said. 'I'll bet you two didn't have such a good time.'

'We did too . . . we had a better time,' I said.

'Doing what?' Wendy asked.

'Me and Tracy put six eggs in Mr Machinist's mailbox.'

'You did not,' Wendy said.

'We did too.'

'I don't believe you.'

130

'We can prove it, can't we, Tracy?'

'Yeah . . . we'll show you.'

'Wait a second. I've got to get my pillowcase on straight,' I said. As I was adjusting it I looked up. And there was Linda, in an upstairs window, watching everything. 'Hey . . . there's Blubber!'

'What a chicken,' Caroline said, '. . . inside on Hallowe'en night.'

'Come on,' Tracy said, 'let's get out of here.'

We raced to Mr Machinist's house and when we got there I pulled his mailbox open while Tracy lit it with her flashlight.

'Well,' I said, 'there's the evidence!'

'You really did it.' Wendy sounded surprised.

'We told you,' I said.

Suddenly a man jumped out from behind a tree. 'Hold it right there!' he called.

'Run!' Wendy hollered, and she and Caroline took off in one direction while me and Tracy ran in the other.

'Don't look back,' Tracy said, breathing hard. 'He's got a camera.'

'And a hose,' I told her, as the water hit me.

When I got home I sneaked in the back door and ran for my bedroom, where I changed into my robe. Then I scooped up the pile of wet clothes from the floor and carried it to the laundry room. I tossed everything into the dryer. Just as I was about to turn it on my mother walked in.

'Oh, hi, honey . . . did you have fun?'

'Yes,' I said, 'lots.'

'I didn't know it was raining out.'

'It's not.'

'Then how come your clothes are in the dryer . . . and your hair's all wet?'

'Oh, that . . .' I said touching my head.

'Or shouldn't I ask?'

'I really wish you wouldn't,' I told Mom.

She smiled and shook her head. Then we went into her bathroom and she dried my hair with her blow-dryer.

six

'The worms crawl in, the worms crawl out . . .'

On Friday mornings, Miss Rothbelle, the music teacher, comes to our classroom. She is tall and skinny with two circles of rouge on her cheeks, hair that is practically blue and fingernails like Dracula. Next to her Mrs Minish looks like Miss America.

I don't know if Miss Rothbelle has just one dress or a lot of dresses exactly alike, but she always looks the same. And every time I pass her in the hall, instead of saying hello, Miss Rothbelle blows her pitchpipe at me.

Today she said, 'We will continue where we left off . . . with lullabies. Remember, you're going to sing at assembly next week and I want a perfect performance. So listen carefully.' She blew into her pitchpipe, then tuned herself up by humming one note until she was satisfied. Her voice is like an opera singer's but it cracks on the high notes.

'Sweet and low . . . sweet and low . . .' Miss Rothbelle sang, walking around the room. When she came to Robby Winters she gave his ear a tug and he sat up straight and tall. Then she tapped Irwin on the head with her ballpoint pen and he put away his comic.

'Low . . . low . . . breathe and blow . . .'

I folded my hands on my desk as Miss Rothbelle came closer to me.

'Sleep, my little one . . . sleep, my little one . . .'

It's very hard to keep a straight face when Miss Rothbelle is singing, especially when she's singing 'Sweet and Low' and comes to the line about 'mother's breast'. She always trills the *br*.

I held my breath until Miss Rothbelle passed my desk.

When she finished her song she was right next to Wendy. 'Wendy . . . can you tell me what was coming out of my mouth as I sang?'

'Out of your mouth?' Wendy asked.

'That's right,' Miss Rothbelle told her.

'Well . . . it was . . . um . . . words?'

'No . . . no . . . no . . .' Miss Rothbelle said.

Wendy was surprised. She can always give teachers the answers they want.

Miss Rothbelle moved on. 'Do you know, Caroline?'

'Was it sound?'

'Wrong!' Miss Rothbelle said, turning. 'Donna Davidson, can you tell me?'

'It was a song,' Donna said.

'Really, Donna . . . we all know that!' Miss Rothbelle looked around. 'Linda Fischer, do you know what was coming out of my mouth as I sang to the class?'

Linda didn't say anything.

'Well, Linda . . .' Miss Rothbelle said.

'I think it was air,' Linda finally told her. 'Either that or breath.'

Miss Rothbelle walked over to Linda's desk. 'That was not the correct answer. Weren't you paying attention?' She pulled a few strands of Linda's hair.

A loud noise came out of Linda then. At first I wasn't sure what it was but then the smell hit me and I knew. I wondered if she'd had sauerkraut for breakfast because that happens to Kenny whenever he eats it.

Miss Rothbelle made a face and stepped away.

I bit my lip to keep from laughing. With Mrs Minish you can laugh out loud and nothing really bad happens. She threatens to send us to Mr Nichols' office but she never does. With Miss Rothbelle you don't laugh, no matter what.

She walked up and down the aisles until she stopped at my desk. 'You're smiling,' she said.

'I am?'

'You are.'

'I don't think so, Miss Rothbelle,' I said.

'We'll see if you've been paying attention . . . suppose you tell me the answer to my question.'

I had no idea what Miss Rothbelle wanted me to say. There was just one thing left that could have been coming out of her mouth as she sang, so I said, 'It was spit.'

'What?' Miss Rothbelle glared at me.

'I mean, it was saliva,' I told her.

Miss Rothbelle banged her fist on my desk. 'That was a very rude thing to say. You can sit in the corner for the rest of the period.'

I pressed my lips together and felt my face turn hot as I carried my chair to the front of the room. I sat down facing the blackboard. Damn that Blubber! I thought. It's all her fault. She's the one who made me smile with her disgusting smell. Miss Rothbelle never would have called on me if I hadn't been smiling. Blubber's the one who should be sitting in the corner. I'd like to tell that to Miss Rothbelle. I really would. Talk about unfair . . .

At the end of music period Robby Winters called out, 'Miss Rothbelle . . . Miss Rothbelle . . .'

'What is it?' she asked.

'You never told us what was coming out of your mouth when you sang.'

'That's right,' Miss Rothbelle said. 'I didn't.'

'It was melody,' Miss Rothbelle said. Then she spelled it. 'M-e-l-o-d-y. And every one of you should have known.' She blew her pitchpipe at us and walked out of the room.

At eleven Mr Kubeck, the custodian, delivers our lunch milk. He leaves it outside the classroom door, in the hall. When I see it standing there my stomach growls and I start thinking about

134

my peanut-butter sandwich, sitting inside my stuffy old locker, getting soggy. By lunchtime the milk is warm. I think it's sour too. I've told my mother to report that to the Board of Health. We'll be able to buy cold milk next year, when the school gym is converted into a part-time cafeteria. Until then we have to suffer through lunch in our classrooms.

At noon Mrs Minish leaves the room. She goes out to lunch every day. All the teachers do. It makes me mad to think of them sitting in some nice restaurant eating hamburgers and french fries while I have to sit at my desk drinking sour milk.

As soon as Mrs Minish is gone we all move our desks around. I push mine next to Wendy's. So does Caroline. Sometimes Donna Davidson joins us and other times she sits across the room with Laurie, which is fine with me. I can't stand hearing her horse stories.

Linda Fischer eats by herself. I watched as she unpacked her lunch and spread it out across her desk. She had a sandwich, a pack of Hostess cupcakes and a big red apple.

'You're going to turn into a real whale if you keep eating like that,' Wendy told her.

'Just shut up,' Linda said, more to her sandwich than to Wendy.

'Well, listen to that!' I said. 'Blubber told Wendy to shut up. Can you imagine!'

'Some people don't know how to talk nice,' Caroline said.

'Didn't your mother teach you any manners, Blubber?' Wendy asked.

'I don't think so,' I said. 'Otherwise Blubber wouldn't chew with her mouth open.'

'Oh yes,' Wendy said. 'I noticed that too. She must want us to see that she has an egg-salad sandwich.'

'On wholewheat bread,' Caroline added.

'And how lovely it looks all chewed up in her mouth,' I said. 'I guess that's why she decided to report on the whale. She has a lot in common with them.' I was beginning to enjoy myself.

'Blub . . . blub . . . blub . . .' Wendy made this funny noise.

Linda took her cupcakes and stuffed them back into her lunch bag. She stood up and headed for the trash basket but Wendy stopped her before she could throw anything away. 'You can't waste those *beautiful* cupcakes, Blubber!'

'I'll take them,' Robby Winters called.

Wendy grabbed the bag out of Linda's hand, took out the package of cupcakes and threw it across the room to Robby. He tossed it to Bill, who passed it to Michael. Michael ate one. The other cupcake was squashed by that time but Irwin stuffed it into his mouth anyway.

Linda went back to her desk. Wendy followed her. 'Oh look . . . Blubber has a shiny red apple.' She held it up for the class to see. Then she put the apple on top of her head and paraded around the room.

Michael stood on his desk and yelled, 'I'm William Tell!'

'Who's he?' Laurie asked.

'The guy who shot the apple off his kid's head, dummy.' Michael pretended to pull back his bow and aim an arrow at Wendy's head.

'Help . . . oh help!' Wendy cried, racing around the room, holding the apple on her head with one hand.

'Help is on the way,' I called, taking off my shoe and throwing it at Michael. It hit him in the leg. He picked it up and ran to the window.

'You wouldn't!' I yelled.

As soon as I said that, Michael raised the window and tossed out my shoe. It landed in the bushes.

'You jerk! You absolute idiot!'

'I'll fix him, Jill,' Wendy called, firing the apple at Michael. It missed him and crashed against the blackboard. Bruce picked it up, polished it off on his shirt, then took a bite.

Donna pointed at him and chanted, 'He ate the poison apple . . . he ate the poison apple . . .'

'Oh . . .' Bruce made this gurgling noise, clutched his stomach and dropped to the floor. He rolled over and played dead while the rest of us circled around him singing, 'The worms crawl in, the worms crawl out, they eat your guts, and they spit them out . . .'

'It's *much* too noisy in here!' Mrs Horvath stood in our doorway with her hands on her hips. She is in charge of us during lunch. She's called a 'lunch teacher' but really, she's more like a policewoman, patrolling the halls and sticking her head in and out of classrooms.

We shut up in a hurry and scrambled back to our desks.

'What is that?' she asked, spying the apple on the floor.

Nobody answered.

'To whom does this apple belong?'

We all looked at Linda.

'Well?' Mrs Horvath said.

'It's mine,' Linda told her in a very weak voice.

'Food does not belong on the floor!' Mrs Horvath shouted.

'I know,' Linda said.

'Then why is it there?'

Linda didn't say anything.

'Do you want me to report you to Mr Nichols?'

'No.'

'Then pick up that apple this instant!'

Linda hurried to the front of the room, picked up the apple, and dumped it into the trash basket.

'That's better,' Mrs Horvath said. 'Now, get into your jackets and go outside.'

As long as it isn't raining we go to the playground after lunch. Rainy days are bad because we have to spend all of lunch hour in our classroom and that is just so boring, even though Mrs Minish unlocks the supply closet and hands out extra vanilla drawing paper.

I prayed that Mrs Horvath wouldn't notice I was wearing just one shoe and all the way down the hall I walked with my sock foot in front of my shoe foot. Outside, instead of jumping rope, like usual, I hunted in the bushes for my shoe. As soon as Tracy heard what happened she came over to help. When we finally found it, it was time to go back to class.

seven

'Doesn't it stick to the roof of your mouth?'

My mother has decided to give up cigarettes. She says if I have
enough willpower to stop biting my nails then she should have
enough to stop smoking. I'm very proud of her. Dad says we've
got to encourage Mom, so Kenny gives her all the bubble gum
from his baseball cards. Mom can blow the biggest bubbles I've
ever seen. She has to keep her mouth busy so she won't crave
cigarettes, which is why she's taken up chewing. I know how
she feels, only with me, instead of chewing, I wiggle my loose
tooth.

On Sunday night, Mom reminded me that I still have
nothing to wear to Warren Winkler's bar mitzvah and it's just
two weeks away. His father lived next door to my father when
they were boys. We don't see the Winklers very often – just
once or twice a year – but that is more than enough for me.
Warren is such a creep! His mother is always making jokes
about how me and Warren will like each other a lot more when
we grow up, which proves that Mrs Winkler doesn't know
anything.

'Do I really have to go?' I asked my mother.

'Yes,' Mom said, trying to scrape the bubble gum off her
chin.

'You need alcohol for that,' I told her.

'Oh . . . thanks.'

We went into the bathroom and I watched Mom clean off her
face. 'I think I'll wear a long dress,' I said. 'Tracy went to a bar
mitzvah last year and she wore one. Her mother made it for
her . . . it's beautiful . . . maybe she'd lend it to me.'

'That's ridiculous,' Mom said.

'What is?' I asked. 'Wearing a long dress or borrowing
Tracy's?'

'Both.'

'Then what am I going to wear?'

'I'll look for something this week.'

'No ruffles or anything like that.'

'Don't worry. I'll get a very simple dress.'

'I hope so,' I said.

We always get off to a slow start on Monday mornings because Mrs Minish has to collect our milk money for the week. I've noticed that she isn't so fast when it comes to arithmetic. If she didn't pay so much attention to thinking the problem through, like it says in our book, she could probably do better.

While Mrs Minish was counting, Robby Winters came over to my desk, holding his hands out like some kind of zombie. He had a pin stuck through the skin of every finger. I used to think it was very brave of him to do that. But when I tried it myself I found out it's easy. It doesn't even hurt. Last time I did it Mrs Sandmeier caught me and made me soak my fingers in Epsom Salt for two hours.

'Robby, you are gruesome,' I told him, as he pushed his pin fingers in my face. As soon as he saw that he couldn't get anywhere with me he went over to Linda Fischer. She screamed.

Mrs Minish looked up. 'What's going on?'

'It's Robby . . .' Linda said. 'He's got pins in his fingers.'

'Take them out, Robby,' Mrs Minish said. 'Right now.'

'But they feel nice,' Robby told her.

'Take them out!'

'Yes, Mrs Minish.'

When she was finished with the milk money, Mrs Minish announced that we would have a social studies test on Wednesday, on the explorers. I get them all mixed up. I can never remember which one is de Vaca and which one is de Soto and who discovered what.

At lunchtime, Wendy and Caroline traded sandwiches. Wendy loves salami and Caroline's favourite is tuna. I had my usual, peanut butter.

'Don't you get sick of the same old thing day after day?' Wendy asked.

'Nope.'

'Doesn't it stick to the roof of your mouth?' Caroline said.

'If it does I just work it off with my tongue.'

'It's good you're so skinny,' Caroline told me. 'Peanut butter's fattening.'

'Jill doesn't have to worry,' Wendy said. 'Not like some people . . .'

We all looked over at Linda. She had her lunch spread out on her desk – two pieces of celery, one slice of yellow cheese and a package of saltine crackers. 'Hey . . .' I said, 'Blubber's on a diet!'

'Is that right?' Wendy asked.

'Yes,' Linda said. 'I'm going to lose ten pounds and then you won't be able to call me that name any more.'

'What name?' Wendy said, and we all giggled.

'You know.'

'Say it!'

'No . . . I don't have to.'

Wendy got up and went over to Linda's desk. She made a fist at her. 'Say it . . .'

'Blubber,' Linda said very low.

'Louder.'

'Blubber,' she said in her regular voice.

Caroline was laughing like a hyena. I've never heard a hyena laugh, but I just know it would sound like Caroline. I think she's really stupid sometimes.

'Now say, *My name will always be Blubber*,' Wendy told Linda.

'No . . . because it won't.'

'Say it!' Wendy told her and she didn't look like she was fooling around any more.

I sat on the edge of my seat, not moving.

'My name will always be Blubber,' Linda said. There were tears in her eyes.

'And don't you forget it,' Wendy said, 'because even if you weigh fifty pounds you'll still be a smelly whale.'

That night, after my bath, I went to my parents' room. Mom was stretched out reading a book. I did a flying leap on to her bed and lay down next to her.

'You're sleepy, aren't you?' she asked, playing with my hair.

'A little . . .'

'You should go to bed.'

'In a minute.'

'Okay.'

'Mom . . .'

'Hum?'

'Remember the time that sixth grader called Tracy a *chink*?'

'I remember,' Mom said.

'And how she socked him right in the nose and he never bothered her again . . .'

'Uh huh.'

'Well, that's what I'd do if somebody called me a name.'

'I wouldn't,' Mom said.

'How come?'

'Because it makes more sense to just laugh it off.'

'I never thought of that.'

'A person who can laugh at herself will be respected,' Mom said.

'Always?'

'Usually . . . what makes you ask, anyway?'

'Nothing special . . . just this girl in our class who lets everybody walk all over her . . . she really looks for it.'

'You should try putting yourself in her place.'

'I could never be in her place!'

'Don't be too sure,' Mom said, as she took off her reading glasses and slid them into their case.

'I think I will go to bed now,' I said, leaning over for my kiss.

eight

'Pass it on . . .'

On Wednesday morning we had our social studies test on the explorers. It was all matching and multiple-choice questions. Mrs Minish handed back the corrected test papers right after lunch. I got a C. I knew I'd forget which one was de Vaca and which one was de Soto and I did. I also goofed up Cortez and Mexico. But what got me really sore was that Wendy and Caroline both got As. And I saw Caroline copy all the answers off Wendy. Sometimes I wish Mrs Minish would wake up.

Miss Rothbelle sent for us at one-fifteen so we'd have time to rehearse before assembly. She made us stand in size places on the stage. I wound up between Rochelle, who is a new girl, and Linda, with Wendy right behind me. All during rehearsal Wendy kept giving me little pokes and pinches, trying to make me laugh. But I kept a straight face the whole time.

We practised singing each of our lullabies twice. Miss Rothbelle seemed satisfied and went down to talk to Mr Vandenberg. He always plays the piano for assemblies. I wish he taught music instead of Miss Rothbelle. He has this funny moustache that he's always twirling and he loves to tell jokes.

As soon as Miss Rothbelle was gone Wendy leaned close and whispered, 'Nobody sings *breast* but Blubber. Pass it on . . .'

I whispered that to Rochelle and she whispered it to Donna, who was on her other side.

Then Mr Vandenburg started playing a march and we watched as all the other classes filed into the auditorium. When everyone was settled Miss Rothbelle blew her pitchpipe at us and we hummed the opening note of 'Brahms's Lullaby'. We sang two more songs before we got to 'Sweet and Low'. The way Miss Rothbelle conducted us you'd have thought she was leading some famous symphony.

In the second verse of 'Sweet and Low', when we came to the

line that goes, 'Rest . . . rest . . . on mother's breast . . .' all of us mouthed the word 'breast' except Linda. She sang it loud and clear with a trill on the *br*, the way Miss Rothbelle does. It was like a one word solo. The rest of us came back in on the next word but by then most of the kids in the audience were laughing so hard no one could hear us sing. Linda turned absolutely purple.

I might have cracked up right on stage except for my loose tooth. Because all of a sudden it wasn't there any more. It didn't fall out of my mouth but I would feel it rolling around on my tongue. I didn't know what to do. I was afraid if I let it stay in my mouth I would swallow it, so I spit it into my hand and stuck my tongue in the space where my tooth used to be. I tasted blood.

After the assembly Miss Rothbelle made an announcement to our class. 'Everybody except Linda will stay after school tomorrow . . . and if this ever happens again you will all fail in music!'

I knew she'd say something like that.

I showed Tracy my tooth on the way home from school. 'It's neat,' she said. 'How much do you think it's worth?'

'I'm not sure,' I told her. 'Last time I got a quarter.'

'If I were you I'd try for more. We haven't got that many baby teeth left.'

'I'll try,' I said.

I didn't know which to tell my parents first – that I have to stay after school tomorrow or that I lost my tooth. I decided on the tooth. I handed it to my father.

'Very nice,' he said, inspecting it. He passed it to Mom.

'Don't forget to put it under your pillow,' she said.

'I won't.'

Mom handed the tooth back to me. 'I went shopping at lunchtime,' she said. 'I found the bar mitzvah dress. It's in a box on my bed.'

'I hope I like it,' I said.

'I hope it fits.'

The dress turned out to be a short knitted thing, with tiny sleeves, a round neck, and three stripes on the skirt. 'It itches,' I told my mother after she'd made me try it on.

'It can't,' Mom said. 'It's acrylic, not wool.'

I wiggled around. 'It itches all over.'

'There's probably a scratchy tag inside. I'll take it out later.'

When Mom and Dad came into my room to kiss me goodnight Mom said, 'Did you put the tooth under your pillow?'

I patted my pillow and said, 'Of course.'

'I hope the Tooth Fairy comes,' Dad said.

'Me too. Do you think she could leave me a cheque this time, instead of cash?'

'A cheque?' Mom asked.

'Yes.' I twisted the edge of my blanket. 'Made out to the Winthrop Stamp Company for two dollars eighty-seven cents.'

'That's a lot of money for one little tooth,' Dad said.

'I know it,' I told him. 'But I haven't got many baby teeth left and I'm sure the Tooth Fairy will understand if you explain it to her.'

Mom and Dad looked at each other. 'We'll try to get the message through,' Mom said. 'Now go to sleep.'

The next morning I felt under my pillow. The tooth was gone and in its place was the cheque I'd asked for. I found Dad in the kitchen, squeezing oranges, and I thanked him.

Then I went looking for Mom. I heard the water running in her bathroom. I figured she was washing up so I tried the door. It was unlocked. 'Mom, thanks for the . . .' I stopped right in the middle. Mom wasn't at the sink. She was crouched in the corner of the bathroom, smoking a cigarette! 'Mom . . . what are you doing?'

My mother tossed the butt into the toilet. Then she stood up and fanned the air, trying to get rid of the smoke. 'I couldn't help it,' she said. 'I really needed one this morning.'

'You promised . . .' I began.

144

'I promised to try and I *am* trying!'

'But . . .'

My mother held up her hand. 'Please get ready for school. I have a very busy day coming up and I don't have the time to drive you if you miss your bus.'

'Oh, that reminds me,' I said. 'I have to stay after school today.'

'Well, this is a fine time to tell me,' Mom said, as she pulled on her pantyhose.

'I forgot to tell you last night because I was so busy trying on the dress and thinking about my tooth and all . . .'

'Damn!' Mom said. 'I just got a run. Now I'll have to wear pants.'

'And anyway, the whole class has to stay after.'

'Why?'

'Oh . . . we were fooling around in music.'

Mom went to her closet. 'Damn again . . . they're at the cleaners.'

'I'll get a ride home with one of the mothers, so don't worry.'

'You're sure?' Mom asked, looking for another pair of pantyhose. 'Because I could call a taxi.'

'Oh no . . . Wendy said either her mother or Caroline's will drop me off.'

'Leave a note for Mrs Sandmeier.'

'I will.'

On the way to school I told Tracy about my cheque and that now I have enough to buy a whole bunch of approvals from Winthrop. When Tracy heard that she started wiggling both of her loose teeth.

nine

'So who won the game?'

Mrs Minish told us to hurry and settle down as we walked into our room because she had to collect the money for our class trip. We're going to the Planetarium next month. I've already been there four times.

I knew it would take Mrs Minish for ever to get our trip money straight so I pulled my chair over to Wendy's desk. She and Caroline had a couple of books spread out in front of them to make it look like they were hard at work on some assignment. But really, they were making up a list. They showed it to me.

HOW TO HAVE FUN WITH BLUBBER

1. Hold your nose when Blubber walks by.
2. Trip her.
3. Push her.
4. Shove her.
5. Pinch her.
6. Make her say, *I am Blubber, the smelly whale of class 206.*

Before I'd had a chance to read the whole thing the office called on the intercom, asking for a messenger from our class and Mrs Minish looked up and said, 'Jill, will you run down to the office please.'

Ms Valdez – that's what the clerk likes to be called – handed me a notice that had to be signed by all the fifth-grade teachers. By the time I got back to our room my class was saying the Pledge of Allegiance. I waited outside the door until they were through. Bruce picked his nose the whole time, which wasn't a very patriotic thing to do.

After that, it was time to line up for gym. I like Mr Witneski, our gym teacher. He treats the girls the same as the boys. This

time of year we usually play kickball. I have this great
daydream where it's the bottom of the last inning and my team
has two outs with the bases loaded. We are losing by three runs
and I'm up. When the ball comes rolling towards me I kick it so
hard and so fast that it goes way into the outfield, over
everyone's head. It's a home run and we win the game. My
whole team starts yelling and cheering and then they pick me
up and carry me around on their shoulders and after that I'm
always the first one picked for a team. So far this has never
happened but I keep hoping it will.

While we were walking down the hall Caroline whispered,
'You missed a good show. When Blubber went up to give
Minish her money, Wendy stuck out her foot and tripped her
and Blubber fell flat on her face . . . and Minish said, *From
now on try to be more careful, Linda.*'

'What'd Blubber say to that?'

'Nothing . . . what do you think?'

I called Tracy as soon as I got home from school.

'What did Miss Rothbelle make you do?' she asked.

'We had to write, *I was very rude yesterday. I will not
misbehave in music again.*'

'How many times?'

'One hundred.'

'Ugh!'

'You can say that again. Did you hear about gym?'

'No . . . what?'

'Well . . . Michael and Rochelle were captains.'

'Yeah . . .'

'And I was on Michael's team and Wendy and Blubber were
on Rochelle's. Blubber was the last one picked.'

'That figures.'

'So . . . on my first time up I kicked a blooper right at
Blubber . . . not on purpose or anything . . . it just
happened . . . you know?'

'Yeah . . .'

'And probably anyone else would have just caught it and I'd have been out. But Blubber missed the ball . . .'

'And?'

'Fell over backwards.'

Tracy laughed.

'So then Wendy started yelling at Blubber, *You dummy, you idiot, you smelly whale* . . . because Wendy really likes to win.'

'I know.'

'So then Blubber started bawling, *It's not my fault* and she grabbed her belly and groaned, *She hit me right in the stomach . . .ohhhh*?'

'Then what?' Tracy asked.

'So Mr Witneski dashed out to the field and said, *Are you hurt, Linda?* which made Blubber start crying harder. She sounded like a sick elephant. And the whole time she kept telling Mr Witneski that I did it on purpose . . . that I aimed right for her . . . as if I could just kick the ball wherever I wanted.'

'Fat chance,' Tracy said.

'Which is what I told Mr Witneski.'

'Did he believe you?'

'I'm not sure because then he turned to me, of all people, and I was already safe at second base . . . and he said, *Jill, take Linda down to see the nurse, please*.'

'Oh no!'

'Oh yes! But I told him, *Mr Witneski, I'm on base*.'

'So he didn't make you go?'

'Wrong! He said, *Someone can run for you* and next thing I know Caroline was sent in to take my place. And I was stuck walking the smelly whale to the nurse's office.'

'Go on . . . go on . . .'

'Well . . . first thing she says is, *Why do you always pick on me?* So I tell her, *I don't pick on you* and she goes, *You do too. You and all your friends. And I never did anything to you.* So I tell her, *You're full of it* and she goes, *Some day you'll be sorry. I'll*

148

get you for this. So I tell her, *I'm really scared* and she goes, *You should be.* So I say, *Yeah . . . I'm shaking all over* and then she goes, *I hate you!*

'She really said that?' Tracy asked.

'Yup. So then we get to the nurse's office and she starts bawling all over again and the nurse asks her where it hurts and Blubber tells her, *In my stomach* and the nurse makes her lie down on the cot and pops the thermometer in her mouth even though I say, *She got hit with a ball. She doesn't have a temperature.* But the nurse doesn't care what I say because she likes to stick thermometers in people's mouths which I happen to know because of that time I sprained my finger and the first thing she did was take my temperature. So while the thermometer is in Blubber's mouth and she can't talk I ask the nurse, *Can I go now?* and she tells me, *Yes, dear . . . and thank you for bringing her.*'

'So who won the game?' Tracy asked.

'Them . . . two to ten.'

That night I struggled over my maths homework for an hour. I should be great at maths since my father is a tax lawyer and my mother works with computers. I don't understand why I have such a hard time with word problems. Dad explained three of them to me but he doesn't set the problems up the way we're supposed to, so even though I got the right answers I knew Mrs Minish would still mark some of them wrong. But I'd done my best and Mom and Dad always say that's what counts.

The next morning, when Linda got on the bus, she stood next to my seat and said, 'You should see my stomach . . . it's all black and blue.'

'I'll bet.'

'It is. My mother had to take me to the doctor.'

'So?'

'He said you knocked the wind out of me.'

'I knew I smelled something bad yesterday!' I turned to Tracy and the two of us absolutely cracked up. I guess nobody ever told Linda about laughing it off.

Right after group science Mrs Minish told the girls to line up alphabetically. 'We're going to the nurse's office to get weighed.'

Everybody groaned. We get weighed every fall and again every spring. If I had known that today was the day I'd have eaten a huge breakfast and worn my fisherman's sweater. It's the heaviest thing I own.

I was first on line, with Donna Davidson right behind me and Linda behind her. Wendy and Caroline were near the end of the line since their last names start with *R* and *T*.

When we got to the office the nurse said, 'Take off your shoes, please.' Then she called, 'Jill Brenner.'

'Right here,' I said. I didn't take off my sneakers. I was hoping that the nurse wouldn't notice. Then I'd weigh two pounds more and she wouldn't be able to give me a lecture about being underweight and how I should drink malted milk shakes every day.

'Please take off your shoes, Jill.'

'I can't.'

She gave me a funny look. 'Why not?'

'I promised my mother I wouldn't. My feet get cold when I go barefoot.'

'It will only be for a minute.'

'I'll get sick if I do.'

'Jill . . . stop being silly and take off your shoes.'

'Oh . . .' I kicked off my sneakers and stepped on the scales. I hoped it was at least five pounds overweight.

'Hmmmm . . .' the nurse said, wiggling the marker all around. 'Sixty-seven and a half.'

I smiled at her to show I was pleased.

She checked the chart. 'That's not much of a gain . . . only half a pound since last spring.'

'Well,' I told her, 'I guess I'm just lucky because I'm always eating.'

'You should try to build yourself up. I'd like to see you weigh about seventy-two. Why don't you start drinking a malted every day?'

'Okay . . .' I said, stepping off the scale. I have never had a malted in my life but what the nurse doesn't know won't hurt her.

The nurse was pleased with Donna Davidson. She has one of those perfect bodies where everything fits the way it should.

Linda was next. I took a long time getting my shoes back on so I heard everything.

'Are you feeling better, Linda?' the nurse asked.

'Yes.'

'Good . . . now, let's see . . . oh my, ninety-one pounds . . . that's too much for your height.'

'I have big bones,' Linda said.

'Even so, according to my chart you should lose some weight.'

'But I'm on a diet.'

'Well, that's a step in the right direction. Remember, no sweets.'

'I know it.'

After lunch we went outside to jump rope and Donna taught everyone this jumping rhyme she used to sing to the fattest counsellor at her summer horse camp.

> Oh, what a riot
> Blubber's on a diet
> I wonder what's the matter
> I think she's getting fatter
> And fatter
> And fatter
> And fatter
> Pop!

Bruce seemed to enjoy jumping to Donna's rhyme best of all. It suits him even more than Linda because he weighs over a hundred pounds and when he jumps his whole body shakes like

Jell-O. He's the one who should be on a diet.

Linda didn't wait her turn on line. She ran back inside and didn't come out at all during recess.

ten

'Not crazy . . . just different.'

'I think you should know that Mr Machinist is showing everybody in Hidden Valley those pictures he took of you on Hallowe'en night.' Wendy told this to me and Tracy on the way home from school. She and Caroline were sitting opposite us on the bus.

Me and Tracy looked at each other. We'd forgotten all about that.

'But don't worry,' Wendy said. 'He only got the back of you and with the pillowcases over your heads nobody will ever be able to identify you.'

'You saw the pictures?' I asked.

'Last night . . . he brought them over himself.'

Caroline said, 'When he came to my house I told him I didn't know who you were even though Tracy's feathers were hanging out.'

'You could see my feathers?' Tracy asked.

'It's all right!' Wendy said, and she gave Caroline a look that made her shut her mouth and turn to the window. 'Nobody's going to say anything. Believe me!'

It's important to be Wendy's friend, I thought. I only hope that what she says is true.

When we got off the bus me and Tracy stopped at our mailboxes, the way we do every day. I got a letter from the Superior Stamp Company. Probably the approvals I sent for last month, I thought.

152

'You don't think Mr Machinist will find out who we are, do you?' Tracy asked.

'Definitely not,' I told her. 'You heard Wendy.'

'I guess you're right. But from now on every time my doorbell rings I'm going to faint.'

'Me too.'

'Listen . . . I'll call you later. I've got to go to the dentist this afternoon.'

'Maybe he can pull out your loose teeth and then you can ask for a cheque.'

'Maybe.'

'Good luck.'

'Thanks,' Tracy said. 'I'll need it.'

As soon as I walked into the house Kenny said, 'Guess what . . . Mrs Sandmeier's going to Switzerland on Saturday.'

I dropped the mail on the hall table and ran into the kitchen. 'It's not true,' I said. 'You wouldn't leave us.'

Mrs Sandmeier put her arm around me. 'Now, now . . . it's only for three weeks.'

'Three weeks! We can't live without you for three weeks.'

'Of course you can.'

'But who'll take care of us?' I asked.

'Oh . . . your mother and father will think of something.'

'I don't see why you can't wait until summer . . . when we're away at camp.'

'Because my mother's going to be eighty-five,' Mrs Sandmeier said, 'and I want to be there for her birthday.'

'Your mother? I never knew you had a mother.'

'Everybody has a mother,' Kenny said.

I shot him a look. 'You know what I mean,' I told Mrs Sandmeier. I never thought of her as somebody's daughter.

'Mama's a wonderful woman. She lives with my sister in Zurich, and I just decided I don't want to miss this birthday.'

'I'll bet they get Grandma to come,' Kenny said, shovelling in a handful of potato chips.

'Oh no!' I said. 'Not Grandma for three weeks!'

'Or they could call the Carol Agency,' Kenny told me.

'What's that?'

'It's the biggest babysitting organization in the world. It's in Los Angeles. They have eight hundred registered babysitters working for them.'

'Why would Mom call a California agency when we live in Pennysylvania?'

'I don't know.'

'Kenny Brenner . . . your facts are driving me up the wall!' I went to my room. If Grandma comes I'm moving to Tracy's for three weeks. Grandma makes me so nervous I get diarrhoea just from being around her. One time, when my mother couldn't find anyone else to watch us, Grandma moved in for a week. And she wouldn't let me or Kenny do any of the things we always do, like ride bicycles or rollerskate, because she thought we'd get hurt. Another thing that got me really sore was the way Grandma made me wear a hat and mittens when it was positively roasting out.

I sat down at my desk and opened the letter from the stamp company. It said:

Dear Friend,

What's wrong? We have noticed that your last few purchases from our approvals have averaged less than thirty-five cents a selection. We certainly do not want to waste your time by submitting selections of stamps that have such little interest to you.

So let's hear from you. Tell us what type of selections would interest you. Please use the reverse side of this note for your suggestions.

Sincerely,
The Superior Stamp Co.

I turned the letter over and wrote my reply,

Dear Superior Stamp Company.

If you got fifty cents allowance a week you'd have trouble ordering a lot of stamps too. Besides, you are not the only stamp company I deal with. You are not even my favourite. Half the stamps you send don't go in my Master Global Album. So you are lucky to get any business from me.

Unsincerely,
Jill Brenner

The second my mother and father got home I asked, 'Is Grandma coming when Mrs Sandmeier goes to Switzerland?'

Mom wriggled out of her coat.

'And how come you didn't tell us Mrs Sandmeier's taking a vacation?' I followed Mom into her bedroom.

'Because she wanted to tell you herself,' my mother said. 'Nothing was definite until yesterday. Please, Jill . . . I'd like to take my shower and then we'll talk about it . . . okay?'

I nodded and waited on Mom's bed. When the water stopped running I stood outside the bathroom and asked, 'Is Grandma coming . . . yes or no?'

My mother opened the bathroom door. She had a towel wrapped around her middle and was brushing her hair. 'No . . . I don't think she's up to spending three weeks with us.'

I looked away and smiled. I couldn't help it. 'Then who is?' I asked.

'Who is what?'

'Who's going to take care of us?'

'Great Maudie.'

'Great Maudie!' I couldn't believe it. Great Maudie is Grandma's sister but they are complete opposites. They haven't talked to each other in ten years, ever since Great Maudie moved in with her friend, Alfred. 'She's really coming?'

'Uh huh. I spoke to her this morning.'

'Is Alfred coming too?' He is a very good magician. He has this one trick where he cuts a grapefruit open and there's a dollar bill inside it.

155

'Alfred can't get away from work so Great Maudie will come without him.'

'What will Grandma think?'

'Well . . .' Mom said, 'I don't see why she has to find out. She's in Pittsburg and Great Maudie is in New York. Hand me my robe, please . . .'

I went to Mom's closet and pulled down her favourite robe. It's pink and there's a hole in one sleeve. I gave it to her, then went into the living room.

Kenny and my father were playing chess. 'Did you hear who's coming?' I asked. 'Great Maudie.'

Kenny nodded and moved his bishop.

I stood over my father's chair. 'I thought she's supposed to be crazy,' I said, while I scratched his back. My father just loves to have his back scratched.

'Not crazy . . .' he said, 'just different . . . mmm . . . that feels good.'

'Because my nails are growing!' I showed him. 'See . . . they're almost past the tips of my fingers.'

Tracy called later. 'No news is good news,' she said. 'Mr Machinist didn't show up.'

'And if he hasn't found out who we are by now we're safe,' I told her.

'I think you might be right,' Tracy said.

And then both of us added, 'I hope,' at the same time.

eleven

'I just can't believe my class would do such a thing.'

School isn't as boring as it used to be. Wendy and Caroline made copies of the *How to Have Fun With Blubber* list and on Monday morning they passed them out.

156

We made Linda say, *I am Blubber, the smelly whale of class 206*. We made her say it before she could use the toilet in the Girls' Room, before she could get a drink at the fountain, before she ate her lunch and before she got on the bus to go home. It was easy to get her to do it. I think she would have done anything we said. There are some people who just make you want to see how far you can go.

Two days later she was saying *I am Blubber, the smelly whale of class 206* without anyone forcing her to. She said it *before* she got a drink at the fountain, *before* she went to the toilet, *before* she got on and off the bus, and during lunch, she said it *before* she started eating.

'Very good,' Wendy told her. 'For that you get a reward. You get to kiss Bruce Bonaventura.'

Bruce wasn't all that willing to get kissed, which is why Robby and Irwin had to chase him around the room and then hold him down while Wendy and Caroline dragged Linda over to him.

Bruce said, 'If she touches my lips I'll spit at her . . . so help me, I will!'

So we had to settle for Linda kissing Bruce on the cheek. If you ask me she enjoyed it.

On Thursday we made Linda show the boys her underpants. She wasn't anxious to do that so Caroline had to hold her hands behind her back while Wendy lifted her skirt.

Irwin found some names for Linda in the Random House Dictionary, which Mrs Minish keeps in the corner on its own table. He's really good at looking things up. He can tell you exactly on what page certain words are found. We called Linda 'flubsy', 'carnivore' and 'bestial'. I didn't recognize any of them, but they all sounded good.

On Friday, Wendy brought a small piece of chocolate to school, wrapped in gold foil. It came from a box of Barricini's somebody had brought her mother. Wendy showed it to Linda after lunch. 'My father had to go all the way to New York for this chocolate-covered ant.'

All of us gathered around Linda's desk. Wendy unwrapped the chocolate. She held it close to Linda's face. 'You're going to eat this ant, Blubber.'

'No I'm not . . . and you can't make me,' Linda said.

'Want to bet?' Wendy asked.

'I could get sick and die and then you'd be in big trouble.'

'I'm willing to take that chance,' Wendy told her.

Linda mashed her lips together and moved her head from side to side, all the time making noises that sounded like she was smothering to death.

Wendy handed me the candy. Then she said, 'Grab her hands, Caroline.'

It's good that Caroline's so strong because Linda was really wriggling around. Once Caroline had Linda's hands behind her back Wendy pinched Linda's nose which made her open her mouth. As soon as she did I shoved in the chocolate.

'Now chew and swallow!' Wendy told her, putting one hand over Linda's mouth so she couldn't spit anything out.

Linda kept her eyes shut and we could see her chewing, then swallowing the candy. Wendy let go of her then and sang, 'Blubber ate an ant . . . Blubber ate an ant . . .'

We all joined in, making a circle around Linda. Even Rochelle, who usually doesn't pay any attention to the rest of us, was enjoying the show.

But after a minute Linda turned this awful greenish colour, gave a big burp, then puked all over her desk and the floor. Wendy ran down the hall for Mrs Horvath.

When Mrs Horvath saw the mess she told the boys to get the custodian.

By then Linda was crying. 'They made me eat an ant.'

'Try to stay calm,' Mrs Horvath told her. 'I'll take you down to the nurse's office.'

If you throw up in school you automatically get sent home for the rest of the day. So Linda didn't come back to class that afternoon. Instead Mr Nichols came to see us.

'We seem to have a little problem, Mrs Minish,' he said,

pretending he was talking just to her but looking at all of us. 'Linda Fischer said your class made her eat a chocolate-covered ant. In fact, she claims they forced it down her throat, causing her to vomit.'

'Well . . . this comes as a surprise to me, Mr Nichols,' Mrs Minish said. 'I just can't believe my class would do such a thing.'

'Neither can I,' Mr Nichols said. 'Nevertheless . . .'

I wondered if something like this could go down on your permanent record card and keep you out of college.

'I'm sure there's a reasonable explanation, Mr Nichols,' Mrs Minish said. 'Can anyone tell us what happened?'

Wendy raised her hand.

'Yes, Wendy?'

'I think I can explain,' Wendy said. 'You see Linda's been on this diet and all she eats is cheese and celery . . . so naturally I knew better than to offer her a piece of my candy.' Wendy looked at Mrs Minish.

'Go on,' Mrs Minish said.

'Well . . . Linda just went crazy. I mean, she wanted my candy in the worst way . . . so I told her it was a chocolate-covered ant . . . I thought she wouldn't want to eat it when she heard that.' Wendy paused and looked around.

'Yes . . .' Mr Nichols said.

'But Linda didn't believe me . . . so I told her how my father goes all the way to New York to get these special chocolate-covered ants that my family loves and that they're very fattening. But she still didn't believe me so finally I gave her a piece of my candy and after she ate it I asked her how the ant tasted and that's when she got sick all over the place.'

'So it wasn't an ant?' Mr Nichols asked.

'No, it was a regular chocolate candy from Barricini's.'

'I see.'

'Linda has a lot of imagination,' Wendy said.

Only Wendy could sit there telling lies to Mr Nichols as if he were a regular person instead of the principal of our school.

'I knew there had to be an explanation,' Mrs Minish said.

'Yes . . . well . . .' Mr Nichols began. 'Thank you for your cooperation in this matter.'

'Any time,' Mrs Minnish told him, as he walked out of the room.

It was drizzling when me and Tracy stopped for our mail that afternoon. There was nothing for either one of us so we ran home.

'We've got to take the dogs to the vet today,' Tracy said. 'I'll see you tomorrow.'

'Not tomorrow,' I told her. 'We're going to a bar mitzvah.'

'Oh . . . I forgot about that.'

'See you Sunday.'

'Right.'

When my parents got home my father said he'd had a really rough day and would I mind scratching his back for a little while. I told him I'd love to and that my nails would soon be long enough to file. When Mom had finished showering she came into the living room carrying two Bloody Marys. She handed one to my father, then flopped on to the sofa. 'Jill, would you bring me the mail?'

'Sure.' I went to the hall table and got it.

Mom sifted through all the letters and sighed. 'Bills and more bills.' Then she picked up a yellow envelope. 'I wonder what this is,' she asked, ripping off the tape. When she saw what was inside she said, 'Oh God . . .' Then she cursed a couple of times. My mother's not shy about cursing. She doesn't even care if me and Kenny use those words around the house as long as we understand there are some people who don't approve of them. I think that's the reason most of the kids I know love to curse. It's because their parents make a big deal out of those words. With me it's different. I don't have to yell and scream them on the school bus every day since I can say them any old time I feel like it.

'Gordon . . . look at this . . .' Mom passed him a letter. I

160

read it over Dad's shoulder, while I was scratching. It said:

> *On Hallowe'en night two youngsters put raw, rotten eggs in my mailbox. Interfering with mail and its delivery is a federal offence. One of these youngsters has been identified as your child. I suggest that you contact me immediately.*
> *William F. Machinist*

I stopped scratching my father. Mom held up a picture. It showed two kids from the back. They were running. One of them had feathers hanging out of her jacket. The other one had a hand on her head to keep her hat from flying off. It was definitely me and Tracy.

twelve

'You really got yourself in big trouble.'

'We only did it because he's so mean . . . he hates kids . . . he won't even give to UNICEF . . .' I told everyone. It was after dinner and Tracy, her mother and father were sitting with me, Mom and Dad in our living room. Mr Machinist also sent the picture and note to their house.

Tracy was crying.

'You know you did wrong, don't you, girls?' my father asked.

Tracy nodded.

I said, 'In one way I know we did wrong, but in another way, he really deserved it.'

'We've always tried to teach Tracy right from wrong,' Mrs Wu said. 'We've always trusted her.'

That made Tracy cry even harder. 'I don't want to go to jail.'

I brought her a box of tissues. 'You won't let us go to jail, will you, Dad?' I asked.

'Nobody's going to jail,' he said. 'But you will have to face the consequences.'

Mom and Dr and Mrs Wu nodded in agreement.

'We'd better call Mr Machinist,' Dr Wu said, 'and see what he has in mind.'

My father went to the phone. I couldn't figure out anything from his end of the conversation. Mr Machinist must have been doing most of the talking.

'What did he say?' my mother asked when Dad hung up.

'He said he'll talk to the police unless the girls admit what they did and show him that they're sorry.'

'Show him that we're sorry . . . how?' I asked.

'He's already cleaned out his mailbox,' my father said, ' . . . it's too late for that. But he's got a yard full of leaves that have to be raked up and bagged.'

With all the trees in Hidden Valley Mr Machinist must have millions of leaves. I thought – maybe even billions.

'When?' my mother asked.

'He wanted them to come tomorrow but I explained that we're busy so we settled on Sunday,' Dad said.

'Sunday!' I shouted. 'That's my only free day this week. Do you think that's fair?'

'I think so,' Mom said. 'After all, he could have called the police first.'

'I think it's fair too,' Mrs Wu said.

'And . . .' my father added, 'maybe this way you'll both learn that it's not up to you to decide who deserves what in this world.'

After Tracy and her parents were gone, I went upstairs to get ready for bed. Kenny was in the bathroom, brushing his teeth. When he finished spitting he said, 'I heard the whole thing. You really got yourself in big trouble.'

'Mind your own business,' I told him. 'And wipe that blob of toothpaste off the counter.'

Kenny ran his towel along the counter-top. 'I hope you like raking up leaves. If you'd stayed home like me you wouldn't be in this mess.'

162

'Oh . . . shut up, you dumb ass, before I bash your face in!'
I heard him laughing all the way to his room.

When I got into bed I thought about who had identified us.
It must have been Blubber! She threatened to get me and she
did.

thirteen

'You can't go around scratching all day.'

We were late starting out for the bar mitzvah because of
Kenny. He didn't want to wear a tie and jacket. 'If I can't go in
play clothes then I'll just stay home!' he said.

My father doesn't yell often, but when he does you can hear
him as far as Tracy's house, maybe even further. Afterwards he
is hoarse for days and has to drink tea with honey. Kenny got
the message and put on his new tie and jacket, complaining the
whole time that he couldn't swallow and might even choke to
death.

I was ready long before anyone else and while they were
rushing around I was in the kitchen, making myself a
peanut-butter sandwich, just in case I didn't like the bar
mitzvah lunch. I wrapped it in silver foil and put it in my
shoulder bag.

By the time we got to the temple in New Jersey it was after
eleven. There was no place to park so Dad dropped us off in
front while he drove around the block.

The temple sat on top of a hill and as we climbed the steps
leading to it Mom said, 'Listen, Jill . . . you can't go around
scratching all day. It doesn't look nice.'

'I can't help it,' I said. 'You're the one who picked out this
itchy dress.'

'It's too late to do anything about that now. Try and keep

your mind on something else.'

'I'll try,' I said, but as soon as Mom looked away I gave myself a quick scratch.

'We just climbed up thirty-seven steps,' Kenny announced, when we reached the top.

Only Kenny would think of counting!

'Whew . . .' Mom said. 'No wonder I'm winded.' She pushed the door open and we walked inside.

I looked all around. 'Wow . . . this is some big place.'

'It certainly is,' Mom said. 'It's enormous.'

'Yeah . . . but it's not the biggest synagogue in the world,' Kenny told us. 'The biggest synagogue in the world is in New York. It's on Fifth Avenue and it's called Temple Emanu-El. It holds six thousand people.'

'Tell the little computer to keep his facts to himself today . . . please, Mom.'

'Kenny's facts are very interesting,' Mom said.

'Yeah . . .'

'Not to me,' I told him.

'Stop arguing . . . we've got to find the sanctuary,' Mom said. 'We're late enough now.'

We walked all around before we came to a man standing in a doorway. He had rosy cheeks and a flower in his buttonhole. He smiled at Mom and handed her a prayer book. Then he put his finger to his lips as if me and Kenny didn't know enough to be quiet. We followed Mom into the sanctuary.

Warren was on the stage. He looked as creepy as ever, except for his hair. That looked worse. Usually it hangs into his eyes but today it was parted and looked like it had been sprayed.

As soon as he noticed us tiptoeing into the sanctuary he stopped reciting, right in the middle of a prayer. Everyone turned around to see who Warren was watching. My mother tried to smile but as she took a seat in the last row she dropped her purse. It had a chain handle so when it hit the floor it made a clinking noise. Mom bent down and picked it up. She had this funny look on her face. I recognized it right away. It meant

164

I don't think I can live through this without a cigarette. I'm very good at knowing what my mother is thinking.

Warren went back to his prayer but he must have lost his place because he stumbled along until the rabbi pointed and said a few words. I was really surprised that Warren could read Hebrew at all. The last time he was over I showed him my book, *Poems for the John*, and he had trouble with every word over two syllables, and that was in English.

When my father walked into the sanctuary a few minutes later, Warren stopped again. This time when everyone turned around there was a lot of whispering. Dad sat down next to me and I could tell he was embarrassed because the back of his neck turned red. That's when Kenny started to sneeze. He never sneezes once like a normal person – it's always twenty or thirty times in a row.

I knew that I shouldn't laugh. I also knew that if I looked at Kenny I would. So I stared straight ahead, right at the back of some girl's head. It reminded me of Linda Fischer's. It was the same potato shape and the hair was the same too – reddish-brown and curled up at the edges.

At least that gave me something to think about so I didn't have to listen to Warren's stupid speech which was something about being grateful to everyone he knew.

After the service we went to a party at Mr Winkler's country club. As soon as we walked into the lobby this woman asked us our names.

'Brenner,' Dad told her.

'Oh yes,' she said, fishing some little white cards out of a pile. She handed them to my father. He passed one to me and one to Kenny.

'What's this?' Kenny asked.

'It tells you what table to sit at for lunch,' Mom said.

'You mean me and Kenny can't sit with you?' I asked.

'We're at Table Nineteen,' Dad told me.

'I'm at Table One,' Kenny said.

I looked at my card. 'I'm at Table One, too.'

'All the young people are probably sitting together,' Mom said.

'But I'd rather sit with you,' I said. 'Suppose I don't like what they have to eat?'

'Just say *no, thank you*,' Dad told me. 'Nobody's going to force you to eat anything.'

'You should have brought your peanut butter!' Kenny laughed. 'Then you wouldn't have to worry.'

'Shut up, you little brat!'

'It won't hurt you to try something new,' my father said.

'Look, Jill . . .' Mom told me, 'you don't have to eat a thing. If you're hungry, that's your problem. Now, I'm going to the Ladies' Room . . . do you want to come?'

'All right.' I didn't want to stand around talking about food any more. I was glad I'd brought a secret sandwich with me.

On the way to the Ladies' Room we passed a big room filled with round tables. In the centre of each one was a bunch of blue and white flowers.

'Look at that!' I said. 'Blue daisies . . . I didn't know there was such a thing.'

'They're dyed,' Mom said.

'They are?'

'To match the tablecloths.'

'This is some party,' I said. 'I'll bet Warren will get a ton of presents.'

'I suppose so . . .'

'Hundreds, I'll bet.'

'Probably.'

'He's lucky. I wish I could get bar mitzvahed.'

'That doesn't necessarily mean big parties and lots of presents, Jill.'

'It doesn't?'

'No . . . it's the ceremony that counts, the tradition of reading from the Torah.'

'Oh.'

We went into the Ladies' Room and took booths next to each

166

other. I watched my mother's feet. It looked like she was dancing.

When we came out there was a woman standing in front of the mirror, putting on lipstick. And next to her was the girl with the potato-shaped head. Only this time I didn't see *just* the back of her head – I saw her whole face in the mirror, including her grey tooth, which is why I suddenly sucked in my breath.

'What's the matter?' Mum asked.

I shook my head a little and whispered, 'Nothing.' I should have known there couldn't be two heads exactly alike. I should have known it was Blubber.

'I have to fix my hair,' Mom said. She stood next to the other woman, who must have been Mrs Fischer.

Linda turned around and faced me then. We stared at each other. I could tell that she was just as surprised to see me as I was to see her. Neither one of us spoke.

Mrs Fischer finished with her lips and started in on her eyes. Mom isn't fussy about anything but her hair. She held a pocket mirror up so she could see the back of it. When she was satisfied she put her comb away and took out a little jar of lip gloss. She rubbed some into her lips. It made them shine. Then she turned to Mrs Fischer and said, 'You look so familiar . . . have we met?'

I wanted to grab my mother's hand and pull her out of the Ladies' Room before it was too late. Of all people, why did she have to start up with Mrs Fischer?

'I was just thinking the same thing,' Mrs Fischer said.

'Where are you from?' Mom asked.

'We live outside of Philadelphia.'

'So do we!' Mom said. 'In Radnor.'

'Well . . . that's how we must know each other. I live there too . . . in Hidden Valley.'

'This is a coincidence!' Mom said. 'We live right near there . . . off Crestview Drive.'

'Isn't this something?' Mrs Fischer said. 'To meet here . . . of all places.'

'Are you related to the Winklers?' Mom asked Mrs Fischer.

'No, Peg was my college roommate.'

'And my husband grew up with Harold.'

'This is just so funny!'

I didn't think it was funny at all.

'I'm Ann Brenner,' Mom said, offering her hand to Mrs Fischer. 'And this is my daughter Jill.'

Mrs Fischer shook Mom's hand and smiled at me. Any second now they're going to introduce me to Blubber, I thought.

'I'm Janice Fischer and this is my daughter Linda.'

Here it comes!

'You two must know each other,' Mom said.

'We do,' I mumbled.

'Oh . . . are you the Jill Brenner in Linda's class?' Mrs Fischer asked.

That did it! 'Yes,' I said, 'but . . .'

'Mom!' Linda tugged at her mother's arm. 'Come on . . .'

When they were gone my mother asked, 'What was that all about?'

And I told her, 'We're not exactly friends.'

fourteen

'I'd rather be a skeleton than a whale.'

We wound up at Table One, sitting next to each other, of course, and right across the table from Kenny. Everyone else sitting there looked about thirteen. They were all friends of Warren's. None of them spoke to us.

I told Linda, 'Just because I'm sitting next to you doesn't mean anything is different. I know what you did.' I wanted to let her know I'd figured out she was the one who told Mr

Machinist on me and Tracy. 'And just wait till Wendy finds out!'

'Finds out what?'

'You know.'

'No, I don't!'

'You're not even a good liar!' I told her.

'Neither are you.'

'I'm not lying!'

'Well, neither am I.'

The waitress served our first course then. It was chunks of fruit in a pineapple boat. It looked pretty but I don't eat stuff like pineapple in public because the threads get caught in my teeth and make me very uncomfortable. It's the same with celery. I did find two pieces of melon though, before I passed the rest to Kenny.

Next came the soup, which would have been all right except for the vegetables. I don't like vegetables. When Mrs Sandmeier makes us soup she strains mine so I won't know what I'm eating. Kenny finished my soup too.

While we were waiting for our main course Kenny asked Linda if she believed in ESP. She told him, 'Yes . . . and reincarnation too.'

'So do I,' Kenny said.

Then they had this long conversation about what they were in their other lives and I muttered, *A smelly whale* and Linda said, 'If you call me that today I'll tell on you. I really will.'

I felt like asking her if Mr Machinist found out about me and Tracy by ESP or did she meet him face to face and identify us that way?

But Kenny was reciting one of his dumb jokes and right in the middle Linda laughed! I couldn't believe it. I didn't know she knew how.

Our main course was rare roast beef, a tomato stuffed with green peas and funny potatoes in some kind of milky sauce. I hate tomatoes, peas make me choke, and I can't even look at meat with blood dripping out of it. Potatoes in sauce are out of the question. I thought about my peanut-butter sandwich and how I might be able to eat it without anyone noticing.

'Don't you eat anything?' Linda asked, after a while.

'Yeah . . .' Kenny told her. 'She eats peanut butter.'

'Butt out!' I said.

'No wonder you look like a skeleton,' Linda said.

'I wouldn't talk if I were you . . . I'd rather be a skeleton than a whale.'

'Not me,' Kenny said. 'Whales are loveable animals . . . skeletons are just dead bony things.'

'Who asked you!'

'You want to share her dinner?' Kenny said to Linda, like I wasn't even there. That fink!

'No, thank you,' Linda said. 'I've got enough.'

'Just a minute,' I said. 'Who told you I was giving you my dinner?'

'Well, it's just sitting there getting cold,' Linda said.

'Yeah, Jill . . .' Kenny told me. 'Pass your plate.'

'You shouldn't waste good food,' Linda said. 'Don't you know there are people starving to death in this world?'

'But you're not one of them and neither is my pig of a brother!'

They looked at each other, then at me. 'Oh, here . . .' I said, shoving my plate at Kenny. 'What do I care if you wind up with a bellyache.' I stood up and went to the Ladies' Room. I was the only one in there besides the attendant. I locked myself into a booth, sat down on the toilet, unwrapped my peanut-butter sandwich and ate it. It made me very thirsty but there was no way I could ask for a cold glass of milk.

Just as I got back to my seat at the table, Kenny yelled, 'Hey, Warren . . . this is a great party.'

One of Warren's friends looked over at Kenny and said, 'You're right, kid . . . I'll bet it's the biggest and best party you've ever been to . . . right?'

'Well,' Kenny said, 'it's big, but it's not the biggest party there ever was.'

'I say it is!'

170

'You're wrong . . . I know all about the biggest party,' Kenny said.

Everyone stopped talking and looked over at Kenny.

'Yeah?' Warren's friend said.

'Yeah,' Kenny told him.

'I suppose it was at your house.' Everybody laughed when Warren's friend said that.

'No,' Kenny told them. 'It was given by Mr and Mrs Bradley Martin of Troy, New York, at the Waldorf Astoria Hotel in New York City.'

'And I suppose you were there . . . right?'

'Hardly,' Kenny said. 'It was in 1897.'

Now everybody laughed at Warren's friend.

After all the tables had been cleared the lights dimmed and two men rolled in the biggest birthday cake I'd ever seen. It was shaped like a book. The icing was blue and white. I hoped the inside was chocolate.

'Wow,' Kenny said, 'that looks delicious.'

'Mmmm . . .' Linda licked her lips.

'What about your diet?' I asked. 'No sweets . . . remember?'

'My mother said I should eat everything today. It's a special occasion.'

'I'll bet that's why your front tooth is grey and rotten,' I said, ' . . . because you eat too much junk.'

'That is not why!'

'Then why is it?'

'Because I ran into a tree and hurt it . . . it's dead.'

'The tree?'

'No, my tooth!'

I started to laugh. 'Whoever heard of a dead tooth?'

'I did,' Kenny said. 'But don't worry,' he told Linda, 'you might grow a whole other set of teeth when you get old. Some people really do.'

'They do?' Linda asked.

'Yeah . . . and did you know some babies are born with teeth?'

'They are?' Linda said.

'Kenny!' I gave him a warning look.

He ignored me. 'For instance, Louis XIV of France was born with two teeth.'

'Nobody's interested, Kenny!' I said.

'I am,' Linda told us.

Kenny didn't have time to say anything else because one of the men who had rolled in the cake started blowing into a microphone. I thought maybe he was getting ready to sing 'The Star Spangled Banner', like at a ball game, and I wondered if I should stand up. But he didn't sing anything, not even 'Happy Birthday'. What he did was call up lots of people to light candles on Warren's cake. First Warren's mother and father, then his grandparents, then his aunts and uncles and cousins. The other man had a camera and every time someone lit a candle he snapped a picture.

Then the man with the microphone looked in my direction and said, 'Representing the friendship of two old family friends, the Brenners and the Fischers . . . two young ladies will light the thirteenth candle on Warren's cake . . . Jill and Linda.'

Both of us were surprised and for a second we didn't move. Finally I pushed my chair back and stood up. Linda followed me. When the man with the microphone held out a lighted candle I took it.

Just as I was about to light the candle on Warren's cake the photographer called, 'Hold it . . . let the other girl put her hand on the candle too.'

The candle really wasn't big enough for both of us to hold but Linda wrapped her hand around it anyway forcing my fingers closer to the flame. I was sure I'd wind up getting burned.

'Ready . . .' the photographer called, 'now smile . . .'

The flashbulb popped and I couldn't see anything but yellow spots. I let go of the candle to rub my eyes and when I did, Linda lit the one on the cake by herself.

172

On the way home Kenny announced, 'I think Linda Fischer's great. She's been reincarnated six times.'

Just to change the subject I told my mother, 'I've got a rash all over my behind from this dumb, itchy dress!'

fifteen

'Nobody else had a reason to get us.'

'Guess who I saw at Warren Winkler's bar mitzvah?' I asked Tracy the next morning, on our way to Mr Machinist's house.

'Who?'

'Blubber!'

'No kidding.'

'And I had to sit next to her all through lunch.'

'Lucky you.'

'I'm sure she's the one who told on us, even though she denied it.'

'You asked her?'

'Not exactly, but I hinted.'

'I don't know,' Tracy said. 'Plenty of kids in Hidden Valley could have recognized me by my costume.'

'But nobody else had a reason to get us,' I said.

'Yeah . . . but if it was Blubber how come she didn't tell on Wendy and Caroline too?'

'They weren't in the picture.'

'You could be right,' Tracy said.

When we got to Mr Machinist's house he was outside, waiting for us. We'd rehearsed exactly what we would say to him. Tracy whispered, 'One . . . two . . . three . . .' and then we both said, 'It was wrong of us to put eggs in your mailbox . . . we're sorry we did it.'

'You'd better be,' Mr Machinist said. He wasn't nearly as old as I'd expected. I wondered if he was married or if he lived in that big house all by himself? He showed us the rakes and the bags and then pointed to all the leaves before he went into his house. As if we couldn't find them ourselves.

When he was gone Tracy said, 'I think he wears a wig.'

'How can you tell?'

'Nobody has hair that thick . . . besides, he didn't have it on straight.'

'Wouldn't you love to pull it off?'

'Yes . . . but I'm not going to.'

'Me neither.'

'He has funny eyes, too.'

'I didn't notice.'

'Well, I did. They turn down at the corners and they're mean. You can tell a lot about people by staring into their eyes.'

By noon we'd been working for three hours and we weren't even halfway through. My mother drove by with lunch for us.

'How are things going?' she asked.

'We'll never finish!' I told her.

'Just do the best you can,' she said. 'But don't fool around and waste time.'

Right after Mom left we decided we had to go to the bathroom. And the more we thought about it the worse we had to go.

'We can ring the bell and ask Mr Machinist,' I said. 'He'll have to let us use his bathroom.'

'Never,' Tracy said. 'I'd sooner die than ask him. I'm going right here.' She pointed to the ground.

'Oh, Tracy . . . you can't!'

'Want to bet?' Tracy unbuckled her jeans and started pulling them down.

'Tracy . . . somebody might see.'

'How?'

I looked around. Tracy was right. It's very woodsy in Mr Machinist's side yard. She crouched down next to a big tree. 'Ah . . . that feels good,' she said.

174

By that time I had to go so bad I was crossing my legs and shifting my weight from one foot to the other. So I undid my jeans too. I crouched like Tracy and watered a tree. 'Oh, Mr Machinist . . .' I sang softly. 'This time you're really getting what you deserve!'

At three o'clock Mrs Wu drove by with some juice and cookies. I showed her my blisters, one on each finger of my right hand, except for my pinky. Mrs Wu took the First Aid kit from her glove compartment and rubbed some ointment on my blisters. She gave me enough Band Aids to cover them. 'Your father's coming to pick you up at five,' she told me.

'Suppose we're not done by then?' Tracy asked.

'Just do the best you can,' Mrs Wu said. 'Nine to five is a long enough working day. Mr Machinist will have to be satisfied.'

We still had two small piles of leaves left when my father pulled up at five. My fingers were killing me and Tracy said she was ready to collapse.

Dad looked around. He said, 'You've done a good job, girls. I didn't think you'd get so much done.' He walked towards the house and me and Tracy followed. We sat on the front step while my father rang Mr Machinist's bell.

When the door opened Dad said, 'I'm Gordon Brenner and I'm taking the girls home now. They've put in a long hard day and I think you'll agree that they've done a fine job.'

'Did they finish?' Mr Machinist asked.

'Just about.'

'Did they learn their lesson?'

Dad looked at me and Tracy.

We nodded.

'I'm sure they have,' my father told Mr Machinist.

'Good . . . that's two more little brats I don't have to worry about . . .'

'They are not brats,' my father said.

'They are to me.' Mr Machinist slammed his door right in my father's face.

'Damn it,' Dad muttered. 'He really is a –'

'I told you, didn't I? I told you he deserved to get eggs in his mailbox.'

'Hmph . . .' was all my father answered.

When I got home I took a long, hot bath. I ached all over. I was too tired to eat any supper. I wanted to go straight to sleep. But then the phone rang. It was Great Maudie, calling from the station. I'd forgotten she was coming. While Mom drove down to pick her up I got comfortable on the sofa, with the pillow and blanket from my bed.

Great Maudie moved in with one small suitcase and one big carton. When Kenny saw the carton, he poked me and grinned. We both thought it was filled with presents for us. So of course we were surprised to find out it was full of food. There were bunches and bunches of carrots – not the kind Mom gets at the supermarket in plastic bags, but the kind that grow in the ground with green tops on them. There was also a whole mess of other vegetable stuff and boxes and jars of funny-looking grains.

'Since when are you on a health food kick, Maudie?' Dad asked.

'Six months,' Great Maudie said, 'and I've never felt better!'

I yawned. Great Maudie sat down beside me. 'What you need is vitamins, organically grown food, and plenty of exercise.'

'I'm not sick,' I said, ' . . . just tired.'

'Jill's had a hard day,' Mom explained.

'Foo . . .' Great Maudie said. 'At her age there's no such thing.'

Later we found out Great Maudie takes twenty-seven vitamin pills a day.

'Are *you* sick?' I asked. 'Is that why you swallow all those vitamins?'

'Just the opposite,' Great Maudie said. 'They keep me very healthy.'

'You should give some to Grandma,' Kenny said. 'She's always got something wrong with her.'

176

'Her troubles are up here.' Great Maudie tapped her head with one finger.

Me and Kenny started laughing because that's what Grandma says about Great Maudie – that she's got something loose in her head.

By the time I went to sleep I decided it would be fun having Great Maudie visit. She laughs a lot. She has a very nice laugh, big and deep.

On Monday morning I changed my mind about her. She had cleaned out our pantry before I woke up. She threw away my Frosted Flakes, Alpha-Bits and Captain Crunch. She made us eat wheat germ mush instead. If this continues, I thought, I might starve to death in three weeks.

sixteen

'If we're going to do this, we're going to do it right.'

'Mr Machinist found out about us,' I told Wendy on the bus. She didn't look surprised. 'And me and Tracy spent all day yesterday raking his leaves to make up for what we did.' I held out my hands and showed her the Band Aids covering my blisters.

'I didn't think she'd do it,' Wendy said. 'I didn't think she'd have the guts.'

'Who?' Caroline asked. 'Do what?'

'Who do you think?' Wendy said.

'Blubber?'

'Naturally.'

'She told?'

'She'd tell on her own mother,' Wendy said.

'Yeah . . .' Caroline agreed. 'She probably would.'

'We'll get her for this,' Wendy told me. 'We'll really get her this time.'

'I don't want to be in on it,' Tracy said. 'I promised my parents I'd stay out of trouble from now on.'

'Who said anything about trouble?' Wendy asked. 'It's just that we can't let her get away with it.'

'Count me out,' Tracy said. 'You can't prove she's the one who told on us.'

'Of course she is,' Wendy said. 'Who else would do it?'

Tracy looked at Wendy and Caroline. Then she shrugged and turned away.

'How dare you accuse us!' Wendy said.

'She's not accusing you . . . are you, Tracy?' I asked.

'I'm not saying anything.' Tracy looked out the window.

'If only we could be sure,' I tried to explain to Wendy. 'I wish we could, but there's no way . . .'

'I don't like what I hear, Jill,' Wendy said. 'Do you like what you hear, Caroline?'

'Not if you don't,' Caroline told Wendy.

'I know,' I said after a minute. 'I know how we can find out the truth once and for all. We'll have a trial! Just like in real life. With a judge and a jury and everything.' I glanced at Wendy to see what she thought of my idea. Personally, I thought it was great.

Wendy smiled. 'I'll be the judge,' she said. 'I'm a very fair person.'

I was really glad to hear that Wendy liked my idea.

'Can I be on the jury?' Caroline asked Wendy, as if she was in charge of the whole thing.

'Naturally,' Wendy said. 'You're my best friend, aren't you?'

By the time our bus pulled into the driveway Wendy wasn't mad any more and everything was settled. She would be the judge, I would be the lawyer and Caroline, Donna, Irwin, Robby and Michael would be on the jury.

'What do you think?' I asked Tracy, as we filed off the bus.

'I think you're scared of Wendy,' Tracy answered.

Wendy planned everything. All we had to do was wait for the

right moment. The only problem was, Linda didn't come to school that day. And she wasn't on the bus Tuesday or Wednesday morning either.

'She's scared,' Wendy said. 'She knows we're going to get her and she's scared to come to school.'

'The smelly whale's a chicken,' Caroline said.

'We've always known that,' Wendy told her.

Just as Mrs Minish was about to take the attendance on Wednesday, Linda came running into the classroom. Wendy flashed me a sign.

'My mother's car wouldn't start,' Linda told Mrs Minish.

'Did you miss the school bus?'

'No . . . my mother's going to drive me to school from now on,' Linda said, 'and home too.'

She really is scared, I thought. She really did tell on us.

At ten o'clock it started to rain. At eleven, when Mr Kubeck delivered our milk, it was pouring. By noon the playground and field were practically flooded. I knew we wouldn't be able to go outside even if it stopped raining, which it didn't.

As soon as Mrs Minish left the room for lunch period Wendy passed the word around we'd have the trial today. We waited until Mrs Horvath checked our room. 'Keep it quiet,' she told us. 'No talking above a whisper.'

'Yes, Mrs Horvath,' Wendy said.

Robby got up and looked out into the hall. He gave us a signal when Mrs Horvath had rounded the corner of the corridor. Then he closed our classroom door.

Wendy stood on her desk and announced, 'The trial of Blubber will begin.'

Linda was drawing a picture on vanilla paper. She looked up when Wendy said that.

'Did you hear me, Blubber? You're on trial!'

'I am not,' Linda said.

Wendy laughed. 'Oh yes you are. And I'm the judge.'

'I don't want to play that game,' Linda said.

'It's not a game,' Wendy told her. 'You're on trial for telling

Mr Machinist about Jill and Tracy on Hallowe'en.'

'I didn't tell anything.'

'Don't lie, you smelly whale!' Wendy said. She got off her desk and stood close to Linda. She held up the picture Linda had been drawing, showed it to the rest of the class, then tore it in half.

Linda looked around at us, then she jumped up so fast that she knocked her chair over backwards. She ran for the door.

'Catch her,' Wendy yelled. 'Don't let her out of the room.'

Robby and Irwin caught Linda and held on even though she was thrashing all around.

'Get the keys to the supply closet,' Wendy told Caroline. 'Quick . . .'

'Where?'

'Mrs Minish's top drawer.'

Caroline ran to Mrs Minish's desk and fumbled around inside the top drawer. She held up a key. 'Is this it?' she asked Wendy.

'Yes . . . throw . . .' Wendy caught the key and unlocked the supply closet. 'Get her in here,' she told the boys.

Robby and Irwin shoved Linda into the closet. Then they slammed the door and Wendy turned the key, leaving it in the lock.

'Let me out of here,' Linda called. Her voice was muffled.

'Just shut up and listen to me, Blubber,' Wendy said. 'You're on trial for being a stool pigeon, a rat, a fink, and a tattletale. How do you plead . . . guilty or not guilty?'

'Let me out of here!' Linda shouted.

'Shut up!' Wendy told her. 'How do you plead . . . guilty or not guilty?'

'Not guilty,' Linda said. 'Open the door . . . please!' She banged on it.

'Ladies and gentlemen of the jury,' Wendy began, 'it is your job to decide if Blubber is lying. Frankly, as the judge, I'm sure she is. We will hear the evidence from Jill Brenner, the class lawyer.'

180

'Open the door,' Linda called, just as I was about to begin giving evidence. 'Open it or I'll scream!'

'You do and you're dead,' Wendy said.

Linda quieted down.

'Hey . . . wait a second . . .' Rochelle said, and everybody turned to look at her because she never says anything. 'Who's Blubber's lawyer?'

'Blubber's lawyer?' Wendy asked. 'She doesn't get a lawyer.'

'Oh yes she does,' Rochelle said. 'Every trial has two lawyers . . . one for the defence and one for the prosecution.'

'Stay out of this, Rochelle,' Wendy said.

I hit my head with my hand. 'You know something . . . she's right. We did forget to give Blubber a lawyer.'

'I want a lawyer!' Linda cried, banging on the door.

'I'm the judge here and I say we do it the way we planned.'

'Look, Wendy,' I began, 'my father's a lawyer and what Rochelle says is true. If we're going to do this we're going to do it right, otherwise it's not a real trial. And since the trial was *my* idea in the first place I say she gets a lawyer!'

'Are you done?' Wendy asked me.

I nodded.

'Good,' she said, raising her voice. 'Because you're ruining everything! You're turning chicken just like your chink friend.'

'Don't you dare call Tracy a chink!'

'I'll call her whatever I damn please . . . and that's what she is.'

I glared at Wendy. Then I turned around and said, 'Rochelle . . . you want to be Blubber's lawyer?'

'I'm not sure,' Rochelle said. 'I'll have to think about it.'

From inside the supply closet Linda called, 'Rochelle . . . please be my lawyer.'

'Okay,' Rochelle said, 'I guess I will. But I'll need some time with my client to get the facts straight.' She stood up.

'Stay right where you are, Rochelle!' Wendy said. 'I'm running this trial.' She looked at me. 'And don't you forget it.'

Rochelle waited to see what would happen next. And the rest

of the class got very quiet. I thought about Tracy and how she said I'm scared of Wendy. And I thought about how worried I'd been on Monday, when Wendy got mad at me, and how good it felt when she wasn't mad any more. And then I thought about Linda. Right that minute it didn't matter to me whether or not she had told on us. It was the trial that was important and it wasn't fair to have a trial without two lawyers. So I faced Wendy and I said, 'I'm sick of you bossing everybody around. If Blubber doesn't get a lawyer then Blubber doesn't get a trial.'

'No lawyer!' Wendy folded her arms across her chest.

'Then no trial!' I shouted, running to the supply closet. Before Wendy knew what I was doing I unlocked the door and flung it open. 'Come out! I just cancelled your trial.'

'You'll pay for this,' Wendy told me. 'You'll be sorry you were ever born, Jill Brenner!'

For the first time I looked right into Wendy's eyes and I didn't like what I saw.

That afternoon Mrs Minnish said, 'You've been such a nice, quiet class since lunch. I wish you'd act this way more often.'

After school I went over to Tracy's. She was cleaning out the chicken coup. 'Need any help?' I asked.

Tracy tossed me a broom and we swept together.

'I'm not hanging around with Wendy any more,' I told her. 'She acts like she owns the whole world.'

'I've always known that,' Tracy picked up Friendly. 'You want to hold him?' she asked.

'You know I do.'

We sat down on the back steps. I held Friendly close and stroked his feathers. We were quiet for a while. Best friends don't have to talk all the time. Finally I said, 'Tracy . . . do you think it was Linda who told on us?'

'I'm not sure . . . it could have been . . . if she was mad enough.'

I nodded.

'Or it could have been Wendy and Caroline.'

'Yeah . . . I guess you're right,' I said. 'It could have been.'

'Or maybe even somebody else.'

I thought about that. 'Do you think we'll ever find out the truth?'

'Probably not.'

Friendly flapped his wings and I let go of him. He ran after a chicken and tried to climb on her back. 'He wants to mate,' I said.

'Oh him . . .' Tracy laughed. 'That's all he ever thinks about.'

seventeen

'What's with her?'

Mrs Wu drove us to school the next morning because Tracy's project on the explorers was too big to carry on the bus. It barely fitted into the car.

I was really glad I didn't have to take the bus because this way I wouldn't have to face Wendy first thing. It's hard not to be scared of her and the things she might do to me. I've made up my mind though. I will act the same as always except I'll just ignore Wendy. That will teach her a lesson about threatening people. She'll never make me feel sorry I was born.

When I walked into class Linda was sitting in my place. 'Your desk is over there now,' Wendy said, pointing to where Linda used to sit.

'Who gave you permission to move my desk, Blubber?' I asked, ignoring Wendy, just like I'd planned.

'Watch how you talk to *my* friend,' Wendy said. 'Her name is Linda and don't you forget it, B.B.'

Everybody laughed. What did B.B. mean? And since when

was Linda Wendy's friend?

Mrs Minish came into the room. I went up to her. 'Mrs Minish . . . somebody moved my desk.'

'Oh . . . the custodian is always moving desks around when he sweeps.'

'Can I move it back where it belongs?'

Mrs Minish looked around the classroom. 'Why don't you move it next to Donna Davidson's . . . there's a space over there.'

I went to my desk, stood the chair on top of it, and pushed it across the room, next to Donna's desk. When I did, she moved hers away and whispered, 'Who wants to sit next to B.B?'

When it was time for gym, Mr Witneski chose Bruce and Linda for the captains. Linda picked Wendy first. I waited and waited but nobody chose me for a team. When I was the only one left Linda told Bruce, 'You get B.B.' And all the kids on Bruce's team moaned.

I'll show them, I thought, I'll show them all. I will play so good I'll kick ten home runs.

But I didn't. I kicked three fly balls right to Wendy and each time I did my team said, 'What can you expect from B.B.?'

At lunch I found out B.B. means Baby Brenner. It could have been worse. Wendy put a diaper pin on my desk with a note attached to it.

Baby Brenner better change her diapers.
She's smelling up the whole room!

After I read the note I said, 'Ha ha . . .' remembering that my mother told me a person should always be able to laugh at herself. I tried to laugh as hard as the rest of the kids to show what a good sport I can be.

'Goo goo . . .' Robby Winters said. 'See Baby Brenner laugh!' He sounded like he was reading from a first-grade book.

'See Baby Brenner eat!' Caroline said.

'Baby Brenner eats only mushy-gushy foods like peanut

butter,' Wendy told everyone, 'because Baby Brenner can't chew big people's food yet.'

I didn't finish my lunch.

That afternoon, when I got on the bus, Wendy stuck out her foot and tripped me. I fell flat on my face and my books flew all over the place. I tried to laugh again but this time the laugh just wouldn't come. Tracy helped me up, collected my books, and led me to the seat she'd been saving.

'See Baby Brenner!' Wendy shouted. 'Baby Brenner hasn't learned to walk yet.'

The next day they all held their noses when I came near them. In the Girls' Room Donna Davidson shoved me against the sink and I got a black and blue mark on my leg. As I was getting a drink from the fountain, Caroline pushed me and I wound up with water all over my face.

During lunch period Wendy wrote on the blackboard, *B.B. loves W.W.*

'What's that mean?' Irwin asked.

'Baby Brenner is in love,' Wendy said. 'Baby Brenner is in love with Warren Winkler.'

That was just too much. 'I am not!' I told everybody. 'That's a big lie!'

Then Wendy whispered something to Linda and both of them laughed.

On the playground we jumped rope. I knew I'd be last on line and I was. I bit my nails the whole time I was waiting.

'What's for dinner?' I asked Great Maudie, throwing my books down.

'Whatever your mother brings home,' Great Maudie said. She was in one of her Yoga positions, with her legs crossed Indian style and her arms out straight.

'I wish you knew how to cook!' I ran for my room, bumping into Kenny on the way.

'Watch where you're going,' he said.

'Shut up, carnivore!' I shouted at him.

I heard him ask Great Maudie, 'What's with her?'

Great Maudie sighed and told him, 'A bad day, I suppose.'

I slammed my bedroom door and sat down at my desk.

Friday, November 22

Dear Mrs Sandmeier,

I hope you're having fun in Switzerland. Nothing is very good at home. Do you believe that bad things always happen in threes? Grandma once told me that and I'm beginning to think it's true. Great Maudie turned out to be a terrible babysitter. She believes in cold showers, morning exercises, and crazy things to eat such as carrot juice and wheat germ mush. She can't cook regular foods at all. That is, she won't! So every night Mom and Dad bring our supper home from a take-out place. I am surviving on peanut butter. Did you know it's not bad with bananas?

I've been thinking that the next time you go on vacation and if it isn't the summer when me and Kenny are at camp, maybe we should ask Grandma to come after all. She's a good cook. She can make soup from real chicken. And besides, her hobby is cleaning. Mom already announced that we are going to spend all day tomorrow doing that.

Things are not the greatest in school either. I am having a special problem. It doesn't have to do with reading or maths or anything like that. It's much worse. A lot of people don't like me any more. And for no good reason. I'm trying hard to pretend it doesn't matter, but the truth is, it does. Sometimes I feel like crying but I hold it in. I wouldn't want to spoil your vacation so I won't say anything else. I hope your mother is having a nice birthday and that you hurry home to us. Tu m'as beaucoup manqué.

Love,

Jill

Mom and Dad brought home Chinese food for supper. 'What about me?' I said. 'What am I supposed to eat?'

'Oh, Jill . . .' Mom said. 'It's time you learned to eat like everyone else.'

'Everyone else doesn't eat that stuff.'

'What your mother means,' Dad said, 'is that practically everyone likes Chinese food. It's very popular in this country.'

'Egg rolls and spare ribs and chow mein are not Chinese foods,' I said. 'If you don't believe me just ask Tracy . . . she'll tell you.'

'Tracy's American,' Kenny said.

'She's Chinese-American.'

'She eats hot dogs.'

'So?' I swallowed hard and nibbled on my nails.

'When did you start biting your nails again?' Mom asked. I didn't answer.

Dad said, 'What about our deal? You haven't forgotten all those stamps at Gimbels, have you?'

I didn't answer him either.

When we sat down to supper I didn't feel like eating anything, not even the bread and cheese I knew Mom had put out just for me. My throat was tight and I had a pain in my stomach. 'I'm not very hungry,' I said.

'Are you getting sick?' Mom asked, touching my forehead.

'No . . .' I managed to say, before the tears came. I pushed my chair away from the table and ran for my room.

'You want to talk about it?' Mom asked, a few minutes later, as she sat on the edge of my bed.

'What?' I said, like I didn't know.

'Whatever's bothering you. It might make you feel better.'

'Nobody likes me any more,' I told her. Then I started crying hard.

Mom held me. 'I know . . . I know how it hurts.'

'I hate them all . . .'

'Now . . . now . . .' Mom said, smoothing my hair.

'I do!'

'Maybe that's the trouble. You can be a pretty tough character sometimes . . .'

'Even so . . . it still isn't fair.'

'Lots of things aren't fair.'

'You told me a person who can laugh at herself will be respected.'

'True.'

'So I laughed,' I said. 'I tried to show I didn't care.'

'That's good.'

'But they don't respect me . . . they don't even like me . . . I need a tissue,' I said, sniffling.

Mom handed one to me and I blew my nose.

'It's rough to be on the other side, isn't it?' she asked.

eighteen

'Never mind spitting.'

We spent all day Saturday cleaning the house, just like my mother promised. My job was dusting everything in sight. Dad scrubbed the bathrooms and kitchen while Mom changed the beds and went to the supermarket. Kenny got to vacuum. Great Maudie watered the plants.

I didn't start my maths homework until Sunday night. I'm not supposed to wait till the last minute but somehow, I always do. It took me over an hour to finish and then I gave the paper to Dad to check. He said it was perfect. I was really pleased.

Talking to Mom on Friday night helped me feel a little better about going back to school on Monday. But even so, I wasn't taking any chances. I wouldn't wear a skirt for anything. Pants were much safer. That way Wendy couldn't force me to show the boys my underwear.

I called for Tracy and told her, 'If they try to make me kiss Bruce I'll spit on them. That's what he said he'd do to Blubber if she touched his lips.'

'Never mind spitting,' Tracy said. 'If they try anything at all you should bite them.'

'I should?'

'Yes. I once read a news article about this woman who bit off another woman's finger. The human bite is very dangerous.'

'I'll remember that,' I said.

When we got to our bus stop a group of kids was coming over the hill, heading in our direction. When I saw who they were my heart started thumping. 'What's going on?' I asked.

'I don't know,' Tracy answered, 'but we better find out.'

Wendy, Caroline, Donna and Linda were first, with Robby, Michael and Irwin right behind them. They looked like an army.

'What're you doing here?' Tracy asked as they got to our corner. 'You get on the bus at Hidden Valley.'

'Not today,' Wendy said and she charged into me, knocking my things to the ground. Before I had a chance to pick everything up Wendy grabbed my maths book and she and the others started playing catch with it.

'Cut that out!' I yelled, trying to get my book back. But they threw it over my head. I couldn't stop them from doing whatever they wanted.

'Give it to her!' Tracy hollered and she bopped Robby with her notebook.

Just as Irwin caught my book I kicked him as hard as I could, figuring he would drop it. But instead, he kicked me back and tossed my book into the street. I won't cry, I thought. I'll never let them see me cry. Never!

Our bus came along then, flashing its red stop lights. I ran into the street to get my maths book, then Tracy helped me put my lunch back together because somebody had pulled it all apart. As I climbed on to the bus the driver yelled at me for taking too long. When I finally sat down next to Tracy I saw that Wendy and Linda were sharing a seat. Caroline sat alone, behind them.

★

Later, when Mrs Minish collected our maths homework, I couldn't find mine. 'But I did it, Mrs Minish,' I said. 'You can ask my father. He checked it for me.'

'Maybe you left it at home.' Mrs Minish didn't seem to care.

I said, 'No . . . I'm positive I put it inside my book.'

'Maybe it fell out,' Mrs Minish told me.

'No!' I said, suddenly sure of what had happened to it. 'It didn't *just* fall out!'

'Well, Jill . . . since this is the first time you've ever forgotten your homework I won't count it against you.'

'But I didn't forget it,' I said. 'I told you I didn't forget it.'

'All right, Jill. Don't worry about it. If you find it you can hand it in tomorrow.'

'I'll do it over,' I said.

'You can if you want to, but it isn't really necessary. Now . . . let's all take out our maths books and open to Chapter Three.'

Wendy turned around and smiled. I wanted to kill her.

When we went to the Girls' Room Wendy blocked the toilets and wouldn't let me use one until I said, *I am Baby Brenner. I'm not toilet trained yet. That's why I stink.*

I shook my head at her.

'You have to say it!' Wendy told me.

'No way,' I said. 'I won't.'

'Then I'll have to check your diapers myself.'

I thought about making a run for it, but Wendy had Caroline, Donna and Linda on her side and I wasn't sure I had anyone on mine. So I said, 'You touch me and you're dead!'

'Grab her, Caroline!' Wendy said. 'Grab her arms and I'll pull her smelly diapers off.'

Caroline is bigger than me and stronger too. As she came towards me I shouted, 'You always do what Wendy says? Don't you have a mind of your own?'

'I have a mind of my own.'

'Then why don't you use it for once! Wendy doesn't even like you any more so why should you follow her orders?'

190

'Shut up, Brenner!' Wendy said. 'Don't listen to her, Caroline.'

'She does too like me,' Caroline said.

'Then how come she's always hanging around Linda? Didn't you see them this morning, on the bus? I'll bet she's not even your partner for the class trip.'

Caroline looked at Wendy. 'We're partners, aren't we?'

Before Wendy could answer, Linda said, 'I'm Wendy's partner.' She hung an arm over Wendy's shoulder.

Caroline bit her lip, turned and walked out of the Girls' Room. Donna followed her.

'Don't you ever answer for me again!' Wendy told Linda.

I didn't wait around to see what Wendy would do next. I opened the door to a toilet and locked myself in the booth. I was really shaking. Before I came out I checked underneath to make sure there were no feet in sight. That way I knew I was safe.

Nobody called me Baby Brenner during lunch. Donna and Caroline moved their desks together and Wendy invited Laurie to eat with her. Linda sat alone at her desk, the way she used to.

I took out my sandwich and looked at it, thinking how much better it would taste if I had someone to talk to. I hate to eat all by myself. I glanced around the room, wondering, should I or shouldn't I? Oh, I might as well try, I finally decided. You sometimes have to make the first move or else you might wind up like Linda – letting other people decide what's going to happen to you.

I stood up, walked over to Rochelle's desk and said, 'Hey, Rochelle . . . you want to eat with me?'

Rochelle didn't answer right away and for a second I was sorry I'd asked her. But then she finished chewing, swallowed whatever was in her mouth, and said, 'Why not?'

I moved my desk next to hers. She had a peanut-butter sandwich too.

nineteen

'Put your money where your mouth is.'

Tuesday morning, on the way to school, Irwin called me some
of his best names. I said, 'The same to you,' and everybody
laughed, but not at me.

That afternoon we had our Thanksgiving programme. The
sixth graders put on a boring play about the Pilgrims, the
Indians and the first Thanksgiving. I wish our school could do
a play like the one in *Harriet the Spy* where everybody pretends
to be a different vegetable. I would like to play the onion. I'd
roll around the floor the way Harriet did in the book. I wonder
if there really are schools where they do that kind of thing?

When we got back to class Mrs Minish stayed out in the hall,
talking to the teacher from the next room. So Robby Winters
had plenty of time to stick pins through his fingers and do his
zombie act. When he shoved his hands in my face I said,
'What's so great about that? Anybody can do it.'

'Oh yeah . . .'

'Yeah . . .'

'Including you?'

'Including me.'

'Put your money where your mouth is, Brenner.'

'How much?' I asked him.

'A quarter.'

'You're on . . . give me some pins.'

Robby took the pins out of his fingers and handed them to
me. I stuck one through the top layer of skin of every finger,
being careful not to flinch as I did. Then I stood up, held my
hands out straight, and walked around making zombie noises.

'Exactly what is going on here?' Mrs Minish stood in the
doorway, watching me. 'Jill . . . you're out of your seat.'

'Yes, Mrs Minish.' I hurried back to my desk, hid my hands

underneath it and pulled the pins out of my fingers.

Robby passed me a quarter.

By lunchtime it was easy to tell that Wendy and Laurie were going to be best friends and so were Donna and Caroline. Some people are *always* changing best friends. I'm glad me and Tracy aren't that way. Still it's nice to have a regular friend in your class, even if it's not a *best* friend. I ate lunch with Rochelle again. She's kind of quiet but I get the feeling that a lot goes on inside her head. So later, when it was time to go home, and we all ran for our lockers, I said, 'Hey, Rochelle . . . you want to be my partner for the class trip?'

She put on her jacket, closed her locker door, and said, 'Why not?'

I didn't bite my nails once that afternoon or night and when Dad tucked me into bed I said, 'You know something? There's still a whole month to go before Christmas.'

'So?' he asked.

'So . . . is our deal still on?' I held out my hands and wiggled my fingers to show him what I was talking about.

'It's still on,' he told me.

'Good . . . because I think I can make it this time.'

We had just half a day of school on Wednesday. On the bus ride home we played Keep-Away with Robby's hat and the sixth graders taught us a song about the girls in France. The bus driver yelled, 'Shut up or I'll report you to the principal.'

Nobody paid any attention.

When we got off the bus, me and Tracy stopped for the mail. Both of us had a packet of approvals from Winthrop.

'Come over and we'll decide what to buy,' I said.

'As soon as I change.'

'Don't forget your album.'

'How could I?' Tracy asked.

Kenny met me at the front door. 'Did you know the longest earthworm in the world measures twenty-one feet when fully extended?'

'I'm really glad to hear that,' I said. 'His mother must be very proud.'

Starring Sally J. Freedman As Herself

For my favourite aunt,
Frances Goldstein . . . who is also my friend

Introduction

When World War II ended I was just seven years old, but the war had so coloured my early life that it was hard to think of anything else. No one I knew had actually experienced the war first hand. There were no bombs dropped on America; we were not starving; we felt reasonably safe. And yet I could not help worrying that it could happen again, could happen to us. I knew that Adolf Hitler was a menace. I knew that he wanted to kill all the Jews in the world. And I was a Jew.

Starring Sally J. Freedman As Herself is my most autobiographical novel. Sally is the kind of child I was, full of imagination, always making up stories inside her head. In a way I think the character of Sally explains how and perhaps why I became a writer. My love of storytelling, although I didn't necessarily share it in those days, has carried through to today.

Some of the Yiddish expressions used by Sally's grandmother in the book are words I learned from my own grandmother. Sally's family is based on my own. And the setting, Miami Beach, Florida, in 1947–48, is real too. I spent two school years living in Miami Beach after the war. Sally's world is the world as I perceived it, at age ten. A world full of secrets, full of questions that no one would answer.

I hope that you can put yourselves into post-war America and enjoy reading about Sally and her family. Sally is one of my favourite characters. I hope she'll become one of yours, too.

Judy Blume

Prologue

August, 1945 – Bradley Beach, New Jersey

'Can I have another jelly sandwich?' Sally asked her
grandmother, Ma Fanny. They were in the kitchen of the
rooming house, sitting on opposite sides of the big wooden
table.

'Such big eyes!' Ma Fanny said, laughing. 'You still have half
a sandwich left.'

'I know, but it's so good!' Sally licked the jelly from the
corners of her mouth. 'I could eat twenty sandwiches, at least.'

'Only twenty?'

'Maybe twenty-one,' Sally said. 'Why don't you make
yourself a jelly sandwich, too . . . and if you can't finish it, I
will.'

'I should eat jelly and have heartburn all night?' Ma Fanny
asked.

'Jelly gives you heartburn?'

'I'm sorry to say . . .' Ma Fanny turned on the radio. Bing
Crosby was singing.

Sally hummed along with him, every now and then singing a
line out loud. 'Or would you rather be a horse? A horse is an
animal . . .' She wiggled around in her chair. The sand in the
bottom of her bathing suit made her itch. Soon she would go
upstairs for her bath. Everyone had to sign up for a bath here,
because all the guests in the rooming house shared the
bathrooms. It was the same with the kitchen. Each family had a
shelf in the pantry and space in the icebox, but no one had to
sign up to cook.

Upstairs, Sally's family had rented two bedrooms for ten
days. One was for Daddy and Mom and the other was for Sally,
her brother Douglas, and Ma Fanny. Sally was the youngest so
she got to sleep on the cot under the window. From it she could
see the organ grinder and his monkey when they were still a

block away. She didn't tell this to Douglas because if he had known he would have wanted to sleep on the cot for the rest of their vacation.

'Drink all your milk,' Ma Fanny said, 'and you'll grow up to be a big, strong girl.'

'I already am big and strong,' Sally answered, making a muscle with her arm.

Ma Fanny reached across the table and squeezed Sally's arm. 'Hoo hoo . . . that's *some* muscle!'

'So can I have another jelly sandwich?'

'Such a one-track mind,' Ma Fanny said, laughing again. She tapped her fingers on the table, keeping in time to the tune on the radio.

Mrs Sternberger, another guest in the rooming house, swept into the kitchen. She took a dish of rice pudding from the icebox and joined Sally and Ma Fanny at the table. As soon as she sat down she noticed the jar of grape jelly with the cap off. 'What are you doing with my grape jelly?' she asked, picking up the jar.

'It's not yours,' Ma Fanny told her. 'It's mine.'

'I just bought this yesterday,' Mrs Sternberger said, replacing the cap. She stood up holding on to the jar, and pointed at Ma Fanny. 'I knew I couldn't trust you the minute I met you.'

'What are you, crazy?' Ma Fanny asked, raising her voice. 'I should use your grape jelly when I have my own? I wouldn't touch yours with a ten-foot pole!'

'And I wouldn't believe you for all the tea in China!' Mrs Sternberger answered, angrily.

'So, who asked you?' Ma Fanny turned to Sally. 'Would you like another jelly sandwich, sweetie pie?'

'Sure.' Sally was surprised that Ma Fanny had changed her mind.

Ma Fanny reached for the jelly jar but Mrs Sternberger said, 'Not with *my* grape jelly!' She held it to her chest.

'Oh . . . go soak your head!' Ma Fanny said.

'Go soak your own!'

Sally wanted to laugh but knew that she shouldn't. 'Can I please have my sandwich?' She shouted to make sure she was heard.

Suddenly, Bing Crosby stopped singing. 'We interrupt this programme to bring you a bulletin from our newsroom,' the announcer said. 'The war is over!'

Ma Fanny and Mrs Sternberger grew quiet. 'Did I hear what I think I heard?' Mrs Sternberger asked.

'Sha . . .' Ma Fanny said, turning up the volume on the radio. Both women listened carefully.

The announcer repeated the news. '*The war is over!*' His voice broke on the last word.

'Thank God . . . thank God . . .' Ma Fanny cried.

Mrs Sternberger plonked the jar of grape jelly on the table and whooped for joy. She and Ma Fanny hugged and kissed. They began to laugh and cry at the same time. 'It's over . . . it's over . . . it's over!' They danced around the kitchen.

Sally felt alone. She wanted to dance with them. She pushed her chair back and ran to Ma Fanny's side. Ma Fanny and Mrs Sternberger dropped hands to make a circle with Sally, and the three of them danced. 'The war is over . . . over . . . over . . .' Sally sang.

The other guests in the rooming house joined them. Daddy and Mom and Douglas were there. It was like a party. A very tall man named Ben held Sally up in the air and twirled around and around with her until she felt dizzy and begged him to put her down.

That night they all marched on the boardwalk, waving small American flags. Daddy carried Sally on his shoulders. He stopped at a stand to buy horns for her and Douglas to toot. Sally's throat felt sore, maybe from cheering so loud.

Douglas said, 'Hey, Dad . . . when we get home can I have your air raid helmet?'

'I don't see why not, son,' Daddy said.

'Won't there be any more blackouts?' Sally asked.

200

'No, dummy,' Douglas said, 'the war is over!'

'I know that!' But Sally didn't know that meant the end of blackouts. So now Daddy wouldn't patrol the streets any more, wearing his white air raid helmet. And she and Douglas wouldn't get into bed with Mom, waiting for Daddy to come home, telling them it had just been practice, that the war was far, far away and nothing bad was ever going to happen to them.

'I'd like your helmet, too,' Sally said. How was she supposed to know that Daddy would be giving it away now?'

'Not fair!' Douglas said. 'I'm older.'

'Tell you what . . .' Daddy said, 'you can *share* it.'

'Her head's so little it'll cover her whole face,' Douglas said.

'Little heads are better than big ones,' Sally told him.

'Children . . . *please* . . .' Mom said.

Daddy put Sally down and went off to sing with a group of men. Sally took Mom aside and said, 'I don't feel so good.'

'What is it?' Mum asked, looking concerned.

'My throat hurts . . . and my stomach feels funny.'

Mom touched Sally's forehead. 'You don't feel warm . . . it's probably all the excitement.'

'I don't think so,' Sally said, 'I feel sick.'

'Let's stay out a little while longer . . . it's warm enough . . . I'm sure you won't get a chill . . .' Mom took Sally's hand.

'But, Mom . . .'

'Try not to think about it,' Mom said. 'Tonight is special.'

'I know, but . . .'

'Think about peace instead . . . think about Uncle Jack coming home . . . think about Tante Rose and Lila . . .'

'Who are they?'

'You know . . . Ma Fanny's sister and her daughter . . .my *Aunt* Rose and my *cousin* Lila . . .'

'Oh, them . . . the ones Hitler sent away . . .'

'Yes. Maybe now we can find out where they are.'

'Do you think they're in New Jersey?' Sally asked.

'No, honey . . . they're far away . . . they're somewhere in Europe.'

'Oh . . . my throat still hurts bad.'

'Please, Sally,' Mom said, 'try for me . . .'

Sally tried to think of other things, as her mother said. She kept marching even though she felt worse and worse. Finally, she couldn't wait any more. 'Mom . . . I think I'm going to . . .' She ran to the side of the boardwalk, leaned over the rail and threw up on to the beach.

'Oh, honey . . . I'm sorry,' Mom said. 'I should have listened.' She wiped Sally's mouth with a Kleenex. 'Don't cry . . . it's all right . . .'

'I didn't mess myself up,' Sally said, sniffing. 'See . . . I was really careful, wasn't I?'

'Yes, you were.'

'I knew you wouldn't want me to get it on my dress.'

'That's right . . . it's just as easy to be careful . . .'

They went back to the rooming house and Mom took Sally's temperature. It was 103°. She put Sally to bed, gave her some ginger ale to sip and laid a cold, wet washcloth on her forehead. 'If only I had listened when you first told me you weren't feeling well . . . I was so excited myself . . . I . . .' She kissed Sally's cheek. 'Try and get to sleep . . . tomorrow we'll go to the doctor . . .' Mom pulled a chair up to Sally's cot and sat beside her. Sally closed her eyes and listened to the sounds outside. Cheering, horns tooting, singing . . . laughter . . . sounds of the celebration. Slowly, she drifted off to sleep.

one

May, 1947 – Elizabeth, New Jersey

Sally had a scab on her knee from falling off her bicycle last week. It itched. She scratched the area around it, knowing that the scab wasn't ready to come off yet. She was sitting on the high-backed chair near the fireplace and her feet didn't quite reach the floor. She wished they would.

'Little pitchers have big ears,' Uncle Jack said, with a nod in her direction. On the far side of the living room Mom, Ma Fanny, Aunt Bette and Uncle Jack were huddled together. They spoke in hushed voices so that Sally could make out only a few words.

'God forbid . . . keep your fingers crossed . . . never should have gone there . . .'

They were talking about Douglas. Something had happened to him. Sally wasn't exactly sure what, but Daddy was at the hospital now, with Douglas, and Mom was waiting impatiently for the phone to ring, with news about him.

Sally ran her hands along the arms of the chair. It was covered in pink and green flowered material, shiny and almost new. The whole living-room was pink and green although Mom didn't say *pink*. She said *rose-beige*. It was a beautiful room, soft and peaceful. Sally loved it. She wished they used it every day and not just on special occasions.

One Sunday her father built a fire in the brick fireplace and he and Sally and Douglas sat around on the floor reading the funnies. But Mom said it made a mess. So they'd had no more log fires. On either side of the fireplace bookcases climbed to the ceiling and between them, and over the fireplace, was a large mirror, reflecting the rest of the room.

Something had to be very wrong with Douglas. Otherwise why were they sitting in the living room tonight?

'Stop picking, Sally . . .' Mom said. 'You'll only make it worse.'

Sally took her hand away from her knee. She twirled a strand of hair around her finger and yawned.

'Why don't you go up to bed?' Mom asked. 'Look how tired you are.'

'I'm not tired.'

'Don't give me a hard time,' Mom snapped. 'Just go on up . . .'

Aunt Bette touched Mom's shoulder, then walked over to Sally. 'Come on,' she said. 'I'll keep you company while you get ready.'

They went upstairs to Sally's room. Aunt Bette flopped across the bed. She was Mom's younger sister. She taught fourth grade and sometimes she brought marbles to Sally and Douglas, marbles that had wound up in her Treasure Chest because someone in her class had been fooling around with them instead of paying attention. And once a marble found its way into Aunt Bette's Treasure Chest the owner could kiss it goodbye. That's why Douglas and Sally had such great marble collections. Sally's favourite was clear green all over.

'Mom's mad at me,' Sally said, 'and I didn't do anything.'

'She's not mad,' Aunt Bette said. 'She's worried about Douglas, that's all.'

'She acted mad . . . she didn't have to holler.'

'Try to understand.'

'What's the matter with Douglas, anyway?'

'He's had an accident.'

Sally knew that. She'd been outside tossing her pink Spalding ball against the side of the house when two boys carried Douglas to the back door. There'd been a big commotion then and Sally was sure of just one thing. Douglas was crying. She'd been surprised about that.

'They were playing in Union Woods,' Aunt Bette said, 'and Douglas tried to jump across the brook but he lost his balance and fell and when he did he dislocated his elbow.'

'We're not supposed to play in Union Woods,' Sally said. There was a strange man who hung out in there. Last month the principal of Sally's school had sent a notice to each classroom, warning the kids not to go into Union Woods any more. That afternoon Sally had asked Douglas, 'Do you know about the strange man in Union Woods?' and Douglas had answered, 'Sure.'

'What kind of strange man is he?' Sally said.

'What do you mean?' Douglas asked.

'Is he a murderer or a kidnapper or what?'

'He's just strange,' Douglas told her.

'What does that mean?'

'You know . . .'

'No, I don't!'

'Well . . . he's kind of crazy,' Douglas said.

'Oh, crazy.' Sally thought about that for a minute. 'Crazy how?'

'In general,' Douglas said.

'What does that mean?'

'I don't have time to explain now . . . I'm busy . . .' and before Sally could ask another question Douglas had run downstairs to his basement workshop and shut the door.

Sally supposed Douglas and his friends weren't afraid to go into Union Woods because they were older. They were thirteen and went to junior high. 'Is it bad to dislocate your elbow?' Sally asked Aunt Bette.

'It's like breaking your arm . . . he'll have a cast when he comes home from the hospital.'

'Like Suzanne Beardsley?'

'I don't know her.'

'She's in my class. She broke her wrist taking out the milk bottles and she had a cast for two months and we all signed our names on it.'

'I'm sure Douglas will let you sign your name on his cast too. Now brush your teeth and hop into bed. It's past ten.'

'Can I listen to my radio?'

'Okay . . . but just for a little while.'

Sally got ready for bed. Her mother came up to kiss her goodnight. 'I didn't mean to scold you,' she said. 'It's just that . . .'

'I know,' Sally said, 'you're worried about Douglas.'

'Well, yes . . . waiting is very hard. I should have gone to the hospital too.'

'Will Douglas be home soon?'

'I hope so. Daddy's going to call as soon as his arm is reset.'

'Reset?'

'Yes . . . to get the elbow back in place.'

'Oh.'

'Good night . . . sleep tight.' Mom bent over to kiss her cheek and Sally could smell the pot roast they'd had for dinner on her hands.

'Night, Mom.'

Sally closed her eyes but she couldn't fall asleep. Even her radio didn't help, so after a while she reached over and turned it off. Then she arranged her covers in just the right way, with both her hands tucked inside, and she closed her eyes again, but still, sleep wouldn't come. So she made up a story inside her head.

Sally Meets the Stranger

Sally is walking in Union Woods, picking flowers and humming a tune. She is wearing a long yellow organdie dress and a picture hat to match. Her hair is blowing in the breeze. Suddenly, she is aware of someone following her. She spins around and comes face to face with the strange man. He has a long, shaggy grey beard and a foolish smile on his face. Saliva trickles out of the corners of his mouth. His clothes are tattered and his bare feet are crusted with dirt.

Oh! Sally exclaims and she drops her flowers. The strange man makes terrible noises and Sally tries to run but finds she can't. Her feet won't move. The strange man comes closer and

206

closer. Sally takes off her hat and swats his face with it but since it is made of organdie it doesn't do any good. He scoops her up and carries her deep into Union Woods.

You're going to be very sorry! Sally tells him, as he prepares to tie her to a tree. He answers. *Ugr harmph vilda phud*, then laughs as he winds the rope tighter and tighter around Sally's small body.

But he is *so* strange he forgets to tie the two ends of the rope together and as soon as he goes back to his hut Sally wiggles free and runs. She doesn't stop until she reaches police headquarters, where she tells her story to the Chief of Police himself. Then she leads him and two of his assistants to the strange man's hut. The strange man is captured at last! Never again will he be able to tie a girl to a tree.

The Chief of Police is so impressed that he makes Sally his number one detective, specializing in strange cases. A Hollywood producer decides to make a movie of Sally's story. But he can't find the right ten-year-old girl to play the lead. He decides he must have Sally herself and that is how Sally gets to be not only a famous detective but also a movie star.

Sometime that night Douglas came home from the hospital. Sally woke to her parents' voices. Mom cried, 'His clothes are wet . . . my God, Arnold, he's soaked right through.'

'From the brook,' Daddy said. 'He fell into the brook . . . remember?'

'But the hospital . . .' Mom said. 'How could they have left him in these wet clothes for so long . . . he'll get pneumonia or something . . . I knew I should have gone too.'

two

Douglas didn't get pneumonia, he got nephritis, a kidney infection. He was very sick and had to stay in bed. Nobody could prove it came from being wet for such a long time but Sally knew that's what her mother was thinking.

Ma Fanny moved into the spare room to help Mom take care of Douglas. And Aunt Bette came over every day after school. She made charts and taped them to the wall in his room. One to keep track of his medicines, another to record his temperature, and a third, showing how many glasses of water he drank each day. If they added up to a quart or more Mom pasted a gold star on that chart at night. Every Thursday afternoon a lab technician would arrive to take some blood from Douglas's arm. Sally wasn't allowed to watch, although she wanted to very much.

Nobody worried about Douglas missing school because he was a genius. He'd skipped third grade which made him the youngest student in eighth. When he was ten he'd built a radio by himself. There wasn't anything he couldn't fix or make from scratch. Still, Sally was glad she wasn't a genius too because Daddy and Mom were never satisfied with Douglas's report card. He didn't get all As or even all Bs like Sally. And his teachers always said the same thing about him. 'Douglas does not work up to his full potential.'

The weather was hot and sticky that May. After school Sally and her best friend, Christine, played together.

'Why can't I see Douglas?' Christine asked Sally.

'Because my mother doesn't want him to get any new germs.'

'I don't have any new germs and besides, I don't want to touch him or anything . . . I just want to see him.'

'Maybe next week . . . I'm not allowed in there myself.'

'Does he look awful?'

'Sort of . . .'

'Did you sign his cast?'

'Not yet . . . I just told you I'm not allowed to get that close . . . but when I do sign it I'm going to draw a *Kilroy Was Here* picture with my name across the brick wall.'

'Let's play Cowgirl today,' Christine said. 'I'm sick of Detective.'

'But we played Cowgirl yesterday and, besides, I've got this really great detective story ready . . .' Sally said. 'We're after this murderer who cuts people up and stuffs the pieces into brown lunch bags . . . he leaves the bags all over town and the people are really scared . . . this is no ordinary murderer . . . this guy is dangerous.'

'Why do you always get to make up the story?' Christine asked.

'Because I'm good at it,' Sally said. 'I'll be in charge of the case and you can be my assistant . . .'

'You were in charge yesterday,' Christine said.

'That was different . . . that was Cowgirl . . .'

'I'll only play if we can be partners,' Christine said.

'Okay . . . we're partners.'

'Good.'

For a while Douglas seemed to be getting better and they made plans to rent a house at Bradley Beach for the summer. Then he got sick all over again and they cancelled their vacation. Mom and Daddy and Ma Fanny spoke in whispers and Sally began to wonder if Douglas might die. If he did she'd be an only child. She could have his bicycle. It was bigger than hers. But then she'd have to learn to ride a boy's bike.

Anyway, she didn't want him to die. And she knew she shouldn't be thinking that way. God could punish her for such evil thoughts. Besides, if Douglas died it wouldn't be fun like when her aunts and uncles and Granny Freedman had died. After their funerals they'd sat shivah for a week, at Sally's house. It was a Jewish custom, to help the family through those difficult first days following a loved one's death. Sally enjoyed sitting shivah very much. Every afternoon and evening friends and relatives would come to visit, bringing baskets of fruit and homemade cakes and cookies and boxes of candy from Barton's. And they would pinch Sally's cheeks, telling her how much she'd grown since the last funeral. Then they'd all sit around and talk and Mom would serve coffee. And as they left they'd always say, 'We must get together on happier occasions.' But they never did.

It seemed to Sally that somebody in her family was always dying. But they were much older or very sick and she didn't know them well enough to really care. The last time they'd sat shivah was in November when Ma Fanny got a letter telling her that Tante Rose and Lila were dead – killed in one of Hitler's concentration camps. And people who Sally had never seen before came to pay condolence calls. People from the old country, who had known Ma Fanny when she was just a girl, before she sailed to America on the banana boat. People who remembered Tante Rose and Lila.

With Douglas it would be different. It wouldn't be like a party at all. Everyone would cry and they would forget all about her. It would be even worse than now. She wished Douglas would hurry and get well so the family could have some time for her too.

When school ended Sally was sent to Day Camp at the Y. And in August Douglas was well again. Towards the end of the month Mom said, 'Daddy and I are going away for a few days.'

'Where to?' Sally asked. 'Bradley Beach?'

'No . . . Florida . . . Ma Fanny will take care of you and Douglas while we're gone.'

'But suppose Douglas gets sick again?'

'He won't . . . the doctor says he's doing fine and we'll just be gone a week . . . maybe less.'

'How will you get there?'

'On the train.'

'But Florida's very far, isn't it?'

'It's a day and a half on the train.'

Sally thought she might start to cry but she wasn't sure why.

'Don't look like that,' Mom said, putting an arm around her. 'Everything's going to be fine . . . and when we come home we may have a big surprise for you.'

'What kind of surprise?'

'If I tell you then it won't be a surprise.'

'Tell me anyway . . . please . . .'

'Can you promise to keep a secret?'

'I promise . . .'

'You won't tell *anybody*?'

Sally shook her head.

'Well . . . Daddy and I are going to look for an apartment in Miami Beach and if we find one then maybe we'll spend next winter there . . . and wouldn't that be fun?'

'You mean all of us?'

'You and Douglas and Ma Fanny and me . . . Daddy would have to stay at home to work, of course . . .'

'But what about school?'

'You'd go to school there . . . wouldn't that be exciting?'

'I don't know.'

'The doctors think it would be very good for Douglas . . . and you always have sore throats in the winter . . . so it would be good for you too.'

'Sometimes I get sore throats in the summer . . . remember the night the war was over . . . remember how my throat hurt then?'

'Yes, but winter is worse . . . and we don't want Douglas to be sick any more, do we?'

'You just said he's fine.'

'He's getting better . . .'

'You said *fine*.'

'I meant the infection is clearing up . . . but Douglas is very run-down . . . he's lost a lot of weight . . . you can see his ribs . . .'

'You always could.'

'But now you can count them . . . he needs time to recuperate . . .'

'I'm not sure I want to go.'

'Well . . . nothing's definite . . . we'll just see what happens. okay?'

'Okay.'

Sally and her friends were in the playhouse in Sally's backyard. It wasn't a baby kind of playhouse for dolls. It was a big sturdy house that her father and Douglas had built. It was painted white with green shutters. Inside there was a table, four chairs, a built-in wooden bed and three windows. There was a Dutch door, too.

Alice Ingram, who had a recreation room and four telephones at her house, didn't have anything to compare with Sally's playhouse. Alice and Christine were both in Sally's class at school. They sat next to each other on the wooden bed. Betsy, who lived across the street, was a year younger than the other girls but two heads taller. She sat on one of the chairs.

'Let's play Love and Romance today,' Alice said. 'Sally and Betsy can be the boys and me and Christine will be the girls.'

'No, thank you,' Betsy said. 'I was the boy last time.'

'That's because you're so tall,' Christine told her. 'You make a good boy.'

'Let's play War instead,' Sally suggested.

'Oh, I'm sick of playing War,' Alice said. 'I always end up being Hitler!'

'Well, you can't expect me to be Hitler,' Sally said. 'I'm Jewish.'

'So . . . everybody expects me to be the boy and I'm really a girl,' Betsy argued.

'That's different!' Sally said. 'But if you don't want to play War I have another idea . . .'

'What?' Alice Ingram asked.

'We can play Concentration Camp instead. And nobody has to be Hitler because he is away on business.'

212

'How do you play?' Betsy asked.

'The usual way . . .' Sally answered. 'First I tell you who you are and then I make up the story . . . Alice, you can be Lila . . .'

'Who's she?' Alice asked.

'This beautiful woman who gets captured and sent to Dachau.'

'What's that?'

'It's the concentration camp where the story takes place.'

'Oh.'

'And Betsy, you can be Tante Rose, Lila's mother . . .'

'Why should I have to be Alice's mother . . . I'm younger . . .'

'Because you're taller . . . now just shut up and listen . . .'

'I don't see why we always have to play Sally's stories,' Betsy whined.

'Because she's good at making them up,' Christine said. 'And besides, it's *her* playhouse.'

'I'll play,' Alice said, 'as long as I can be Lila . . . you did say she was beautiful, didn't you?'

'Yes, very . . . we've got pictures of her. She has long, dark hair and big eyes.'

'Is her mother beautiful too?' Betsy asked.

'Of course. And she's not even *that* old because she had Lila when she was just sixteen.'

'My sister's sixteen,' Betsy said.

'I know . . . I know . . .' Sally was anxious to get on with the game.

'Who am I supposed to be?' Christine asked.

'You can be the concentration camp guard. You hand the pretend soap to Tante Rose and Lila and tell them to go to the showers.'

'Why do they get *pretend* soap?'

'Because it's a trick. They're not really going to get showers, they're going to get killed in a big gas oven.'

'I'm going home,' Betsy said. 'I don't like this game.'

'It is kind of scary,' Christine said. 'I'd rather play Love and Romance.'

'If we do, then I'll stay,' Betsy said.

'Let's take a vote,' Christine said. 'All in favour of Concentration Camp, raise your hands.'

Sally and Alice raised their hands.

'All in favour of Love and Romance, raise yours . . .' Christine and Betsy raised theirs. 'It's a tie.'

'Oh, all right . . .' Sally said, 'we'll play Detective instead. That way nobody wins.'

Later, after Alice and Betsy went home, Christine and Sally sat on the glider swing. 'How long will your parents be in Florida?' Christine asked.

'A week . . . they're looking for an apartment.'

'You're moving?'

'No, silly . . . I'd never move . . . it's just for next winter . . . so Douglas doesn't get sick in the cold weather. And if you tell anybody anything about it I'll kill you . . . it's supposed to be a secret.'

'Who would I tell?'

'I don't know . . . just promise that you won't.'

'Okay . . . I promise . . . I've got to go now . . .'

Sally walked Christine to her bicycle.

'You know who goes to Florida in the winter?' Christine asked.

'No . . . who?'

'Millionaires! I read it in my mother's magazine.' She coasted down Sally's driveway.

'Hey . . . my father's just a dentist,' Sally called, 'not a millionaire . . .'

Christine laughed and waved.

'Hey . . . remember your promise . . . not a word to anyone.'

'My lips are sealed,' Christine called back.

Bounce . . . catch . . . bounce . . . catch . . . Sally was tossing

214

her Spalding ball against the side of the house. The supper that Ma Fanny was cooking smelled good. Sally guessed it was roast chicken. Bounce . . . catch . . . bounce . . . catch . . . She had time for just a short story before Ma Fanny called her in to eat. At least when she made up the stories inside her head she didn't have to worry about who would play what. That was such a waste of time. Let's see, Sally thought, thinking up a title.

Sally Saves Lila

It is during the war. President Roosevelt asks for volunteers to go to Europe to help.

Sally is the first on line.

How old are you? the Head of Volunteers asks.

I'm ten, Sally tells her, *but I'm smart . . . and strong . . . and tough.*

Yes, I can see that, the Head says. *Okay, I am going to take a chance and send you . . . your ship leaves in an hour.*

Thank you, Sally says, *you won't be sorry you chose me.*

Good luck, the Head says.

Sally salutes, slings her duffle bag over her shoulder and boards her ship.

When she arrives in Europe she realizes she has forgotten her toothpaste. She goes into the first Rexall's she sees and selects a tube of Ipana, for the smile of beauty. Then she feels hungry. It must be lunchtime. She finds a deli and orders a salami sandwich on rye and a Coke to go. She takes her lunch to the park across the street and finds a sunny bench. She unwraps her sandwich but before she takes her first bite she hears someone crying.

Sally investigates. After all, she has come to Europe to help. It is a woman, huddled on the ground next to a tall tree. Her hands cover her face, muffling her sobs. She is dressed in rags.

Sally goes to her side. *Are you hungry?* she asks.

The woman does not respond so Sally holds out her

sandwich. *It's salami*, she says. *Doesn't it smell good?*

Kosher? the woman asks.

Yes, Sally tells her. *Kosher salami is the only kind I like.*

Me too, the woman says. She reaches for the sandwich and wolfs it down, her back to Sally.

How long has it been since you've eaten? Sally asks.

Days . . . weeks . . . months . . . I don't know any more.

Where do you live?

I have no home . . . no family . . . no friends . . . all gone . . . gone . . . Finally she turns around and faces Sally. Even though her hair is filthy and her big eyes are red and swollen and most of her teeth are missing, Sally knows her instantly. *Lila!*

At the sound of her name the woman tries to stand up and run but she is so weak she falls to the ground, beating it with her fists. *I knew you would catch me . . . sooner or later . . . I knew I could never escape . . . but I won't go back to Dachau . . . not ever . . . I'll die right here . . . right now . . .* She pulls a knife from her pocket and aims it at her heart.

No! Sally says, springing to her feet. She wrestles the knife away from Lila. *You don't understand . . . I'm here to help . . .*

You are not with the Gestapo? Lila asks.

No, I'm with the Volunteers of America. I'm Sally J. Freedman, from New Jersey . . . I'm your cousin, once removed . . .

You mean you're Louise's daughter?

Sally nods.

You mean you're Tante Fanny's granddaughter?

Sally nods again.

I can't believe it . . . I can't believe it . . . just when I'd given up all hope. Sally and Lila embrace.

Where's Tante Rose? Sally asks.

Lila begins to cry again. *My mother is dead. We dug the hole together. For five months, every night, we dug the hole . . . until finally it was ready . . . and just when we were going to escape they caught Mama and sent her to the showers. That night I crawled through the hole myself and came out in the forest and I ran and ran*

and I've been running ever since . . . but not any more . . . I'm too
tired . . . too tired to run . . .

It's all over now, Sally tells Lila. *You're safe. I'm taking you*
home with me. You can share my room. My father will make you
new teeth. He's a very good dentist.

How can I ever thank you? Lila asks.

Don't even try . . . I'm just doing my job.

The next day, after Lila has a bath and shampoo, a good
night's sleep and a big breakfast in bed, she and Sally board the
ship for New Jersey. On the way Lila develops a sore throat and
a fever of 103°. Sally puts her to bed, gives her ginger ale to sip
and keeps a cold cloth on her forehead. She sits at Lila's
bedside and tells her stories until Lila is well again.

When they get home Sally is a hero. There is a big parade in
her honour on Broad Street and everyone cheers. The people
watching from the windows in the office buildings throw
confetti, the way Sally did when Admiral Halsey came home at
the end of the war.

That night, Sally was soaking in the tub trying to keep cool.
When she and Douglas were small they played in the tub
together on hot summer days. But Douglas didn't let her see
him undressed any more. She lay back in the tub and squeezed
her sponge. The water trickled on her legs and belly.

There were four bedrooms in Sally's house but just that one
bathroom, unless you counted the one that was off the kitchen,
and Sally didn't. That one had only a sink and toilet, while this
one had a tub, a separate shower, a hamper, a mirrored cabinet,
plus a sink and toilet. The tile was lavender, with black trim.
The wallpaper matched and all the woodwork was painted
black, including the door. Sally loved it.

Her father didn't. He said it looked like a bordello. 'What's
that?' Sally had asked at the time. 'Never mind,' Daddy and
Mom had answered together. Then Mom went on to say,
'There's not much you can do with lavender tile, Arnold . . .
beside, lavender and black are the newest colours but if you feel

that strongly about it we can always rip out the tile and fixtures and start all over . . .' Then Daddy said, 'Hell, no . . . I'll get used to it in time . . . I guess.'

The only thing wrong with the bathroom was you couldn't powder in it because the powder flew all over and made the black woodwork dusty and Mom didn't like that.

The phone rang as Sally was drying herself. If you didn't dry carefully between your toes you could get something called Athlete's Foot and your skin would peel off.

'Sally . . .' Ma Fanny called, 'hurry . . . it's your mother on the line.'

Sally jumped into her robe and dashed to the telephone

'Hi, honey . . . how're you doing?' Mom asked.

'Okay . . . how's Florida . . . and when are you coming home?'

'Day after tomorrow and it's beautiful!'

'Did you find a place?'

'Yes, just this afternoon.'

'Then we're really going?'

'Most likely . . . but the lease isn't signed yet so don't tell anyone.'

'I won't . . . I won't . . . what's it like?'

'Oh, it's very interesting. How's Douglas?'

'He's fine.'

'Good . . . put him on and then you can say hello to Daddy.'

The next day Sally told Christine, 'They found a place. My mother says it's really interesting.'

'When are you going?'

'I don't know . . . when it gets cold, I guess . . . nothing's definite yet.'

Sally ate lunch at Christine's house. Mrs Mackler made them bologna sandwiches with mayonnaise and lettuce and thick chocolate malteds to drink. Sally wondered if she'd dropped an egg in while they weren't looking the way Ma Fanny did.

Mrs Mackler said, 'I heard you're going to Florida.'

218

'You did?' Sally gave Christine a *look*.

'Or am I wrong?' Mrs Mackler asked.

'Wrong?'

'Yes, wrong.'

'Well, I don't know . . . I don't know anything about any of that.'

'Oh, I see.'

After lunch, when they went outside, Sally told Christine, 'Next time don't *seal* your lips . . . *sew* them!'

And Christine said, 'Oh, Sally . . . I only told my mother . . . I can keep a secret as good as you . . . honest!'

three

'I had to pay under the table,' Sally's father said, 'but I think it's worth it . . . besides, I had no choice . . . there's so little available.'

They were having Sunday supper at Aunt Bette and Uncle Jack's place, which was over a beauty parlour on the other side of town. Sally tried to picture her father under the table in Miami Beach. Probably the apartment landlord, Mr Koner, was with him. Daddy would take out his money and hand it to Mr Koner. He'd count it, nod, and then they'd both crawl out from under the table together. It didn't make much sense to Sally but she supposed that was the way they did business in Florida.

'Finish the tongue, Sally,' her mother said.

'I'm eating the potato salad first.'

'Finish the tongue, *then* eat the potato salad.'

'Do I have to?'

'You know the poor children are starving in Europe . . . besides, Aunt Bette will be insulted if you don't finish the tongue. She made it herself.'

Aunt Bette was learning to cook now that Ma Fanny, who lived with her and Uncle Jack, was going to Florida. Ma Fanny had always done the cooking. Aunt Bette was gathering recipes on her own these days and trying them out on the family. The tongue was covered with a sweet sauce that had raisins floating in it. Sally couldn't stand the idea of eating some cow's tongue. She looked at Aunt Bette and tried to smile. 'I like the potato salad a lot.'

'Ma Fanny made that,' Aunt Bette said, softly.

'Oh.'

'I'll finish your tongue,' Douglas said. 'I think it's great.'

Aunt Bette beamed.

Sally handed him her plate and was grateful when her aunt changed the subject. 'I still think you should consider getting them there in time to start school,' she told Daddy and Mom. 'It's difficult enough to adjust to a new school situation without coming in mid-term . . .'

'On the other hand,' Daddy said, 'I really don't want them there during the hurricane season . . . it's too risky.'

'So when do you think we should leave?' Mom asked.

'Mid-October . . . that way the danger of the storms will be over and we can still get our money's worth.'

'But we'll come home as soon as winter's over, right?' Sally asked.

'No . . . I think we'll stay and finish the school year,' Mom said. 'Anyway, you'll probably like it so much you'll never want to come home. Just wait till you see those palm trees!'

'But I'll miss Daddy and Aunt Bette and Uncle Jack and Christine and my bed and the bathroom and my other friends and my playhouse and school and . . .'

They all started to laugh. Even Douglas laughed, with his mouth full of food. Sally hated it when the family thought she'd said something funny when she was being serious.

'And I'll miss you, too,' Daddy told her, 'and Douglas and Mom and Ma Fanny . . . but I'll fly down whenever I can.'

'On a plane?' Sally asked.

'He hasn't got wings,' Douglas said and they all laughed again.

'But planes crash,' Sally told her father.

'So do cars . . . but we ride in them every day.'

'But it's more dangerous up in the sky,' Sally argued.

'Not true,' Douglas said. 'You're a lot better off up there.'

'Douglas is right,' Uncle Jack said. 'Planes are more safe than cars.'

'Just as long as I don't have to try it,' Mom said. 'I'll leave the flying to the more adventurous members of the family.'

'Louise . . .' Daddy said, 'I wish you wouldn't talk that way in front of Sally. How will she ever learn to be adventurous?'

'Little girls don't need to be adventurous,' Mom said.

'But I want to be adventurous,' Sally told her.

'Fat chance!' Douglas said. 'You're scared of your own shadow.'

'I am not!'

'So how come you won't go down to the basement by yourself?'

'That's different,' Sally said. 'That has nothing to do with my shadow.'

'That's enough, children!' Mom said.

Aunt Bette and Uncle Jack looked at each other.

Sally turned to her father. 'Will you come for my birthday?'

'I'll try.'

'You'll have to promise!'

'I'll try my very, very best . . . how's that?'

'Okay . . . I guess.'

Mom took Sally and Douglas to their father's office to have their teeth checked and cleaned before they left for Florida. Ma Fanny didn't have to worry about her teeth because they weren't real. At night she took them out and soaked them in a glass. They clicked when she talked.

Sometimes, when Sally came to her father's office, Miss Kay, Daddy's nurse-secretary, would let her sit at the typewriter, but today she was busy so Sally had to wait with everyone else.

She was glad her father was a dentist. It was fun to have him clean her teeth even though the little brush tickled her gums and made her wiggle around. She'd never had a cavity and Christine said she was really lucky because she had had twenty of them and it didn't tickle to have them filled.

While he cleaned her teeth, Daddy sang to her. He always sang while he worked. He made up the songs as he went along. He could also whistle just like a bird. So Sally gave him the name, Doey-bird. Douglas said it was dumb to name a grown man Doey-bird but Sally's father didn't mind. She liked giving special people special names. She was the one who'd started calling her grandmother Ma Fanny and now everybody called her that. Douglas was just jealous because she hadn't given him a special name too.

If Sally could sing like her father, or even whistle, she wouldn't be in the listener group in music class. It wasn't much fun to mouth the words while practically everyone else got to sing them. Sometimes Sally would forget just to listen and she would sing too. Then Miss Vickers would ask, 'Sally Freedman . . . are you singing out loud?' and Sally would go back to mouthing the words.

After her father finished with her, it was Douglas's turn. Sally hung around until Miss Kay asked, 'Would you like to type for a while?' She gave Sally some yellow paper and adjusted the stool so she could reach the keys. As she typed she heard her father start another song.

Now that he'd had a series of whirlpool treatments, Douglas could use his hands to build things again. He still had to spend a lot of time resting, but instead of lying on his bed reading his favourite magazines, *Popular Science, Popular Mechanics* and *Model Airplane News,* he was making cartoon characters out of eggshells. He had a whole row of them standing on a shelf in his bookcase – Mickey Mouse, Pluto, Donald Duck, Bugs Bunny. Sally liked to watch Douglas blow the insides out of eggshells.

222

And she liked the cakes that Mom and Ma Fanny baked to use up the eggs, too.

As soon as Mom let him go down to his basement workshop again, Douglas abandoned his eggshells in favour of his oscilloscope. He was determined to finish it before they left. It was some kind of machine that let you see electrical waves on a green screen. Sally didn't understand how it worked but everyone else was impressed that Douglas had built it himself.

Mom had a special lamp installed over the workbench. It was supposed to give Douglas extra vitamin D, like sunshine, until he got to Miami Beach, where they had the real thing. Douglas got a very nice tan on the back of his neck.

During the last week in September Sally invited six school friends home for a farewell lunch. Her mother fixed egg salad sandwiches in different shapes, but Alice Ingram said she was allergic to eggs so Sally's mother made a grilled cheese bun for her. Christine gave Sally a small silver pin with two Scottie dogs on it and said, 'This one's you and this one's me and we're together . . . see . . . best friends for always.' They promised to write at least twice a week.

On October eighth, Sally said goodbye to her classmates and teachers and got her transfer card from the school office. She and Douglas spent the next week at home, in isolation, because Mom didn't want to take any chances that they might come down with something before their trip.

Aunt Bette and Uncle Jack gave up their apartment and arranged to move into Sally's house so her father wouldn't be lonely while the family was away. Sally was glad about that. She didn't like the idea of Daddy living all alone.

It was hardest to say goodbye to him. She sat on his lap with her head on his chest and played with the curly dark hairs on his arm.

'I'm going to finish the basement while you're away,' Daddy told her.

'You are?'

'Yes . . . that's going to be my special project . . . and when you come back we'll have a recreation room.'

'Like Alice Ingram's?'

'I've never seen hers.'

'It's nice,' Sally said. 'Can I have a party in ours?'

'As many as you want.'

'I hope the time goes fast,' Sally said. 'I hope it flies by . . .'

'It will. You'll see. This is going to be an adventure . . .'

'How do you know?' Sally asked.

'Because every new experience is an adventure. Life's full of them. Do you think you can remember that?'

'I'll try . . . but I'll miss you, Doey-bird.'

Daddy hugged her. 'And I'll miss my little gal, Sal.'

'You're so silly!'

'So are you.'

'I wish Mom was silly.'

'She loves you . . . you know that . . . not everybody can be silly.'

'I know . . . but I wish it anyway . . . at least sometimes.'

'You take good care of her, okay?'

'Okay . . .' Sally said. 'Are you ready for your treatment?'

'You know I am.'

'Ready . . . set . . . go . . .' Sally gave him a sliding kiss, three quick hugs and finished with a butterfly kiss on his nose.

'Don't forget to write to me,' Daddy said.

'How could I forget?'

Daddy looked away then. He had tears in his eyes. Sally pretended not to notice. She was having enough trouble holding back her own.

four

They left on a Saturday morning, from the railroad station in Newark, on a train called *The Champion*. Douglas was

224

disappointed. He'd wanted to fly. 'Flying is fine for people in a hurry,' Daddy had explained, 'but it's much more expensive and you'll have a good time this way.'

Sally was relieved. She didn't want to fly anywhere but if she told that to her father he might get the wrong idea and think she wasn't adventurous after all. Why wasn't Douglas afraid of anything? That didn't seem fair. Sally felt safe on trains. She was used to them. It bothered her that in this respect she was like her mother.

Daddy came on board, carrying a wicker lunch basket, and helped them get settled in their seats, with Sally and Douglas facing Mom and Ma Fanny. Then he kissed them goodbye for the hundredth time and went back to the platform where he waited with Aunt Bette and Uncle Jack. When the train started Sally waved and blew kisses. And she kept waving until she couldn't see them any more.

'I'll trade seats with you,' Sally said to Douglas.

'Not now . . . we've only been gone five minutes.'

'You promised you'd share the window seat with me.'

'I'll switch in an hour.'

'Make it half an hour and I won't nudge you.'

'Sit back in your seat, Sally,' Mom said, sounding sharp.

'What for?'

'Because I said so.'

'But I like to sit up . . .'

'Stop that right now,' Mom said, 'or you won't get the window seat at all.'

'Stop what?'

'She can have mine,' Ma Fanny said. 'What do I need with a window seat?'

'No, Ma . . . she can stay right where she is.'

'Yeah,' Douglas muttered.

'Who asked you?' Sally said. She was annoyed at Mom. If Ma Fanny wanted to switch places what did Mom care? Sally turned around and adjusted the white linen napkin clipped to the top of her seat so that her head rested against it. The seats were soft and comfortable, not like the hard ones on the train to New York. These cushions were covered in blue velvet.

Ma Fanny pulled out her knitting. She was the fastest knitter Sally had ever seen. Her needles clicked together as the wool flew off her fingers. Mom knitted more slowly, but her sweaters turned out just as good. Ma Fanny had taught Sally to knit. She could do knit-one-purl-one, and knit-two-purl-two, but her squares always came out with holes in the middle where she'd dropped stitches by mistake.

The train picked up speed and Sally and Douglas watched the scenery whiz by. After a while Douglas took out the latest issue of *Popular Mechanics* and Sally browsed through the two new Nancy Drew books Aunt Bette had given to her as a going-away present. She'd been really surprised to find them inside the pretty package because Aunt Bette didn't approve of Nancy Drews. She thought Sally should be reading the books about the prairie girl.

Sally wrote Christine a postcard.

Dear Christine,
   We are on the train now. We've been gone about an hour. That's about all that's new. Write soon.
   Love and other indoor sports,
   Your very best friend,
   Sally Jane Freedman (The First)

Sally didn't know what *Love and other indoor sports* meant but she used to have a babysitter named Carolyn who signed all her letters that way. Sally didn't like Carolyn because she was always writing letters. She never had time to play games. One time, when Carolyn left the room for a few minutes, Sally looked at one of her letters and saw how it was signed. When Carolyn came back Sally asked, 'What does *Love and other indoor sports* mean?'

'Have you been reading my letters?' Carolyn asked.

'No.'

'Then how do you know about *Love and other indoor sports*?'

'I saw it, on the bottom of your letter, but I didn't read anything else . . . I promise . . .'

'I hope you're telling the truth,' Carolyn said, 'because you know what happens to nosy little girls, don't you?'

'No . . . what?'

'Nothing very good!'

'Can't you just tell me what *Love and other indoor sports* means?'

Carolyn laughed. 'Some day you'll find out.'

So far she hadn't. But Christine wouldn't know that Sally didn't know.

They ate lunch in their seats. The wicker basket was filled with roast chicken sandwiches, chocolate chip cookies and fresh fruit. When they'd finished, Ma Fanny offered some of the extras to the soldiers sitting behind them.

After lunch Mom and Ma Fanny dozed off and Sally and Douglas walked to the club car. It was fixed up like Alice Ingram's recreation room, with a bar, sofas, and tables and chairs. Douglas bought two Cokes and he and Sally sat at a card table and played a few hands of Go Fish. Douglas won every time.

'Are you glad we're going to Florida?' Sally asked.

'I don't know yet.'

'Same here.'

Douglas reminded Sally of a grasshopper. His legs were growing very long and the shape of his face was long too, and thin, with big brown eyes. He had very nice hair, blond and wavy, the kind Sally would have liked because then Mom wouldn't have to set hers in rag curlers each night.

'Did you know when I first got my kidney infection it burned when I pissed?'

'It did?' Douglas was always trying to shock her with bad words.

'Yeah . . . something awful . . . I wanted to climb the walls.'

227

'You said funny things when you had your fever,' Sally told him.

'Like what, for instance?'

'Oh, I don't remember exactly . . . a lot of mumbo-jumbo stuff . . .'

'No kidding?'

'Honest.'

'Could you make anything out?' Douglas asked.

'No . . . I didn't get to listen that much . . . I was at school all day and then they wouldn't let me in your room most of the time . . .' Sally took a sip of her Coke and promptly got the hiccups.

'You shouldn't drink that stuff.'

'But I like it.'

'Yeah . . . but you get the hiccups every single time.'

'They'll go away.'

'I thought I was going to die,' Douglas said. 'And I didn't even care . . . that's how bad I felt.'

'I thought so too . . . for a little while.'

'No kidding?'

'Really.'

'Were you sorry?'

'Well, naturally . . . who'd want to be an only child?'

'I figured you'd inherit my bicycle.'

'Why would I even want your bicycle?'

'It's newer than yours . . . and bigger . . .'

'So . . . I wouldn't want you to die just because of that . . . don't you think I have any feelings?' She hiccupped loudly and the bartender started to laugh.

When they got back to their seats Mom was still dozing and Ma Fanny was reading *The Forward*, her Yiddish newspaper. Across the aisle and two seats ahead of them was a Negro woman with two little boys and a baby girl. The boys had been watching Sally all morning and now she took some cookies out of the basket and crossed the aisle, offering them to the children.

228

'How nice,' their mother said. 'Say, *thank you*, Kevin and Kenneth.'

'Thank you, Kevin and Kenneth,' they said at the same time, making Sally laugh. She wasn't as interested in them as she was in the baby, who sat on her mother's lap.

'My name's Sally Freedman and I'm going to Miami Beach because my brother Douglas, who's sitting right over there, has been sick with a kidney infection . . .'

'Oh, that's too bad. I'm Mrs Williamson and this is Kevin and this is Kenneth.' She touched each boy on the head as she said his name. 'We're going to Miami, too. We're going to visit our granny, who's never seen Loreen.' She held up the baby.

'She's so cute,' Sally said. 'How old is she?'

'Eight months.'

'Hi, Loreen . . .' Sally said. The baby smiled at her. 'I think she likes me. Can I hold her?'

'Sure . . . if you sit down. Kevin, come sit by me and we'll let Sally hold Loreen for a while.'

'You'll be sorry,' Kevin said. 'She makes pooeys.'

'So did you when you were a baby,' his mother reminded him.

Sally got comfortable with Loreen on her lap. As soon as she did the baby grabbed a fistful of her hair and tried to get it into her mouth.

'No, no . . .' Sally said, forcing the baby's fist open.

'And she eats hair,' Kevin said. 'That's how dumb she is.'

Loreen laughed and made gurgling noises.

'She's teething,' Mrs Williamson said. 'Here . . . give her this.' She passed a teething ring to Sally. Loreen put it in her mouth and went, 'Ga-ga.'

'That's all she ever says,' Kenneth told Sally.

Sally held Loreen until the baby fell asleep. Then she gave her back to Mrs Williamson and went to her own seat.

'What were you doing over there?' Mom asked.

'Playing with the baby.'

'You shouldn't be bothering them.'

'I wasn't . . . I was helping . . .'

'From now on just stay in your own seat and read a book or something . . . it's almost time for dinner.'

'Okay . . .' Sally said.

They ate in the dining car, and after took a walk to the club car, where they played checkers. Then it was time to get ready for bed. Sally, Mom and Ma Fanny changed into night clothes in the Ladies' Room and when Sally brushed her teeth Mom warned her not to put her mouth on the fountain when she rinsed. 'You could get *trench mouth* that way, God forbid.' Sally was careful.

There were sleeping compartments on *The Champion* but Sally and her family slept right in their seats. The porter gave them each a pillow and a blanket and showed them how to tilt their chairs way back. The lights in the car dimmed and the steady rhythm of the train soon put Sally to sleep.

She half awoke sometime in the middle of the night, vaguely aware that the train had stopped and that Ma Fanny was snoring softly.

In the morning Loreen and her family were gone. 'But they're going to Miami too,' Sally said. 'Mrs Williamson told me.'

'They had to change cars,' Mom said.

'But why?'

'Because they're Negro.'

'So?'

'We're in a different part of the country now, Sally . . . and coloured people don't ride with white people here.'

'That's not fair.'

'Maybe not . . . but that's the way it is.'

Sally was bored without Loreen, and angry that Mom didn't seem to care that the Williamsons had to change cars. The day dragged on and on. Breakfast turned into lunch and lunch turned into supper. Douglas kept pointing out the change in the scenery. They had to be getting close, he said. There were palm trees everywhere. Sally was tired of just sitting. She wished she could get off the train and run around.

Finally the conductor called, 'Next stop . . . Miami . . . Miami, Florida . . .'

Finally they were there.

Sally stepped off the train, stretched, and yawned loudly. Now her adventure would begin. But what did that mean? Maybe I don't want an adventure, Sally thought. Maybe I'd just rather go home. Her stomach rolled over, and tears came to her eyes. 'I want to go home,' she said, but no one heard. They were too busy trying to find a porter.

five

They took a taxi to 1330 Pennsylvania Avenue, a pink stucco, U-shaped building, with a goldfish pool in front. Their apartment was ugly. Ugly and bare and damp. Mom opened the windows while Sally went looking for the bedrooms, but all she could find was a tiny kitchen, a breakfast nook, a bathroom and an alcove.

'I thought you said this place was interesting,' Sally said to her mother.

'And it is,' Mom answered. 'Look at this . . .' Sally followed her into the alcove and watched as Mom opened a door in the wall and pulled down a bed. 'You see . . . it fits right into the wall . . . it's called a Murphy bed . . . isn't that clever . . . and interesting?' But she didn't sound as if she really thought so herself.

'Who sleeps on that?'

'Me and Ma Fanny,' Mom said. 'You and Douglas get the day beds in the living room.'

'You and Ma Fanny are going to sleep together . . . in the same bed?'

'Why not?' Ma Fanny asked. 'I don't take up much room.'

'But what about when Daddy comes?'

'Oh, well . . . when Daddy comes Ma Fanny will sleep on the bed that's tucked away *under* your day bed. We have plenty of room . . . plenty . . .' Mom brushed some loose hairs away from her forehead.

Sally thought of the four big bedrooms in her house in New Jersey. Of her own room with twin beds so she could have friends sleep overnight. And then she remembered how Christine had said that only millionaires spend the winter in Florida and she felt like laughing, not because it was funny but because if Christine could see this place she'd change her mind pretty quick.

'So what do you think?' Mom asked Ma Fanny.

'With new slipcovers and curtains, a few plants, some knick-knacks, a throw rug here and there, a picture or two on the wall . . . not bad. Maybe not worth what you had to pay under the table, but not bad. It could be worse.'

'We had no choice,' Mom said, her voice breaking. 'Everything's so scarce right now.'

'Don't worry,' Ma Fanny said, touching Mom's arm, 'as soon as my Singer gets here you'll never recognize the place.'

'Where's the telephone?' Douglas asked.

'We ordered one,' Mom said, 'but it takes a long time . . . there's one in the lobby for emergencies though.'

Douglas nodded.

'At home we have two,' Sally said, suddenly angry. Why were they pretending? Why didn't one of them just admit the truth. This place was a dump. Then she added, 'And we have rose-beige carpeting too!'

'Why don't you just shut up?' Douglas said.

'Who's going to make me?'

'Enough!' Mom said. 'It's been a long trip. Let's get ready for bed. We'll all feel better in the morning.'

It was hard to fall asleep even though Sally felt tired. She tried a story inside her head but that didn't work either. She wasn't used to the smells here, to the strange night noises, to the day bed or having Douglas in the same room, breathing heavily. She missed her father. She wished he was there to tuck her in, although she wasn't under any covers. It was too warm. Just a sheet was more than enough. She wished Daddy was there to give her a treatment.

Two days later Sally got ready for school. She wore her red loafers, her Gibson Girl skirt and blouse and the pin Christine had given to her. Mom braided her hair, then pinned it on top of her head in a coronet because it was too warm to let it hang loose. Ma Fanny kissed her cheek and said, 'Such a shana maidelah.' Sally understood Ma Fanny's Yiddish expressions well enough. Shana maidelah meant pretty girl.

Outside, Sally stopped for a look at the goldfish pool, then she and her mother walked up the street, past yellow and blue and other pink stucco apartment houses.

'One of the reasons we wanted this apartment so badly is that it's very close to school,' Mom said. 'Just one block up and two blocks over . . .' At the corner they crossed the street. 'That's where Douglas will go,' Mom said, pointing to Miami Beach Junior-Senior High.

'When will he start?' Sally asked.

'Tomorrow, I think. First I want Dr Spear to give him a good going-over.'

'Who's Dr Spear?'

'He's going to be our doctor here . . . he was highly recommended . . . he's the best . . .'

'Do I really need this jacket?' Sally asked. 'It's so warm out.'

'I guess not. Give it to me and I'll take it home.'

Sally wriggled out of it.

'You're not nervous, are you?' Mom asked.

'No . . . why should I be nervous?'

'I don't know . . . you didn't eat any breakfast and you've been picking at your cuticles.'

'I'm not used to eating here yet and my cuticles itch . . . that's why I pick at them.'

'I know you'll do just fine,' Mom said, 'so don't be scared.'

'Who's scared?' Sally snapped a big red flower off a bush next to the sidewalk.

'That's a hibiscus,' Mom said.

'It's pretty.' She tucked it behind one ear and twirled around. 'How do I look?'

'Just like Esther Williams,' Mom said.

Sally smiled. Esther Williams was her favourite movie actress. Some day she was going to swim just like her, with her hair in a coronet and a flower behind her ear. Swimming along underwater, always smiling, with beautiful straight white teeth and shiny red lipstick. Esther Williams never got water up her nose or had to spit while she swam, like Sally, who didn't like to get her face wet in the first place. And Esther Williams never splashed either. Not even when she dived off the high board. You'd never know you had to kick to stay afloat from watching Esther Williams. And when she swam in the movies there was always beautiful music in the background and handsome men standing around, waiting. It would be great fun to be Esther Williams!

'This is it,' Mom said. 'Central Beach Elementary School . . .'

'It doesn't look like a school,' Sally said and her stomach growled. 'Oh, be quiet,' she told herself.

'It doesn't look like your school at home,' Mom said.

'That's what I meant.'

'It's Spanish style . . . see the red tile roof . . . and all the archways . . . it's very pretty . . .'

'But it's so big,' Sally said. At home there was just one class for each grade. She knew all the teachers and they knew her. She'd had the same kids in her class since kindergarten. This school was one floor, but it extended for a full block. It was U-shaped too, and made of white stucco. 'And look at all those trailers,' Sally said. 'What do you suppose they're for?'

'They're portable classrooms,' Mom told her. 'The schools down here are crowded.'

234

'A person could get lost in a school like this.'

'You'll find your way around in no time.'

'And it looks about five hundred years old, too.'

'I doubt that it's *that* old,' Mom said, looking around. 'Now, first of all we've got to find the office.' She stopped a freckle-faced boy. 'Can you tell us where the office is?'

'Yes, ma'am . . .' he said, 'right around the corridor and second door to your left.'

'Thank you.'

'He called you *ma'am*,' Sally said.

'Yes, he was very polite.'

'That sounds so funny.'

'I think it sounds nice.'

They found the office and Mom presented Sally's transfer card and school records. The clerk said, 'Well, Sally . . . you'll be in 5B, Miss Swetnick's class . . . and she's one of our nicest fifth-grade teachers. I know you'll like her.'

'Thank you,' Sally said, wondering if she should add *ma'am* but deciding against it.

'Now then . . .' the clerk went on, 'the nurse's office is around the corridor to your right, past the portables and the library, until you come to the art room, then turn left and continue down that corridor until you come to the fourth room on your right . . . it says *Nurse* on the door . . . got that?'

'I think so,' Mom said.

'Why do I have to go the nurse?' Sally asked.

'It's just a formality,' the clerk told her.

The nurse was fat, with bleached blonde hair in an upsweep. Sally knew it was bleached because the black roots were showing along the part, like when Mom needed a touch-up. She had two chins and a huge bosom, the kind that went straight across her chest with no space in between. 'Good morning . . .' she sang, taking the folder from Mom. 'And who do we have here?' She looked inside the folder. 'Sally Freedman?' she asked, as if she were guessing.

'Yes,' Sally said.

'Just get in from New York?'

'New Jersey . . .' How did she know?

'Okay, Sally . . . your mother can wait right here while you come with me . . .' They went into another room. It smelled like alcohol. There were small cots lined up against the wall, with white curtains between them. In the corner was a doctor's scale and next to it, a glass cabinet filled with bandages, bottles and instruments. Sally hoped she wasn't going to get a shot.

'Shoes off, Sally . . . and step on the scale,' the nurse said. As she weighed her she added, 'Don't eat much, do you?'

'Enough,' Sally answered.

'Not very tall either.' The nurse adjusted the marker so that it just touched the top of Sally's head.

'I'm still growing,' Sally said.

'Let's hope so.'

After that the nurse handed Sally a piece of cardboard. 'Cover your left eye, look at the chart on the wall and tell me which way the E is pointing . . . up, down, left or right . . .'

'Don't you have the alphabet here? At home we have charts with all the letters . . .'

'Up, down, left or right . . . if you don't know your left from your right just point . . .'

'I know my left from my right,' Sally said and she began to read the chart. 'Up . . . left . . . right . . . up . . . down . . .'

When both her eyes had been tested and the nurse was satisfied that Sally could see, she said, 'Now have a seat and unbraid your hair.'

'But my mother just fixed it for me . . .'

'And it looks very pretty . . . but I have to check your head before you can be admitted to class, so the sooner you take down those braids the sooner you can get going . . .'

Sally reached up and unpinned her coronet. Then she took the rubber bands off the ends of her braids and unwound them.

The nurse started picking through Sally's hair, messing it up. Sally hoped Mom had a hair brush in her purse. 'Oh, oh . . .' the nurse said, clicking her tongue against the roof of her mouth. 'You've got them.'

'Got what?'

'Nits.'

'In my hair?'

'Where else?'

'What are they?'

'Lice eggs . . . I can't admit you to school with them . . . you'll spread them everywhere . . .'

'But how could I have them? My hair's very clean . . . my mother washed it last night and gave me a vinegar rinse besides . . .'

'No matter . . . shampooing can't get them out . . . you need something much stronger . . . they're nasty little critters. Put your shoes back on while I tell your mother what to do.' She walked out of the room.

Sally jumped into her loafers and listened at the doorway.

'I've never heard anything so outrageous!' Mom said. 'I've always kept my children immaculate. Anyone with eyes can see that. Why, just last night I shampooed her hair . . .'

'Look, Mrs Freedman . . . don't take this personally . . . you've been travelling . . . you're in another part of the country . . . she could have picked them up anywhere . . . it's very common . . . that's why we check the new children so carefully . . . she's not alone . . .'

Mom shook her head. 'You don't understand.'

'Take her home and use the treatment,' the nurse said, 'and in a few days I'll be happy to check her again.'

When Sally heard the word *treatment* her throat tightened and tears came to her eyes.

'I hate it here!' Sally and Mom were walking home from school. 'I hate the nurse and the school and Miami Beach!' She bit her lip to keep from crying.

Mom said, 'Listen, honey . . . that nurse is crazy . . . she doesn't know what she's talking about. You don't have nits. And we'll never tell anyone about it, okay?'

'Then I don't need her treatment after all?' Sally asked brightening.

'Oh, I suppose it can't hurt to go along with her . . . otherwise she might not let you into school . . . but between you and me, there's nothing wrong . . . absolutely nothing . . .'

When they got home Sally went into the bathroom and carefully examined her hair in the mirror. She didn't see anything unusual. She came out and found her mother, Douglas and Ma Fanny talking quietly in the kitchen. They stopped when they saw her.

'Well . . .' Mom said, 'I think I'll go down to the drugstore . . . I'll be back as fast as I can.'

As soon as she'd left Douglas said, 'I hear you got the cooties.'

'I do not have cooties. Mom said there's nothing wrong . . . that nurse is crazy . . . besides, she didn't say *cooties*, she said *nits*.'

'What do you think cooties are?'

'Cooties are make-believe . . . there's really no such thing.'

Douglas started laughing. 'Baloney . . . they're lice . . . little bugs that fly around in your hair . . .' He rubbed his thumb and second finger together.

'You're lying,' Sally said.

'Cootie . . . cootie . . . cootie . . .'

'Ma Fanny,' Sally cried, 'did you hear what he said?'

'Dougie . . . be a good boy,' Ma Fanny said. 'Don't tease Sally.'

'Oh, it was just a joke,' Douglas said. 'Can't she even take a joke?'

'Some joke!' Sally ran across the room and shook her hair at Douglas. 'Have a cootie . . .' she said. 'Have two or three or four . . .'

Douglas ran to the bathroom and locked himself in.

Ma Fanny called, 'Cooties . . . schmooties . . . stop it right now . . .'

238

Dear Doey-bird,

I miss you very much. Miami Beach is not as great as the ads say. I have a lot to tell you. The nurse wouldn't let me into school because she says I have nits. Do you know what they are? Douglas says they're cooties but I don't believe him. I have this special ointment on my hair now. It's blue and pretty disgusting. I hope it doesn't make my hair fall out. I'm trying to think of this as an adventure, like you said, but so far, it doesn't seem like one because everything is going wrong. Don't feel too bad that I hate it here and want to come home. After all, it's not your fault.

Your loving daughter,
Sally F.

six

Two days later Sally went back to school. This time the nurse didn't find anything wrong with her hair and she was admitted to Miss Swetnick's fifth-grade class.

The desks were lined up in rows and attached to the floor. Each one had an inkwell in the corner. At home they'd had light-coloured wooden desks that moved around and chairs that came in different sizes. And sometimes they'd push their desks together to make tables or else sit two-by-two. Sally knew now that she'd been right about Central Beach Elementary School in the first place. It *was* about five hundred years old.

But Miss Swetnick wasn't. She was young and pretty with red-framed eyeglasses shaped like hearts. She had long black hair tied back with a ribbon and a lot of the girls in the class wore theirs the same way. A few had long braids like Margaret O'Brien, the movie star, but nobody else had a coronet. Another thing Sally noticed right off was their shoes. They all wore sandals – white or gold – and no socks. Sally looked down at her red loafers and thick white socks, which were so popular in New Jersey, and felt foolish.

'Could I please be excused?' Sally asked Miss Swetnick.

Miss Swetnick smiled. Her front tooth was chipped at an angle. Sally liked the way it looked and wondered if her father could fix her front tooth the same way. 'Already?' Miss Swetnick said. 'You just got here.'

'I know . . . but it's important . . .' Sally shifted her weight from one foot to the other so Miss Swetnick would think it was a real emergency.

'Well . . . I suppose it's all right. But from now on you'll have to go with the rest of the class.'

'I'll remember that,' Sally said.

'The Girls' Room is down the corridor and on your right. Would you like someone from the class to show you the way?'

'No . . . I can find it myself.'

'Hurry back now . . .'

'I will.'

Sally unpinned her coronet on the way to the Girls' Room and put the bobby pins in her dress pocket. Her hair hung below her shoulders in braids. She felt better already. She found the Girls' Room but couldn't believe that there were no doors, not on the outside and not on the inside either. The toilets were separated into stalls but not one of them had a door for privacy. Sally made up her mind never to use the bathroom at school, no matter what. She took off her shoes and socks, then stepped back into her loafers, barefoot. She rolled her socks up in a ball and tried to stuff them into her pocket but they wouldn't go. She had to get rid of them somehow, and fast, so she tossed them into the trash basket, hoping that her mother would never find out. It was a terrible sin to throw away clothing when everyone knew the poor children in Europe were going half-naked. God could punish a person for throwing perfectly good socks away. She hoped he'd understand just this one time.

If Miss Swetnick noticed that Sally had changed her hair or removed her socks, she didn't say. 'We're doing a project on ancient Egypt . . . we're working in committees . . . do you like to draw?' she asked Sally.

'Yes . . . a lot.'

'Good.' Miss Swetnick led her to a group working on the floor, painting a mural. 'Boys and girls . . . this is Sally Freedman. She's from New Jersey and she's going to be in our class. So let's make her feel welcome.'

They looked up at Sally and began to sing.

'We welcome you to Central Beach
We're mighty glad you're here
We'll send the air reverberating
With a mighty cheer
We'll sing you in
We'll sing you out
To you we'll give a mighty shout
Hail, hail, the gang's all here
And you're welcome to Central Bee . . . eeach!'

A boy held a paint brush out to Sally. 'You can put in the woman carrying the jug of water . . . right here . . .' He tapped the paper. 'And make it good . . .'

As she began to sketch, a chubby girl leaned over and put her face so close that Sally could smell her breath. 'I don't like you,' she whispered. 'Get it?'

'I don't like you either,' Sally whispered back because what else could she say to a person who started out that way?

They had Bathroom before lunch and Sally had to go but she wasn't about to use those toilets without doors, although the others did, as if it didn't matter that everyone could see and hear what they were doing. She found out that the girl who didn't like her was Harriet Goodman. Barbara Ash, another girl in the class, told her. She also said that Harriet Goodman could play 'Peg O' My Heart' on the piano. She thinks she's really great because she lives here all year round,' Barbara said. 'She doesn't like winter people.'

'Oh . . . where do you come from?' Sally asked.

'St Louis originally . . . but I live here all the time now . . . only I'm not a snob like Harriet. You want to come to lunch with me?'

'Sure,' Sally said. Barbara had straight blonde hair cut like a Dutch boy's with long bangs. Her skin was suntanned and she had eyes like a dog's, sad but friendly.

Sally had never been in a school cafeteria. In New Jersey she went home for lunch every day. 'Is the food any good?' she asked Barbara, looking around. It was hot and noisy.

Barbara stuck out her tongue and pointed her thumbs down. 'But you're lucky . . . today's spaghetti . . . it could have been meat loaf and that really rots.'

'I don't like spaghetti,' Sally said. 'Can I get something else?'

'Are you kidding? You take what they give you . . . just tell the woman behind the counter you want a small portion . . . and watch for Mrs Walker . . . she's our table monitor this month.'

'A small portion, please,' Sally said, when it was her turn, but the woman behind the counter dumped a load on her plate anyway. Sally picked up a milk carton and followed Barbara to their table.

As soon as they sat down Mrs Walker drawled, 'What's your name, dearie?'

'Sally Freedman.'

'I have certain rules at my table, Sally . . . for one thing, we never wash our food down with our milk. We take small sips after every two mouthfuls. That aids our digestion. And we always clean our plates because so many children are starving in Europe. We have to show we care by not wasting our food. And, of course, we never talk with food in our mouths. Do you have any questions?'

'No,' Sally said.

'No, what, dearie?'

'No . . .' Barbara gave her a kick under the table and mouthed the right word to her. 'No, *ma'am* . . .' Sally said, feeling stupid.

242

'That's better. Now you may begin . . .'

Sally ran all the way home from school. She had to go to the bathroom in the worst way. She raced up the stairs and past Mom and Ma Fanny, who were waiting at the apartment door, but by then it was too late. Her legs were already wet and as she sat down on the toilet she began to cry. She had never been so ashamed! Maybe God was punishing her for throwing her socks in the trash basket.

'What's wrong?' Mom asked, banging on the bathroom door. 'Are you sick? Sally, let me in.'

Sally flushed the toilet and opened the door. 'I'm never going back!' she cried. '*Never!* There are no doors on the toilets . . . they made me eat a whole plate of spaghetti and I had to sip warm milk after every two bites . . . a girl named Harriet Goodman hates me . . . I wore my hair the wrong way . . . I need sandals . . . I . . .'

Ma Fanny put her arms around Sally and held her until she stopped crying. Then she said, 'So that's the bad news, mumeshana . . . now tell us the good news . . .'

'What good news?' Sally asked.

'Something good must have happened . . . you can't go a whole day without one good thing happening . . .'

'Well,' Sally said, sniffing, 'I met a girl named Barbara. She seemed pretty nice.'

seven

There were two other apartments in their section. The Daniels lived next door. They had one daughter who was a junior in high school. Her name was Beulah but everybody called her Bubbles. She had rheumatic fever and had to go for check-ups and blood tests every week, like Douglas. The Daniels were very religious and from sundown on Friday till sundown on Saturday they wouldn't answer their doorbell, ride in a car, smoke, turn on the radio or even the light switch. Sally worried that their Sabbath candles would burn the house down.

The Daniels had a mezuzah hanging at the side of their door, like most of the families in the house, but every time they went in or out of their apartment they'd kiss their fingers, then touch their mezuzah. Sally had never known such orthodox Jews.

On Friday, after supper, Sally was sitting on the floor cutting out ballet paper dolls when Mrs Daniels came by with a honey cake for them. 'I'm just on my way to synagogue,' she said. Mom whispered, 'Quick, Sally . . . put away the scissors . . .' Sally thought it was silly of Mom to pretend that they observed the Sabbath like the Daniels. Just because Mrs Daniels wouldn't use a pair of scissors after sundown didn't mean that Sally couldn't. But when she questioned her mother Mom said, 'It doesn't look nice . . . what would they think?'

The Rubins lived across the hall. They were winter people, from Brooklyn – a grandmother, a mother and two kids, like Sally's family. Linda was in second grade and Andrea was in sixth. She and Sally played potsy after school. At home they'd called it hopscotch and had used a rubber heel from the shoemaker. Here it had a different name and they used a stone or a bobby pin, but it was still the same game. Andrea was much taller than Sally – she was even taller than Betsy – with short, dark, curly hair and light blue eyes under heavy brows. She had a dimple in her left cheek and braces on her teeth. When she opened her mouth wide Sally could see the rubber bands way in back.

The Rubins had an all-white cat, called Omar, who slept under the covers with Andrea. He was the most beautiful cat Sally had ever seen but Mom said, 'He may be very pretty but cats can be full of worms so watch out . . . no use looking for trouble.'

Ten days after Sally and her family got to Miami Beach, Ma Fanny's sewing machine arrived, along with their bicycles, a

244

trunkful of clothes and several cartons of household items.

Andrea stood outside with Sally and watched as the movers unloaded their things from the van. 'Now we can go bike riding together!' Andrea said.

'Can I, Mom?' Sally asked.

'Not now,' Mom said, 'it's already close to four.'

'Just to Flamingo Park,' Andrea said, '. . . it's only a few blocks from here . . . my mother lets me go . . .'

'Oh, please, Mom!'

'You're not an experienced bicycle rider, Sally.'

'I'm experienced enough . . . I hardly ever fall off any more.'

'I'll watch out for her, Mrs Freedman,' Andrea said.

'And you'll bring her back in an hour?'

'Anything you say . . .'

'Well . . . I guess it's all right then . . .'

'Great!' Andrea said. 'I'll be right back . . . my bike is in the storage room.' While she was gone Sally tried out her own bicycle, making circles in the street. Andrea returned, calling, 'Hey, Douglas . . . want to come to the park with us?'

'Uh uh . . .' Douglas said. 'I'm going exploring on my own.' And he jumped on his bicycle and rode off in the opposite direction.

Sally and Andrea rode to the park on streets lined with palm trees, just like their own.

'Did you know the Pittsburgh Pirates come to Miami Beach in the winter?' Andrea asked.

'You mean the baseball team?' Sally said.

'No . . . I mean the bad guys who rob ships!'

'You *do* mean the baseball team, don't you?'

'Of *course* I mean the baseball team!' Andrea coasted down a small hill.

'I didn't know they came to Miami Beach in the winter.'

'That's what I've been *trying* to tell you . . . they practise in Flamingo Park.'

'I've never been to a big league baseball game,' Sally said, avoiding a stone in the road.

'I have . . . I've seen the Pittsburgh Pirates play . . . at Ebbets Field.'

'Where's that?'

'In Brooklyn . . . right near my house . . . we go to Dodger games all the time.'

'The Brooklyn Dodgers?'

'No . . .' Andrea said, clenching her teeth, 'the Jersey City Dodgers!'

'You *do* mean the Brooklyn Dodgers, don't you?'

'Sally . . . will you quit acting dumb!'

'I'm not acting.'

Andrea took Sally on a bicycle tour around Flamingo Park. The grass was darker green than in New Jersey, but coarse, and Sally already knew, from the yard beside their apartment house, that if you walked on it barefoot, it would scratch the bottoms of your feet.

A group of kids were playing kickball in one of the open areas and some teenagers were stretched out on the grass, soaking up the Miami Beach sunshine. And there were many old people. Sally had never seen so many old people in one place. There were women sitting on park benches, knitting and chatting. There were men, reading and playing cards or checkers.

'Let's go down the bike path,' Andrea said. 'Follow me . . .' It was a narrow path, surrounded by lush shrubbery. Sally saw a tree with a trunk that looked exactly like the outside of a pineapple. It was strange to see everything so green in October. In New Jersey the leaves would be turning fall colours by now.

Sally noticed the man first. He was sitting alone on a bench next to a clump of trees. As they approached he stood up and blocked their path. 'Hello, little girls,' he said. 'Would you like some candy?' He held a small brown bag out to them.

Andrea reached in and helped herself to a handful of rock candy. 'Thanks . . .' she said, as if she were talking to just anybody.

'You want?' he asked Sally.

After years and years of her mother's warnings it was finally happening. A strange man was offering her candy! Sally took a hard look at him so she could describe him to the police. The police would ask for details and she wanted to be ready to help. Of course, if he murdered her, then she wouldn't be able to help the police at all, but if he murdered only Andrea, then Sally would be able to identify him. He looked familiar, somehow. Who was it that he resembled? Sally chewed on her lower lip and cocked her head to one side. With slick, dark hair and a small black moustache . . . he'd look a lot like . . . like Adolf Hitler! He really would. And the longer she studied his face the more she could see the resemblance.

He shook the bag of candy at Sally. 'Go on . . . take . . .'

'No!' Sally said and rode off, almost knocking the man over.

'What's wrong with you?' Andrea said, pedalling hard to catch up with Sally.

'Don't you know better than to take candy from strangers? He could be a kidnapper or a murderer . . . or worse!'

'He's not a stranger . . .' Andrea said. 'He's Mr Zavodsky.'

'You know him?'

'Sure . . . he lives in our building.' Andrea bit down on a piece of rock candy.

'He could still be a murderer,' Sally said.

'So could anybody!'

'That's what I mean.'

Sally couldn't fall asleep. She tossed and turned, trying out different positions. Legs outside the bed sheet, arms at her sides; arms outside the sheet, legs inside. One leg out, one arm out; curled in a ball; spreadeagled on her stomach. Nothing worked. I need a story, she thought.

Sally F. Meets Adolf H.

It is during the war and Sally is caught by Hitler in a round-up of Jewish people in Union County, New Jersey. She has secret information from the head of the east coast underground but she refuses to tell. Hitler can't send her to a concentration camp because he is just building one in Bayonne and it won't be ready for a month. He orders the Gestapo to bring her to his private office. *Tell me, you little swine*, Hitler hisses at her. *Tell me what you know or I'll cut off your hair.*

Your threats don't scare me, Adolf, Sally says.

Oh no? We'll see about that! Hitler grabs a pair of scissors and Sally's hair falls to the floor in slow motion until there is a great pile at her feet. *Now you will talk!* Hitler screams.

Never! Sally answers and she sticks her tongue out at him.

That makes him still angrier. He lights a match and one by one burns each of Sally's toes. *Talk . . . talk, you pig . . .*

Sally shakes her head. *I'll never tell you anything . . . never!*

So Hitler goes to his desk and gets his knife and he slowly slashes each of her fingers. She watches as her blood drips on to his rug, covering the huge swastika in the middle.

Look what you've done, you little swine, Hitler cries hysterically. *You've ruined my rug!*

Ha ha, Sally says. *Ha ha on you, Adolf . . .* And then she passes out.

When she comes to, Hitler is asleep and snoring, with his head on his desk. Sally crawls out of his office, then dashes down the hall to the secret passageway of the underground. She gives them valuable information leading to the capture of Adolf Hitler and the end of the war.

On Saturday morning Sally and her family walked to the 15th Street beach with the Rubins. Ma Fanny packed a lunch in the wicker basket and Mom and Douglas each carried a folding chair from Burdines. Sally got to take the old army blanket and the bag with the towels, suntan lotion and dry suits.

At Bradley Beach, on the Jersey shore, the waves were very high and the undertow pulled you in if you weren't careful. Sally clung to the rope there. In Miami Beach there was no boardwalk and no rope. But there were miles and miles of soft yellow sand, bordered by palm trees, and the ocean, even though it was still the Atlantic, wasn't the same at all. The water here was warm and clear and blue-green and when it was low tide you could walk way, way out and still you would only get wet up to your knees.

It took a very long time for Mom to lotion Sally and Sally lost patience and began to wiggle around. 'You could get sun poisoning or a third-degree burn, God forbid,' Mom said, 'so stand still . . . you have to be very careful here . . . the sun is different . . . you should wear your hat . . .'

'Not now . . . maybe later,' Sally said.

'This isn't New Jersey, you know . . .'

'Please, Mom . . .'

'All right . . . one hour without your hat, but don't come crying to me if it's already too late.'

'I won't . . . I promise . . .'

When Mom was finished with Sally she called to Douglas. 'You're next . . .'

'I'll do it myself,' Douglas said, reaching for the lotion.

'You can't get your back . . . you want to wind up in the hospital, God forbid?'

'Dammit! I'm not a baby,' Douglas said, 'so stop treating me like one.'

'Don't you ever let me hear you use that language again!' Mom turned to Ma Fanny. 'He's so stubborn lately,' she said, as if Douglas weren't right there, listening. 'How am I going to manage such a stubborn boy all by myself? He needs his father . . . sometimes I wonder why we ever came here . . .'

'Don't get yourself worked up, Louise,' Ma Fanny said. 'Everything will be all right . . . give it a little time.' She looked across the blanket at Douglas. 'Come, Dougie . . . let me do your back.'

He let Ma Fanny help him without another word.

The Rubins spread their beach blanket next to Sally's, and after Andrea was fully lotioned she and Sally went off together, with Linda running behind them.

Andrea turned perfect cartwheels up and down the beach. Sally tried her best to copy them but she couldn't get both legs up for anything. 'Didn't you ever take acrobatics?' Andrea asked.

'No . . . did you?' Sally knew the answer before Andrea told her.

'I've taken acrobatics since I was seven and ballet since I was eight.'

'I take ballet at home too. I'm in Junior Advanced . . . that is, I would be if I was still in New Jersey.'

'Can you do a backbend?' Andrea asked.

'I don't know . . . I've never tried.'

'Watch this . . .' Andrea bent over backwards and when her hands touched the sand she flipped up her legs, stayed like that for a second, then stood up and started all over again.

'You're really good,' Sally said.

'I know . . . I'll teach you, if you want . . .'

'Okay . . .'

Andrea put her hands around Sally's waist. 'Now bend over backwards . . . go on . . . I'm holding you . . . don't worry . . . just touch the sand with your hands . . .'

'I'm trying,' Sally said.

'But you're not doing it . . . you're hardly bending at all.'

'I don't think my body goes that way.'

'You have to tell it to . . . you have to send a little message to your brain . . .'

'I'm trying . . . but my brain's not listening.'

'Hi, Sally . . . what are you doing?'

Sally straightened up. It was Barbara. 'Oh, hi, Barbara . . . I'm learning to do a backbend. Andrea's teaching me. Andrea, this is Barbara . . . she's in my class at school.'

'Hi,' Barbara said.

'Hello,' Andrea answered.

'Andrea lives across the hall from me,' Sally said.

'I'm in *sixth* grade,' Andrea told Barbara.

'You look older,' Barbara said.

250

'I am.'

'Oh, you stayed back?' Barbara asked.

'No! I'm older than you, is what I meant. I'm almost twelve.'

'Oh, I get it,' Barbara said. 'Well, I've got to go now . . . I have to be home by noon. Bye, Sally . . . see you Monday.'

'Bye . . .'

'Eeuuww . . . how can you stand her?' Andrea said, when Barbara was out of earshot. 'She's so . . . so . . . stupid!'

'Not usually,' Sally answered. 'Usually she's very nice. So . . . you want me to try another backbend?'

'No . . . let's get wet instead.'

They ran down to the ocean's edge. 'Can you swim?' Andrea asked.

'Some,' Sally told her. 'Can you?'

Andrea sat in the wet sand and held her knees to her chest. 'I could if I wanted to but I feel better with my feet on the bottom . . . do you know what I mean?'

Sally tried not to smile. She picked up a handful of wet sand and let it ooze through her fingers. 'I can float on my back. I might be able to teach you.'

'Maybe,' Andrea said, shielding her eyes from the sun. 'Look . . . there's the Goodyear Blimp.'

Sally looked up and saw a big grey bubble floating over the ocean, in the sky. The word GOODYEAR was printed on its side.

Linda ran in front of them then, splashing. 'Ha ha . . .' she called, 'got you wet . . . got you wet . . .'

'Go back to Mommy,' Andrea yelled. 'You know you're not allowed in by yourself.'

'*Tinsel Teeth,*' Linda called, '*Railroad Tracks . . .*'

Andrea picked up a handful of sand and tossed it at Linda. 'Get out of here, you little brat!'

Linda ran toward her mother.

'She's getting so spoiled,' Andrea said. 'I can't stand it. Just because she almost died my mother lets her get away with murder . . . and my grandmother's just as bad . . .'

'I didn't know she almost died,' Sally said.

'Last April . . . she had polio . . .'

'Really? You can't tell . . .'

'I know it . . . she's fine now . . . but that's why we're
here . . . they don't want her to get sick again . . .'

'Sounds like us,' Sally said, 'except if I ever called Douglas
Tinsel Teeth or *Railroad Tracks* I'd really get it . . . my father's
a dentist!'

'Mine manufactures bras and girdles.'

'Really?'

'Uh huh . . . he's coming down for Thanksgiving . . . want
me to ask him to bring you some bras?'

'I don't wear them yet.'

'I noticed . . . but some day you might.'

'I hope so.'

'I don't miss my father at all . . . do you miss yours?'

'Yes, a lot. He's coming down for Thanksgiving too. I can't
wait!'

'My father's very busy . . . I hardly ever see him at
home . . .'

'My father's busy too but he always has time for me.'

eight

Dear Doey-bird,
   Miami Beach is full of bugs. You never saw so many bugs.
Big ones, little ones, they are everywhere. I especially hate water
bugs. They give me the creeps. Also, outside you can see
salamanders. They are lizards that change colours. Or did you
already know that? Douglas wants to keep one for a pet but Mom
won't let him. But here is the biggest news yet. We had to set
mouse traps in the kitchen! Ma Fanny discovered the mice. That
is, she heard them running around at night. She says in Miami
Beach it doesn't mean you don't keep a clean kitchen. Just about

*everybody has them, and bugs too. Mom bought three mouse
traps. We caught our first mouse this morning. Douglas got
elected mouse remover and had to throw him in the garbage. He
picked him up by the tail!*

*I like the beach here very much except Mom makes me change
out of my wet suit before lunch. She says Douglas got his kidney
infection from sitting around in wet clothes. I told her, Mom, this
is the beach . . . you're supposed to get wet. She didn't think that
was very funny. I wouldn't even mind changing if she'd just let
me go to the bathhouse to do it. But she says I might pick up
something very bad there. I asked her What? but she says it's
better if I don't know. Andrea's mother told her the same thing.
We think it's some kind of disease.*

*Do you know of a special disease you can get from bathhouses?
If so, write and tell me. If not, write and tell Mom so I don't
have to change out in the open any more. Mom says no one can
see anything because she holds up a towel to cover my front and
Ma Fanny holds one up to cover my back, making a little closet
for me. I keep my eyes shut the whole time because if anyone is
looking I don't want to know. Douglas doesn't have to change
because he never gets wet!*

*Do you know about Man O'Wars? They are bluish bubbles
that sometimes float around in the ocean. When there are a lot of
them the lifeguards won't let you go in the water. They're pretty
dangerous. They can sting you. Douglas poked one that had
washed up on the beach, with a stick, and Mom got sooo mad.
She said Douglas chases trouble. But the Man O'War was
already dead. Douglas was just interested in its insides.*

*In school we are studying the history and geography of
Florida. Can't wait to see you.*

Your loving daughter,
Sally F.

Sally folded her letter, put it in an envelope, and sealed it.
Then she took another piece of paper from her box of Bambi
stationery and wrote:

Dear Mr Zavodsky,

You don't know me or who I am and you'll never find out, not if you guess for twenty years. But I think I know who you are. I think you are a person people hate. I think you are a person who is wicked and evil. I think you are worse than a regular murderer or kidnapper. I think you are a person with the initials A.H.

She folded that letter and put it in her keepsake box, under the day bed. Tomorrow she might mail it.

Sally got a special letter from her father. It was written in red ink on a yellow balloon. She had to blow it up before she could read it.

Dear Sally,

How's my gal? Thought you might like to get a different kind of letter so here it is. I saw Christine yesterday. She asked for your address so she can write to you. I miss you too! Soon it will be Thanksgiving and I'll be there for my treatment. Stay well. Take good care of Mom for me.

Love and kisses,
Doey

Dear Doey-bird,

Hi! I loved your balloon letter. I'm saving it in my keepsake box, along with my marble collection, some shells from the beach and a very pretty flower I picked up on my way home from school. I'm glad the balloon didn't pop when I blew it up. You didn't answer my question about the bathhouse disease. Please tell me what you know. It's very important! I have a new friend. Her name is Shelby and she lives at the corner. Don't get her mixed up with Andrea, who lives across the hall. Andrea is in sixth grade and has a cat called Omar. Don't get her mixed up with Barbara either. Barbara is my friend from my class. Shelby is in fifth grade too but not in my section. Her classroom is in a portable. She lives with her grandmother and has a neat game called Jolly Roger. I sure wish I had it too. We met because she goes home for lunch every day, like me. We both got special permission because we are allergic to the food at school. Well, not really allergic, but that's what we said. Finally we decided to walk back and forth together. When I'm done eating lunch I call for her and if there's time we play some Jolly Roger before heading back to school. Shelby's mother and father are getting a divorce. That's how come she's here. They're having a big fight over who gets her and she's not supposed to know about it. She hates them both. I don't blame her.

Next week is Hallowe'en. There's going to be a parade in Flamingo Park at night. A flamingo is a tall pink bird with skinny legs. Or did you already know that? Anyway, Andrea is going to dress up like one. She's tall enough!

Mom came up with an idea for my costume. I'm going to be a peanut girl. She is sewing peanuts all over my old green dress. And she's making me a crown out of cardboard that will have peanuts glued to it. Even my socks have peanuts on them. Mom has two infected fingers from pushing the sewing needle through the peanuts, but don't worry. Ma Fanny knew just what to do and Mom is soaking her fingers right now.

I am still blotchy red from the sun, but Douglas is already very tanned. The pimples on his chin are clearing up. Mom says the Miami Beach sunshine is really some medicine. But she is worried that Douglas isn't making new friends here. At home he didn't have that many either so I think she should just leave him alone. He likes to explore by himself. He is also busy inventing a coconut catcher. He wants to get coconuts off the trees when they are just ripe enough, but before they get rotten. He loves to eat them and drink their milk. I tried one the other day but yuck . . . I spat the whole thing out. Does that mean I'm not adventurous? I hope not! When you take the shell off a coconut it looks like it has a face. Or did you already know that?

I miss you very, very, very much! I can't wait until Thanksgiving either. I will give you such a treatment then. Say

*hello to Aunt Bette and Uncle Jack and Miss Kay and anyone
else you think might miss me.*

Your loving daughter,
Sally F.
P.S. Jolly Roger is the best game I've ever played!

nine

On Sunday mornings, at exactly ten o'clock, Sally, Douglas
and Mom went down to the lobby to wait for Daddy's phone
call. The phone was too high on the wall for Sally to reach so
she stood on a chair. This was her Sunday to answer.

'Doey-bird!' Sally shouted, when the phone rang and she
heard her father's voice at last.

Douglas hissed, 'Will you shut up with that dumb name
before everybody hears it.'

Sally motioned for Douglas to shut up himself.

'How's my little gal?' Daddy asked.

'Fine . . . but I miss you.'

'I miss you too.'

'Last night we went to the movies and nobody wanted to sit
next to me because they say I ask too many questions . . . but if
you don't ask questions then you'll never learn anything . . .
isn't that right? And did you hear about Hallowe'en? There was
this huge thunderstorm in the middle of the parade and all the
lights in the park went out and you should have heard all the
screaming but I wasn't scared because it was an adventure . . .'

Douglas muttered under his breath, 'Not much . . .'

'Anyway, Doey . . . I wasn't *that* scared . . . and we got
home okay . . . just all my peanuts got soggy and we had to
throw away my whole costume.' She paused for a breath. 'And
in school the music teacher lets me sing . . . she even likes the
way I sing . . .'

Douglas mumbled, 'Ha ha . . .'

'Well, she does . . . not like dumb old Miss Vickers who always made me be in the listener group . . .'

Douglas tried to grab the phone away but Sally held on and told her father, 'Douglas is trying to take the phone from me and I don't know why because he never even has anything to say and I have a lot to say and listen, Doey . . . the goldfish in the pool in our courtyard are *so* big . . . you never saw goldfish *so* big in your life and . . .'

Douglas grabbed again. 'Okay, Douglas! Just one more thing, Doey . . . my friend Andrea has a cat . . . I wrote you about him . . . he's so soft and he purrs when you pet him and I know he hasn't got any worms. So will you please tell Mom it's okay for me to play with him? And what about the bathhouse disease? Oh . . . well, don't forget . . . okay, I'll listen to her . . . yes, I promise . . . Douglas is practically *breaking* my arm . . . I love you too. Here, Douglas,' Sally said, shoving the phone at him. 'I hope you have something important to say this time.'

'Hi, Dad . . .' Douglas said. 'I'm okay . . . they're okay . . . it's okay . . . yeah, I feel fine . . . yeah, I'm trying . . . yeah, I know . . . yeah . . . well, here's Mom . . .' He passed the phone to his mother.

'Oh, Arnold . . .' Mom said, sniffling. Douglas went outside. Sally stayed where she was, hoping to hear the rest of the conversation but Mom waved her away, saying, 'Go play . . .'

'Do I have to?'

'Yes . . . hurry up . . . outside . . .'

'Oh, all right!' Sally went outside, in time to catch Douglas, walking his bicycle from the storage room to the street. 'Hey, Douglas, wait up . . .' she called. 'I'll ride with you.'

'No, thanks . . .'

'Where are you going, anyway?'

'Exploring.'

'Exploring where?'

'All over,' he said and pedalled away.

Sally sat on the edge of the goldfish pool. It was so quiet this morning. Where was everybody? Probably still sleeping. It was going to be hot today, a real sizzler, as Ma Fanny would say. Later they'd go to the beach. Sally watched a salamander work its way up a bush, changing its colour to blend in with its surroundings. Lucky salamander! It would be nice to become invisible like that, sometimes. If she had been able to blend right into the sofa in the lobby she could have listened to Mom talking to Daddy. And what did Mom have to say to him that was so private anyhow? Yes, it would be very nice to be invisible whenever you wanted.

Sally looked into the goldfish pond. I am invisible . . . I can see you, fish, but you can't see me . . . She tossed a pebble at her own reflection and watched as the ripples distorted her face. Invisible . . . invisible, she thought, closing her eyes.

When she opened them another reflection appeared in the pool, next to hers. She turned around and caught her breath. *Mr Zavodsky!* He was standing very close to her. Close enough to reach out and touch her. Close enough to push her into the goldfish pool.

'Hello, little girl . . . you want some candy?'

'No!' Sally jumped up and tore off into the house. She rushed up the stairs and burst into her apartment. 'Do you know Mr Zavodsky?' she asked Mom.

Mom was sitting in the stuffed chair in the corner, one hand covering her eyes. 'I know of him . . . why?' She sniffled and took her hand away from her face.

'I don't like him!' Sally said.

'Why . . . did he do something to you?' Mom looked concerned.

'He offered me candy.'

'I hope you didn't take any.' Mom wiped her nose with a Kleenex.

'I didn't . . . but one time Andrea did.'

'She should know better.'

'That's what I told her.'

'Stay away from him,' Mom said, '. . . and where's your brother?'

'Out on his bike . . . exploring . . .'

'Oh, God . . . what am I going to do?' Mom asked, her voice breaking.

'About what?' Sally asked.

But Mom didn't answer. She ran to the bathroom.

On Thursdays schools were closed because of a teachers' meeting. Sally went down to the lobby to wait for Shelby, who was coming over for lunch. She wondered if Mr Zavodsky would be there, with his bag of candy. If he was, she'd have to warn Shelby. She'll tell her he was a dangerous stranger, but no more.

Mr Zavodsky wasn't in the lobby but Bubbles Daniels from next door was, talking on the pay phone. Sally sat down on the sofa. Bubbles had pretty hair, the colour of carrots. She was almost seventeen. Sally wound her braid around her finger, thinking, Bubbles is older than Tante Rose when she had Lila.

Bubbles put her hand over the mouthpiece and spoke to Sally. 'I'll just be another minute.'

'That's okay,' Sally told her, 'I'm not waiting for the phone.'

'Oh . . . then could you possibly go outside?'

'What for?'

'So I can finish my conversation.'

'I don't mind if you finish.'

'I'd like to finish in *private*,' Bubbles said.

'Oh . . . why didn't you say so in the first place?' Sally walked outside. As she did, she heard Bubbles say, 'Will I be glad when we finally get a phone upstairs!'

'Everybody's got secrets these days,' Sally muttered to herself.

Sally met Shelby out front. 'I brought my Jolly Roger game,' Shelby said.

'Good.'

They went into the lobby. Bubbles was still on the phone. 'Just a minute . . .' she said into it, giving Sally and Shelby a nasty look. When they were on the stairs, Bubbles went back to her conversation. 'The *children* in this house are driving me crazy!'

'She's my next-door neighbour,' Sally told Shelby.

'Lucky you!' Shelby said.

Sally opened the door to her apartment and called, 'Shelby's here . . .'

Shelby looked around. 'Your place is so pretty!'

'Thanks . . . you should have seen it before . . .' Sally had to admit that Mom and Ma Fanny had done a nice job. The apartment was bright and cheerful now, with plants and curtains and plaid slipcovers on the day beds. There were pictures of boats and sunsets hanging on the walls and Ma Fanny's collection of family snapshots standing on all the small tables. There were twenty-two photographs in silver frames, four of them showing Tante Rose and Lila at different ages. Sally picked up her favourite. 'This is Lila, my cousin, once removed. She died in a concentration camp.'

'That's too bad.'

'Doesn't she have big eyes?'

'Yes.'

'You can tell she's happy even though she isn't really smiling, can't you?'

'Sure.'

Sally wanted to grow up to look just like Lila. She hoped her eyes would get bigger and her hair heavier, and that you would know she was smiling even when her mouth was closed. And then, when she finally parted her lips – what a surprise – a beautifully chipped front tooth, exactly like Miss Swetnick's.

Sally and Shelby had sour cream and cottage cheese for lunch and for dessert, ladyfingers with grape jelly. After, they played three games of Jolly Roger.

'Would you like to play something else now?' Sally asked.

'Like what?'

'Oh, I don't know . . . we could play Pretend . . .'

'Pretend what?'

'Cowgirl or Detective or War . . . something like that.'

'I wouldn't mind playing Cowgirl,' Shelby said. 'What are the rules?'

'There aren't any . . . I make up the story and we play . . . it's easy . . .'

'I don't know . . . I'm not very good at games without rules.'

'Well . . . if you don't want to . . .'

'What about marbles?' Shelby said. 'I like to shoot marbles.'

'I have a great collection!' Sally said, jumping up. 'Wait till I show you my favourite . . . clear green all over . . .' She pulled her keepsake box out from under the day bed, opened it, and took out a small cloth bag. She emptied it on the floor, in front of Shelby.

'Next time I'll bring my collection over,' Shelby said. 'I've got one that's pure black!'

That night Mom took Sally and Douglas to the movies to see *The Farmer's Daughter*. Even though Sally loved movies she missed seeing them with her father, because without Daddy there was no one to act out scenes with her after the show. And when she asked questions during the movie, Mom and Douglas just said, *shush* . . .

But there were some things in Miami Beach that were better than in New Jersey. One of them was Herschel's Sweet Shoppe. Mom always took them to Herschel's after the movies. Herschel knew just how to make Sally's sundae. She never had to remind him. One scoop of chocolate ice cream, one scoop of vanilla, lots of fudge sauce, a great pile of whipped cream and just a touch of cherry juice on top, but not the cherry itself. Herschel got it right every time.

ten

It was Wednesday afternoon and Miss Swetnick was dictating a poem to the class. They would be graded on spelling and handwriting. Sally dipped her stick pen into the inkwell in the corner of her desk. She glanced across the aisle at Barbara. Barbara had the best handwriting in the class. At least Miss Swetnick thought so. She always gave her an E for excellent while Sally never got more than a G for good. She was hoping for an E today. She watched Barbara form her letters and she tried to make hers look the same. Big and round with lots of space between each word. She didn't worry much about spelling because she never got more than one or at the most two words wrong. Not like Peter Hornstein. He sat behind her and got five or six words wrong every week and since you had to write every misspelled word twenty-five times in the back of your book he never caught up and had to stay after school at lot.

When Miss Swetnick had finished dictating they folded their hands on their desks and she walked up and down the aisles grading their papers. Sally dug her nails into her palms. She hoped, she prayed, that today would be the day she'd get an E, but when Miss Swetnick came by she hardly glanced at Sally's paper. She just made a big G in red pencil at the top, smiled, and said, 'Your letters are too big and there's too much space between each word.'

Barbara got another E for excellent.

As soon as Miss Swetnick moved to another aisle Sally felt a tug on her right braid. She whipped around in her seat to tell Peter Hornstein to leave her hair alone once and for all and when she did her braid hit her face.

'Miss Swetnick . . . Miss Swetnick . . .' Sally called, wiping ink off her cheek. 'I've got ink all over me . . .' She held up her hand to show Miss Swetnick.

Barbara leaned across the aisle. 'It's on the back of your dress, too,' she whispered.

'Oh . . . and it's on my dress . . . my mother's going to kill me!'

'How did that happen?' Miss Swetnick asked.

'I don't know,' Sally said.

'Peter . . . did you dip Sally's hair in your inkwell?'

'Yes, ma'am,' Peter said. 'By accident.'

Sally turned round in her seat. 'You dipped my braid in your ink?'

'It got in the way,' Peter said. 'It's always in the way . . . hanging on to my desk . . . tickling my fingers . . .'

'Peter,' Miss Swetnick said, 'Sally's braids hang straight down her back, not on to your desk. You must have reached out for one of them . . .'

Sally glared at him.

He smiled back.

'Oh, Peter . . .' Miss Swetnick sighed and took off her glasses. 'What am I going to do with you?'

'I don't know, ma'am,' Peter said.

From the back of the room, where the tallest kids in the class sat, Harriet Goodman called, 'You should send him to the office, Miss Swetnick.'

'When I want your advice, Harriet, I'll ask for it,' Miss Swetnick said.

'I thought you did . . . you said that you don't know . . .'

'I *know* what I said. Thank you, Harriet!' Miss Swetnick came over to Peter's desk and shook her head. 'You'll have to stay after school again. This time the blackboards get washed, the plants get watered and you'll write *I will not misbehave in class* twenty-five times in your best handwriting.'

'But, Miss Swetnick . . .' Peter said, 'I have six spelling words to write. I'll never get done.'

'Maybe you'll remember that before you start fooling around again.'

'Yes, ma'am.'

'Sally, go and wash off your face.'

'What about my hair and my dress?'

'You can do that at home.'

'Yes, Miss Swetnick.' She still couldn't bring herself to say *ma'am*.

As they were lining up to go home Harriet Goodman stood behind Sally and said, 'Miss Swetnick will never send Peter to the office because she goes with his brother. Everybody knows that . . . and I still don't like you . . .'

After school Sally went to Barbara's. She lived a few blocks up from Sally in a yellow building with hibiscus bushes out front. Her apartment was on the first floor and had a damp smell. Sally remembered Mom saying that first floor apartments were no good in Florida because of the dampness. There was nobody home.

'My mother works,' Barbara said. 'She gets home at five-thirty.'

'Oh.' Sally didn't know anybody who had a working mother.

'She's a secretary for National Airlines.'

'My father might fly National at Thanksgiving.'

'My mother says they're all the same. Want a glass of milk?'

'If you do.'

'I do if you do.'

'Well, it doesn't matter to me.'

'Okay . . . then I'll have some.'

'Okay . . . me too.'

'Want a fig newton with it?' Barbara asked.

'They're my favourites.'

'Mine too.'

'My sister likes butter cookies best.'

'I didn't know you have a sister.'

'Yes . . . her name's Marla . . . she'll be home later . . . she's in tenth grade.'

'My brother's in ninth . . . but he should only be in eighth . . . he's a genius.'

'My sister's not . . . but she's a majorette . . . she can twirl two batons at once.'

264

'I can't even twirl one.'

'Me neither . . . but I'm going to learn.'

'Maybe I can too,' Sally suggested.

'Yes, we could learn together.'

'That'd be fun,' Sally said. 'Except I don't have a baton.'

'Maybe you can get one . . .' Barbara said. 'Want to see my room?'

'Sure.'

They grabbed a few more cookies and carried their milk glasses through the small living room to the bedroom.

'Peter Hornstein likes you,' Barbara said.

'He does?'

'Yes . . . otherwise he wouldn't dip your hair in his inkwell.'

'Really?' This was certainly news to Sally.

'Yes . . . my sister's an expert on this stuff and she told me that if a boy teases you it means he likes you.'

'Well . . . I don't mind,' Sally said. 'I think he's cute . . . don't you?'

'No . . . I think he looks like a chimpanzee.'

'Just because his ears stick out?' Sally asked.

'That and the shape of his mouth.'

'Harriet Goodman says Miss Swetnick goes with Peter's brother . . .'

'She does,' Barbara said. 'Everybody knows . . .'

'I never knew.'

'You do now!' Barbara sat down on a bed. 'This is my side of the room . . . I like my things neat and Marla's a slob so my mother divided the room for us.'

Barbara's bed was covered with a white spread and on her shelves were rows of miniature dolls and jelly glasses filled with sharpened pencils. Marla's side of the room was a mess, with an unmade bed and clothing all over the floor.

'Where does your mother sleep?' Sally asked.

'In the living room . . . on the sofa.'

'How about your father . . . when he comes down?'

'My father's dead,' Barbara said, slurping up the last of her milk. She brushed the crumbs off her hands into the waste basket. 'You want to see his picture?'

'Sure.' Sally didn't know what else to say.

Barbara took a silver framed photo from the top of her dresser and handed it to Sally. The picture showed a handsome man in a uniform and across the bottom he had written, *For my darling daughters, Marla and Barbara, Love always, Daddy*. 'He got it in the Pacific,' Barbara said. 'Right in the gut . . .' She punched herself in the stomach. 'They sent us his dog tags.'

'Who?'

'Washington . . . the marines . . . you know . . .'

'Oh.'

'I can show them to you if you want . . . I know where my mother keeps them.'

'Okay.'

Sally followed Barbara into the living room where she opened a desk drawer and pulled out a velvet jewellery box. She handed it to Sally. 'Go on . . . open it . . .'

Sally raised the lid. Inside was a chain with Barbara's father's dog tags.

'His name was Jacob Ash . . . but my mother and everyone else called him Jack. We moved here after . . . she needed to get away . . . she cried a lot . . . he had big hands . . . when I was little he carried me on his shoulders so I wouldn't get tired . . . at first I hated him for dying but now I understand it wasn't his fault . . .' Barbara closed the box and put it back in the drawer. 'Let's go outside,' she said. 'We can play statues.'

When Sally got home her mother said, 'Sally Freedman . . . what happened to your dress?'

'Nothing much . . . it's just ink,' Sally said.

'How did that happen . . . ink won't come out . . . the dress is ruined . . .'

'It was an accident,' Sally said. 'My braid got into Peter Hornstein's inkwell by mistake and then I shook my head and the ink splattered . . .'

266

'That's no excuse . . .'

Sally looked around. 'Where's Ma Fanny?'

'At her card game . . . why?'

'Because *she'd* know what to do!'

'I know what to do, too,' Mom said. '. . . soak it in seltzer water . . . but that's not the point. You've got to learn to take care of your things . . . I can't afford to replace them . . . money doesn't grow on trees!'

'There are some things that are more important than money,' Sally shouted, 'or clothes!' And suddenly she started to cry. She ran for the bathroom. When Mom knocked on the door Sally opened it halfway and handed her the soiled dress.

eleven

Sally was stretched out on the floor, drawing. 'How old is Daddy going to be on his birthday?' she asked her mother.

'Forty-two,' Mom said, looking up from her book. 'Why?'

'I want to put it on this card I'm making him,' Sally said, pulling a green crayon from her box of Crayolas. 'How soon do I have to mail it?'

'Tomorrow, to be safe,' Mom said. 'His birthday's the fifteenth.'

'What do you think of my rhyme?' Sally asked. *'Forty-two and I love you!'*

'Original . . .' Douglas said, munching on a piece of coconut. 'Very original.'

Sally made a face at him and thought harder. 'How about this? *Don't be blue just because you're forty-two.'*

'Oh, God . . .' Mom jumped up and ran into the bathroom.

'Smart,' Douglas said to Sally. 'Very smart . . .'

'What'd I do?'

'You had to go and bring up the subject.'

'What subject?'

'Dad's age.'

'So, it's his birthday.'

'Yeah . . . but Uncle Eddie and Uncle Abe were both
forty-two when they died . . . did you know that?'

'No,' Sally said. 'That's impossible . . . I remember
them . . . they were both old . . .'

'It seemed that way to you because you were only four or
something . . .'

'I don't believe you,' Sally said, standing up.

'Why else do you think she's in there crying?' Douglas
nodded in the direction of the bathroom.

'Who says she's crying?' It made Sally uncomfortable to
think of Mom crying.

Douglas shrugged and headed for the door.

'Where are you going?' Sally asked.

'Out.'

'Can I come?'

'No!' He let the screen slam shut.

Sally wished Ma Fanny were home instead of out walking
with Andrea's grandmother. They walked together just about
every night, after supper.

Later, when Sally went to bed, she couldn't stop thinking
about her father, and then about Barbara. Barbara was the only
friend she had with no father. Even though very few of her new
friends lived with their fathers, they still had them. But not
Barbara. Her father was dead . . . killed in the war. How
would it feel to know your father was dead and not coming
down for Thanksgiving . . . that you would never see him
again . . .

Sally prayed hard. *Please, God, let Doey-bird get through this
bad year . . . this year of being forty-two . . . we need him,
God . . . we love him . . . so don't let him die.* She started to cry
quietly, worrying that her father was lonely, that something
terrible would happen to him. *Keep him well, God . . . you
wouldn't let three brothers die at the same age, would you?* But

268

somewhere in the back of her mind she remembered hearing
that bad things always happen in threes. If only she was home
in New Jersey now . . . she'd watch her father carefully . . .
she'd make sure he got plenty of rest and if he caught cold or
something she'd make him go straight to bed and stay
there . . . and she'd get him to stop smoking two packs of
Camels a day . . .

Finally she drifted off to sleep. She dreamed Miss Kay had
died. It was raining and they were all at her funeral – Sally,
Douglas, Mom, Aunt Bette, Uncle Jack, Ma Fanny. Miss Kay
just lay in her coffin, dressed in her nurse's uniform. She had a
kind of smile on her face and was wearing bright red lipstick.
But where was Daddy? Why wasn't he there too? Sally called
out and sat up.

'Shut up,' Douglas said, 'some people are trying to sleep.'

'I had a bad dream,' Sally told him.

'Well, it's over now so go back to sleep.'

At breakfast the next morning Sally said, 'I dreamed Miss Kay
was dead.'

'That means she's going to get married,' Ma Fanny said,
pouring the juice.

'It does? But how would *I* know that she's going to get
married?'

'When you dream somebody dies it means they're going to
get married,' Ma Fanny said. 'Everybody knows that . . .
right, Louise?'

'Yes,' Mom said, 'of course . . .' She was browsing through
the morning paper, sipping a cup of tea.

'But suppose the person is already married and you dream
that?' Sally said, mashing her shredded wheat.

'That means the person will stay happily married for years
and years,' Ma Fanny answered. 'Right, Louise?'

'Right,' Mom said, looking up from the paper. 'And Miss
Kay would be very happy to hear about your dream because
she'd like to meet a nice man and get married.'

'You think I should write and tell her about it?'

'Oh, you don't have to do that,' Mom said. 'You can wait until the next time you see her.'

'But I won't see her for a very long time.'

'That's okay,' Mom said. 'It'll keep.'

Douglas was reading the back of the cereal box. He never had anything to say in the morning.

'Ma Fanny . . .' Sally said.

'What, sweetie-pie?'

'Do you believe that bad things always happen in threes?'

'Not always . . . but sometimes,' Ma Fanny said.

'How can you tell when it will be like that . . . when something bad will happen three times?'

Now Douglas looked over at Sally, as if to warn her to cut it out.

'You can't tell,' Ma Fanny went on. 'You wait and see . . . then if it happens three times, you know . . .'

'But that doesn't make sense,' Sally said.

'Finish your cereal,' Mom told her, 'or you'll be late for school.'

'It's all superstition anyway,' Douglas said, yawning.

'I'm superstitious?' Ma Fanny asked.

'Yes,' Douglas said. 'You knock on wood and all that stuff.'

'Just to be careful . . . just in case . . .' Ma Fanny said, 'but not because I'm superstitious.'

'You told me once if a bird craps on you it's good luck,' Douglas said.

'Douglas!' Mom sounded shocked, but not angry. 'Watch your language.'

'Sorry . . . if a bird lets out his stuff on you . . .'

'Douglas!' Now she sounded angry.

'Well, how else can you say it?' Douglas asked.

'If a bird *plops* on you,' Sally suggested.

'That's enough!' Mom told them both and Sally and Douglas smiled at each other. He could be such fun when he wanted to. Sally wished he'd want to more often.

270

'How do you know all those things, Ma Fanny?' Sally asked.

'My mother told me . . . when I was a little girl.'

'Some people respect what their mothers say.' Mom aimed this remark at Douglas.

'Bully for some people,' Douglas answered.

Sally got a letter from Christine.

Dear Sally,

Hi! How are you? I am fine. Alice Ingram showed the boys her underpants in the cloakroom. They were light blue with lace around the edges. I always knew she was a show-off! Miss Vickers put me into the listener group in music. I guess I am taking your place. My mother is really mad and is going to complain to the principal. I already know all the Thanksgiving songs by heart and I want to sing them, not just pretend. Our programme is the usual, with Pilgrims and Indians and stuff. I hope you are having fun with the other millionaires. You are still my best friend, but until you come home I am pretending that Joan is.

Love and other indoor sports (what does
that mean, anyway?),
Chrissy (this is what I now call myself)

After supper all the neighbourhood kids came out to play hide and seek. It didn't get dark as early here as in New Jersey and Sally was allowed to stay outside until eight o'clock on school nights. Mom wouldn't let Douglas ride his bicycle after supper so he sometimes joined the hide and seek game too. Lately, Andrea tried to hide with Douglas. Sally didn't like that and was pleased when Douglas told Andrea, 'Quit following me . . . go and hide with Sally.'

Tonight, Shelby was It. She had to hide her eyes by the big palm tree and count to 120. Sally and Andrea ran off to hide behind the row of bushes near the sidewalk. The bushes grew so high and thick it was easy to stay out of sight.

'Ready or not, here I come . . .' Shelby shouted and went off to search on the other side of the house.

'Should we run in?' Sally asked. 'I think we can make it.'

'Not yet,' Andrea said.

'Hello, little girls . . .'

They turned around. *Mr Zavodsky, again!*

'Shush . . .' Andrea said, putting her finger to her lips. 'We're in the middle of a game.'

He made a hand motion to show he understood and went away.

'I don't like him,' Sally said. 'He's always sneaking up on people.'

'No, he's not.'

'How about just now?' Sally asked.

'He wasn't sneaking up on us . . .'

'I say he was.'

'Home free . . .' they heard Douglas call.

'Doesn't he remind you of somebody?' Sally whispered to Andrea.

'Who?'

'Mr Zavodsky.'

'Not especially.'

'Picture him with a small black moustache and slick dark hair . . .'

'Oh yeah . . .' Andrea said, 'I guess he does look a little like my grandfather . . . come on . . . let's run in . . .'

Dear Mr Zavodsky,

I know you are in disguise. You have shaved off your moustache and let your hair grow in grey but I am not so easy to fool. I happen to be one of the best detectives around and I am working on your case. So watch it!

They were at the beach on the Saturday before Thanksgiving. Mom had been dieting and with her hair in an upsweep and dressed in her new bathing suit she looked taller and slimmer than before. Her skin was very white so she always sat under an umbrella or in the shade of a palm tree. She never went near the water because when she'd been a little girl her father had thrown her into the ocean in Atlantic City, saying that was the best way to learn to swim. She'd been so scared she'd nearly drowned and never tried again.

Sally couldn't imagine a father throwing his child into the water. Certainly her father would never do such a thing. And if Ma Fanny had been along that day, long ago, in Atlantic City, she never would have allowed Grandfather to throw Mom in. Sally was sure of that. Sally hardly remembered her grandfather. He had died when she was just three years old, the year before Uncle Eddie and two years before Uncle Abe. Her other grandmother had died when Sally was eight, the same year as Aunt Ruth, Daddy's older sister, which was six months before Aunt Lena, Daddy's younger sister.

Ma Fanny liked the beach. She had just one bathing suit and Sally admired it. It had purple flowers all over and a skirt bottom. Sally found it much more interesting than Mom's new suit which was plain black. Ma Fanny didn't swim but she did get wet. She'd stand at the ocean's edge and splash herself and when she did the loose flesh of her arms wiggled.

On this day Sally and Andrea had finally convinced their mothers to let them go to the public bathhouse to change before lunch. But they'd had to promise not to use the toilets there.

'Douglas looked down my bathing suit this morning,' Andrea told Sally, as she stepped out of her wet suit.

'What for?' Sally asked.

'To see my tits . . . what do you think?'

'So how come you let him?' Sally dried carefully between her toes.

'I didn't let him . . . he just did it.'

'I don't believe you,' Sally said.

'I don't *care* what you believe. It's true! You're just jealous because you don't have tits yet.'

'I have them,' Sally said.

'You have buttons, that's all . . . you're still a child.'

'If I'm such a child how come you play potsy with me every day after school?'

'That's different,' Andrea said. 'You're the best potsy player in our house.'

Sally smiled. At least Andrea admitted *that*. She *was* the potsy champion of 1330 Pennsylvania Avenue and she intended to keep it that way.

'I've already kissed two boys,' Andrea said on their way back from the bathhouse. 'Did you know that?'

'Real kisses . . .' Sally asked, 'like in the movies?'

'One was and the other wasn't,' Andrea said.

'Tell me about the one that was . . .'

'Well . . . he was this friend of my cousin Gary's from Long Island . . . he's in eighth grade now but this was over the summer . . . he thought I was thirteen . . . at least . . .'

'What'd it feel like?' Sally asked.

'Oh, you know . . . nothing much . . . he put his face real close to mine and then I closed my eyes . . .'

'Was he *that* ugly?'

'No! You're supposed to close your eyes . . . you never watch . . . that's bad manners . . .'

'Oh.'

'And then he put his lips on mine and we kissed.'

'Did you like it?' Sally kicked at the sand. If you did it just right you could make it squeak.

'I told you . . . it was all right . . . I didn't especially like *him* though . . . Latin lovers are the best . . .'

'How can you tell if a lover is Latin?' Sally asked.

'Oh, he'll have dark, flashing eyes and he'll talk with an accent.'

'You talk with an accent,' Sally said.

'I do not!'

'You do too! You say *mothah* and *fathah* instead of *mother* and *father*.'

'That's not an accent!' Andrea said, annoyed. 'Everyone

from New York talks that way. You sound just as strange to me, if you want to know the truth. Besides, I thought you loved the movies . . . I thought Esther Williams was your favourite movie star . . .'

'She is,' Sally said, 'but what's that got to do with it?'

'Because you should know about Latin lovers . . . her boyfriends are all Latin.'

'The ones who stand around and sing?' Sally asked, surprised.

'Yes . . . the ones who kiss her . . . like Fernando Lamas . . .'

'He's Latin?'

'Of course . . . you should pay closer attention to details,' Andrea said.

'From now on I will.' Sally thought about Peter Hornstein. He had dark eyes. She wasn't sure if they were flashing though. She'd have to pay closer attention to details, as Andrea said. Maybe Peter Hornstein would grow up to be a Latin lover. And he liked her. Barbara said so. Wouldn't Andrea be surprised to hear that Sally had her own Latin lover!

During supper that night, Sally said, 'Mom . . . where's Latin?'

'Latin what?' Mom asked.

'You know . . . Latin . . .'

'There's no such place as Latin,' Mom said.

'Then where do Latin lovers come from?'

'Who's been filling your head with Latin lovers?' Mom asked, laughing.

'Nobody special . . . me and Andrea were just talking.'

'She means Latin America, I guess,' Mom said.

'Where's that?'

'South . . .'

'Like here . . . like Miami Beach, you mean?' Sally asked.

'No,' Mom said, 'south of the border . . . more like Cuba or Mexico or South America.'

'Oh.' Sally picked up her lamb chop bone. She liked to suck on it after the meat was gone.

'Latin lovers . . .' Douglas mumbled, chuckling.

Sally didn't answer him out loud but to herself she said, you're just jealous because you'll never be one, so ha ha on you, Douglas.

Mom was singing in the shower. Sally hadn't seen or heard her so happy in a long time, not since before Douglas had his accident. Tonight Mom was going to Miami, to the airport, to meet Daddy's plane. It was due in very late.

Ma Fanny was in the tiny kitchen, baking.

'Ummm . . . smells good,' Sally said.

'I don't trust this oven,' Ma Fanny said. 'I hope it doesn't ruin my pie or God forbid, my turkey.'

'Oh, Ma Fanny . . . you're such a good cook . . . you couldn't ruin anything if you tried.'

'Maybe yes, maybe no,' Ma Fanny said.

'I'll knock on wood for you,' Sally suggested, 'just to make sure everything comes out delicious.'

'You knock on wood *after* it comes out delicious . . . not before,' Ma Fanny said.

Sally thumped the wooden table anyway.

When she and Douglas were in bed and all the lights were out, Sally said, 'I wish Daddy's plane landed earlier so they wouldn't have to stay overnight in that hotel near the airport.'

'That's not why they're staying in a hotel,' Douglas said.

'It's not?'

'No.'

'Then, why?' Sally asked.

'So they can be alone.'

'But why would they want to be alone?'

'You know . . .'

'No, I don't.'

'So they can do it,' Douglas said.

276

'Do what?'

'You're so dumb sometimes . . .' Douglas sounded disgusted. 'Don't you know anything?'

'How can I know anything if nobody ever tells me!'

'Oh . . . go to sleep.'

Sally thought about Fernando Lamas kissing Esther Williams, then about her father kissing her mother the same way. Not that she'd ever seen them do that. But it was possible, she supposed. Could that be it then? They wanted to be alone so they could kiss for a long time? Maybe. But that seemed so silly . . . couldn't they kiss just as well right here . . . in the Murphy bed?

twelve

'Doey-bird!' Sally cried, jumping into her father's arms. 'I'm so glad you're here.' She kissed him on both sides of his face.

'My little gal,' Daddy said. 'How I've missed my little gal . . .' He hugged her hard and returned her kisses.

'Hi, Dad,' Douglas said.

Her father put Sally down, then hugged Douglas. 'How are you, son?'

'Pretty good. I invented a coconut retriever . . . you want to see it?'

'Sure . . . just as soon as I get settled.' He rumpled Douglas's hair. 'Growing taller and taller . . .'

'Yeah . . . my pants are getting too short again.'

'Arnold!' Ma Fanny called, rushing out of the kitchen, wiping her hands on her apron.

'Ma Fanny!' Daddy said, holding her at arm's length for a minute. 'Just look at that tan! You look about twenty-five.' He pulled her to him.

'Always with the compliments,' Ma Fanny said, laughing.

'For you . . . why not?' Daddy said.

On the radio, comedians like Bob Hope and Jack Benny were always telling mother-in-law jokes but Sally knew that her father and Ma Fanny really liked each other. They're much more alike than Ma Fanny and Mom, Sally thought. How strange, since they aren't even blood relatives.

Mom stood in the doorway, watching and smiling. She has such a pretty smile, Sally thought. If only she'd show it more often.

Daddy had presents for all of them – a handbag for Ma Fanny, a gold necklace for Mom, a special tool kit for Douglas and for Sally, the Jolly Roger game. She wasn't as surprised as she pretended to be. There were so many things to tell her father, so many things to show him. She'd never catch up in a week and then he'd be gone again.

They sat down to Thanksgiving dinner at four o'clock. After she'd tasted the turkey, Ma Fanny said, 'It's too dry.'

'No, it's fine,' Mom told her and Daddy added, 'It's delicious!'

'I overcooked it . . . half an hour earlier it would have been perfect.' Tears came to her eyes.

'It's good this way,' Mom said, but Ma Fanny had already pushed back her chair and was heading for the kitchen.

Daddy and Mom exchanged looks, then he got up and went after Ma Fanny.

'Just keep eating,' Mom told Sally and Douglas, but Sally didn't feel hungry any more. She could hear her father talking softly and Ma Fanny blowing her nose.

In a little while Daddy and Ma Fanny came back to the table. He had his arm around her. 'I'm sorry,' Ma Fanny said, taking her seat. 'I was being silly . . . who cares about the turkey as long as we're all well . . .' She sniffled. 'I just wish Bette and Jack could be with us.'

'Next year,' Mom said, patting Ma Fanny's hand. 'Next year we'll all be together.'

'Knock wood,' Ma Fanny said.

'Anyway,' Sally said, '. . . who likes juicy turkey?'

They all laughed but this time Sally was hoping they would. Suddenly she felt hungry again.

The next night her parents were going to a nightclub with somebody named Wiskoff that Daddy had met on the plane. Mom wore a dark blue dress that rustled as she walked and high heeled shoes. New rhinestone combs held her upsweep hairdo in place. Sally sat on the Murphy bed and watched as Mom put some more rouge on her cheeks, went over her lips a second time and dabbed a drop of perfume behind each ear. 'You smell good,' Sally said. 'Like lilies of the valley.'

'It's called White Shoulders,' Mom said. 'It's my favourite . . . here, I'll put some behind your ears too.'

'Ummm . . . I like that,' Sally said, wondering if Latin lovers would be attracted to it. Maybe she'd try it out on Peter Hornstein.

Sally went into the living room. 'Smell me,' she said to Douglas, putting her face close to his nose.

'Uck! Get out of here . . . you stink!'

'I do not.'

'That is a matter of opinion!' Douglas said.

'Do I get my treatment now?' Daddy asked, putting down the *Miami Herald*, 'or should I wait until I get home?'

'I'll probably be asleep by then,' Sally told him, arranging herself on his lap. 'I better give it to you now.' She put her face next to his. 'Do you like the way I smell?'

'Like White Shoulders,' Daddy said.

'How'd you know?'

'I've been enjoying it for a long time.'

'Oh . . .' Sally gave him a sliding kiss, up one cheek, across his forehead, down the other cheek, three quick hugs, and a butterfly on the nose.

'That was very nice,' Daddy said. 'I've really missed my treatments.'

'Me too,' Sally said. 'Doey-bird . . .'

'Yes . . .'

'How are you feeling?'

'Very, very nice.' He closed his eyes for a minute.

Sally traced his eyelids with her fingertip. 'I mean, how are you feeling, in general?'

'In general, I'm feeling just fine.' He opened his eyes and looked concerned. 'Why do you ask?'

'I was just wondering . . .'

'How about you?' Daddy said. 'Are you feeling all right?'

'Me?' Sally said. 'I'm fine. You know that. Douglas is the one you should be asking.'

'I thought maybe you were trying to tell me something.'

'No . . . nothing like that.' But inside Sally was saying, I am trying to tell you something, Doey . . . please make it through your bad year . . . please don't die!

'Have a wonderful time,' Ma Fanny said, when Mom and Daddy were ready to leave. 'And don't worry about a thing. Sally's going to teach me and Dougie to play Jolly Roger. Who knows . . . maybe I'll like it better than rummy.'

At ten, Sally, Douglas and Ma Fanny got ready for bed.

Sally fell asleep quickly and had a strange dream.

She is sitting in a movie theatre on Lincoln Road. The lights dim, the curtain rises, the music begins and the title of the motion picture everyone has been waiting for flashes on to the silver screen in glorious technicolour. *The White Shoulders*, starring Sally Jane Freedman as Lila and Mr Zavodsky as Adolf Hitler. You know right away it's going to be a war story because of the soldiers on the street. Lila is one of them. She is petting a turkey. All the soldiers are talking and laughing because it is rest hour. But then the whistle blows and it is time to get back to the battle.

Good luck, they say to Lila. *Remember, you're the only one who can do it . . . we're counting on you.*

One soldier lingers after the others are gone. *Oh, Peter . . . Peter . . .* Lila sighs. *I'm frightened . . . not for myself, but for you. If I fail . . . if I . . .*

No ifs or buts, my darling, Peter whispers, holding Lila close.
Soon it will be all over . . . soon we will be together again.

And will there be a parade? Lila asks.

Yes, my darling . . . a parade for you.

I'll try my best, Peter . . . I only hope that's enough.

It's all anyone can ask, Peter says, with tears in his eyes.
Goodbye, Lila . . . for just a little while.

Goodbye, Peter . . . we'll meet again in Latin. They kiss.
The turkey flies away.

And now Lila is alone on the street. She waits, her hand in
her pocket, ready for action. At last he approaches. Adolf
Hitler, monster of monsters.

What is that delicious smell? he asks, his nostrils twitching like
a rabbit's.

It is me, Lila says in a husky voice.

He runs toward her. *Such a smell . . . I can't stand it . . . it is
too good.*

It is called White Shoulders, Lila says, *an old family perfume,
handed down from my mother and before her, my grandmother . . .*

Hitler's face is almost touching Lila's. She feels sick to her
stomach but she has a job to do. She whips her pistol out of her
pocket, points it at Hitler's gut and says, *From all of us on the
other side . . .* and she pulls the trigger . . .

Sally awakened hours later to voices in the hall. It was Mom
and Daddy. Mom was laughing and saying something silly.
Something that sounded like *willya . . . willya . . . willya . . .*
Daddy was laughing too, but more quietly. She heard the key
in the door and then they were inside the apartment. Daddy
said, 'Shush, Louise . . . you'll wake the kids . . .'

'Willya . . . willya . . . willya . . .'

Ma Fanny snored and Douglas rolled over in bed and hit the
wall.

Sally lay very still but she opened her eyes. Daddy was

holding Mom up, with his arm around her waist. Mom was carrying one of her shoes and wearing the other. 'Willya . . . willya . . . willya . . .' she said, laughing harder.

'Shush . . . come on, Lou . . .'

'What's wrong with Mom?' Sally whispered to her father.

'Too much champagne . . . go back to sleep now.'

'Willya . . . willya . . . willya . . .'

Sally pulled the bedsheet up around her ears and closed her eyes.

In the morning Mom couldn't get out of bed. Daddy made an icepack for her head and brought her a glass of tomato juice. She wasn't laughing any more.

Daddy took Sally and Douglas to the beach. He helped Sally collect shells, built a beautiful sand castle, then fooled around with them in the ocean. Later, he sat on their blanket and played gin rummy with Andrea's father, while Sally and Andrea ran off to practise cartwheels.

Sally was soaking in the tub. Her shoulders were sunburned again and Ma Fanny had put some vinegar in her bath water, to take the sting away. Her parents were in the sleeping alcove, arguing, because Mr Wiskoff had invited them all out to dinner and Mom didn't want to go.

Sally could hear everything. That was the good thing about this apartment. At home, in New Jersey, her parents could talk privately and Sally couldn't make out a word. She had to imagine it all.

'Seven hours on a plane and they're your best friends?'

'I didn't say best friends . . . I said *friends* . . . why can't you get that straight? The other night . . .'

'The other night I got drunk,' Mom said. 'For the first time in my life . . . I still don't see how you could have let me . . .'

'Oh, come on, Lou . . . you enjoyed it . . . and they enjoyed you . . . you should try letting go more often . . .'

'I'm telling you . . . I just can't face them tonight.'

'Because you're embarrassed?'

'Partly . . . and I certainly don't think it's wise to expose the children to them.'

'Nobody has to know they're not married,' Daddy said.

'It's not just that . . . they aren't our kind of people, Arnold.'

'Do we always have to associate with the same kinds of people?'

'I'd rather go out with the Rubins . . . they asked us to join them.'

'We've already accepted Ted's invitation.'

'You could call and say I'm sick.'

'You're being unreasonable, Louise.'

'I have a feeling about him . . .'

'Look . . . he gambles a little and he plays the market in a big way . . . but so what?'

'I don't know,' Mom said. 'I'm just not comfortable with them.'

'You could try . . . for me . . .'

'All right . . . I'll try . . . it's just that we have so little time together . . . I hate sharing you with them.'

'Lou . . . Lou . . .'

Sally listened hard but she couldn't hear anything after that.

Daddy wanted Ma Fanny to join them too, but she said she had her card game and he should please understand that she couldn't disappoint her friends. So Sally and Douglas and Mom and Daddy took a taxi to The Park Avenue Restaurant near Lincoln Road.

The Wiskoffs were waiting at the table. Daddy introduced them, saying, 'Ted . . . Vicki . . . these are my children, Douglas and Sally.'

Mr Wiskoff stood up and shook hands with Douglas. He was tall, with slick black hair, turning grey around the ears. He wore a dark, striped suit and in the middle of his tie was a diamond stick pin. A red silk handkerchief showed out of the top of his jacket pocket and Sally wondered if he actually used it to blow his nose. 'Hooloo, sweetheart,' he said to Sally.

'You're as adorable as your daddy promised.' He leaned across Sally then, and kissed Mom's cheek. 'How're you doing, doll?' he asked her.

All this time Douglas was staring at Vicki. Sally didn't blame him. Because Vicki looked just like Rita Heyworth, the movie star, with long red hair and a wide, beautiful smile. She was wearing a green silk dress, the same colour as her eyes, and more jewellery than Sally had ever seen, all of it sparkling.

Sally got to sit next to her and could see that Douglas would have given anything to trade places, including his orange marble, because Sally could look right down the front of Vicki's dress and Vicki wasn't wearing anything under it!

When the waiter took their order, Mr Wiskoff said, 'And a bottle of your best champagne for the doll over there.' He nodded in Mom's direction. 'She really enjoys her bubbly.'

Mom held up her hand. 'Not tonight, Ted . . . really.'

Mr Wiskoff winked at the waiter. 'Bring it anyway . . .'

'Yes, sir.'

Sally ordered fruit cup supreme, roast beef, mashed potatoes, carrots, and chocolate ice cream. When he served dessert, the waiter brought a big silver bowl of whipped cream to their table and they each got to spoon as much as they wanted on to their plates. Sally loved whipped cream, especially over chocolate ice cream, but she wouldn't have minded it plain either. Just a plate of whipped cream would do any day. Nothing tasted as good. This was definitely her favourite restaurant. In the whole world there couldn't be another restaurant this good. She felt just a little bit guilty, thinking of all the starving children in Europe.

After the coffee had been served Vicki said, 'I got to go to the little girls' room . . . anyone need to join me?'

'No, thanks,' Mom said, but Sally quickly answered, 'I will . . . I mean, I do,' and she stood up and followed Vicki.

A lot of people turned to look at them as they crossed the dining room and Sally knew it was because of Vicki, not her. As Vicki walked, her backside wiggled from side to side and her breasts bounced up and down. It was exciting just to be near her.

In the Ladies' Room, Vicki sat down at a small dressing table and pulled a make-up kit out of her purse. Sally stood next to her, watching. Vicki put green eye shadow on her lids. 'You want to try some, honey?' she asked.

'Okay,' Sally said.

'Very nice,' Vicki told her as she rubbed it on to Sally's lids. 'It brings out the colour of your eyes.'

'But my eyes are brown, not green.'

'Brown and green are a good combination.' Vicki zipped up her make-up bag and shook out her hair.

Sally shook hers, too.

'Do you like my ring?' Vicki asked. She held it to her mouth and breathed hard on it. 'It's twelve carats . . .'

'I like carrots,' Sally said.

'Me too.' Vicki laughed. 'My necklace is emerald and diamond. Isn't it pretty?'

'Yes, very . . .'

'Would you undo the clasp for me, honey . . . I need to wash it.'

Sally stood behind Vicki and undid the clasp of her necklace. Vicki caught it as it dropped, and spread it out on the dressing table. Then she took another bag out of her purse and unzipped it. She pulled out a small bottle and a soft, white cloth.

'My mother has combs for her hair that sparkle like that,' Sally said, admiring Vicki's necklace.

'That's nice, honey . . . but these are the *real* things . . . now, I'm going to show you how to wash diamonds . . . every girl should know how to do it the right way . . . watch carefully . . .' Vicki poured some liquid on to the white cloth. 'You see how nice they look now? You see how they sparkle?'

'Yes. Did Mr Wiskoff give them to you?'

'Of course! Teddy and I have been together almost six years.'

Sally noticed that she didn't say *married*.

'I do for him and he does for me,' Vicki said. 'That's the way it should be . . . don't you think?'

'Oh, yes!' Sally said. 'That's the way it is with my parents too.'

'Really?' Vicki sounded surprised.

'Yes . . . like tonight, my mother didn't want to come but my father . . .' Sally put her hand to her mouth and blushed. 'I mean . . .'

'I know just what you mean,' Vicki said.

'But, I . . .'

'It's all right. I'll pretend I never heard a word. You know something, Sally?'

'No . . . what?'

'I like you!'

'I like you too.'

'How would you like to wear one of my bracelets for a little while?'

'Well, I don't know . . . I have my own . . . you see . . .' She held out her wrist so Vicki could see her shell bracelet. 'I bought it in Woolworth's . . . they're real shells too . . . from the beach.'

'Very pretty,' Vicki said. 'I guess you don't need mine after all, then.'

'I guess not,' Sally said. 'But thank you anyway.'

Vicki was going through her make-up bag again, deciding which lipstick to use. She chose a bright pink one, applied it, then blotted her lips with a tissue.

'Is Mr Wiskoff, by any chance, Latin?' Sally asked.

'Latin?' Vicki said.

'Yes . . . from Cuba or Mexico or someplace south of the border?'

Vicki laughed. 'Teddy is New York all the way, honey. He's a very important man back east . . . and don't you forget it . . . you've had dinner with Big Ted Wiskoff and that means a lot!'

'Wash that goo off your eyes before you go to sleep,' Mom said, in the taxi, on the way back to their apartment.

'Do I have to?' Sally asked.

'Yes!'

'But it looks so pretty.'

'Pretty awful!' Douglas said.

Sally gave him an elbow in the ribs. 'Do you know they call Mr Wiskoff, *Big Ted*?' Sally asked her father.

Mom answered, 'And not because he's tall, I'll bet.'

'I really liked him,' Douglas said. 'And that Mrs Wiskoff . . . what a dish!'

'She showed me how to wash diamonds,' Sally told them.

'That's wonderful!' Mom said. 'Every girl should know how to wash diamonds.'

'That's exactly what Vicki said!'

Mom snorted and looked out of the window.

Daddy laughed. 'Did you enjoy dinner, kids?'

'Oh, yeah . . . it was great,' Douglas answered.

'When they got out of the taxi they saw the Goodyear Blimp in the sky. It was all lit up. Douglas said, 'Oh, boy . . . would I like to fly around in that!'

Mom said, 'Some people don't have enough trouble . . . they have to go looking for it.'

'Was tonight an adventure, Doey?' Sally asked. She was already tucked into bed and Daddy sat on the edge, waiting for his treatment.

'I'll say . . .'

'I thought so.'

'I'm glad you had a good time, Sal . . .'

'Mmm . . . I really did.'

When her mother came over to kiss her goodnight Sally reached up and put her arms around Mom's neck. 'You know something . . . I wouldn't want a mother who looks like Vicki . . . she's nice and all that but I don't think she'd know how to love a kid the way she loves her diamonds . . .' She kissed Mom's cheek.

Mom hugged her back. 'Thank you, Sally . . . I really needed to hear that tonight.'

thirteen

Dear Doey,

    I miss you already! I hope you had a good trip home. Next time I think you should fly National Airlines because Barbara's mother works for them. You remember who Barbara is, don't you?

    I forgot to tell you something very important when you were here. My teacher, Miss Swetnick, goes out with Peter Hornstein's brother. Peter Hornstein sits behind me in class. I also forgot to ask if you could fix my front tooth like my teacher's. It looks very pretty when she smiles.

    I am still trying to get my first E for excellent in penmanship. Doesn't my writing look better? I don't make my o's like a's any more.

    Well, that's it for now. Send my love to Aunt Bette, Uncle Jack and Miss Kay.

    Your loving and only daughter,
    S.J.F.

She folded the letter and placed it in an envelope. Then she took out another piece of paper. As long as she was writing letters she might as well write one to *him* too.

Dear Mr Zavodsky,

    I had a dream about you. I am almost sure I know who you really are. Give yourself up before I report you to the police. I will be watching and waiting. Don't think you can get away with this disguise of yours. Nobody feels sorry for you just because you lost.

★

Sally and Andrea were sitting at the edge of the goldfish pool in the courtyard, playing the initial game. Omar had his front paws on the edge of the pool and was peering over the side.

'You can look but don't touch,' Andrea warned Omar. 'No goldfish for you!'

Omar purred and stuck his tail straight up in the air.

'Look at that,' Sally said. 'I never saw him do that before.'

'Oh, sure . . . it means he wants affection.'

'How do you know?'

'I read it in this book called *Getting To Know Your Cat*,' Andrea said. 'When they stick their tails up like that you should pet them.' She reached out and stroked Omar's back. 'It's your turn . . .'

Sally petted Omar too.

'Not for that!' Andrea said, annoyed. 'For the initial game.'

'Oh,' Sally said, '. . . okay, I'm thinking of a famous person and his initials are A.H.'

'A.H.,' Andrea repeated, 'Let's see . . . is he a movie star?'

'Nope.'

'A radio personality?'

'Nope.'

'Uh . . . a political figure?'

'I guess you could say that . . .'

'Let's see . . .' Andrea put her finger to her lip and looked up at the sky. 'I've got it . . . Admiral Halsey!'

'Nope,' Sally said. 'But did I ever tell you that I saw Admiral Halsey's parade when he came home from the war?'

'You did?'

'Yes . . . I threw confetti and everything . . . but that's not who I'm thinking of . . .'

'Well,' Andrea said, 'then I give up . . . I can't think of anybody else with those initials . . .'

'How about Adolf Hitler?' Sally was pleased that she'd stumped Andrea.

'Adolf Hitler!' Andrea said, and she leaned over the side of the goldfish pool and spat into it. 'How can you even say that name without spitting?'

'I never spit,' Sally said.

'Well, you should . . . every time you say that name . . . every time you even hear it you should spit . . . he made lampshades out of Jewish people's skin!'

'He did?' Sally leaned over and spat into the pool too. 'There,' she said, wiping her mouth with the back of her hand.

'And don't you ever use that filthy name on me again,' Andrea said, 'or I'll never play the initial game with you!'

'All right,' Sally said. 'I'm thinking of a . . .' She was interrupted by a high, shrill scream, coming from the side yard. Both girls jumped up and ran to see what was happening. It was Mrs Richter, a small, thin woman with white hair. Other people rushed outside to see what the commotion was about. Through it all Mrs Richter kept screaming, with one hand clutching her chest and the other pointing to the bushes.

Mr Koner, the landlord, who also lived in their building, said, 'Tell us what's wrong . . .'

Mrs Richter just shook her head, took a breath and let out another scream.

'Try to tell us what it is . . .' Mr Koner said. 'How can we help you if you won't tell us . . .'

Mrs Richter began to cry and talk at the same time. 'It's the second one this week . . . and two last week . . . that makes four . . . and the week before another one . . . that makes five . . . my heart isn't what it used to be . . . I can't take much more of it . . . it's that cat's fault . . .'

'What cat?' Mr Koner asked.

'That cat!' Mrs Richter said. 'That white cat . . .' She pointed to Omar. 'I've seen him running through these bushes. I've seen him chasing birds.'

Everyone looked towards the bushes and there, on the ground, lay a bird's head. The crowd that had gathered began to chatter.

Andrea grew pale and scooped Omar into her arms. 'It's *not* Omar,' she told everyone. 'He gets enough to eat at home . . .

he doesn't need any old birds!'

'You keep him locked up . . . you hear?' Mrs Richter shouted. 'Because if I see him again . . .'

Andrea turned and ran back to the courtyard. Sally followed. Andrea held Omar to her. 'It wasn't you . . . I know it wasn't you . . .' she told him, kissing his face. 'I love you, Omar . . . don't you listen to that old witch . . .'

'Everybody knows she's crazy,' Sally said. 'Just ask my grandmother . . . she'll tell you . . . just because she's from Boston she think's she's so great . . . she won't ever play rummy with the rest of the ladies . . .'

'I hate her!' Andrea said.

Sally was thoughtful for a minute. 'You could get Omar a collar with bells . . . then he'd scare the birds away and Mrs Richter wouldn't be able to blame him any more.'

Andrea looked at Sally. 'That's a very good idea . . . sometimes you really surprise me . . . for a fifth grader you're pretty smart.'

Sally smiled.

They took Omar upstairs, then walked to the Five and Dime, where they chose a blue collar with three tiny bells.

'Don't you think this collar will go nicely with his eyes?' Andrea asked.

'Yes . . . he'll look really pretty in it.'

'Let's hurry home and try it on him,' Andrea said.

'Okay . . . I just want to stop at the fountain for a drink of water . . . I'm so thirsty . . .'

'Yeah . . . me too . . . it's really hot today,' Andrea said. 'We could stop at the corner and get a glass of orange juice instead.'

'The orange juice at the corner has too many pieces in it.'

'It's not pieces . . . it's pulp,' Andrea said. 'I love my juice pulpy.'

'Not me . . . pulp gags me.'

'You have to open your throat wide.'

'I can't.'

'You could ask the man to strain it for you,' Andrea suggested.

'I did once . . . I was with my mother and the man behind the counter said he wouldn't do it because all the vitamins are in the pulp and why should my mother pay for a fresh orange juice with no vitamins . . . so if you don't mind I'll just get a drink of water . . .'

'I don't mind.'

They walked to the drinking fountain at the back of the store and Sally stood on tiptoe. Andrea held the button down for her. As Sally was drinking a woman came up from behind and yanked her away.

'Hey . . .' Andrea said.

'What's the matter with you girls?' the woman asked. 'Can't you read?' She pointed to a sign above the fountain: *Coloured*. 'Your fountain is over there.' She spun Sally around by the shoulders. 'You see . . . it says *White* . . . what would your mothers say if they knew what you'd been doing? God only knows what you might pick up drinking from this fountain . . . you better thank your lucky stars I came along when I did. Now here,' she said, reaching into her purse for a Kleenex. She handed it to Sally. 'You wipe your mouth off real good and from now on be more careful . . .'

Sally was shaking. When the woman was gone she turned to Andrea. 'Did you know why they had two fountains?'

'No,' Andrea said. 'I never even thought about it.'

'Me neither . . . but I know Negro people have to sit in the back of the bus here.'

'Everybody with dark skin has to . . .' Andrea said. 'That's why my mother always makes me sit up front.'

'Do you think that's fair?'

'I don't know, but my mother says you have to follow the rules.'

'So does mine.'

They began to walk home slowly.

'We had a Negro lady who came in to clean three times a

week in New Jersey,' Sally said, 'and here we have one every Friday . . . she's half Seminole Indian . . . my mother told me. She has dark skin but she eats off our dishes and drinks from our glasses and all that . . .'

'It's not the same thing,' Andrea said.

'I don't see the difference . . . she's very nice . . . and she's got the prettiest name . . . Precious Redwine . . . isn't that a beautiful name?'

'Yes, but I wouldn't want it,' Andrea said. 'Nobody in Brooklyn has a name like that.'

'Nobody in New Jersey has either.'

Dear Doey-bird,

   Right now Douglas is listening to the radio. Jack Armstrong, All American Boy *is on. I haven't been following Jack Armstrong lately so I don't know what's happening. Did I tell you that I'm not as scared of* The Shadow *as I used to be? I still don't like it when he laughs and says* The Shadow knows . . . *but I don't have to stuff my ears with cotton the way I do when Douglas listens to* Inner Sanctum.

   This afternoon me and Andrea went to the Five and Dime and I took a drink from the wrong water fountain. They have two of them here. One is marked White *and the other is marked* Coloured. *What would happen if a person with dark skin, like a Negro or a Seminole Indian, took a drink from our fountain? Do they really have different germs? Since you went to Dental College I'm sure you know these things . . .*

Dear Sally,

   In your last letter you raised some questions that are very hard to answer. I have always believed that people have more similarities than differences, regardless of the colour of their skin. While the south continues to practise outright segregation, the north is not much better. We just don't admit we do it. For instance, how many Negro children were in your school in New Jersey? . . .

293

Dear Doey-bird,

One. He was in sixth grade. And you forgot to tell me if people with dark skin have different germs in their mouths. And can they give trench mouth to white people? I have decided that if I ever have a daughter I will name her Precious. Don't you think that's a beautiful name? I wish it could be my name even though Precious Redwine sounds a lot better than Precious Freedman . . .

Dear Sally,

Trench mouth has nothing to do with the colour of your skin. Anyone can get it. As for germs in people's mouths, we are all the same . . .

Dear Doey-bird,

Then why does the Five and Dime have two fountains and why do they drink only from theirs and we drink only from ours? And you didn't tell me what you think about my favourite name . . .

Dear Sally,

Your questions are very hard to answer. At the moment it is simply the way things are. I doubt that they will remain that way forever, but for now, you have to abide by the rules. I'm glad that you're questioning those rules though. Yes, I think Precious is a lovely name and that is exactly what you are, even though we call you Sally . . .

fourteen

Sally, Shelby and Andrea were walking home from school. Sally was careful not to step on any cracks in the sidewalk. Shelby went out of her way to step on *every* one. When they reached the corner Shelby said, ''Bye . . . see you tomorrow . . . I've got to go to the dentist this afternoon.' She went up the walk to her house.

As soon as she was gone, Andrea said, 'Can you keep a secret, Sally?'

'Yes.'

'You're sure?'

'Of course!' Sally said.

Andrea stood still and faced Sally. 'Okay . . . I've decided to tell you and *only* you because you came up with the idea for Omar's collar . . . but if anybody ever finds out . . .'

'I can keep a secret!' Sally insisted.

'Okay.' Andrea took a big breath. 'I'm in love.'

'You are?'

Andrea started walking again. 'Yes . . . hopelessly.'

'Is that good or bad?' Sally had to hurry to keep up with her, skipping over every line in the pavement.

'It all depends,' Andrea said.

'On what?'

Andrea shrugged, as if she wasn't sure herself.

'Who is he?' Sally asked.

'He's called Georgia Blue Eyes . . . he's new . . . he's in Mrs Wingate's portable.'

'Oh . . . that's right next to Shelby's . . . maybe she knows him . . .'

'This is a secret, remember?'

'Don't worry . . . I won't give you away,' Sally said. 'What's his real name?'

'I don't know . . . but he's from Georgia and he has the most beautiful blue eyes you ever saw.'

'Nicer than Omar's?'

'Omar is a cat.' Andrea said this as if Sally didn't already know.

'I thought you like Latin lovers best . . . with dark and flashing eyes.'

'I do sometimes,' Andrea said quietly, and then she became

annoyed. 'Will you stop jumping like that . . . you look like a kangaroo.'

'I don't want to step on any cracks.'

'Don't tell me you believe that garbage about your mother's back . . . that's the silliest superstition.'

'I don't believe it.'

'Then stop jumping!'

'I like to jump.'

'Sometimes you act younger than a fifth grader . . . you know that . . . and I *was* going to ask you to come to the park with me this afternoon . . . but now I'm not so sure . . .'

'And sometimes I act older . . . you said so yourself.' Sally waited for Andrea to agree with her. When she didn't, Sally asked, 'So what's at the park today?'

'Georgia Blue Eyes . . . I heard he's playing ball there this afternoon.'

'Oh,' Sally said and she stopped jumping.

'Can I go to the park with Andrea?' Sally asked her mother. 'Please . . . I'll be very careful.'

'Walking or on bicycles?' Mom asked.

'Bicycles . . . but I'll watch out for cars . . . I promise . . . please . . .'

'All right,' Mom said. 'But be back by five . . . that means you have to leave the park no later than quarter to . . .'

'Okay . . .'

She and Andrea rode their bicycles to Flamingo Park. When they got to a field where a bunch of boys were playing ball Andrea's face flushed and she said, 'There he is!'

'Which one?' Sally asked.

'On first base . . . isn't he the most beautiful boy you've ever seen?'

'I don't know.'

'How can you not know? Look at that hair . . . oh, I'd love to run my fingers through it.'

'He might have nits.'

'Are you crazy?' Andrea asked.

'Some people do, you know.'

'Not *nice* people.'

'Even them . . .' Sally said.

'Never! Nits are what dirty disgusting people get from not shampooing and Georgia Blue Eyes isn't dirty *or* disgusting!'

'Maybe . . .' Sally paused for a minute, not wanting to go deeper into that subject. 'So, you want to ride around or just sit here and watch?' she asked Andrea.

'Hmm . . . I guess we should ride around for a while. We can circle the field . . . that way he might notice me.'

They rode around three times but if Georgia Blue Eyes noticed Andrea he kept it to himself. Then Andrea decided they should ride around the rest of the park and come back to the field later, when Georgia Blue Eyes wasn't quite so busy.

They rode past the tennis courts, past the food stand and through the wooded area. Mr Zavodsky was there, sitting on a bench, reading *The Forward*. Andrea called, 'Yoo hoo . . . Mr Zavodsky . . .' and when he looked up she waved.

Sally caught Andrea's arm and held it down. 'Cut that out!' Andrea said, shaking Sally off. 'Got any candy today?' Andrea called to Mr Zavodsky.

'For you . . . always . . .' He beckoned to her.

'Don't go,' Sally said, under her breath.

'Why not?' Andrea said.

'I don't trust him.'

'Why?'

'He offers us candy and we're . . . practically strangers . . .'

'We are not . . . he knows us.'

'He doesn't know *me* at all!'

'Oh, Sally . . . quit being such a jerk!' Andrea got off her bicycle, kicked down the stand and ran across the grass.

You monster! Sally thought. *Reading* The Forward, *a Yiddish newspaper . . . pretending to be Jewish . . . and after you've made lampshades out of Jews' skin! I hate you . . . I hate you . . . you think you're so smart, coming to Miami Beach to retire, like*

297

everybody else . . . I'll bet you think this is a great hiding place . . . well, you're wrong . . .

Andrea came back with a handful of rock candy. 'Want some?' she asked Sally.

'No!' Sally said and rode off.

Andrea caught up with her. 'What's wrong with you this time?'

Sally didn't answer. She just kept pedalling.

'Are you sick or something . . . you look funny . . .'

'I . . . I . . .'

'Do you have to throw up? Because if you do I'm getting out of the way . . . I can't stand it when somebody throws up . . .'

'I'm not going to throw up!' Sally said.

'Then what?'

'I just got hot . . . that's all . . .' Sally mopped her forehead with the tails of her shirt.

'Well, don't fall off your bike,' Andrea said. 'You're riding so wobbly.'

'I won't.'

'Have a piece of candy . . . it'll make you feel better.'

'No! I already told you I wouldn't eat his candy . . . it could be poison.'

'Are you crazy?' Andrea said.

'No, I'm careful . . . and you should be too . . . I've never seen *him* eat his candy, have you?'

'How can he . . . he's got false teeth!' She crunched another piece of rock candy.

'You're going to ruin *your* teeth and wind up with false ones too!'

'Since when are you my mother?' Andrea asked.

The next morning at breakfast, Sally said, 'Whatever happened to Hitler?'

'Nobody's sure,' Douglas answered, his mouth full of cereal. 'Some people say he killed himself and others say he escaped to South America.'

'What do you think?' Sally asked Mom.

298

'I think he's dead.'

'He should be,' Ma Fanny said. 'If anybody deserves to be dead it's him.'

'I think he got away,' Douglas said. 'I'll bet he's in Argentina right now . . .'

'Or he could be here, in Miami Beach,' Sally said. 'I'll bet you never thought of that.'

Douglas coughed some cereal out of his mouth. 'Boy, are you a card.'

'What an idea,' Mom said. 'Hitler in Miami Beach . . .'

'God forbid,' Ma Fanny added.

fifteen

Dance, ballerina, dance . . . Sally sang softly. She twirled around and around in her black inner tube, her head back, her eyes closed. The ocean was calm and blue and the sun hot on her face. Earlier, she had talked to Daddy on the phone. He had wished her happy Hanukkah and said he'd be down to visit in just two more weeks. She wished he could be there tonight, to light the first candle on the menorah. It was hard to believe that Hanukkah was beginning. Usually the weather was very cold for her favourite holiday. Sometimes it even snowed. She laughed out loud at the idea of celebrating Hanukkah in the middle of summer, then opened her eyes to make sure no one had heard. It was okay. There was no one near enough to have noticed.

Dance, ballerina, dance . . . what a good song! No wonder it was number one on the hit parade. After Christmas vacation she and Andrea were going to take ballet lessons. Their mothers had already signed them up at Miss Beverly's School of Classic Ballet. Sally could hardly wait. Her hands skimmed the water, keeping time to her music. She hoped that at Miss

Beverly's ballet school she'd get to wear a tutu instead of an exercise dress. She pictured herself in pink net with pink satin toe slippers to match, like Margaret O'Brien in *The Unfinished Dance*, the best movie Sally had ever seen. Mom bought her the colouring book and the paper doll set because she'd enjoyed the film so much.

Some people, like Mrs Daniels from next door, thought fifth graders were too old for that stuff. Sally heard her say so to Mom. 'When my Bubbles was that age she was sewing her own clothes and reading fine literature from the library.' What Mrs Daniels didn't know was that you could play with paper dolls like a baby or you could play with them in a very grown-up way, making up stories inside your head. Like *Margaret O'Brien meets Mr Zavodsky* . . . This takes place before she becomes a famous movie star. She's just a regular kid, like Sally. Margaret finds out Mr Zavodsky is Adolf Hitler in disguise and reports him to the police. They capture Mr Zavodsky and award the Medal of Honour to Margaret O'Brien. At the medal ceremony a well-known Hollywood producer says, *We're looking for a girl just like you to play the lead in a new movie. How are you at ballet? Well, sir* . . . Margaret answers, *I'm in the Junior Advanced class and I hope to be in Advanced next year at the latest.* She then performs for him and gets the part.

It bothered Sally that Mom had said to Mrs Daniels, 'Each child matures at her own rate.' But Mom didn't know about Sally's stories, so maybe she thought Sally played like a baby too.

Suddenly Sally felt a sharp, stinging pain on her leg. She cried out and reached. Something was there. Something was on her leg. She tried to pull it off but the same pain hit her hand and wrist. 'Stop . . .' she cried, 'stop it . . . stop it . . .' She began to kick and scream as the painful sting spread. She couldn't stop the stinging pain. 'Help . . .' she called. 'Please . . . somebody help me . . .'

It seemed like hours before the lifeguard reached her. He

lifted her out of the tube, trying to hold her still, but the pain made her squirm and cry even though she knew it was important to be quiet during a rescue. She moaned and closed her eyes.

'You'll be okay now . . .' the lifeguard said. He sounded very far away. Sally wondered why. And then, everything went black.

When she opened her eyes again she was on the beach, wrapped in a blanket, and Mom was at her side. She could hear Ma Fanny and Douglas talking to her, but she couldn't turn her head to see them. A crowd had gathered around her. 'Oh, my baby . . . my poor little girl . . .' Mom cried.

'It hurts,' Sally said. She closed her eyes again, too tired to say any more.

'How could such a thing have happened?' she heard her mother ask, and was surprised that Mom sounded so angry.

'I don't know, ma'am . . .' the lifeguard answered. 'We had no warning . . . you can look through my glasses yourself . . . there's not another Man O'War in sight.'

'Are you absolutely sure that's what it was?' Mom asked.

'Yes, ma'am . . . positive . . . wrapped itself right around her leg and when she tried to pull it off it got her hand. I've seen plenty of cases and it hurts like hell . . . pardon my language . . . but she'll be okay. You can call the Board of Health . . . they'll tell you what to do.'

'Come . . .' Ma Fanny said, 'let's get her home.'

'But how?' Mom sounded confused now and frightened. 'She can't walk . . .'

'Never mind,' Ma Fanny said. 'Dougie . . . go and ask that woman if we can borrow her baby stroller . . . tell her we'll bring it back right away.'

'For Sally?' Douglas asked.

Sally tried to open her eyes again, tried to speak, but she hadn't the strength. The pain was less acute now but she could still feel the stinging and she couldn't move her fingers or toes.

'Just go and do it, Douglas!' Mom said.

'Okay . . . but Sally won't like it.'

'Never mind,' Mom said. 'She'll never know . . . she's only half-conscious . . . you can see that . . .'

I am not, Sally wanted to say. I can hear every word and I'll die if you take me home like a baby!

'I'll carry her for you, ma'am,' the lifeguard said and Sally felt his arms around her again.

He lowered her into the stroller. Sally kept her eyes tightly shut. If any of her friends were around she didn't want to know.

'Watch her legs,' Mom said. 'Let them dangle over the sides . . . that's it.'

'Can you make it home now, ma'am?' the lifeguard asked.

'Yes, I think so . . . and thank you very much.'

'Anytime.'

'I'll push her,' Douglas said.

'No,' Mom told him, 'I will. You walk at her side and make sure she doesn't fall out.'

Sally felt herself moving, first on grass and then on concrete. 'Listen, Ma . . .' Mom said to Ma Fanny, 'you better walk home slowly. I don't want you to get out of breath and have a spell.'

'Spell . . . schmell . . .' Ma Fanny said. 'I can keep up with anybody.'

The Board of Health told Mom that Sally should sit in a tub of tepid water with baking soda. She soaked so long, the skin on her fingers and toes got crinkly. The pain eased up and soon she could move her fingers again. The family took turns sitting in the bathroom with her. She didn't mind because she was still wearing her bathing suit. Besides, she was grateful for the company. She watched as Mom filed her nails, as Ma Fanny worked on her afghan, and as Douglas blew the insides out of an egg.

'You were pretty brave,' Douglas said, pausing for a breath. 'You really surprised me.'

'I screamed in the water,' Sally said. 'I remember . . .'

'Yeah . . . but once you were on the beach you shut up.'

'Because it hurt too bad to do anything,' Sally said.

'Worse than a shot?'

'Much worse.'

'Worse than a bee sting?'

'I don't know . . . I never got stung by a bee . . . but Christine did once, on the bottom of her foot. She cried a lot.'

'She would!' Douglas held his eggshell up to the light. 'I wonder if it hurt worse than my kidney infection?'

'I can't say . . . I've never had a kidney infection.'

'It looked like it hurt worse.'

Sally shrugged.

'I hope I never get stung by a Man O'War,' Douglas said.

'I hope you don't either . . . I wouldn't wish that on anybody . . . not even Harriet Goodman and I hate her.'

'Who's Harriet Goodman?'

'This jerk in my class who hates me for no reason.'

'Oh.'

Three hours later Mom said, 'Okay . . . you can get out now.'

Sally pulled the stopper from the tub. 'At last!'

'I'll help you,' Mom said. 'I don't want you to faint again.'

'Is that what happened before . . . when everything got black?'

'Yes, you passed out . . . and the lifeguard said it's lucky you did . . . because you were fighting him so badly he could hardly handle you.'

At sundown they lit the first candle on the menorah and sang the Hanukkah blessing. Sally was lying on the sofa with a thick, baking-soda paste covering her hand and leg, where she'd been stung. It felt yuckiest between her toes.

All the neighbours came to visit that night.

Andrea said, 'Of all days to go to Monkey Jungle . . . and just when something exciting happened . . .'

'How was it?' Sally asked.

'To tell the truth, it wasn't that great . . . and you could smell monkeys everywhere.'

'My mother thinks you can get diseases from monkeys so I'll probably never get there,' Sally said.

'Well, you're not missing much.'

'But I like chimps . . .'

'So do I . . . but not *that* many at one time . . . besides, I'd have rather been at the beach with you.'

'Then you might have been stung by a Man O'War too.'

'I know . . .'

'And it wasn't any fun . . . I'll tell you that . . .'

'So I hear . . .'

'But Douglas says I was really brave.'

'Brave is a matter of opinion,' Andrea said. 'Everyone acts differently in an emergency . . . passing out isn't necessarily brave.'

'I didn't *want* to pass out . . . it just happened.'

'Don't get me wrong . . . I'm not saying it *wasn't* brave to pass out . . . who knows, I might have done the same thing.' She looked down for a minute. 'Anyway, I'm glad you're okay now.'

'Thanks.'

Mrs Daniels came over with a honey cake. 'My Bubbles was stung two years ago . . . on her foot . . . we went straight to the hospital . . . when it comes to my Bubbles we don't fool around.'

'We don't fool around when it comes to our children either,' Mom said. 'When Douglas had nephritis we went to the biggest specialist in New Jersey. And today, we called the Board of Health about Sally.'

'The Board of Health!' Mrs Daniels said. 'Who'd trust them?'

'What did they do for Bubbles in the hospital?' Mom asked.

'Told us to put her in a tub of baking-soda water.'

'Well, that's exactly what the Board of Health told us.' Sally could tell that Mom was pleased. 'And now she's just fine, as you can see for yourself.'

'So this time you were lucky,' Mrs Daniels said.

'Knock wood!' Ma Fanny thumped the dining table.

'Knock wood,' Mrs Daniels repeated.

Later, before she went to sleep, Douglas gave Sally a freshly painted eggshell. 'It's supposed to be Margaret O'Brien.'

Sally held the fragile shell in the palm of her good hand. 'I can tell by the braids,' she said. 'It's a beautiful shell . . . the best one you've ever done.'

Douglas half smiled. 'It'll stand by itself on your shelf . . . the feet are supposed to be ballet shoes but I had to make them kind of wide to support the weight . . . so they might not look like ballet shoes to you . . .'

'Oh, no . . .' Sally said. 'I can tell they are . . .'

'Good.'

'Thank you, Douglas.'

'Goodnight . . . I'm glad you're okay,' Douglas said.

sixteen

'No school for you today!' Mom said the next morning.

'But I'm fine,' Sally told her.

'We're not going to take any chances. A day of rest can't hurt.'

'But I don't want to miss school today . . . we're having a Hanukkah party with songs and games . . .'

'I know, honey . . . but your health comes first,' Mom said.

'Please, Mom . . . please let me go to school . . .'

'We'll have our own Hanukkah party, right here,' Mom said.

'That's not the same!'

'Tell you what . . . I was saving your Hanukkah present until Daddy gets here, but I'm sure he'll understand if I give it to you now . . .'

'My Hanukkah present?' Can it be a baton? she wondered.

Mom went into the sleeping alcove and came back with a slender box. 'I haven't even wrapped it yet.'

It can't be a baton, Sally thought, opening the box. It's much too small. Instead, she found a Mickey Mouse watch with a red patent leather strap. 'Oh, Mom . . . I love it! It's exactly what I wanted. It's even better than a baton. Oh, thank you . . . thank you . . .' She jumped off the day bed and hugged her mother.

'I didn't know you wanted a baton,' Mom said.

'You didn't?'

'No . . . you never mentioned it.'

'You mean I forgot? Oh well . . . it doesn't matter . . . because this is even better . . . and now I've just *got* to go to school . . . I've got to show all my friends my new watch.'

'Tomorrow . . .' Mom said, laughing. 'Today you stay on your bed and rest.'

So Sally rested. She watched the hours go by on her new watch. She read a Nancy Drew mystery. She studied Ma Fanny's collection of family photos. She always had trouble believing that the chubby baby on Ma Fanny's lap was once her mother. And then there was her favourite picture. Lila. She held it, running her hands along the silver frame, then tracing Lila's features with one finger – her eyes, nose, mouth – beautiful Lila.

Dear Mr Zavodsky,

  I'm thinking about you. I know you didn't get my other letters because I didn't send them yet. But that doesn't mean I'm not going to send them because I am. They are safe, inside my keepsake box. I am just waiting for the right moment. A detective has to get evidence and that is what I'm doing now. I know plenty about you. I know you killed Lila. So don't think that just because you haven't heard from me you're safe.

Two weeks later, when Sally's father arrived, they joined the Seagull Pool Club. Mom said it had nothing to do with the Man

O'Wars in the ocean but Sally didn't believe her.

'Does this mean we can't go to the beach any more?' she asked.

'Of course not,' Daddy said. 'This is just something extra.'

'And you can take swimming lessons,' Mom said. 'I hear they have an excellent instructor.'

'I can already float on my back.'

'But there are lots of other strokes,' Daddy said.

'I don't want swimming lessons. I'd rather learn by myself,' Sally said.

'Well, that's all right too,' Mom told her. 'You know I don't believe in forcing children when it comes to swimming.'

'And neither do I,' Daddy added.

'I'm hoping Douglas will make some friends at the pool,' Mom said, more to Daddy than Sally. 'He's always alone, riding his bicycle . . . even on the beach he keeps to himself . . .'

'Douglas doesn't need friends,' Sally said.

'Everybody needs friends,' Mom said. 'Even Douglas.'

It wasn't that Sally objected to joining the Seagull Pool Club. Shelby belonged there and so did a lot of other kids from school. It was just that she wanted to make sure she could still go to the beach. In spite of the Man O'Wars, she loved the ocean – the smell of it, the sound of it, the salty taste – her toes squishing into the sand at the water's edge . . .

On her first day at the Seagull Pool Club, Shelby taught Sally how to hold her nose and sit on the bottom. Then Sally showed Shelby how she could float on her back. While she was demonstrating, someone swam so close she felt a foot brush the side of her face. 'Hey . . .' Sally called, losing her balance. She stood in waist-high water. 'Why don't you watch where you're going?'

He turned to face her. 'Why don't you watch out yourself?' he drawled. It was Georgia Blue Eyes.

'Did you see that boy who kicked me?' Sally asked Shelby.

'Yes.'

'Well, Andrea is hopelessly in love with him.'

'She is?'

'Oops . . .' Sally covered her mouth with her hand. 'That's supposed to be a secret. I shouldn't have told you.'

'It's okay,' Shelby said. 'I know how to keep secrets.'

'How was the Seagull?' Andrea asked that night. They were sitting at the side of the goldfish pool, watching Omar stalk a salamander.

'It was pretty good,' Sally said, stirring the fish pool with a long stick.

'Any interesting boys?'

'I haven't looked around yet.' Sally was surprised by her own answer. She had expected to tell Andrea about Georgia Blue Eyes right away. But having a secret from Andrea was so exciting she decided to keep her news to herself. Someday she would tell Andrea. Someday when the time was right. She would say, *Oh, by the way . . . Georgia Blue Eyes once put his foot in my face.*

'We might join in March,' Andrea said. 'My father's going to think about it. He got me and Linda a raft for Hanukkah . . . we rode the waves all day . . . it was so much fun.'

'Shelby taught me to hold my nose and sit on the bottom of the pool.'

'I don't like water in my eyes.'

'Me neither . . . but Shelby told me to keep them closed and I wouldn't feel a thing.'

'Yes . . . but you could bump into someone that way.'

'Listen . . .' Sally said, 'you could bump into someone just floating on your back . . . you never know . . .'

'That's true,' Andrea said.

'I don't want to fly to Cuba,' Mom said.

'Just for the weekend, Louise,' Daddy told her.

Sally sat at the table in the breakfast nook, shelling lima beans for Ma Fanny, who was in the kitchen, fixing dinner. She and Ma Fanny were very quiet so that they could hear the conversation between Daddy and Mom, who were in the sleeping alcove.

'No . . . I don't want to go, Arnold.'

'Because of Vicki and Ted?'

'Because I'm afraid to fly . . . and you know it.'

'Is that the whole reason?' Daddy asked.

'It's reason enough.'

'There's nothing to be afraid of . . . I've flown three times since you've been down here . . .'

'And I wish to God you wouldn't . . . I wish you'd take the train down and back.'

Sally nodded. She worried so each time her father flew.

'I'd lose two days that way,' Daddy said.

'But at least you'd be safe,' Mom told him.

Sally nodded again.

'If your time's up, it's up . . . it doesn't matter where you are,' Daddy said.

'You don't have to take chances though . . . you don't have to go looking for trouble.'

'That's right,' Sally mumbled to herself. 'Especially this year.' She finished shelling the beans. She dumped them out on the table and began dividing them into five equal piles.

'I want to go to Cuba for the weekend.' Daddy sounded very firm. 'And I want you to come with me.'

'No!' Mom said, sounding just as firm.

'I'm going, Lou . . . with you or without you.'

'Then I guess you don't love me very much.' Mom's voice broke.

Sally paused, feeling herself choke up.

'This has nothing to do with love,' Daddy said, quietly.

'It has everything to do with love.' Mom was crying now.

'If you loved me *enough* you'd come too,' Daddy said.

Sally was afraid to look up from the table. She didn't want to meet Ma Fanny's glance.

'You only want to go because of Ted and Vicki . . . they put the bug in your head . . .'

Daddy sighed, 'Oh, Lou . . . why can't you understand . . .
I need to get away with *you* . . . I need that badly . . .'

'I need it too,' Mom said, sniffing. 'But I'd rather move up to
a hotel on Lincoln Road. Why do we have to fly to Cuba?'

'Because Ted will pick up the tab, for one thing . . . and for
another, it's an adventure . . .'

'I'm not Sally,' Mom said. 'You can't convince me by calling
this an adventure!'

Sally sat up straight.

'Shush . . . she'll hear you.'

'I don't care!'

'Maybe you should be more like Sally,' Daddy said. 'At least
she's willing to try.'

Sally couldn't help smiling.

'You're ruining our time together, Arnold . . . I don't
understand why you're doing this to us.'

'Why *I'm* doing it!' Daddy said. 'Okay . . . not another word
on the subject . . . but next Friday night I'm flying to Cuba
with Ted and Vicki. I'll have two tickets in my pocket. I hope
you'll change your mind and come with us.'

Daddy clumped out of the sleeping alcove, still wearing his
wooden beach shoes. Sally pretended to be busy with the lima
beans as he walked over to her. He put his hand on her head.
'How's my little gal?' he asked.

'Oh . . . just fine,' Sally told him.

'Good . . . that's good . . .'

'We each get twenty-six lima beans for supper.'

'Suppose I eat twenty-seven?' Daddy asked.

'Then we'll all point and call *pig* . . .'

Daddy laughed and took a lima bean from one of the
carefully arranged piles. He ate it raw.

The next morning Sally went grocery shopping with Mom and
Ma Fanny. She needed a new box of Crayolas and she also
wanted to make sure Mom bought enough Welch's grape juice.

'Get smart, Louise,' Ma Fanny said. 'Go to Cuba for the weekend. There's nothing to worry about here.'

'I don't know, Ma . . . both of us on the same plane . . . if anything happens what will become of the children?'

'Nothing will happen.'

'You can't be sure.'

'So who's ever sure of anything in this crazy world? Go with Arnold . . . don't send him away without you.'

'I'll think about it, Ma.' Mom looked over at Sally. 'Don't you know better than to listen to grownups when they're talking?'

'I wasn't listening,' Sally said. 'I don't care if you go to Cuba or not.' She pushed her cart down the aisle. Actually, Sally was torn between wanting Mom to go because Daddy seemed so anxious and wanting them both to stay home. After all, it would be more than a month before she'd see her father again. It bothered her that he wanted to get away with just Mom.

Sally and her family went to the Seagull Pool Club every day that week. It was such fun to have Daddy with them! He never tired of playing games. He played dolphin with Sally, letting her ride on his back as he swam underwater. He lifted her on to his shoulders and had chicken fights with Douglas, who carried Shelby as his partner. He played Keep-Away, tossing a brightly coloured beach ball from one to the other. He rented flippers for their feet, showing them how to use them. And suddenly, to Sally's surprise, she found that she could lift both feet off the bottom of the pool and not go under. She was learning to swim! It was easy. All she had to do was kick her feet and move her arms. She was actually *swimming* and without ever having had a lesson!

Mom stood at the edge of the pool snapping pictures.

On Thursday, Sally brought Barbara as her guest. 'Barbara . . . you know Shelby, don't you?' she said, when they met in the pool.

'Oh, sure . . .' Barbara said. 'You're the other one who's

allergic to the school food, right?'

'Right!' Shelby answered and all three of them laughed together.

That afternoon Sally spoke to Georgia Blue Eyes. She said, 'You know something . . . you're a good swimmer but you're aways bumping into me when I'm floating on my back.'

He said, 'If you'd turn over once in a while you wouldn't have that problem.'

She said, 'You're the one with the problem.'

He said, 'I've seen you around, haven't I?'

She said, 'Maybe . . .'

He said, 'You're always with that other one . . . that jerk with the frizzy hair.'

She said, 'Her name is Andrea and her hair's not frizzy . . . it's curly.'

He said, 'And what's your name?'

She said, 'Mine?' and she looked over at Shelby and Barbara who were giggling like crazy. 'I'm Sally.'

'Sally what?' he asked.

'Never mind,' Sally said.

'Sally Nevermind . . . that's a pretty jerky name . . . but it fits you . . .' He laughed and swam away.

'Oh . . . he's so cute!' Barbara said. 'Don't you think he's the most adorable boy you've ever seen?'

'Yes,' Shelby said. 'And I love his accent . . . I'd let him kiss me any day.'

'Me too,' Barbara said. 'Any day and any place.'

'What about you, Sally?' Shelby asked. 'Would you let him kiss you?'

'I'd have to think about it,' Sally answered. 'I usually prefer Latin lovers . . . they're the best.'

On Saturday afternoon Sally and Douglas went to the beach with Ma Fanny and the Rubins. There were no Man O'Wars in sight. Mrs Rubin sat on her blanket rubbing suntan oil on to Mr Rubin's back. 'Your mother's so lucky . . .' she said to

Sally. 'Going off to Cuba for the weekend . . . I wish somebody would take me to Cuba . . . hint, hint . . .' She tickled Mr Rubin's belly.

He said, 'Somebody's already paying to keep you in Miami Beach . . . remember?'

'Oh, Ivan . . . I was just teasing,' Mrs Rubin said. 'You know that.' She kissed his cheek.

'My mother didn't even want to go,' Sally explained. 'My father practically had to force her . . .'

'Sally,' Ma Fanny called, 'come and have a sandwich.'

'I'm not hungry yet.'

'Come and have it anyway . . .' Ma Fanny said.

When Sally sat down next to her, Ma Fanny leaned close and whispered, 'Don't tell family secrets.'

'But I . . .'

'Think, mumeshana . . . always think before you speak.'

'I try to . . .' Sally said.

'I loved it, I loved it, I loved it!' Mom sang, when she and Daddy returned from Cuba on Sunday night. 'It was even more exciting than Daddy promised.'

'Did you see any Latin lovers?' Sally asked.

'Oh, dozens . . . everywhere you looked . . .' She and Daddy laughed. 'And we rhumbaed until three in the morning . . .' She put her arms around Daddy's neck and they danced across the room. 'And we drank Crème de Cacao . . . and it was so delicious . . .'

'As good as champagne?' Sally asked.

'Oh, better . . . much, much better . . .' Mom laughed some more. 'It makes you feel like you're walking on air.'

'And what about flying?' Sally said. 'How was that?'

'Well . . .' Mom answered, 'once we got up I never even knew we were moving . . .'

'Once she opened her eyes, that is,' Daddy said, '*and* stopped digging her nails into my hand . . .'

'Oh, Arnold . . .' Mom gave him a playful punch. 'Not that

313

I'd want to do it all the time, mind you . . . but once in a while . . . in good weather . . .'

Sally noticed that her parents looked at each other and laughed a lot in the next few days. On New Year's Eve they all went to the Orange Bowl Parade. Mr Wiskoff had a box, right up front, so Sally had no trouble seeing all the marching bands and floats go by. And after the parade Big Ted took Sally by the hand, to his car, and gave her a special gift – a baton. 'Someday we're going to see *you* march in the Orange Bowl Parade,' he said.

'But how did you know . . .' Sally asked, 'how did you know I've been dying for a baton?'

'A little bird told me,' he said.

And then it was January second and Daddy had to fly back to New Jersey. They went to the airport to see him off. Sally waved and blew kisses and prayed hard as the plane took off.

And then it was January third and time to go back to school.

seventeen

Sally couldn't find her library book. 'It's due today,' she said. 'I can't go to school without it.'

'Did you look under the day bed?' Mom asked.

'I've looked everywhere . . .' Sally picked at her cuticles. 'I'm going to be late.' If you were late to Central Beach Elementary School you had to go to the Vice-Principal's office for a late slip and Sally had heard that the Vice-Principal was so mean three kids had fainted and two had thrown up just from being late to school last month.

'Think . . .' Ma Fanny said. 'Where was the last place you saw it?'

314

'I don't remember . . . in the kitchen, maybe . . . before Daddy came.'

Ma Fanny walked away. In a few minutes she came back with Sally's book. 'So . . .' she said, handing it to Sally.

'You found it!' Sally had searched so carefully she couldn't believe it. 'Where . . . where was it?'

'In the pantry,' Ma Fanny said, as if that were the logical place for a book to be.

'How did it get in there?' Mom asked.

Sally raised her shoulders and held up her hands. She and her mother looked at Ma Fanny.

'So what's wrong with reading a book in English now and then?' Ma Fanny said. 'How is a person supposed to learn if she doesn't practise?' She kissed Sally's forehead. 'Hurry to school now, sweetie pie . . .'

Sally ran all the way but the second bell rang just as she reached her corridor. She knew the rules. She was supposed to go straight to the office. But maybe she could sneak into her classroom. Maybe Miss Swetnick wouldn't notice. Of course, if they'd already started opening exercises she'd have no choice. She'd have to go to the office. And she'd eaten scrambled eggs for breakfast. Just the thought of throwing them up in front of the Vice-Principal was enough to make her feel sick. Maybe she'd get lucky. Maybe she'd faint instead.

She stood outside her classroom. It was very noisy. They weren't having opening exercises yet. Miss Swetnick was standing at the front of the room waving her hand around. She noticed Sally, standing in the doorway.

Sally felt her stomach roll over. Now she would be sent to the Vice-Principal.

'Well . . . good morning, Sally.'

'Good morning,' Sally said. 'I'm late . . .'

'So I see,' Miss Swetnick said. She was wearing her pale blue blouse and her hair was tied back with the same colour ribbon.

Sally didn't move.

'Well . . . don't just stand there . . . come in and take your seat,' Miss Swetnick said.

'But I'm late.'

'You've already said that . . . but this is the first time you've been late, isn't it?'

'Yes.'

'And I'm sure you've a good reason . . .'

'Oh, I do . . . my library book is due today and I couldn't find it . . .'

'You see . . .' Miss Swetnick said.

'Then I don't have to go to the office?'

'Not this time.'

Sally thought, Miss Swetnick is the nicest, most fair teacher in the whole world. And also, the prettiest.

'Besides,' Miss Swetnick said, 'today is a special day . . . I've just told the class I'm engaged to be married.' She smiled and held out her hand, showing Sally a gold ring with a tiny diamond in the centre.

'Congratulations!' Sally said, wondering if Miss Swetnick knew how to wash diamonds. She took her seat.

'Now . . . let's get on with our geography,' Miss Swetnick said. 'Page eighty-seven . . . Harriet, would you begin, please.'

Peter leaned close to Sally and whispered, 'She's marrying my brother!' Before Sally had a chance to answer him, Harriet called out, 'When's the wedding, Miss Swetnick?'

'We're doing geography now, Harriet . . .'

'But you haven't told us when you're getting married.'

'Over Easter vacation,' Miss Swetnick said. 'Please begin with the first paragraph, Harriet . . .'

'But you'll still be our teacher, won't you?' Harriet asked.

'Yes, of course.'

'Where are you going on your honeymoon?'

'Harriet . . . we're doing our geography now,' Miss Swetnick said.

'But that *is* geography . . . you're going *some place*, aren't you?'

'Yes, we're going to Cuba. Now that's the last question I'm

going to answer . . . so please begin, Harriet.'

'Okay,' Harriet said, opening her book. 'Florida is a land of great beauty . . .'

During recess Peter Hornstein said, 'It sure is great to have your sister-in-law for a teacher.'

'She's not your sister-in-law yet,' Harriet reminded him.

'Yeah . . . but she can't keep her *almost* brother-in-law after school . . . how would that look?'

'Miss Swetnick is very fair,' Sally said. 'She doesn't play favourites.'

'Just because she didn't send you to the office this morning . . . that doesn't mean anything.'

'We'll see,' Sally said.

'We sure will,' Peter told her.

That afternoon, during a spelling bee, Sally missed the word *Pacific* on the fourth round and had to take her seat. Peter had missed on the second round so he was seated too. As soon as she felt the tug on her braid Sally knew that Peter was about to dip her hair in his inkwell, but this time she didn't have to say anything because Miss Swetnick saw the whole thing.

'Peter Hornstein! How many times have I told you to keep your hands off Sally's hair? Three days after school and thirty *I will nots* in your notebook.'

'But, Miss Swetnick . . .' Peter began.

'You know better, Peter.'

'But, Miss Swetnick . . .'

'Did you think I wouldn't keep you after school just because we're practically related?'

'No, ma'am . . . I never thought that.'

'I'm glad . . . now, let's get back to our spelling bee. Barbara, can you spell the word, *university* . . .'

'U-n-i-v-e-r-s-i-t-y.' Barbara won the spelling bee. She won almost every week. She would certainly be the class representative to the school spelling bee and if she won that she'd go to the state spelling bee and get her picture in the newspapers. Sally wished she could spell the same way Barbara could. Or was it just that Miss Swetnick gave Sally harder words? No, she wouldn't do that . . . after all, she was a very fair teacher.

'Who's that fat girl with Douglas?' Barbara asked Sally. They were taking a short cut to Barbara's house, after school, across the grounds of Miami Beach Junior-Senior High.

'Where?' Sally asked.

'Over there . . . see . . .' Barbara pointed to a palm tree.

'I don't know,' Sally said, spotting them on the grass. 'I've never seen her before.'

'Probably his girlfriend,' Barbara said.

'No . . . Douglas doesn't have any friends.'

'Everybody has friends.'

'Not Douglas . . . he's different,' Sally said. 'He had two in New Jersey but he doesn't have any here.'

'I'll bet he does,' Barbara said, 'and that he just doesn't tell you about them.'

'Douglas doesn't tell us about anything!'

'You see . . .' Barbara said.

When Douglas came home for supper, Sally was outside, waiting for him. 'Who was that girl?' she asked.

'What girl?'

'Under the tree . . . this afternoon . . . I saw you . . .'

'Oh, that girl . . . that was Darlene.'

'Who's Darlene?' Sally said.

'The girl under the tree.'

'I mean *who* is she?'

'A friend . . . why?' Douglas asked.

So, Barbara was right after all, Sally thought. 'How do you know her?'

'From school . . . what is this . . . twenty questions?'

'I'm just curious . . . does she live around here?'

'No, she lives on an island in Biscayne Bay.'

318

'Isn't that where the millionaires live?' Sally asked.

'Yeah . . .'

'Is she a millionaire?'

'You know something, Sally . . . you're starting to sound just like Mom!'

'I am not . . . I just want to know what's going on for a change!'

Sally sat down at the table in the dining alcove. Aunt Bette had sent her a new box of stationery. *Sayings From Sally* was printed across the top of every sheet. She wrote a short thank you note to Aunt Bette, then put the box back on her shelf and took a piece of paper from her old Bambi stationery.

She couldn't write to *him* on name paper.

Dear Mr Zavodsky,
   You haven't seen me around much lately because I've been very busy. But that doesn't mean I don't know what's going on. I'm still on your case even when I don't see you. So don't get any wrong ideas and think you're home free.

The next day Sally went to Barbara's house again. They were going to practise twirling batons. 'You were right,' Sally said. 'Douglas does have a friend. Her name's Darlene.'

'You see . . .' Barbara said, 'I told you so.'

'She lives on an island in Biscayne Bay.'

'Oh . . . one of those!'

'Douglas wouldn't tell me anything else about her.'

'I'll get Marla to find out for us,' Barbara said. They practised twirling in Barbara's front yard. Barbara was getting very good. She could toss her baton into the air and catch it as it came down without missing a beat. Sally hadn't mastered that trick yet. She always closed her eyes at the last moment, sure the baton would hit her in the head, and usually it did. But she could twirl it under her leg and switch hands.

'I want to twirl in the Orange Bowl parade next New Year's Eve,' Barbara said.

'Oh, me too,' Sally said, and she marched across the yard

with her knees high and her head back. 'How do I look?'

'A lot better,' Barbara said, as Sally strutted in front of her. 'I hope I get to wear the same uniform as my sister . . . I love her white boots and her red dress.'

'I like her hat best,' Sally said, 'with all that gold braid.'

Barbara did her figure eights so fast her baton looked like it had a motor.

'We could march together in the parade,' Sally said tentatively, not sure if Barbara considered her an equal in twirling.

'Yes . . . and be the first and only Central Beach kids *ever* in the parade.'

Sally felt more sure of herself then. 'They'll announce the debut of Barbara Ash and Sally Freedman and we'll march in front of the best float like this . . . *dum dum dee dah dah* . . .' she sang as she strutted across the yard.

'Did you hear where Miss Swetnick's going on her honeymoon?' Barbara asked, tossing her baton into the air.

'Yes, to Cuba.'

'Isn't that a dumb place to go for a honeymoon?'

'I don't know . . . my parents were there over Christmas vacation and they said it was great.'

'If you like cigars . . .'

Sally laughed. 'My parents don't like cigars . . . especially my mother.'

'But that's what Cuba's famous for.'

'That's not the only thing,' Sally said. 'They have this drink called Crème de Cacao that's supposed to be really something . . . it makes you feel like you're walking on air . . .'

'I've never heard of it.'

'My mother told me . . .'

Barbara sank to her knees, whipping her baton from hand to hand. 'We've got cocoa and cream . . . we could make some . . .'

'It's got something else in it too,' Sally said. 'Some kind of whisky, I think.'

320

'We've got whisky,' Barbara said. 'And I'm getting thirsty . . .'

They went inside, to the kitchen, where Barbara gathered the ingredients. She mixed the cocoa and cream, then added a dash of whisky.

'Are you allowed to drink that?' Sally asked, eyeing the whisky bottle. It was called Johnnie Walker.

'I've never asked,' Barbara said, stirring in some sugar. 'This is instant cocoa . . . we don't need to heat it.' She handed Sally a cup. 'Well . . . here's looking at you,' she said, clinking cups with Sally.

Sally took a sip, then waited for Barbara to do the same.

'What do you think?' Barbara asked.

'Not bad,' Sally said, afraid of hurting Barbara's feelings.

'I don't like it,' Barbara said, wiping her mouth with the back of her hand. 'It doesn't make me feel like I'm walking on air . . .'

'Me neither,' Sally said.

'Let's have grape juice instead.' Barbara rinsed out their cups and poured the grape juice.

'It might have tasted good without the whisky,' Sally said.

'But then it would have been just plain cocoa.'

'I suppose you're right.'

'I could tell you a secret about whisky,' Barbara said.

'Tell me . . .'

'Only if you promise never to breathe a word . . .'

'I promise . . .'

'Swear it?'

'I swear . . .'

'Every Saturday night my mother gets drunk.' Barbara took a long drink of juice.

'She does?' Sally asked.

'Yes . . . she drinks until she passes out. She listens to records . . . the ones she and my father used to play . . . and she gets out the old scrap-books . . . and she cries and she drinks . . . she thinks me and Marla don't know because she

gives us money for the movies . . . to get us out of the
house . . . but we know . . . and on Sundays she says she
thinks she's catching cold and she stays in bed all day . . . she
doesn't touch a drop the rest of the week though . . .'

'That's sad . . .' Sally didn't know what else to say.

'Yes . . . it would be better if she'd come out and tell us how
she's feeling . . .'

'Grownups always keep things to themselves, don't they?'
Sally said.

'They seem to.'

'But it's better to share your problems with a friend, don't
you think?'

'Well . . . I feel better since I told you about my mother,'
Barbara said, quietly.

Sally looked away for a moment, then said, 'I've got a secret
too . . .'

'About your mother?'

'No . . . my father.'

'He drinks?'

'No . . .'

'Well what is it?'

'Cross your heart and hope to die you'll never tell?'

'Cross my heart . . .'

'I've never told anyone about this . . .' Sally said,
reconsidering.

'You'll feel better when you do,' Barbara told her.

'Okay . . . I'm scared my father's going to die this year.'

'Why, is he sick?'

'No . . . but both his brothers died when they were
forty-two and that's how old my father is.'

'Were they sick first?' Barbara asked, pouring more juice.

'One was and the other wasn't . . . he just dropped dead.'

'That's pretty scary,' Barbara said.

'I know . . . I pray for him every night.'

'I prayed for my father during the war . . .'

'But you were just a little kid then.'

322

'So? I prayed with my mother and Marla every single night . . . but it didn't do any good.'

eighteen

Sally caught Virus X. It was going around. Her head hurt and she felt weak and dizzy when she tried to stand. Ma Fanny sat beside her and showed her a story in *The Forward*. 'You see . . .' she said, tapping her paper, 'all the famous people in Hollywood have Virus X too. You're right in style.'

'I don't feel in style.'

'Three days and you'll be better. It says so right here.' She began to read. 'Virus X strikes movie stars, Esther Williams and Margaret O'Brien . . .'

'Where . . . where does it say that?' Sally asked, sitting up. 'Show me those names.'

Ma Fanny laughed. 'Okay . . . so maybe not both of your favourites at once but a lot of famous people just the same.'

'Famous schmamous,' Sally said, imitating Ma Fanny. She rolled over in her bed and moaned, 'I'm not *longed* for this world . . .'

Dr Spear came to the house to examine Sally. 'You'll be just fine,' he said, handing her a lollipop from his black bag.

'What about medicine?' Mom asked.

'None needed . . . three days and she'll be as good as new.'

'I told you,' Ma Fanny said. 'I read it in my paper.'

Mom ignored Ma Fanny's remark and asked the doctor, 'What about Douglas . . . it could be dangerous for him to come into contact with Sally's germs . . . should I send him to stay with friends until she's well?'

'I wouldn't bother,' Dr Spear said. 'Virus X is a relatively

mild bug . . . and even if Douglas comes down with it there's
not much we can do . . . let's just wait . . . no need to worry in
advance.'

'Easier said than done,' Mom told him.

'Look, Mrs Freedman . . . all of Douglas's blood tests have
been normal. You really have two fine, healthy children . . .'
He looked over at Sally and winked. 'So why do you worry so?'

'It's my nature,' Mom said.

'Try to relax . . . I can prescribe something to help if you
like . . .'

'No, no . . . I don't need anything. I just want my children
to stay healthy . . . that's all I ask.'

'Take each day as it comes,' Dr Spear advised.

'I'll try,' Mom said. 'And thanks for coming . . . I know how
busy you are.'

Later when Ma Fanny went to the kitchen to make a fresh
orangeade for Sally, she said, 'Maybe the doctor's right,
Louise. You should try to relax more.'

'I play mah-jong twice a week,' Mom said.

'But the rest of the time you sit home and read . . . you'll
ruin your eyes.'

'My eyes are fine.'

'Maybe you should get out more with people . . . not just me
and the women in this house . . . they could drive anybody
crazy . . . one, two, three . . .'

'Look, Ma . . . I enjoy Eileen's company . . . she's a very
good friend to me down here . . . and other than that I'm busy
with the children . . . they're my life.'

'And mine, you please shouldn't forget,' Ma Fanny said.

On Sally's third day home from school Andrea woke up with
Virus X too and Mrs Rubin was so concerned about Linda she
sent her to stay at the Shelbourne Hotel with her grandmother.
Sally thought Linda was very lucky because the Shelbourne
Hotel was one of the prettiest on Collins Avenue.

Ma Fanny made chicken soup with rice for Sally's lunch. It
was the first time Sally had felt hungry since coming down with

Virus X. While she was having her second bowl, the doorbell rang. It was the man from the telephone company, ready to install their phone.

'At last!' Mom said. 'I'd just about given up hope.'

'You and everybody else,' the telephone man said. He had a toothpick in his mouth and when he spoke he kept his teeth together so that he sounded like Humphrey Bogart, the movie star.

'Now we'll be able to talk to Daddy without the whole world listening,' Mom told Sally.

'And I won't have to stand on a chair to reach *this* phone,' Sally said.

'That's right.' Mom smiled and ran her fingers through Sally's hair.

When he'd finished, the telephone man said, 'Okay . . . this is a four-party line so when you . . .'

Mom interrupted him. 'But we requested a private line . . . we've always had a private line . . .'

'Listen, lady . . . you're lucky to be getting any kind of line . . . we have a long list of people who'd be happy with this set-up.'

'It's not that I'm unhappy,' Mom said, 'it's just that I thought . . .'

'It won't be as bad as it sounds,' the telephone man said. 'You'll get used to it.' He took the toothpick out of his mouth and put it in the ashtray. 'Okay . . .' he said, opening and closing his mouth a few times, as if he were testing his jaw to make sure it worked. 'Your signal is one long ring, followed by two short ones.'

'What do you mean?' Sally asked.

'It'll sound like this,' he said, 'brrriinngg . . . brring, brring . . .'

Sally laughed. 'What a funny telephone!'

'It may be funny, sister, but it works!'

'What will the other signals sound like?' Sally asked.

'The only one you need to worry about is your own,' he said.

'I don't have time for long demonstrations. I've got to hook up your neighbours too.'

'The Rubins?' Sally asked.

The telephone man checked his book. 'No . . . the Daniels.'

'Oh, them . . .' Sally said. 'That should make Bubbles very happy.'

'So . . . if you'll sign right here,' he said to Mom, tapping his paper, 'I'll leave you a phone directory and be on my way.'

Mom signed and said, 'Thank you very much.'

'Don't mention it.' He looked over at Sally.

'Goodbye, sister . . .'

'Goodbye,' Sally said, 'and don't forget your toothpick.'

'Sally!' Mom said.

'What?'

The telephone man shook his head and went out the door.

'Oh . . . never mind,' Mom said.

'Can I make the first call?' Sally asked. 'Pretty please . . .'

'Who are you going to call?'

'Barbara . . . I want to find out what's new in school.'

'She won't be home yet . . . it's just one-thirty.'

'Oh.'

'But you can call her later.'

'As long as I get to try it out before Douglas,' Sally said.

'Okay . . . you can be the first,' Mom said.

'Thanks!'

Sally looked up Barbara's number in the directory. She wrote it down and waited until three-fifteen, then she dialled. Barbara answered.

'Hi, it's me . . .' Sally said. 'I'm trying out our new phone . . . how does it sound to you? . . . oh, I had Virus X . . . but I'm better now . . . what's new in school? . . . really? . . . a new girl . . . what's she like? . . . oh . . . from Chicago . . . really a blood disease . . . oh . . . um, let's see . . . it's Central 4-6424 . . . okay . . . I'll be right here, waiting . . .'

Sally hung up the phone. 'She's going to call me back,' she told Mom.

326

'I have to do some shopping,' Mom said. 'I'll only be gone an hour. Do you need anything, Ma?'

'Corn flakes,' Ma Fanny said. 'And maybe another quart of milk . . .'

'Okay . . .' Mom said. 'Rest up, Sally.'

'I will.'

The phone rang. One long followed by two short rings. 'I'll get it,' Sally said, 'it's probably Barbara.' She lifted the receiver off the hook. 'Hello . . . oh, hi . . . I knew it would be you . . .'

'I've got information about Darlene,' Barbara said, 'but I had to wait for Marla to go outside so she wouldn't know I was telling you. Darlene's in ninth grade, she belongs to the Model Airplane Club, she's always on a diet, her father's a movie producer, they have a butler and two maids, they have three cars, one is a convertible, and she's not popular with the kids at school . . . listen, I've got to hang up now . . . see you tomorrow . . . 'bye . . .'

'Wait . . .' Sally started to say, but it was too late. She looked at Ma Fanny. 'I forgot to ask if I missed a lot of work in school . . .'

'So, you'll call her back,' Ma Fanny said. 'I'll be in the kitchen, making you another drink . . .'

Sally lifted the receiver again. But this time, instead of the dial tone, she heard Bubbles talking. She hadn't realized she'd be able to hear the other people on their line. How interesting! Bubbles was talking to a boy. Sally held the receiver to her ear. Bubbles said, 'I don't know how I'll live until Saturday night.' The boy said, 'I think of you every second . . . I can't think of anything else.' Bubbles said, 'Can you get the car?' The boy said, 'I've got it all arranged.'

Ma Fanny came back into the living room, carrying an orangeade for Sally. Sally replaced the receiver. 'I was trying to get Barbara,' she said, 'but the line was busy.'

Ma Fanny nodded.

That night, after supper, Mom placed a call to Daddy.

Douglas and Sally each got to say hello. Then, when Mom took the phone, Douglas automatically went out the door. Mom told Sally, 'Go out to play now . . .'

'I can't,' Sally said. 'I have Virus X . . . remember?'

'Then go to the bathroom.'

'I don't have to.'

'Go anyway . . .'

'Oh . . .' Sally said, stomping across the living room, through the sleeping alcove and into the bathroom.

She heard Mom sigh. 'She's such a funny little girl . . . always afraid of missing out . . . and I miss you too, Arnold . . . Sally, will you *close* the bathroom door, please!'

The next day Sally went back to school. She met Jackie, the new girl, during recess. Jackie was small and frail, with very pale skin and long straight dark hair. 'My brother Douglas had nephritis,' Sally said.

'I'm sorry to hear that,' Jackie answered.

'He's okay now.'

'That's good.'

'So what did you have?'

'Mine's very complicated . . . it doesn't have a name . . . it's got to do with my blood . . .'

'Oh.'

'I was in hospital three months . . . I almost died.'

'That sounds serious.'

'Yes . . . that's what everyone said . . . but I'm going to be all right now . . . my mother promised . . .'

While they were talking Peter ran up to Sally and pulled her braids. 'Oh . . . he makes me so mad!'

'I think he's cute,' Jackie said. 'I wouldn't mind if he pulled my hair.

Andrea was sick for a week. One afternoon Sally asked Mom if she could go to the park with Shelby.

'Walking or riding?' Mom asked.

'Riding . . . but we'll be very careful.'

328

'And be back by five on the dot?'

'Yes, five on the dot . . . I promise,' Sally said.

Sally and Shelby rode to the park and watched Georgia Blue Eyes and his friends play ball.

Shelby said, 'I really want to kiss him . . . don't you?'

'I wouldn't mind,' Sally answered.

'We could chase him until he drops,' Shelby suggested, 'and then both of us could jump on him and you could hold him still while I kiss him and then I'd hold him still for you . . . what do you think?'

'I don't want to kiss him *that* much,' Sally said.

'Oh, well . . . too bad . . .'

They circled the field on their bicycles, then tried out a new bike path. 'Watch this . . .' Shelby said, pedalling faster and faster. 'No hands . . .'

'Be careful,' Sally called, trying to catch up with Shelby. But it was too late. Shelby fell and her bicycle toppled over her. 'Oh, no . . .' Sally jumped off her bicycle and freed Shelby. 'Are you okay?' she asked.

'No,' Shelby whimpered.

'What hurts?'

'Everything.' Shelby began to cry. 'Everything hurts . . .'

Shelby's knees and one elbow were badly scraped and bleeding. 'Oh, boy . . .' Sally said, 'are you going to have good scabs!'

That made Shelby cry harder.

'Can you ride?' Sally asked.

'No . . . how can I ride . . . I'm bleeding.'

'Well . . .' Sally thought fast. 'You stay right here and don't move an inch. I'll go for help and be right back.'

Shelby nodded and squeezed her nostrils together to keep them from dripping.

Sally hopped on her bicycle and took off. As she rounded the corner of the path she spotted Mr Zavodsky on a bench, reading his newspaper. Don't look up, Sally said under her breath. Don't notice me . . . just keep reading your paper. I don't have time for you now, Adolf . . . I've got other things to worry about, like Shelby . . . She rode with her head down and her shirt collar up. What good luck, she thought as she passed him, he didn't see me. She checked her new Mickey Mouse watch. It was two minutes to five. Mom would be really angry if she was late. She pedalled as fast as she could, all the way home. When she got there she burst in the door, calling, 'Mom . . . Mom!'

'What is it . . .' Mom asked, 'and do you know you're five minutes late?'

'Shelby fell off her bike and she's bleeding.'

'Where?'

'Her knees and her elbow . . .'

'I mean, where is she?' Mom said.

'In the park . . . I told her to stay right there and I'd get help.'

'You left her in the park . . . bleeding?'

'Well, you told me to be home by five . . .'

'But, Sally . . . how could you leave your friend that way . . . I'm surprised at you . . . how would you feel if you'd had an accident and Shelby left you alone?'

'I didn't know what else to do,' Sally said.

'So now *I* have to go to the park . . . is that right?' Mom asked.

'Well, yes . . .' Sally didn't understand her mother. She'd come home for help. What else should she have done?'

Mom ran into the bathroom, muttering, and threw some supplies into a paper bag. 'Okay . . . let's go.'

'To the park?' Sally asked.

'Honestly, Sally . . .' Mom let the screen door slam and raced down the stairs.

Sally followed.

'How are we going to get there?' she asked, trying to keep up with her mother.

'On bicycles,' Mom said.

'Both of us on mine?'

330

'No . . . I'll ride Douglas's.'

'You know how to ride a boy's bike?'

'Of course.'

'I never knew that.'

'There are many things you don't know.'

They rode to the park, side by side. Mom gathered her skirt between her legs and after a wobbly start became more sure of herself and rode as fast as Sally.

Sally led her mother to the bicycle path where she had left Shelby, but both Shelby and her bicycle were gone.

'Well . . .' Mom said. 'Where is she?'

'I don't know.' But Sally had an idea – an idea so horrible it was almost too scary to think about. *Mr Zavodsky*. He had found Shelby. Yes, he had found her lying there, helpless and bleeding. And then, when he saw that she was wearing a Jewish star around her neck he couldn't control himself any more. He reached into his pocket and pulled out a rope. He tied it around Shelby's neck, pulling it tighter and tighter, until Shelby's face turned blue. She died with her eyes open, staring into space. And then, while her body was still warm, Mr Zavodsky pulled out his knife, sharp and shiny, and he peeled off Shelby's skin, slowly, so as not to rip any. And then he went home to make a new lampshade.

'Sally . . . what *is* wrong with you?' Mom asked.

'What . . . me . . . nothing . . .' Sally said.

'You look funny . . .'

'It's Shelby . . . I . . .'

'Now you see why you shouldn't have left her?'

'Oh, yes,' Sally said, unable to hold back her tears. 'And I'm sorry . . . I really am . . .'

'I know you are,' Mom said. 'You must never leave the scene of an accident. Do you understand that?'

'Yes . . .'

Mom put her arm around Sally. 'It's all right now . . . you've learned your lesson . . . stop crying and let's go . . .'

'It's not all right . . .'

331

'It will be . . . once we find Shelby.'

'But we can't . . . she'll be . . .'

'We can and we will . . . and when we do, we'll tell her we're sorry . . .'

'But you don't understand . . .'

'We'll go to her house first,' Mom said. 'Her grandmother is probably worried sick.'

'But, Mom . . .' Who should Sally tell first . . . Shelby's mother or her father? And how would she ever find them? All she knew was they lived somewhere in New York. They'd be sorry now . . . sorry they'd spent so much time fighting over Shelby . . .

'Follow me, Sally . . . and no more buts . . .'

Sally could just imagine what would happen next. Shelby's grandmother would answer the door and say, *Hello, Sally . . . come in . . . come in . . . have a cookie . . . have a piece of Challah, fresh from the oven . . .*

Then Sally would say, *I really can't stay, Mrs Bierman . . . you see, I've come with bad news . . . very, very bad . . .*

Mrs Bierman would clutch her chest and Sally would take a big breath and say, *I'm sorry to tell you that Shelby has been murdered by Adolf Hitler.* No need to tell Mrs Bierman the gruesome details.

Adolf Hitler? Mrs Bierman would say, unbelievingly.

Yes.

Not the Adolf Hitler?

The very same one.

But how?

He came here to retire, you see.

Oh, I didn't know.

Nobody does.

Then Mrs Bierman would begin to cry. She would sob and yell and scream and beat her fists against the wall.

It's all my fault, Sally would tell her. *I hope you'll forgive me some day but if you won't I'll understand because I know you're old and Shelby is all you had in the whole world and now there's*

*nothing left to live for . . . but I really didn't do it on purpose . . .
in fact, I was sure I was doing the right thing . . . going home to get
my mother and all . . . but now I realize that I must never ever
leave the scene of an accident . . . and maybe I should have gone
straight to the police about Mr Zavodsky . . .*

Zavodsky . . . who's Zavodsky?

*That's what Hitler calls himself now . . . but you see, the police
would want evidence . . . they always do . . . and until Shelby's
murder we didn't have any . . . now, of course, they'll arrest him
and stick him in the electric chair where he belongs and he won't kill
any more children, ever.*

Mrs Bierman would nod.

*Maybe you could adopt a poor orphan from Europe and then
you'd have someone to live for again . . .*

'Here we are,' Mom said. 'Which apartment?'

'2C,' Sally said, feeling her legs shake.

Mom rang the bell.

Shelby's grandmother answered. 'Hello, Sally,' she said.
'Come in . . . come in . . . have some Challah, fresh from the
oven . . .'

Sally shook her head. 'I really can't stay . . .' she began, but
then, as Mrs Bierman opened the apartment door all the way,
Sally saw Shelby, sitting on the floor, shooting marbles. 'Hi,'
she said. 'I got tired of waiting in the park so I rode home.
Granny cleaned up my knees . . . there were pebbles stuck to
them.'

'I had *some* job,' Mrs Bierman said.

Sally started to cry again.

'What's wrong with you?' Shelby asked.

'Nothing . . .'

'Listen,' Shelby said, 'I'm really sorry . . . Granny told me it
wasn't right that I left the park after you went to get help for
me . . . she explained how I should have waited right there
until you came back . . . and we've been calling your
house . . . but your grandmother didn't know where you
were . . .'

'That's not it,' Sally said, fighting to control herself.

'Then what?'

'I thought you were dead, that's what!'

'God forbid!' Mrs Bierman said.

'God forbid!' Mom repeated, and then, sounding embarrassed, she added, 'Sally has an active imagination.'

'Such an imagination!' Mrs Bierman shook her head.

Shelby laughed and laughed. 'Why would I be dead? I just fell off my bicycle . . . you don't die from that . . . that's the silliest thing I ever heard.' She shot her black marble across the room. It hit Sally in the foot.

Dear Mr Zavodsky,
I know what you were thinking of doing to Shelby today. I always know what you are thinking! Any day now I will have the evidence I need and then you will get what you deserve!

nineteen

Before Miss Beverly dismissed the Saturday morning ballet class she announced a contest, sponsored by Raymond's Shoe Store. Raymond's had the very pair of pink satin toe slippers that Margaret O'Brien had worn while filming *The Unfinished Dance*. Sally had now seen the movie three times and it was still her favourite. Everyone who took ballet lessons in Miami Beach was invited to try them on. And the person who fitted best into Margaret O'Brien's shoes would win the contest and get a free trip to Hollywood – *and* a screen test – *and* lunch with Margaret herself!

Sally just *had* to win. Then she would be discovered and get to be a famous movie star too. And when she caught Virus X again, it would say so in all the papers, including *The Forward*. And Miss Swetnick would say, *Isn't it wonderful . . . two girls*

from my class becoming famous in the same year . . . Barbara Ash
for spelling and Sally Freedman for the movies!

'Let's go over to Raymond's right after lunch,' Andrea said,
as she and Sally walked home from ballet class. They each
carried a package. Andrea hugged hers and said, 'Don't you
just love our new ballet dresses?'

'They're okay,' Sally said, shifting her package from one arm
to the other. She tried to hide her disappointment, because
instead of the pink net tutu she'd been hoping for, her ballet
dress turned out to be white cotton, with red smocking.

'In Brooklyn I had this ugly exercise outfit for acrobatics,'
Andrea said. 'A blue skirt and a beige jersey top. This one is
beautiful. We're so lucky!'

'In New Jersey I had a pink dotted Swiss ballet dress.'

'Dotted Swiss!' Andrea said. 'That's so fancy.'

'I went to a fancy dancing school.' Sally couldn't tell if
Andrea was impressed or if she thought *fancy* meant bad. 'My
teacher had ballet slippers in every colour.'

'Even red?'

'Yes . . . and green and blue and yellow, too.'

'I never saw ballet slippers in those colours . . .' Andrea
said, giving Sally a sceptical look.

'Well, Miss Elsie had them . . . you can ask my mother . . .
with a different ballet costume every week, to match her
slippers . . .'

'Hmmm . . . I'll bet you anything my feet will fit into
Margaret O'Brien's toe slippers,' Andrea said.

'What makes you so sure?'

'We have the same build . . . haven't you noticed?'

'No,' Sally said.

'Take a good look.' Andrea stood still.

Sally looked her up and down. 'I can't remember Margaret
O'Brien's build.'

'I'm surprised you haven't noticed how much alike we look,'
Andrea said.

'Who . . . you and me?'

Andrea made a sound with her tongue. 'No . . . me and Margaret O'Brien.'

Sally hid a smile.

'You don't think so?' Andrea asked.

'Nope.'

'We both have dark hair . . .'

'So does Hitler.'

Andrea spat. 'How many times have I told you *never* to say that name in front of me!' She spat again.

'I'm sorry . . . I forgot . . .'

'You better spit, Sally . . . you better spit right now or I'm never speaking to you again.'

'Okay . . . okay . . .' Sally went to the kerb and worked up some saliva. Then she took a big breath. 'Hoc-tooey,' she said, spitting into the street. At the same moment, a bird, flying overhead, plopped on Sally's arm. 'Look at this!' she said to Andrea.

'Eeuuwww . . .' Andrea held her nose. 'How disgusting!'

'That's how much you know . . .'

Sally ran the rest of the way home. When she got there she raced up the stairs, kicked open the door, tossed her package on the floor and shouted, 'Look at this . . . a bird made on me . . . look . . .' She held out her arm for Douglas and Mom and Ma Fanny to see.

Ma Fanny clapped her hands together. 'Good luck for a year!' she said, hugging Sally. 'And it couldn't happen to a better person.'

'It's not just superstition . . . is it?' Sally asked.

'No more than *knock on wood* or *bad things always happen in threes*,' Douglas said, sarcastically.

'Good luck for a year,' Ma Fanny repeated. 'You can take it or leave it.'

'I'll take it!' Sally thought of what this could mean. That her father would be all right. That the police would arrest Mr Zavodsky. That she'd win the contest at the shoe store. That Miss Swetnick would start asking her easier words during spelling bees. That Georgia Blue Eyes would kiss her, voluntarily. That Peter Hornstein would grow up into a Latin Lover and want *her* for his partner. That Big Ted would give Daddy such good tips in the stock market they'd get rich. That Harriet Goodman would get transferred to another class. That . . .

'So . . . I'm going to the Roney,' Douglas said, stretching.

'Not so fast,' Mom told him. '. . . I haven't decided yet.'

'When we were interrupted by Miss Bird Crap . . .'

'Douglas!'

'When my dear, sweet little sister came home we were in the midst of a . . .'

'We were *discussing* the situation,' Mom said.

'Some discussion!' Douglas said. 'It was more like the Spanish Inquisition . . .'

'What's that?' Sally asked.

'Mind your own business, for once!' Douglas told her.

'You know,' Mom said, 'I'm on your side, Douglas.'

'Good . . . then it's all settled . . .'

'Such a *swell* my son picks for his friend,' Mom said, sounding half-annoyed and half-pleased.

'I don't get you,' Douglas said to Mom. 'First, it's *Douglas make friends . . . try harder . . . don't sit around by yourself so much* . . . so I find a friend . . . so now all I hear is *The Swells* . . . so they're rich . . . so what's wrong with that . . . aren't you the one who's always saying it's just as easy to fall in love with a rich person as a poor one?'

'That's enough, Douglas!' Mom said and Sally could tell by the look on her face that she wasn't just angry but that her feelings were hurt too.

'When you can't think of anything better to say it's always, *That's enough, Douglas!*' He mimicked Mom and sounded surprisingly like her.

'Dougie . . .' Ma Fanny said, 'don't talk like that to your mother . . . she loves you . . .'

'Love-schmov . . .' Douglas retreated to the bathroom.

'What am I going to do with that boy?' Mom asked.

'Sha . . .' Ma Fanny said, 'everything will turn out fine . . . he's a good boy . . . he's got growing pains, that's all.'

'Does it hurt when your bones begin to grow fast?' Sally asked.

'It hurts inside,' Ma Fanny said.

'How about breasts . . . does it hurt when they start to grow?'

'You shouldn't be thinking about breasts at your age,' Mom said.

'Why not? Some girls in my class have them already . . . and take a look at Andrea . . . she wears a bra . . . did you know that . . . and she's just one year older than me.'

'They don't hurt, mumeshana . . .' Ma Fanny said. 'They grow quietly, when they're ready.'

Mom cleared her throat. 'Sally . . . go and wash off your arm before it starts to smell.'

'But I can't . . . then I won't have good luck for a year.'

Ma Fanny laughed. 'All that counts is the bird picked *you* . . . nothing can stop your good luck now . . .'

'Oh . . . I didn't know that,' Sally said. She went to the kitchen to wash because Douglas was still locked in the bathroom and she didn't want to mess with him.

Sally and Andrea stood on line at Raymond's Shoe Store. There was just nine more girls ahead of them. They'd been waiting for thirty-five minutes. Sally could feel the sweat trickling down her back. She thought of Douglas, swimming at the Roney Plaza, and of Shelby, holding her nose and sitting on the bottom of the Seagull pool, and of the ocean, with the tide rushing in.

'Boy, am I thirsty,' Andrea said.

'Same here.'

'I could really go for a tall glass of orange juice, couldn't you?'

'Make mine grape,' Sally said, licking her lips.

'Oh . . . I always forget about you and the pulp.'

338

Ten minutes later it was Andrea's turn to try on Margaret
O'Brien's ballet shoes. She sat down and kicked off her sandals.
Sally stood at her side. Would Andrea's foot fit? Would she win
the contest? Sally hoped not. She knew it was wrong to wish
Andrea bad luck but she wanted to win so much. If *she* couldn't
win the contest then she certainly didn't want Andrea to win.

The shoe man held out the slipper. Andrea slid her foot in as
far as it would go but the heel was still sticking out. 'Oops . . .'
the shoe man said. 'It's a little too small for you . . . sorry,
sweetheart . . . next,' he called.

'Right here,' Sally said.

'Listen,' Andrea said. 'It's not really too small for me. Miss
Beverly told us toe shoes should hug the foot . . . and if I just
bend my toes a little . . .'

'Really, sweetheart . . . take it from your Uncle Joe . . . it's
just not your size . . .'

'You're not my uncle,' Andrea said, standing up and
pouting.

She and Sally changed places. Sally knew exactly how
Cinderella must have felt when it was her turn to try on the
glass slipper. She closed her eyes for a minute. Thank you,
bird . . . thank you for choosing me to plop on. She took off
her sandal and held out her foot, digging her fingernails into
the upholstered arms of the chair. The shoe man held out
Margaret's pink slipper. It didn't have a boxed toe, like Sally's
toe shoe. This toe was covered with satin, like a professional
ballerina's. She eased her foot into the shoe. It fitted! She
didn't have to bend her toes or anything. Her whole foot went
in easily. She smiled. But, wait . . . there was too much space
around her foot. Maybe the shoe man wouldn't notice. 'It's very
comfortable,' Sally said, glancing at Andrea. Andrea looked
concerned. Her lips were scrunched up and her brow was
wrinkled. She doesn't want me to win, Sally thought. She
doesn't want me to win any more than I wanted her to win.

'Sorry, sweetheart . . .' the shoe man said to Sally. 'It's too
wide for your narrow little foot.'

'I could stuff the sides with lamb's wool,' Sally said, 'I usually do that anyway.'

'Lamb's wool is okay for the toe, sweetheart . . . but not for the rest of the foot . . . don't look so glum . . . maybe you'll win some other time . . . next,' he called and Sally knew it was over, that she had to put on her sandal and stand up and let someone else try on Margaret O'Brien's toe slipper.

She felt like crying. Some good luck that bird was bringing her! She couldn't speak. If she did her voice would break and then nothing would stop the tears. And she wasn't going to make a fool of herself like that blonde girl in the corner, bawling her eyes out.

She and Andrea went outside. 'Who wants a trip to Hollywood anyway?' Andrea asked. 'All they let you eat there is parsley sandwiches.'

'Says who?'

'I read it in a movie magazine . . . they feed all the movie stars parsley sandwiches so they'll stay skinny. Imagine no bologna or cupcakes or spaghetti . . .'

'I don't like spaghetti,' Sally said.

'But you like bologna, don't you?' Andrea said.

'Yes . . . and cupcakes too.'

'Well, then . . .'

'That bird didn't bring me good luck at all,' Sally told Ma Fanny. They were in the breakfast nook waiting for Douglas to return from the Chinese restaurant with a take-out supper.

'How do you know it's not good luck?' Ma Fanny asked.

'I didn't win the contest, did I?'

'But in the long run that could be good luck.'

'How?' Sally asked.

'Suppose you won,' Ma Fanny said. 'Suppose you went to Hollywood and while you were there the hotel burned down, God forbid . . .'

'I don't get it,' Sally said.

'Think, mumeshana . . . think and you'll understand.'

Sally thought about what Ma Fanny had said but it still didn't make any sense to her.

Douglas came home with the food. Ma Fanny fixed the tea while Mom opened the containers – first the rice, then the noodles, and finally the chow mein. But when Mom saw the chow mein she screamed and put the lid back on its container.

'What . . . what is it . . . what's the matter . . .' they all asked at once.

'A cockroach,' Mom said. 'A cockroach right on top . . . sitting on the chow mein.' The colour drained from her face.

'Let me see that . . .' Douglas said. He opened the container slowly. 'Hot damn! Look at that . . .' He held the container open for Sally and Ma Fanny to see.

'Close it up, Douglas,' Mom said. 'For God's sake . . . close it up before he gets out . . .'

'I'm taking it back,' Douglas said. 'I'm taking it back and telling them what I think of their restaurant . . '.

'No, don't . . .' Mom said. 'We'll have tuna instead.'

'That's not the point,' Douglas said, his face turning more and more red. 'We can't let them get away with this . . . just because I'm only fourteen they can't put a cockroach in my chow mein and get away with it!'

He stormed out of the door, carrying the container of chow mein.

Mom called after him but Ma Fanny said, 'Let him go, Louise . . . let him handle it himself.'

'Ma Fanny . . .' Sally said.

'What, lovey?'

'Does it mean something special if you find a cockroach in your chow mein?'

'Yes . . .'

'What?'

'It means the chow mein comes from a very dirty restaurant!'

twenty

Dear Doey,

    I am waiting and waiting for my luck to begin. I hope it starts soon because I sure could use it.

    I hope you are feeling fine. I am almost fine, except for the fungus on the bottoms of my feet. At first Mom said it came because I didn't dry between my toes, but then she changed her mind and decided it came from walking barefoot on the rug in the living room. She says we don't know who rented this place before us and what kinds of germs they may have left. Dr Spear said my fungus came from the air. I believe him. He gave me a salve to rub into my feet three times a day and I have to wear white cotton socks until it is gone. Nobody, but nobody, wears socks to school here. I feel like a jerk!

    Did you hear about the rain? It came down in buckets, as Ma Fanny would say. The gutters were flooded in a few minutes and all the big kids walked home from school carrying their shoes. They had so much fun! I can't wait to be a big kid. Mom almost killed Douglas though. She yelled that he would catch pneumonia or worse from getting his feet so wet. She made him soak them in a hot tub for an hour. He was so mad he didn't talk to her for two days!

    Did you hear about Douglas's friend? Her name is Darlene. Mom calls her family The Swells *because they are very rich, maybe even millionaires, and they belong to the Roney Plaza instead of the Seagull Pool, like us. Don't tell Douglas that I said this, but Darlene is fat. My friend Barbara and I saw her outside the high school one day, talking to Douglas. They are building a model airplane together. Darlene reads every issue of* Popular Science *and* Popular Mechanics *and she is giving Douglas a subscription to* Model Airplane News *for his birthday.*

    I understand why you can't come down for my birthday. It will be more fair if you come in between mine and Douglas's, like you said. I am disappointed but I will try to have fun anyway. I'll miss you a lot at my party. Mom is taking me, Andrea, Barbara and Shelby to The Park Avenue Restaurant. I'm going to eat twenty bowls of whipped cream, at least! See you soon.

Love and kisses and a big treatment,
Your favourite and only daughter,
Sally F.

Besides the fungus and the fact that Daddy wouldn't be down for her birthday, something else was bothering Sally – Peter Hornstein liked Jackie, the new girl in her class.

Peter began to write notes to Sally.

How come you don't wear halters like Jackie?

How come you don't wear your hair like Jackie?

How come you don't have tiddly winks, like Jackie?

This last note was the worst. All the boys in school called breasts *tiddly winks* and when Sally wore her pinafore with the open sides, they teased her all day. She was never going to wear it again! But Jackie didn't have anything to show either. She was just as flat as Sally, maybe even flatter because she was so skinny.

Peter was driving her crazy with his *how come* notes. Finally, Sally wrote one back to him. *If you like Jackie so much how come you don't write notes to her?*

He answered, *How come you care?*

More and more Sally found herself daydreaming about kissing Peter instead of Georgia Blue Eyes.

Besides the fungus and Daddy not coming down for her birthday *and* Peter liking Jackie, Sally was disturbed that Mr Zavodsky was still walking around a free man. It was time to do something about that!

Dear Chief of Police,

You don't know me but I am a detective from New Jersey. I have uncovered a very interesting case down here. I have discovered that Adolf Hitler is alive *and has come to Miami Beach to retire. He is pretending to be an old Jewish man. He uses the name Zavodsky and lives at 1330 Pennsylvania Avenue. He is in disguise so don't expect him to look just like his pictures. I know that you want evidence. Well, I'm working on it. Any day now I will be able to give you the exact details. In the meantime I just wanted you to know what's going on. Do not put any other detectives on this case. If you do you might ruin . . .*

Andrea was knocking on the door, calling, 'Sally . . . Sally . . .'

'Hi,' Sally said, letting her in.

'What're you doing?' Andrea said.

'Writing a letter.'

'To who?'

'Oh . . . somebody you don't know . . .'

'Want to play potsy?'

'Sure.' Sally put her letter in her keepsake box and she and Andrea went outside.

The following Friday morning Sally woke up with a stomach ache. 'I warned you yesterday that too much bologna would make you sick,' Mom said.

'I only ate six pieces.'

'That's five pieces too many.'

'I won't do it again.'

'Ma Fanny and I are supposed to go to a Hadassah meeting this afternoon,' Mom said.

'I'll be better by then.'

'Don't worry, tootsie,' Ma Fanny said. 'I'd rather stay home with you any day.'

'Oh no, Ma,' Mom told Ma Fanny. 'If anybody has to stay home with her, it's me. I know how much you've been looking forward to today's lecture. She wouldn't listen when I told her to stop eating that bologna . . . and she stuffed herself full of pickles . . . how many did you have, Sally . . . four, five . . .'

'Just three,' Sally said.

'But I'll bet they were big dills, weren't they?'

'Pretty big.'

'I certainly hope you've learned a lesson.'

'I have . . . I have . . .' Every time Mom said bologna or pickles Sally felt worse.

At noon Precious Redwine came to iron. When Precious heard that Mom was going to miss her meeting because of Sally's stomach ache she said, 'I've got eight kids at home, Mrs Freedman . . . so you go on and get ready and I'll watch Sally for you . . .'

'Well, that's very kind of you, Precious,' Mom said. 'You're sure you don't mind?'

'I don't mind.'

'I feel better anyway,' Sally said. 'They were just gas pains.'

Mom touched Sally's forehead three more times before she left with Ma Fanny, telling Precious, 'If there's an emergency I can be reached at Temple Beth-El, on the corner of Fourteenth Street.'

'She'll be just fine . . . don't you worry,' Precious said.

As soon as Mom and Ma Fanny left, Sally lay back on her day bed and made up a story inside her head . . .

Esther Williams Finds a Sister

Esther Williams is searching for a girl to play her younger sister in a new movie. She comes to Miami Beach but she can't find anyone suitable at the Roney Plaza, so she tries the Seagull Pool. When she spots Sally, floating on her back, she says, *That's her . . . that's the girl I want to play my little sister! We'll teach her to swim just like me. I can tell she's got real talent by the way she floats on her back. We'll need a boy to play opposite her . . . someone with dark, flashing eyes.*

Oh, I know just the boy, Sally tells Esther Williams, and she introduces her to Peter Hornstein, who happens to be visiting at the Seagull Pool that very day. Then Sally and Peter fly off to

Hollywood with Esther Williams and they have to practise kissing three times a week.

Sally sighed. 'What is it, sugar?' Precious Redwine asked, licking her finger, then touching it to the iron.

'Nothing . . .' Sally said.

The phone rang. Three short rings. Sally already knew that one long ring was Mrs Purcell, who lived in their building, but it wasn't much fun to listen in on her conversations because they were always about her headaches and backaches and hot flashes. And she knew the Daniels' ring too. One long, one short, then another long. She'd listened to Bubbles and her boyfriend plenty of times. But this was the first time she'd heard three short rings. She picked up the receiver very quietly and covered the mouthpiece with one hand, while raising it to her ear with the other.

'Hey, Zavodsky . . . that's you?' It was a man's voice.

'That's me, Simon,' Mr Zavodsky answered.

Sally sucked in her breath. She didn't know *he* was on their party line too. What good luck! At last the bird plop was working.

'So how's by you?' the man named Simon asked.

'By me, it's okay,' Mr Zavodsky said.

'By me, too.'

'So . . . it's all set for tonight?'

'All set . . . just like I promised,' Simon said.

'Good . . . so, you'll come by about eight?' Mr Zavodsky asked.

'About eight sounds good. We'll walk over from your place.'

'You should please be careful walking,' Mr Zavodsky said.

'I'm not always careful?' Simon asked.

'I should know?' Mr Zavodsky asked him.

'Goodbye.'

'Goodbye, yourself.'

Sally waited until she'd heard the click, then she replaced the receiver. It has to be a code, she thought. Yes, a secret code!

Otherwise it made no sense. And Simon was probably one of Hitler's old cronies, from the war. And probably what they were planning for tonight at eight was somebody's murder!

'Why do you listen to other people on the telephone?' Precious Redwine asked.

'I like to,' Sally told her.

'You shouldn't do that.'

'I know.'

'It's not nice.'

'I know.'

'Then why do you do it?'

'I told you . . . I like to . . . I like to know what's going on . . .'

Precious Redwine laughed then – a big, deep laugh that came right out of her belly. 'You're a nosy little girl . . . you know that?'

Sally nodded. 'Please don't tell on me.'

'I won't tell on you if you don't tell . . .'

'Tell what?' Sally asked.

'That I'm going to sit down and have a little rest.'

'It's a deal,' Sally said.

Precious lowered herself into the chair in the living room, kicked off her shoes, and put her feet up on the footstool. 'Oh my . . . that feels good . . . off my aching feet at last . . .'

'You better not walk barefoot in here,' Sally said. 'There might be a fungus in our rug.'

'I've got tough old feet,' Precious said, closing her eyes.

There were so many questions Sally wanted to ask Precious Redwine, starting with her beautiful name. And then she wanted to ask about drinking from the *Coloured* water fountain and about riding in the back of the bus and about her eight kids and about how she learned to be such a good ironer and about how she touched her wet finger to the iron without burning herself and about which half of her was Seminole Indian . . . but while Sally was working up the nerve to speak, Precious fell asleep, and when she woke up, half an hour later, Sally had lost her nerve again.

So Precious went back to her ironing and Sally went back to
Esther Williams Finds a Sister, Part Two.

twenty-one

'But I have to go out tonight,' Sally told her mother. 'Just for a
little while.'

'No . . . you stayed home from school with a stomach ache
so you can't possibly go outside until tomorrow.'

'But, Mom . . . my stomach ache is all better. It was better
before you left for your Hadassah meeting.'

'The answer is still *no*, Sally.'

'But, Mom . . . it's very warm out and I'll come in by
eight . . . I promise . . . and you always let me stay out until
nine on Fridays.'

'Stop begging,' Mom said. 'If I let you go out you'll only run
around and get all sweated up and then you'll get thirsty and
want to drink a quart of juice and then, bingo, another stomach
ache.'

'I won't run. I'll sit very quietly by the goldfish pool.'

'This discussion is over,' Mom said. 'Tonight you're going to
bed early and that's that.'

If Sally couldn't go out tonight then she wouldn't get to see
Mr Zavodsky's friend, Simon. And this could be just the
evidence she'd been waiting for! But there was no point in
arguing with her mother. Mom wasn't going to change her
mind. Sally wrote another note.

Dear Mr Zavodsky,
  Okay. Enough is enough! I know all about you and Simon.
You better not try anything funny. I'm closing in on you. This is
your last chance to give yourself up.

348

Sally was going to put this letter into Mr Zavodsky's mailbox the next morning, on her way to the Seagull Pool Club. But the Rubins had recently joined the Seagull and today was to be their first day and both families were going over together. So there was no chance for Sally to mail her letter without being noticed. She would just have to wait until later.

'I'm so excited!' Andrea said. 'Do you like my new suit?'

'It's very nice,' Sally said, putting the letter into her beach bag. Andrea's new bathing suit was two-piece, with green stripes. The top was the same kind of halter that Jackie wore to school. The same kind that Peter Hornstein admired.

When the girls were in the changing room at the Seagull Sally told Andrea, 'You have to wear a bathing hat here.'

'I hate bathing hats!'

'Me too . . . they make my head itch . . . but you can't go in without one . . . it's a rule.'

'I hate rules!'

'Me too . . . and that's not the only one either . . . you have to wash your feet before they'll let you in . . .'

'My feet!'

'Yes.'

'You're the one with the fungus,' Andrea said.

'I have to wash mine too . . . besides, my fungus is cleared up . . . you want to see . . .' She sat on the bench and held her bare feet up so that Andrea could see the bottoms.

'They're peeling!'

'I know,' Sally said. 'That's the fungus part coming off.'

'Euueewww . . .' Andrea made her 'disgusting' face.

Sally was worried. She had never told Andrea that Georgia Blue Eyes belonged to the Seagull Pool. The only thing to do now was pretend that she had never seen him there before. She'd act as surprised as Andrea. Of course, she'd have to explain this to Shelby but she was sure Shelby would go along with her. Or better yet, maybe Georgia Blue Eyes wouldn't show up today. Maybe he'd stay home with Virus X or something.

Sally, Andrea and Shelby were dunking in the shallow end of the pool when four boys surrounded them. One of them was Georgia Blue Eyes! But before Sally had a chance to say anything he sneaked up behind Andrea and untied her bathing top. 'Tiddly winks . . . tiddly winks . . .' he called and the other boys joined in, chanting, 'Tiddly winks . . . tiddly winks . . .'

Luckily for Andrea her halter top was tied in two places, around her back *and* around her neck. Georgia Blue Eyes got only the string around her back. Andrea held her suit to her as the boys splashed, cutting the water with their hands so that it hit the girls in their faces. 'Stop it . . . stop it . . .' the girls cried.

'Hey . . . it's Sally Nevermind,' Georgia Blue Eyes shouted. And the other boys began to call, 'Sal-ly Nevermin-d . . . Sal-ly Nevermin-d . . .'

Finally, the lifeguard blew his whistle and the boys swam away. They were still laughing when they reached the other side of the pool.

Andrea ran for the changing room, with Sally and Shelby on her trail. When they got there, safe at last, Sally could see that Andrea was close to tears. 'Want me to tie your top for you?' Sally asked.

'Don't you touch me!' Andrea said. '*He* knows your name.'

Sally was surprised that Andrea was angry about that now. What the boys did was so much worse. She was sure Andrea would be too mad at them to care about Georgia Blue Eyes knowing her name. 'No, he doesn't,' she told Andrea.

'Don't lie to me . . . I heard him call you *Sally*.'

'Oh, that . . . he knows my first name but not my last.'

'You never told me *he* belongs here!'

'I didn't know myself.'

'Liar!'

'I've seen him here a few times but I didn't know he was a member.'

'You never said you *saw* him here.'

'I didn't? I guess I forgot.'

'How could you . . . how could you keep such a secret from me? I hate you! I'm never going to speak to you again!' She ran into a toilet stall and slammed the door.

'Whew . . .' Shelby said, 'she's really mad.'

'I know.'

'I think she might *really* hate you.'

'I know.'

'Have you got any suntan lotion?' Shelby asked. 'My back is killing me.'

Sally opened her locker and took out her beach bag.

'What are you going to do?' Shelby asked.

'I don't know.' Sally couldn't find the lotion. She turned the bag upside down and shook. Everything fell out on to the wet floor, including her letter to Mr Zavodsky.

'I sure wouldn't want to trade places with you!' Shelby said.

Sally picked up her letter. It was ruined. The ink had blurred.

'Could you do my back?' Shelby asked.

'In a second . . .' Sally mashed up her letter and threw it into the trash basket. She could write a better one later. Right now she had other things to worry about, like Andrea hating her.

Sally got a letter from her father, written on pink dental wax, the same day that Douglas got one written on toilet paper. Daddy never ran out of ideas for funny letters. Sally also got a letter from Christine.

Dear Sally,

You probably don't remember me but I used to be your best friend. My name is Chrissy. We used to live on the same street. I haven't heard from you in ages. It is too bad that some people go away and forget their old friends. In case you are wondering, we survived the ice storm. My mother says it will go down in history. In case you are wondering, we have a new girl in our class. Her name is Pearl and she comes from Ohio. She thinks she's great

because she can do fractions. Nobody likes her. She's a real jerk.
Do you remember Tommy Byers? In case you're wondering, I like
him. So does Pearl. I guess you must be having a great time with
all the other millionaires. If you can find time to write, in
between all your parties and dances, I might be able to find the
time to read your letter.
Your old friend,
Chrissy

Miss Swetnick and Peter Hornstein's brother, Hank, rented an
apartment in the building next to Sally's. Sally could look out
her living-room window and see into their bedroom. They were
painting it themselves. On Thursday after supper Sally waved
to them and they waved back. 'Need any help?' Sally cried. 'I
love to paint.'

'Sure . . . come on over,' Hank called back, leaning out the
window. 'We're going to do the bathroom tonight.'

Sally ran next door. 'We have a *beautiful* bathroom back
home,' she told Miss Swetnick and Hank. 'It's black and
lavender.'

'We're doing ours in blue,' Miss Swetnick said. She had on
shorts and a man's shirt, with the tails hanging out. Sally was
used to seeing her in dresses.

'Black and lavender looks really pretty . . .' Sally said, 'just
like a bordello.'

Miss Swetnick and Hank looked at each other and laughed.
'Who told you that?' Miss Swetnick asked.

'My father,' Sally said. 'Have you ever been to a bordello?'

'No,' Miss Swetnick said, 'I haven't.'

'Me neither.'

They laughed again. 'Do you know what a bordello is?' Hank
asked.

'No . . . do you?'

Miss Swetnick cleared her throat and said, 'Come on . . .
let's get busy . . . we have a lot to do tonight . . .'

They went into the bathroom. Hank handed Sally a paint

brush. 'You can start under the sink,' he said. 'I can't get in there because of my size.'

'I'm going to work on the curtains, darling,' Miss Swetnick said.

'Okay . . .' Hank told her. 'My partner and I will see how far we can get . . .'

Sally crawled under the sink. 'Does your brother ever help you paint?'

'No . . . Peter would rather play ball.'

Sally dipped her brush into the tray of blue paint and started on the wall. 'Does Peter talk much about his school friends?'

'Not too much.'

Some paint dripped on the floor. Sally wiped it up with a cloth. 'Does he ever mention them by name?'

'Now and then.'

Sally paused, her brush on the wall. 'Does he ever mention Jackie?'

'Jackie . . . let's see . . . is he the one who plays third base?'

'No . . . Jackie's a girl!'

'Oh, a girl! No, I don't think he's ever mentioned her . . .'

Sally smiled to herself and went back to painting.

After a while, Hank said, 'The only girl I've heard him talk about is Sally . . .'

'*Sally* . . . that's me!'

'Oh . . .' Hank said. 'I didn't realize you were *that* Sally.'

'Yes, I'm the only one in the class.' She wanted to ask, *What did Peter say about me?* but she couldn't. That would be too nosy.

Miss Swetnick came back into the bathroom. 'I've got the curtains up . . . come and see . . .'

Sally and Hank followed Miss Swetnick into the bedroom. The new curtains were drawn, making the room dark.

'Very nice!' Hank said, putting his arms around Miss Swetnick's waist.

'They're pretty,' Sally said. 'I like the colours.' They were made out of heavy cotton material, in yellow, orange and brown print. 'But you won't be able to see into our living room any more.'

'Yes, we will . . .' Miss Swetnick said. 'See . . .' and she pulled the cord, opening the curtains.

'I meant you won't be able to see when the curtains are closed,' Sally said.

'Oh . . .' Miss Swetnick answered. 'I guess you're right.'

At eight o'clock, Sally said goodbye to Hank and Miss Swetnick. Too bad Hank hadn't told her anything else about Peter. Maybe next time.

'Thanks for helping,' Hank said.

'It was fun,' Sally answered. She was glad she'd done the hardest part for him. Getting the wall under the sink just right wasn't easy.

She had to walk to dancing class by herself, because Andrea still wasn't speaking to her. Sally had tried to explain. She'd said, 'I meant to tell you about him . . . I really did . . . it's just that I had so many other things on my mind . . . I forgot . . . that's all . . .'

'Don't waste your breath,' Andrea had said, 'because I'm not listening.'

Their mothers tried to get them back together but Andrea recognized this and told her mother to mind her own business. So their grandmothers tried to fix things up but Andrea saw through that too and told her grandmother to worry about her own friends.

On the way home from dancing school Sally tried again. 'Can I walk with you?' she asked Andrea.

Andrea didn't answer.

'Miss Swetnick is moving in next door.'

No response from Andrea.

'I'll tell you a secret . . .' Sally said, looking for some kind of expression on Andrea's face, but Andrea acted as if she hadn't heard a word. 'I like Peter Hornstein . . . nobody else in the whole world knows that, except maybe Barbara.'

354

Andrea didn't even look her way.

'I'd like to kiss him . . . I really would . . . Andrea, can you hear me?'

'No.'

'Remember the day we were walking home and the bird plopped on me?' Sally laughed, hoping Andrea would too. 'Andrea, please say something!'

'Something.'

They saw Omar at almost the same moment. He was lying in the middle of the street, in front of their building. Andrea cried out and ran to him. 'Omar . . . Omar . . .' She sank to her knees and gathered Omar's broken body into her arms. She held him close. 'Oh no . . . my baby . . . my poor baby . . .' She stroked his head. Omar's eyes were staring into space and his beautiful white fur was all bloodied. Sally knew he was dead.

Andrea sobbed, her body shaking, her cries growing louder and louder. Sally didn't know what to do, what to say. She touched Andrea's shoulder but Andrea shook her away. Sally ran into the house, calling, 'Omar's dead . . . Omar's dead . . .'

Andrea's mother heard Sally and so did many of the other neighbours. They all rushed outside, in time to see Andrea stand up and walk slowly towards the house, with Omar cradled in her arms.

'I didn't do it,' Mrs Richter said to no one in particular. 'I never liked that cat but I didn't do it.'

'Of course you didn't,' another woman said. 'You don't even have a car.'

'Hit and run . . .'

'Such a shame . . .'

'Getting his blood all over her dress . . .'

Mrs Rubin put her arms around Andrea and cried with her. Andrea's sister, Linda, became so hysterical her grandmother had to slap her and carry her upstairs.

'I'm sorry, Andrea,' Sally said, as Andrea walked by. 'I know how much you loved him.'

'No one will ever know how much I loved him,' Andrea wept.

twenty-two

The phone rang. One long ring followed by two short rings. It was for them. Douglas answered. He'd been expecting Darlene to call. But it wasn't Darlene this time, because Douglas said, 'Yes . . . yes, this is the Freedman residence . . . just a minute, please . . .' He put the receiver down and called, 'Mom . . . hey, Mom . . . hurry up . . . it's long distance for you . . . person to person . . .'

Mom ran out of the bathroom, pulling her robe around her. 'Oh, my God . . . oh, my God . . . something's happened to Arnold . . .'

Ma Fanny rushed to her side and Sally and Douglas stood close by, waiting. Sally felt her stomach turn over. This is it, she thought. This is it. It's Daddy. Something terrible has happened. She wanted to scream. Scream because she'd been praying so hard. And for what? Barbara was right. It didn't help to pray. In that moment she knew she would never see her father again. Never feel his arms around her. Never give him another treatment. She let out a small cry, then clapped her hands over her mouth. *Bad* things always happen in threes, she thought. First, Omar . . . and now, Daddy . . .'

'Yes, this is Louise Freedman,' her mother said into the telephone. Then, 'Bette . . . Bette, is that you?' She covered the mouthpiece with her hand and told the three of them, 'It's Bette.' They nodded. 'Yes,' Mom continued, 'yes, I can hear you . . . yes, yes . . . what is it?'

Sally tried to swallow but found she couldn't.

'Oh, thank God,' Mom said. 'Thank God everything's all

356

right.' She covered the mouthpiece again and told the family, 'It's all right.'

Sally tasted the beans she'd had for supper.

'Yes, I'm okay now,' Mom said, sounding stronger. 'I was just so worried getting a person to person phone call . . . how are you? . . . you do? . . . you are?' Mom turned to Ma Fanny. 'It's an addition,' she said. Ma Fanny slapped her hand against the side of her face. 'Oh, God . . . that's wonderful,' Mom said into the phone. 'I'm so happy for you . . .' She started to cry and handed the phone to Ma Fanny.

'Bette . . .' Ma Fanny said. 'So tell me the good news . . . I want to hear it straight from the horse's mouth . . . I couldn't be happier . . . for all the money in the world I couldn't be happier . . . When? . . . August? . . . I'll be there with bells on . . . mazel tov, my darling . . .' She handed the phone back to Mom.

'Jack . . .' Mom said, 'Jack, is that you? Congratulations! It's wonderful news . . . the best.'

An addition, Sally thought. What does that mean? It's got to be something good, they're all so happy. An addition. Maybe Aunt Bette has passed some kind of arithmetic test. No, that's silly . . . it has to be something else. I'm so sick of secrets! Why doesn't anybody ever tell me what's going on!

When Mom and Ma Fanny were off the phone, Douglas said, 'That's great news for them but, personally, I wouldn't want one.'

'I should hope not, at your age,' Mom said and she and Douglas and Ma Fanny laughed together.

So, Sally thought, Douglas understood about the addition too. So, she was the only one who didn't know. Well, she wasn't about to admit it. Then Douglas would make fun of her, saying her mind was a blank, or that she was just a baby. 'What will the addition look like?' Sally asked, figuring she could find out what it was by playing twenty questions.

'Who can say?' Ma Fanny answered. 'As long as it's healthy we won't complain.'

357

'I still can't believe it,' Mom said. 'Just when I was expecting the worst it turned out to be the best.'

'And she's already four months?' Ma Fanny asked.

'Yes, I guess she didn't want to get our hopes up until she was sure . . . remember last time?'

'How could I forget?'

'The last time, what?' Sally asked.

'The last time Aunt Bette was pregnant she lost the baby after two months,' Mom said.

'Oh . . . she's going to have a baby.' Suddenly it all made sense.

'You dummy!' Douglas said. 'What'd you think she was going to have, an elephant?'

'No!' Sally said. 'An addition!'

'It *is* an addition,' Mom said, 'an addition to the family.'

'Oh . . . an addition to the family,' Sally said. 'Now I get it.'

Mom gave Sally a hug. 'You're so funny sometimes . . .'

Later, while Mom was setting her hair, Sally asked, 'How does a woman get pregnant, anyway?'

'Oh, you know . . .' Mom said.

'But I don't . . .'

'Well,' Mom began, 'the husband plants the seed inside the wife . . .'

'I know about *that*,' Sally said. 'But how does he get the seed and where does he plant it?'

'Well . . .' Mom said. She made three more pin curls before she spoke again. 'I think you need a book to explain that part. Tomorrow I'll go to the bookstore and see what they have on the subject.'

'Tomorrow's Sunday.'

'Oh . . . you're right. Well, I'll go first thing Monday morning.'

'But, Mom . . . I want to know now!'

'I can see that, Sally. But you'll just have to wait until Monday.'

'You mean you don't know either?'

358

'I know,' Mom said, 'it's just that I don't know how to explain it to you . . . if Daddy were here he would, but I'm not very good at those things . . .'

> *Dear Aunt Bette,*
> *Congratulations! I'm very glad to hear that Uncle Jack got the seed planted at last. It will be nice to have a baby cousin. I hope it's a girl and that you name her Precious, which is what I would like my name to be. Monday, Mom is getting me a book explaining how you got the baby made. I'm really curious!*
> *Love and other indoor sports,*
> *Sally J. Freedman, your friend and relative.*

Monday morning, on her way to school, Sally called, 'And, Mom . . . don't forget about that book!'

That afternoon, Sally found a brown bag on her day bed. Inside was the book and a note from Mom saying, *Don't show this to Douglas!*

twenty-three

Andrea refused to leave her room. Mrs Rubin was worried about her. She came to Sally's house to discuss the situation with Mom.

'Promise her a movie . . .' Mom suggested.

'I've already tried that.'

'A new dress?'

'That, too . . .'

'A record album?'

'Even that . . .'

'Hmmm . . . what about a sundae at Herschel's every night for a week?'

'I know what she needs,' Sally said, and Mom and Mrs

Rubin looked up, as if remembering for the first time that she was sitting at the table too.

'What's that?' Mrs Rubin asked.

'Something to love . . . like a kitten.'

'What a nice idea,' Mrs Rubin said. 'I wonder if it would work?'

'It will . . . I just know it,' Sally said. 'And I'd like to be the one to give her the kitten.'

'I must say, Sally . . . that's very generous of you, considering the way Andrea's been treating you this week.'

'She had a right to be mad at me.'

'Maybe so . . . but she's carried it too far,' Mrs Rubin said.

'In a way I don't blame her, though,' Sally said.

Sally and her mother went to the pet shop next to the movie theatre, where *The Outlaw*, starring Jane Russell, was playing. 'Can we go to see it?' Sally asked.

'No.'

'Not today . . . maybe Friday night or Saturday, I mean . . .'

'Absolutely not,' Mom said.

'But why . . . it looks good . . .'

'Never mind why.'

'Because you can see down Jane Russell's blouse when she bends over?' Sally said.

'Who told you that?'

'Douglas . . . he's going to see it.'

'Over my dead body!'

'Oh, please, Mom . . . don't tell him I said anything about it . . . he'll kill me.' Why did she have to go and open her big mouth? She'd promised Douglas she could keep his secret.

'I won't tell him how I found out,' Mom said.

'Anyway, I don't see what's so bad about looking down Jane Russell's blouse . . . when Vicki bends over you can do the same thing.'

'Sally!'

'Well, it's true. That night I sat next to her at The Park

360

Avenue Restaurant I could look down her dress and see everything.'

'Sally!'

'What?'

'Stop talking that way.'

'What way?'

'You know very well what way!'

Sally chose a ginger kitten for Andrea and Mom didn't say one word about it having worms. Ma Fanny lined a basket with blue velvet and tied a matching blue ribbon on the handle. Sally put the kitten in the basket and went across the hall, to Andrea's.

Mrs Rubin said, 'She's still in her room.'

Sally walked through the living room, past the kitchen, to Andrea's room. It was no bigger than the foyer closet in Sally's house in New Jersey but at least it was all Andrea's. Andrea was lying face down on her bed.

'Hi . . . it's me . . . Sally.' She put the basket on the floor. 'I'm sorry about Georgia Blue Eyes . . . I should have told you before . . . and I'm sorry about Omar . . . I didn't love him as much as you but I did love him.'

'I know you did,' Andrea said, into her pillow.

'Will you be my friend again?' Sally asked.

'Yes.'

'Good . . . I've got something to show you.'

'What?'

'You can't see it that way.'

Andrea rolled over and sat up. Sally was surprised at the way she looked, with dark circles under her eyes and her hair matted to the side of her face. Sally picked up the basket and put it on the bed, next to Andrea.

Andrea looked into the basket. 'Oh no . . .' She shook her head and began to cry.

'But . . .'

'Did they think I'd forget about him just like that?' She buried her face in her hands.

'No,' Sally said, 'and anyway, it was *my* idea, not *theirs*.'

'Take it away,' Andrea cried. 'Take it far, far away . . .'

'You're impossible, Andrea Rubin . . . you know that? You're really impossible! It's hard to even like you sometimes . . .' Sally picked up the basket and stomped out of Andrea's room. She was shaking all over. She went home.

Mom said, 'What a shame . . . I guess we'll have to take the kitten back.' 'Please, Mom . . . can't we keep him?' Sally asked.

At first Mom didn't answer and Sally took her silence to mean *maybe*. 'Just feel how soft he is,' Sally said.

Mom stroked the kitten. 'He is soft, isn't he?'

'Yes . . . and I'd take care of him . . . really . . . you wouldn't have to do a thing . . .'

'I know, honey . . . but we can't take a chance on a kitten . . . we have too many allergies . . .'

'Name one person in this family who's allergic to cats . . .'

'It could be dangerous for Douglas.'

'Baloney!' Sally said, holding back tears.

'I'm sorry,' Mom said. 'I really am.'

'If you meant that you'd let me keep him.'

'We shouldn't have bought him in the first place . . . not without asking Andrea . . .'

'But I wanted to surprise her.'

'Sometimes surprises don't work,' Mom said.

They sat down to a dairy supper. 'What's this about going to see *The Outlaw*?' Mom asked Douglas.

Sally put her spoon down. 'Don't look at me,' she said to Douglas, before he'd even glanced her way.

'I want you to stay away from that movie,' Mom told him.

'It's a cowboy story,' Douglas said. 'What's wrong with cowboys all of a sudden?'

'Nothing.'

'Then why can't I go?'

'We both know the answer to that, Douglas!'

'It's not like I've never seen a breast . . . you know.'

'Douglas!'

'Suppose I want to be a doctor . . . I'm going to have to see plenty of them then.'

'This has nothing to do with being a doctor,' Mom said.

'You act like there's something wrong with the human body.'

'There's a time and a place for everything.'

'I think I'll ask Dad about it when he calls on Sunday . . . I'll bet he'll let me go!'

'Children . . .' Ma Fanny said, holding up a bowl, 'have some more carrots . . . they'll make you see in the dark.'

'I can't trust you with anything,' Douglas said to Sally, after supper. They were on the floor, playing with the kitten.

'I didn't tell on you . . . it just came out . . .'

'You better learn how to keep secrets or you're going to wind up with no friends.'

'I have friends. I have Shelby and Barbara and Andr . . .'

'Guess again.'

Sally let the kitten nibble on her finger. 'I'm sorry . . . from now on I'm going to try harder. I'm going to learn how to keep secrets if it kills me . . . really.'

'This time it doesn't even matter,' Douglas said, 'because I'm going whether *she* likes it or not.'

Sally nodded.

The doorbell rang while Sally was getting ready for bed. She was in the bathroom, brushing her teeth, when Mom came to get her. 'It's Andrea,' Mom said.

Sally wiped her mouth with the corner of a towel and went into the living room.

Andrea said, 'I hear you have to take the kitten back.'

'Yes.'

'Can I have another look?'

'Help yourself.'

The kitten was curled up in the basket, sound asleep. Andrea lifted him out and put her face next to his soft body. 'Hello, you little darling . . . hello, you precious angel . . .' She looked up at Sally. 'I think I'm going to call her Margaret O'Brien the

Second, if that's all right with you.'

'But, Andrea,' Sally said, suddenly laughing, 'it's a *boy* cat.'

'Oh . . . in that case I'll call *him* Margaret O'Brien the Second!' And she laughed with Sally.

Aunt Bette wasn't the only one pregnant. Two weeks later Andrea said, 'Did you hear about Bubbles?'

'No . . . what?'

'She's going to have a baby!'

'But how can she . . . she's not even married.'

'You don't have to be married,' Andrea said.

'But my book says . . .'

'Never mind what your book says . . . I'm telling you . . . you don't have to be married . . . and Bubbles did it with a *goy* . . . so now Mr and Mrs Daniels are sitting shivah . . . pretending Bubbles is dead . . . and I think it's horrible . . . she's their only child . . . God should punish them for what they're doing.'

'If she'd done it with a Jewish boy would they be sitting shivah?'

'No, silly . . . then they'd be making a wedding.'

'I don't get it,' Sally said.

'It's all very complicated.'

Sally went home and told her mother, 'My book was wrong. You don't have to be married to get a baby.'

'If you're a nice girl you do.'

'Isn't Bubbles a nice girl?'

'I don't want to talk about that.'

But everybody else in their house was talking about it. Sally listened to Mrs Purcell on their party line. She said, 'I'd do the same thing if, God forbid, one of my children ran off with a goy. Thank God I don't have to worry . . . all three are married very well.'

Ma Fanny and Andrea's grandmother were talking about it. 'And her with scarlet fever yet,' Andrea's grandmother said.

'A pox on them!' Ma Fanny said, pointing to the Daniels'

364

apartment. 'Sitting shivah for Bubbles . . . meshuggeners!'

Sally had never seen her so angry.

'Fanny . . . don't be so hard on them,' Andrea's grandmother said. 'Remember, they're orthodox Jews . . . they're doing what they feel is right.'

'Orthodox, schmorthodox.'

'Listen,' Andrea's grandmother said, 'plenty of goys disown their children for marrying Jews . . .'

'Your child is your child,' Ma Fanny said, 'no matter what . . . I could tell you plenty, but I won't . . .'

Sally wished she would.

'So, you'll make a donation through the temple?' Andrea's grandmother asked.

'Not a penny . . . not one cent . . . they should only rot in there,' Ma Fanny said, her face tightening.

Mom and Mrs Rubin and Andrea's grandmother were going to pay a condolence call on the Daniels that evening. Ma Fanny refused to join them, even though Mom said, 'They're our neighbours . . . how will it look?'

'They should only know what it's like to *really* lose a child! Whatever they think, I couldn't care less . . .'

'What did you mean?' Sally asked Ma Fanny, after the others had left. Sally was sitting in the big chair, a hank of wool wrapped around her outstretched arms.

Ma Fanny sat on the footstool, facing her, rolling a wool ball. 'About what, sweetie pie?'

Sally watched as the wool flew off her arms. 'About losing a child . . . you sounded like you knew about that.'

Ma Fanny nodded.

'You lost a child?'

She nodded again.

'I never knew that,' Sally said.

'It's not something I advertise.'

'When did it happen?'

'A long time ago . . . before your mother was born . . . I had a baby boy and one day he died . . .' She snapped her fingers.

'Just like that!'

'From what?'

'We never found out . . . he was only five months old . . . his name was Samuel . . .' She sighed. 'Such a long time ago . . .'

'Is it a secret?' Sally asked.

'Not a secret . . . just something I don't like to talk about.'

'Thank you for telling me, Ma Fanny. I understand better now.'

Ma Fanny cupped Sally's chin in her hand. 'You're worth a million . . . you know that . . . more even . . .' She went back to winding her wool.

twenty-four

Class 5B was having an election for King and Queen of Posture. The winners would go on to compete in the All-Fifth-Grade contest and the winners of that election would represent the entire fifth grade in the All-School contest. Barbara had nominated Sally, and Peter had seconded the motion, so Sally stood out in the corridor with the other five nominees, waiting, while the rest of the class voted.

In a few minutes Miss Swetnick opened the door and said, 'You can come back in now . . .'

The winners' names were written on the blackboard. *Gordon and Beatrice, King and Queen of Posture of Class 5B.* Sally tried to hide her disappointment. On her way back to her desk Harriet Goodman leaned over and said, 'I didn't vote for you . . . I'd *never* vote for you!'

'I'd never vote for you, either,' Sally answered.

She took her seat. Barbara whispered, 'You got six votes . . . that's pretty good . . . you came in third . . .'

Third and last, Sally thought. But at least she hadn't lost by just one vote. Then she'd have even more reason to hate

Harriet. And, there was always next time. Maybe she'd do better then. There were so many contests in Miami Beach. The newspapers were full of them. *Miss Bright Eyes, Miss Complexion, Miss Long Legs*. Even Central Beach Elementary School had contests all the time. *Girl of the Week, Tumbler of the Month, Smile of the Year*. Maybe they'd have a *Queen of Toenails* contest, Sally thought. Yes, she could win that one. Then she'd get to be fifth-grade representative to the *All-School-Queen of Toenails* election. And if Harriet Goodman didn't vote for her this time it wouldn't matter because everybody else in the class would. She looked down at her feet and wiggled her toes. She *did* have nice toenails!

'Sally . . .' Miss Swetnick said, 'would you please take out your arithmetic book and open to page ninety-two.'

When Sally got home from school she found Mr Zavodsky sitting on the porch with another old man. This one had white hair, suntanned skin and wore a flowered cabana shirt. Simon! Yes, it had to be. They were sharing some kind of book – reading, pointing and laughing together. Mr Zavodsky was so involved he didn't offer her candy, didn't even notice her.

'Look . . .' Mr Zavodsky said to Simon, tapping a page of his book. 'Do you remember her?'

'Do I remember her?' Simon answered. 'She's one I'll never forget.'

Their scrapbook of the war! Sally thought, running into the lobby and up the stairs. She tore a piece of paper from her notebook and scribbled:

Dear Mr Zavodsky,
    I have seen you with Simon. His cabana shirt and suntan may fool some people but not me. He is the monster who was in charge of Dachau! I know plenty about Dachau and what you and Simon did to the prisoners there. You will pay for laughing about it.

I'll copy this note over later, she thought. For now she folded

367

it in half and put it in her keepsake box. She'd have to hurry.
Andrea would be waiting to play potsy.

Daddy made some money on one of Big Ted's stock tips and
came down to visit for five days in March, and again, over
Easter vacation.

Sally was curled up in his lap, running her middle finger up
and down his arm. She felt happy and relaxed like Andrea's
kitten when he purred. '. . . and the recreation room is almost
finished,' Daddy said. 'All that's left to do is the floor and the
trimmings . . . what do you think of green and black tiles?'

'Alice Ingram has red and black.' She wondered how long it
would take to count all the hairs on his arm.

'Everybody has red and black . . . that's why I thought of
green and black . . . but if you don't like green . . .'

'Oh no . . . green is nice . . .'

'And green leather on the built-in seats . . .'

'I like green a lot.'

'And a green top on the bar . . .'

'We can call it the Green Room,' Sally said.

Daddy smiled at her.

'Can I have a party in it right away . . . as soon as I get
home?'

'I think you should wait an hour or two.'

'You know what I mean,' Sally said, laughing.

'As soon as you want.'

'And can I have boys, too?'

'We better discuss that with your mother.'

'Why . . . what's wrong with having boys?'

'Nothing . . .'

'Then why do we have to ask Mom?'

'Okay,' Daddy said. 'You can have boys to your party.'

'Thanks . . . but the boy I like is here, in Miami Beach.'

'Then you don't have to have boys to your party after all.'

'But I might find some boys to like when I get back to New
Jersey.'

368

'Then you *can* invite boys to your party . . .'

'Oh, Doey . . . you're being so silly!'

'Who's being silly?' he asked, tickling her in the ribs.

Ma Fanny called, 'Supper . . .'

Daddy sniffed in three times. 'Could that wonderful, fragrant aroma emerging from the depths of the kitchen by any chance be Fantastic Fanny's Fabulous Borscht?' he asked, leaping to his feet so that Sally rolled off his lap on to the floor. He scooped her up and flung her over his shoulder.

'Put me down . . . put me down . . .' Sally cried, loving every minute of her father's nonsense.

As they sat down to eat, Ma Fanny said, 'I don't know one single person who enjoys his borscht as much as you, Arnold . . .' She reached over and pinched his cheek as if he were a little boy.

Sally wished she could learn to like borscht. It looked so pretty – bright pink soup with tiny white potatoes floating in it. But the taste – cold beets – ugh! She drank a glass of tomato juice instead.

While the rest of them were enjoying their borscht, Mom said, 'Didn't you leave your recipe with Bette, Ma . . . so she could make it for Arnold?'

'More or less,' Ma Fanny said. 'I told her, a pinch of this . . . a pinch of that . . .'

'Bette tries hard,' Daddy said, 'but her pinches aren't like your pinches yet . . .' Now *he* leaned over and gave one back to Ma Fanny. 'Only you make the real thing . . . the genuine article . . .'

'How did I get myself such a son-in-law?' Ma Fanny asked.

'You were lucky,' Sally said.

'Sometimes I think he married me for my mother,' Mom said, and it didn't sound like she was joking.

At the end of the meal, when Daddy was sipping his coffee, he said, 'I have an announcement to make.'

'Yes . . .'

'What is it?'

'Tell us . . .'

'No,' Daddy said, 'I think I'll make you guess . . .'

'Oh, Doey . . .'

'You first, Sally.'

'What am I supposed to guess?'

'Guess where we're going . . .'

'Umm . . . Monkey Jungle?'

'Nope . . . your turn, Douglas.'

'To see *The Outlaw*?'

'Douglas!' Mom said.

'Only joking . . .'

'Your turn, Fanny,' Daddy said.

'I should know?'

'Your turn, Lou . . .' Daddy said and Sally could see how much he was enjoying his game.

'I'm afraid to even think about what you've got up your sleeve this time . . .'

'Aha . . .' Daddy looked around the table slowly, a smile spreading across his face. 'How about a ride in the Goodyear Blimp?'

'The Goodyear Blimp!' Douglas said, knocking over his dish of tapioca pudding.

'Twenty minutes over scenic Miami,' Daddy said.

'Hot dog!' Douglas said. 'That's what I've been wanting to do more than anything!'

'I know,' Daddy said. 'You've only mentioned it three or four hundred times.'

'Hot dog!' He slapped his thigh under the table. 'The Goodyear Blimp . . . wait till I tell Darlene.'

'Would you like to bring her along?'

'Would I? Oh, boy, Dad . . . you're the greatest . . . you think of everything!'

Sally, trying to match Douglas's enthusiasm, jumped up and down in her seat, saying, 'Hot dog . . . the Goodyear Blimp . . . wowie!' But the idea of it frightened her. She liked watching it, but riding in it was something else.

'Would you like to bring a friend, too?' Daddy asked her.

'Oh, sure . . . that's great . . . boy, am I excited!'

'Do you think it's a wise idea, Arnold?' Mom asked. 'After all . . . remember *The Hindenburg* . . .'

'This is 1948, Lou . . . besides, the Goodyear Blimp runs on helium, not hydrogen.'

'Some difference!' Mom said.

'There is.'

'Not to me.'

'That's because you don't understand the scientific facts, Mom . . .' Douglas said. 'I'll explain them to you. You see, the . . .'

Mom held up her hand. 'You know I have no head for science,' she said.

'Is it expensive?' Sally asked her father.

'About ten dollars a person . . .'

'Then I guess I'll invite Barbara,' Sally said, thinking out loud, 'because Andrea's father can afford to take her . . . and Shelby's grandmother probably wouldn't let her go anyway . . .'

'And I wouldn't blame her one bit,' Mom said.

'How about you, Fanny,' Daddy asked, '. . . going to give it a try?'

'Ha, ha,' Ma Fanny said, 'such a comedian! I like my feet on the ground.'

'How about you, Lou?' Daddy asked.

'No thank you!'

'Come on, Mom,' Douglas said. 'Live it up for once.'

'Remember, you enjoyed Cuba,' Daddy reminded her.

'I was very lucky,' Mom said. 'My first plane trip was a good one . . . let's just leave it at that . . .'

'I'd really like you to come with us,' Daddy said.

Sally looked from one to the other.

'I am *not* setting foot in that blimp,' Mom said, 'and I wish you'd have discussed the whole idea with me before you went ahead and told the children . . . after all, they're mine, too . . .

don't I have anything to say about what happens to them?' She pushed her chair away from the table and ran for the bathroom.

Daddy cleared his throat.

Ma Fanny carried the pudding bowl back into the kitchen.

'Well . . .' Douglas said, 'I think I'll give Darlene a call and tell her the good news.'

Sally just sat there, watching, waiting and wondering.

'Would you like to take a little walk?' Daddy asked her.

'I have to call Barbara first . . .'

'You can call when we get back . . . Douglas is on the phone now.'

'Okay,' Sally said.

They went outside. It was just turning dark. The air was warm and sweet smelling.

'Your mother worries a lot,' Daddy said, as they passed the goldfish pool.

Sally nodded.

'She can't help it . . . she loves us all so much . . . but I don't want you to grow up worrying that way.' He took her hand in his.

'Miss Swetnick is moving in there,' Sally said, pointing to the next building. 'Did I tell you I helped her and Hank paint their bathroom?'

'That's nice,' Daddy said, but Sally could tell he had something more serious on his mind. And it made her uncomfortable.

'Some people worry away their whole lives . . .' He looked down at her. 'Do you know what I mean?'

'I think so.'

'Your mother, for instance, spends too much time worrying about what *might* happen.'

'Why does she do that?'

'I don't know . . . that's just the way she is.'

'Don't you ever worry?' Sally asked.

'Sure . . . everybody worries sometimes . . . it's just that some people worry so much about tomorrow they have no time to enjoy today. Do you understand?'

'I think so.'

'You don't worry, do you?' Daddy asked.

'Well . . . only if it's very important . . .'

'At your age you should be free of worries.'

'There are some things I *have* to worry about.'

'I know,' he said, squeezing her fingers, 'spelling tests and boyfriends . . .'

She squeezed back without saying anything. How could she tell him that *he* was the one she worried about most?

'I'm going to tell you a secret, Sally . . . I think you're ready to hear it . . . both my brothers were exactly my age when they died . . .'

'They were?' Sally tried to sound surprised.

'Yes . . . your Uncle Eddie and your Uncle Abe . . . and I used to worry that the same thing would happen to me . . . that I would die when I was forty-two . . . I didn't want to . . . I didn't want to leave you and Douglas and Mom . . .'

Sally tried to keep her breathing quiet, while inside she felt ready to explode.

'But now I realize how foolish it was for me to worry about that . . . because it was just a coincidence . . . it has nothing to do with me. It's taught me something, though . . . I've learned what's really important . . . to experience everything that life has to offer . . . to be near the ones I love . . .' He looked down at her. 'Don't cry, Sally . . . don't, honey . . . I didn't mean to make you cry . . . stop now . . . stop, Sally . . .' He held her to him.

But Sally couldn't stop. It felt so good to let it all out. 'I don't want you to die,' she said, hugging her father.

'Everybody has to die, Sal . . .'

'Promise me you won't.'

'I can't promise that . . . we live and we die . . . it's a fact we have to accept . . .'

'But you won't die until I'm old, will you?'

'I hope not . . . but I'm not going to worry about it and I don't want you to either.'

When they went back upstairs, Douglas was sitting at the kitchen table, listening to *Inner Sanctum*. Ma Fanny was sitting in the stuffed chair in the living room, working on a red sweater, and Mom was stretched out on the Murphy bed, holding a magazine upside down. The only sound in the apartment, beside the radio, was the click-clack of Ma Fanny's knitting needles.

Sally couldn't get to sleep. Couldn't stop thinking that one day *she* would be dead, too. What would it feel like? It could be nice. It could be that she'd turn into an angel and fly around and watch what was going on down on earth. Suppose she knew she was going to die in one month, like in that radio programme she'd heard last week. What would she do? See a lot of movies, for one thing. And eat whipped cream at every meal and have a party every week, with boys, and never do anything she didn't feel like doing. And she'd get a kitten. Maybe two or three of them. And she'd get all the cut-out books she wanted, and if Mrs Daniels said, *Cut-out books at her age? Why, when my Bubbles was her age she* . . . this time Sally wouldn't let her finish. She'd say, *I know all about your Bubbles . . . she did it with a goy and got a baby . . . so ha ha on you.*

And then she'd fly up to heaven and be a beautiful angel with long blonde hair. Or maybe she'd keep her own hair because who says angels can't have brown hair? But if it turned out that there were no angels and when you died there was nothing . . . because you were just plain dead . . . dead and cold . . . lying in the ground . . . *oh!* She moaned at the idea of that. There had to be angels. There just had to be!

TWENTY MINUTES OVER SCENIC MIAMI IN THE GOODYEAR BLIMP the sign said. They sat in a small compartment on the underside of the blimp: Sally and Barbara, Douglas and Darlene, Daddy and two strangers, who also had tickets for the 2 p.m. ride. Sally was scared and excited at the same time. So was Barbara. 'This could be it,' she said. 'We could crash during take-

374

off . . . or burn up, like *The Hindenburg* . . .' She and Sally
held hands. 'Do you believe in life after death?' Barbara asked.

'Yes . . . do you?'

'Today I do.'

'I believe in angels,' Sally said.

'Me too . . . Jewish angels,' Barbara said. 'Not the Christian
kind who go around blowing bugles.'

'Right,' Sally said. 'Jewish angels . . .' It had never occurred
to her that angels had to be one religion or the other.

Suddenly they lifted up . . . up, up, into the sky. They were
floating. And down below them was scenic Miami and the
Atlantic Ocean. It was fun looking down. Scary but fun.
Everything seemed so small.

Darlene and Douglas talked on and on about helium and how
it works and that it was too bad the U.S. government wasn't
smart enough to build lots of blimps. And that some day the
two of them would build their own and possibly start a
magazine called *Blimp News.*

Daddy looked across the compartment at Sally and smiled.
She smiled back and let go of Barbara's hand. Her own was all
sweaty.

When they were down again, when the ride was over,
Barbara leaned close to Sally and whispered, 'I don't believe in
angels after all. When you're dead, you're dead, and that's it.'

twenty-five

Sally was home with Ma Fanny. Douglas and Mom and Daddy
had gone to Lincoln Road to buy a suit for Douglas because
Darlene had invited him to her house for dinner and Mom said
The Swells dress up when they eat.

Sally had the phone to her ear. Ma Fanny knew she listened
in to other people's conversations but she never told on her.

'Papa . . . Papa is that you?' A woman's voice asked.

'It's me,' Mr Zavodsky answered.

'Oh, I'm so glad you got a phone . . . I worry about you . . .'

'Don't worry . . . I couldn't be better.'

'Papa, I wish you'd come to live with us . . . Murray wants you and so do the boys. We'd fix up the attic room so you'd have privacy . . .'

'I like it here, Rita . . . who needs the cold?'

'Are you still having pains?'

'Not a one.'

'That's wonderful! And you're going to the doctor?'

'When I feel like it.'

'But, Papa, you're supposed to go every two weeks . . .'

'You shouldn't worry, Rita . . . I'm fine . . . I'm enjoying . . .'

'That's good. You take care of yourself . . . promise?'

'I promise . . . I promise . . .'

'I'll call you again in a few weeks.'

'Did Hitler have any kids?' Sally asked that night.

'Not that I know of,' Mom said. 'And what's this sudden fascination with Hitler?'

'I'm just trying to get the facts straight,' Sally said. 'Was he married?'

'He had a girlfriend,' Mom said.

'Was her name Rita?'

'No . . . Eva.'

'Oh, Eva.'

So . . . the phone conversation had been in code again, Sally thought. He didn't have a daughter. And Rita was probably Eva. And they were making plans. And Murray and the boys were probably his old cronies, like Simon. Too bad the police weren't smart enough to crack Mr Zavodsky's code.

Douglas was angry. He'd worn his new suit to Darlene's house for dinner and Darlene's father had worn a golf shirt and Darlene's brothers had worn bathing suits and Darlene's

376

mother had worn a bathrobe – a pretty fancy one, but still a bathrobe – and Darlene had worn dungarees and sneakers. 'Only the maid was dressed up,' Douglas told them.

'How was I to know *The Swells* have no manners?' Mom asked.

'They have manners,' Douglas said. 'They say *please* and *thank you* and all that and they were really nice to me. Her father even offered me a tee shirt.'

'Next time you'll know better,' Daddy said. 'But your mother was right to want you to make a good impression . . . not just on them, but on everyone.'

'Yeah . . . sure . . .' Douglas answered.

Sally and Barbara were hot from playing statues in Sally's side yard. They lay down under the trees to rest. Across the yard, Ma Fanny and some of her friends were talking and knitting.

'Miss Swetnick's getting married tomorrow,' Sally said.

'I know.'

'I wish we could go to the wedding . . . she probably wanted to invite the whole class but there wasn't enough room.'

'Probably . . .' Barbara said. She rolled a coconut toward Sally. 'We could go to the temple and stand outside . . . you don't have to be invited for that . . .'

'And see her dressed as a bride?' Sally sat up.

'Sure.'

'Let's do it!' Sally rolled the coconut back to Barbara.

'Okay . . . and I know something else we could do at the same time.'

'What?'

'Kiss Peter,' Barbara said.

'*You* want to kiss Peter?'

'No . . .' Barbara said, 'I mean you . . . *you* could kiss him.'

'Who says I want to?'

'Don't you?'

'Well . . . I wouldn't mind . . . but not in front of a lot of people.'

'We'll get him away from the people.'

'How?'

'Oh . . . we'll say you have a surprise for him or something.'

'And you'll do all the talking?' Sally asked.

'Sure . . . all you'll have to say is *congratulations* . . . and then kiss him . . . it'll be easy . . . everybody kisses at weddings.'

'I don't know . . .'

'If you don't want to . . .' Barbara began.

'It's not that . . .'

'. . . or if you're *chicken* . . .'

'I'm *not* chicken!'

'Then it's all set,' Barbara said, standing up. She brushed off her hands. 'I'll meet you at the corner at noon . . . and Sally . . .'

'What?'

'Don't wear your hair in braids . . . let it hang loose for a change.'

Sally and Barbara stood outside Temple Beth-El, waiting. Each of them had a bag of rice. It was very hot and Sally wore her new off-the-shoulder midriff. She had a hibiscus tucked behind one ear and her hair hung loose, below her shoulders. She checked herself in the mirror and was surprised that she looked so much like Lila. When Miss Swetnick and Hank came out of the temple everyone cheered and threw rice. Miss Swetnick looked beautiful but she wasn't wearing her glasses and Sally could tell that she was having some trouble without them by the way she squinted at the crowd. She laughed as she tossed her bouquet. Sally hoped to catch it but Miss Swetnick aimed it at her bridesmaids. Then she and Hank got into a shiny car and drove away.

Peter was wearing the same kind of blue suit that Douglas had worn to *The Swells'* house for dinner, but he had already loosened his tie and unbuttoned his shirt collar.

'So, Petey . . .' a fat, older woman said, 'you're next?'

'Like fish!' Peter told her.

378

Sally and Barbara went over to him. 'Hi, Peter . . .'

Barbara said, 'Sally has something for you.'

Peter said, 'Oh, yeah . . . what?'

Barbara said, 'Something she can only give you in private.'

Peter said, 'Okay . . . let's have it.'

Barbara said, 'Over there . . .' And she nudged Sally toward the side yard of the temple. 'Come on, Peter . . . or you'll never find out what it is.'

It was too late to back out now. She never should have come to the wedding. She never should have let Barbara get things going.

When the three of them reached the side yard Peter said, 'Okay . . . we're in private now.'

'Well . . .' Sally said, taking a deep breath, 'in honour of your brother's wedding, congratulations!' She leaned over and kissed him on the mouth.

He turned bright red. 'What'd you do that for?'

Sally blushed too. 'I told you . . . it was in honour of your brother's wedding . . .' She chewed on her bottom lip and pulled at her midriff.

Peter leaned over and kissed Sally back.

'What's *that* for?' she asked.

'For letting me copy off you on our last spelling test.'

'Petey . . . hurry . . .' the fat woman called.

'See you,' Peter said, running off.

'See you . . .' Sally called, waving.

'Well . . .' Barbara said. 'You really did it!'

'Uh huh . . .'

'Tell me about it.'

'You were standing right here,' Sally said. 'You saw the whole thing.'

'But what did it *feel* like?' Barbara asked.

'Nice.'

'I always knew he liked you.'

'I wish Jackie knew it.'

'She will . . .'

When Sally got back to her house there was an ambulance and a police car outside and a crowd of people standing around. Oh no . . . Sally thought, please, God . . . don't let it be Doey . . . She pushed her way into the crowd. He's going to be all right . . . he promised . . .

'Let me in . . . let me in . . .' Sally said, using her elbows. The hibiscus fell from behind her ear and she tramped over it. 'Everybody has to die . . .' she could hear her father saying. 'We live and we die . . .' 'But you won't die until I'm old, will you?' she asked. And he had answered, 'I hope not . . .' She forced her way through until she reached the front of the crowd.

Andrea was there. 'Did you hear the news?'

'No . . . what?' Please, God . . . please . . .

'It's Mr Zavodsky . . .'

Sally felt dazed, as if she might pass out.

'You know . . .' Andrea added, 'that old guy who gives us candy . . .'

'What about him?' Sally asked. So, the police had found out on their own . . .

'He's dead!' Andrea said.

'He can't be.'

'Well, he is. He had a heart attack on the stairs. He just keeled right over . . . my grandmother's friend found him and called the ambulance. They're bringing him out any second . . . I'm not going to look . . . are you?'

'Yes!' Sally said. Thank you, God . . . Thank you for not letting it be Doey.

'There . . .' Andrea pointed and started sniffling, as two attendants carried out a stretcher.

'How can you cry?' Sally asked. 'You should be glad it's him and not . . . not . . .'

'He was a little touched,' Andrea said, 'but he was nice `. . .'

'That's how much you know!'

'Poor Mr Zavodsky . . .' Andrea cried, 'all covered up with a blanket . . .'

'I have to go now . . .' Sally said. 'I'll see you later.' She walked away slowly, through the lobby, up the stairs, to her apartment. She pulled her keepsake box out from under the day bed, opened it, rummaged through the shells, marbles, withered flowers, notes from Peter, and letters from Daddy, and fished out her Hitler letters, including the one she had written, but never mailed, to the Chief of Police.

She carried her letters back downstairs. The street was empty now, and quiet, except for a small group of old men and women, talking softly, where the crowd had stood a few moments before. She went to the trash bins, next to the storage room, and tore each letter into tiny pieces. So, it was over! She dropped them into the bin one by one. There was no more Mr Zavodsky. He was dead.

She sat down on the step. But maybe he's dead *not* from a heart attack! Maybe Simon and Rita murdered him. Yes, they'd found out someone was hot on his trail and the only thing to do was kill him to protect themselves! They'd injected poison, the kind that works fast and leaves no trace. And now Adolf would rot in hell. He'd shovel coal down there for a million years. He'd find out how it felt to get shoved into an oven, like Lila. God would see to that!

Douglas rode up on his bicycle, finished exploring for the day.

'Mr Zavodsky's dead!' Sally told him.

'Who's he?'

'Oh, Douglas . . . don't you have any imagination?' Sally stood up and walked away.

twenty-six

Dear Chrissy,

I'm coming home soon. My father is driving down next week and then we are going to take the scenic route back to New Jersey. We will visit St Augustine, Bok Tower, Silver Springs and other exciting places in Florida that I have studied about this year. You probably never heard of any of them. We will wind up in Washington, D.C. where I will inspect the FBI, as I am thinking seriously of joining it.

As soon as I get home I'm planning on having a party. I may or may not invite boys. I may or may not invite Alice Ingram, since I haven't heard from her once. Have you grown any this year? I've hardly grown at all. Not up and not out, either. But I have learned a lot. Do you know the difference between helium and hydrogen? Do you know how babies get made? Have you kissed any boys? I have. I will tell you about that too. It's more interesting than the difference between helium and hydrogen. Have you heard about television? My father says we are going to get a set when we get home. You can come over to watch. My father says it's going to be a big thing. My mother says nothing will ever replace the radio. I am in between my mother and my father, not just about television, but about a lot of things. That is something else I've found out this year.

Well, see you soon. Don't do anything I wouldn't do.

Love and other indoor sports,

Sally F.

Sally was packing a carton with Crayolas, books, her keepsake box and her toe slippers.

'And when we get home . . .' Douglas was saying, tying up his carton, 'I want you to stay away from Union Woods.'

'I'm not the one who plays in Union Woods,' Sally said, trying to decide on whether or not to pack her Margaret O'Brien paper dolls.

'I mean it . . . you stay out of there,' Douglas said.

'I will . . . I will . . .'

'Because some really bad things could happen to you in Union Woods . . .'

'I know . . . I could trip jumping across the brook and dislocate my elbow and wind up with a kidney infection and then . . .'

'That's not exactly how it happened,' Douglas said, interrupting.

'It's not?'

'No . . .'

'How did it happen then?'

'If you could keep a secret I'd tell you.'

'I can . . . I can . . . I've finally learned . . .'

'How can I be sure?' Douglas asked. 'How do I know I can really trust you this time?'

'You can, Douglas . . . I swear it . . . I've changed a lot.'

'Since when?'

'Since that time about *The Outlaw* . . .'

'Well . . .'

'Oh, come on, Douglas . . . I'll tell you a secret too.'

'Okay,' Douglas said. 'You go first.'

'I kissed Peter Hornstein on the lips . . . and that's a real secret because if Mom ever found out she'd kill me . . . a person could get trench mouth that way, or worse . . .'

Douglas laughed.

'It's not funny.'

'Trench mouth . . .' He rolled around on the floor, laughing and holding his stomach. 'You're so dumb . . . you believe everything Mom tells you.'

'I do not!'

'Name one thing she's told you that you don't believe . . .'

'I don't believe my fungus came from the living-room rug.'

This made Douglas laugh harder.

'Stop it!' Sally said. 'You promised to tell me your secret . . .'

Douglas lay flat on his back, panting. 'Okay . . . the real reason I was running in Union Woods . . .' He paused.

'Go on . . . go on . . .'

'It was the crazy guy.'

'What crazy guy?'

'You know . . . the one who hangs out in the woods . . .'

'You mean the one they warned us about in school . . . the *crazy* one?'

Douglas nodded. 'That's what I just said . . . he was chasing us . . .'

'Oh, Douglas . . . that's so exciting! Could you identify him for the police?'

'I'm not sure.'

'Did he, by any chance, have a small black moustache?'

'Why . . . do you think he was Hitler?' Douglas doubled up with laughter. Sally had never seen him this way.

'It's not funny!'

'It is . . . it is . . . Hitler in Union Woods . . .'

'Stop it, Douglas!'

'I can't . . . I can't . . . it's just too much . . .'

Sally started laughing too. She couldn't help it either. It *was* funny . . . *Hitler in Union Woods* . . . why would he bother to go there? 'You know something, Douglas . . . when we get home I'm going to give you a special name, like I did for Doey-bird and Ma Fanny . . .'

'That's really big of you, Sally . . . but if you don't mind I think I'll just stick with plain old Douglas . . . that's good enough for me.'

'If I didn't know better I'd take that as an insult.'

'Insult . . . schminsult,' Douglas said, and he stood up, still laughing, and headed for the bathroom.

Sally leaned back against the day bed, holding her Margaret O'Brien paper dolls. Just one more story before I finish packing, she thought. Yes, this will be a good one. I'll call it *Margaret O'Brien Meets the Crazy One*.